SHORT STORY AMERICA

VOLUME V

EDITED BY T.D. JOHNSTON

SHORT STORY AMERICA PRESS

Volume V

Short Story America
31 Great Contemporary Short Stories
Edited by T.D. Johnston

ISBN: 978-0-9882497-9-0
Library of Congress Control Number: 2017901214

Published by
Short Story America Press
www.shortstoryamerica.com
editors@shortstoryamerica.com
843-597-3220

FIRST EDITION

Printed in the USA

Book design by Soundview Design Studio

TABLE OF CONTENTS

INTRODUCTION

When I created Short Story America in January of 2010, my sense of the state of short fiction was that quality short stories were being missed or rejected far too often by the "gatekeepers" of literature in America. I wanted to build a home for new, emerging and established authors to gather their work together in a selective anthology series. With this fifth volume, that home is now five stories tall, fully furnished both with variety and quality.

It has been a pleasure to develop friendships with fellow writers of short fiction from around the country and the world. I consider these friendships to be lifelong, and have come to see, with no surprise, that writers of short fiction are among the most genuine and inclusive people I have ever known. The best writers of fiction care deeply about individuals, about society as a whole, and about the curious reader. This affection shows up in their "construction of human souls," as Ortega y Gasset so aptly described the job of fiction writers who take this work seriously.

Perhaps most satisfying about the Short Story America project has been the discovery, in my travels as writer and editor, of people everywhere who deeply appreciate short fiction, and who want others to discover or re-discover this great original American literary art form. Thank you, dear reader, for joining us on this fifth step in our mission, and for helping us to keep this journey moving forward.

T.D. (Tim) Johnston

HEAVEN
Michael Matson

It was nearly nine when Amalia Pedrosa entered the portales, those covered walkways fronting the hotels, restaurants and businesses along the north side of Morelia's Avenida Madero. By then, most of the tables along the arcade were occupied, predominantly by middle-aged men taking their morning coffees, reading newspapers, smoking or chatting with friends.

As she had for the past two years, since she was five, Amalia held her small tray of chewing gum, nuts and cheap chili-flavored candies in front her and set out toward the nearest table. Reaching it, she would stand silently until the men glanced up and, as often as not, waved her away. It was easier now to accept the indifference, the rejection. Two years ago it had been hard. Frequently, then, she had cried knowing she had failed and wouldn't be able to provide the pitiful few extra pesos her grandmother and her brother, who washed the windshields of passing cars, depended on. On a good day, working six hours, her brother Luis might make 200 pesos, a tenth of which he'd have to share with others who "owned" the corner where he worked. Amalia might provide another 15 or 20 pesos. Because her grandmother was old and unable to work, it was all they had.

Amalia's grandmother, her abuela, had tried to comfort her those first days by reminding her that Morelia's cathedral stood across the street from the portales. "It is the house of God," she'd said, "so you see, you are close to God. Like your dear mother."

Her grandmother had told her that when a person died and went to heaven, they were "close to God." That was good, Amalia supposed. But when she asked questions about heaven…where it was and what one did there, her grandmother could provide no details. Was it like a city? No, it wasn't. Were there streets? No, there weren't. Were there things to eat there? No, there weren't. You were only "close to God."

On any day the portales were busy. Aside from the passersby and the bustling meseros bearing trays of coffee or food, there were other vendors: shoe shine men with their wooden boxes of rags and wax, men selling maps, older women begging for alms or trying to sell small cloth dolls dressed in native costume. Sometimes there were troubadours dressed in medieval costume or young men and women playing guitars and flutes. At the end

1

of the first arcade was a man in a wheelchair selling chewing gum who always scowled at her. She always stopped short of the kiosk selling newspapers and magazines where he usually sat.

Throughout the morning, Amalia wended her way from the first arcade to the second and back several times. Frequently she glanced across the avenue at the cathedral. Many times she had wondered... if she was "close to God" as her abuela said, was God inside? If she crossed the avenue, looked inside and found him, would God tell her more about heaven? About her mother? She knew she would be afraid to ask.

At noon Amalia walked to the portales on the west side of the cathedral and offered her meager wares to the people seated outside the Hotel Virrey de Mendoza and, farther on, at the tables outside Trico. This day, she had sold more than usual, enough to buy a refresco and still have a few pesos extra. She crossed the street to the Plaza de Armas and hoisted herself up on one of the concrete benches to eat her lunch, a bolillo with a thin slice of queso blanco, an inexpensive soft white cheese. She enjoyed watching the students who gathered there, the girls on cell phones and flirting, the boys showing off on skateboards they rode up and down the broad western perimeter of the plaza. On most days there was a man who walked in circles around the plaza's bandstand, reading from a bible. Mostly he shouted and frightened her.

The woman and the girl were already there when she returned to the portales. The woman might have been the same age as Amalia's mother, had she lived. She was wearing crisp, new designer jeans, a fresh, sleeveless white blouse, simple gold earrings and chain and black heels. She was kneeling down in front of a slender little girl, tucking back an errant lock of the girl's hair that had escaped from a white, butterfly barrette. Fascinated, Amalia edged back behind one of the walkway's thick columns and peeked out. The girl, slender and near Amalia's age, wore spotless, shiny black shoes and the most beautiful dress Amalia had ever seen. It was entirely pink, made of some rich material that seemed to glow in the diminished light of the portales. A wide sash of the same material circled the girl's waist and tied in back into a huge bow.

The woman finished re-clipping the stray tress. She smiled and gently caressed the girl's face. Amalia gasped. It was as though her own face had been touched and she felt her heart make a sudden unexpected jump.

The woman stood, took the girl's hand and laughed at something the girl said. Hand in hand they crossed the avenue. As if drawn by an irresistible tide, Amalia followed, forgetting completely her tray of small treats. Staying as close as possible, she trailed behind the couple as they passed through the Plaza, turned right, then left again into a series of small, narrow streets. Mezmerized and with no thought to what she was doing, Amalia followed. She was dimly aware of the slap-scuffle of her yellow rubber flip-flops on the stone sidewalk, of other people on the street and passing cars. But she was acutely aware of how oddly warm her hands felt. It was almost as though the woman held her hands instead of the other little girl.

Time seemed to float away, to cease to express itself in seconds and minutes. Still, it was perhaps only ten minutes after leaving the Plaza de Armas when the woman paused in front of a tall, elaborately carved door. Releasing the girl's hand for a moment, she fished in her purse and withdrew a key. She opened the door, placed a hand on the little girl's shoulder and the pair entered.

And the world stopped. As suddenly as though dropped from a cloud, Amalia found herself alone on a cold, gray-stone street staring at a massive, uncommunicative door. For long minutes she stood there, uncertain what to do, hoping the door would magically swing open and the woman and the girl would step out. A half-hour passed. Finally, realizing the woman and girl would not reappear, she turned slowly and began to retrace her steps. There had been many turns and, focused as she'd been on following the pair, she had not paid strict attention. For a while she feared she was lost and it was all she could do to choke back tears. Eventually, however, after many wrong turns, she managed to find herself back to the Plaza de Armas.

She entered the Plaza and slowly crossed it, finally taking a seat on a hard, stone bench facing the cathedral. For a long time she stared at the graceful twin towers, the elaborate stonework, now framed by a background of darkening clouds. Feeling empty. Lonely. Immensely sad.

She no longer needed to ask God about heaven, she realized.

Heaven was a place where mothers touched your face and smiled. Where mothers laughed and held your hand.

Amalia touched the worn fabric of her faded dress.

And dresses, she thought. In heaven you wore pretty, pretty dresses.

DRIVING THE DODGE OVER FIFTY

Beverly Jean Harris

The first time I met Declan, on the twenty-third floor of Boston's State Street Bank Building, I saw words above his head—words that looked like the lighted headlines that gird the New York Times Tower—and I *read* them. The words were in capital letters that spit and fizzled, neon-like: "THIS GUY IS TROUBLE. STAY AWAY."

I was only twenty-two. I didn't know about trouble. It was 1980.

* * *

A year earlier I had graduated from a reasonably good university only five miles from my parents' house in New Jersey, where I had always lived. Since graduation, I had ushered at a local theater, sliced cheese at a deli, and groomed horses, and now that it had opened for the season, I was working at the local amusement pier, making cotton candy and frozen lemonade. One day I had just returned from an afternoon shift at the pier, my fingers sticky with dried pink spun sugar, when my older sister's best friend from childhood, Annie, called my parents' phone and asked for me. Annie lived in Allston, Massachusetts, a working-class neighborhood east of Harvard Square and southwest of Boston proper. She said her boyfriend had moved out and asked if I wanted to be her new roommate. I surprised myself by saying yes.

I'd been in Boston once, in 1972, when I was fourteen. Annie didn't live there then, but my sister, Vivian, did, before she took off for Santa Cruz. A twenty-year-old college student, Vivian was studying math and statistics. My sister and I had never been especially close—my family was reserved, even with each other. But during that visit Vivian talked to me about her love for her boyfriend and her yearning for a job that would make the world a better place. I didn't respond in kind because I didn't yet know what I yearned for. As always, I was reticent with her, but I was glad that she hadn't been reticent with me.

During my visit, the city had mirrored the possibility of hopes and dreams that I might someday hold. I remembered standing outside my sister's brownstone apartment on a warm May morning, watching the Coolidge Corner trolley head toward us from the west; I remembered the screech of the wheels against the curved track, the trolley's metallic green side bright against the background of ginkgo trees and red brick row houses across Beacon Street. Behind me, the yellow marigolds in a bay-window box caught the sun, and a passing breeze brought with it the hissing smell of spent electricity, hot off the trolley's overhead lines. Ever since that moment, I had wanted to live in Boston — or Brookline, or Cambridge, or any one of the old Boston neighborhoods that I found both redolent of history and bustling with life.

After Annie's phone call, it took me three days to gather enough courage to tell my parents that I planned to move and to ask if I could borrow the old family car — permanently. Throughout my college years at home, I'd been driving the 1966 Dodge station wagon, still the apple of my father's eye. The car was green, solid, and long. That particular model, the Polara, was possibly the greenest, the most solid, and the longest station wagon ever built. My dad allowed me to drive the Dodge around our hometown; taking the car to a different state, however, was another matter altogether.

After my dad reluctantly agreed to relinquish the car, he was going to do everything he could to ensure that the Polara was properly maintained while it was out from under his watchful eye. On the morning before my departure, he called me to our driveway, opened the hood of the Dodge, and handed me a pen and a graphed engineer's pad.

"Is this a test?" I asked him, with dread.

He focused his blue eyes on mine and ran one hand back across his thinning gray hair. "Actually, Paige, now that I think about it — yes, it is a test. It's a test of character. Owning a car is a serious responsibility."

I wrote that down. For the next ninety minutes my father leaned over the open hood and pointed at various parts of the engine, staring intently at me as he explained the mechanics of the carburetor, the purpose of the spark plugs, the movement of the pistons.

An inventor of transistorized devices and computer functions, my dad was as comfortable with the engine of a car as he was with math and physics. His comfort with the engine was in inverse proportion to his comfort with me. I sometimes wondered if he ever felt lonely inside his immense intelligence, unable to share the intricacies of his ideas with anyone, his mind doomed to be disappointed by mankind, in general, and by his youngest daughter, in particular.

As I took copious notes, I thought: I'm not going to be able to do this.

He described the sound a fan belt makes when it's loose. Raising his glasses to his forehead, he leaned closer to the engine and examined whether the belt was, in fact, tight enough. My eyes wandered toward our house. My mother, at the open kitchen window, was washing dishes. The comforting sound of running water and plates gently clinking against each other carried across the cool spring air. My mother had once told me that when I was five she'd overheard my dad explaining the theory of electromagnetism to me, and she had stopped him. Part of me wished she would stop him now.

My dad unhooked the metal rod from the hood's underside, laid it horizontally, and snapped it into place. With two hands he lowered the heavy hood and let it fall with a thud. He wiped his palms together briskly. "Now for that test."

My heart dropped like a dead weight.

He quizzed me on all the details we'd gone over, but I couldn't remember any of them. And my notes were no help. Most of what I'd written was indecipherable—obscure words and half sentences: "Combustion," "Pistons, 4 moving," "Slide stick out from," "Remember to" and then a blank space, and "Under no circumstances" at the top of an empty page.

When I answered the seventh question incorrectly, he lifted his chin, almost stoically, crossed his arms, and sighed, "Ah, yes."

He must have been thinking: Ah, yes. I had forgotten that this child of mine is such an idiot.

"When is it, again, that you intend to leave for Boston?" he asked.

I looked around at the familiar tall locusts in our backyard. The wind stirred, and the trees' barely budding branches knocked against each other, sending out the scent of their white pollen blossoms. I loved these trees. I loved this town. I loved my parents. I wanted so badly to not be here anymore. "Tomorrow."

His smile tightened as if he were reassuring himself that everything would be fine in spite of my abysmal capabilities. "Well, I suppose this is the best we are going to do." He sounded deeply disappointed.

I felt flat and inept, embarrassed that his efforts had been wasted. "Thanks for your help, Dad." I just hoped the car would carry me to Boston and that I wouldn't destroy it in the process.

The Dodge Polara was an integral part of my parents' world. No trade-in models for them—they held onto a car much longer than other families in our neighborhood would, not so much out of thriftiness as out of an appreciation for what good fortune and hard work had brought them. From the South, my parents were traditional, modest, and prudent. They went to church every Sunday. They didn't go to parties. I didn't go to parties either. It wasn't that they forbade me—but I intuitively knew that I was held to a higher standard than other kids my age. I was expected to not fail at anything. The disillusion and distress my parents would feel if I were to get into a scrape or make a fool of myself would be too much for them to bear—and too much for me to bear. My sister had ended up on the other end of their disapproval. Since I didn't even know what she had done wrong, I wasn't taking any chances: I just had to be perfect.

We lived a peaceful life. My parents assumed that I would not disturb that quietude and that I was content with a tranquil life as well. I had acquiesced to their assumption.

My dad was watching me.

"Are you sure it's sensible to move all that distance away?" he asked, his voice inflecting downward as if implying an answer in the negative.

Doubt overcame me, as it always did whenever he questioned my intentions. Of course it wasn't sensible. Didn't he know that?

I nodded, despite my trepidation.

"Well, all right, then, Sweet Pea." He gave me an extra key to the car. "I guess it's all part of growing up. You do what you need to do."

I felt relieved that he hadn't noticed my instant of inner wavering.

"The main thing to remember is to drive defensively."

"Okay, Dad."

"Anticipate danger."

"Okay, Dad."

"And don't drive the car over fifty miles per hour. If you do—"

"I won't, Dad," I interrupted him. I couldn't listen to another word of advice.

He looked tired and unsettled. It had been a long session. I hoped he didn't think that I was ungrateful.

"I'll call you when I get to Boston," I offered.

"Perhaps you could call me from the road at the halfway point to let me know how you're doing."

I said I would. I just had to figure out where the halfway point would be.

* * *

The next morning, I filled the old Dodge with most of my possessions and my cat. As I was about to leave, my mother, slight of figure and still sprightly at sixty, jogged to the car holding a brass table lamp from our living room. She'd wrapped it in newspaper.

"Your father and I have entirely too many lamps," she said, handing it to me through the open passenger window. "You can use this more than we can."

I thanked her and placed it on the floor of the front seat. It would look nice on my little desk, which was now on its side in the back of the Dodge. She'd also loaned me a small bureau of my aunt's.

"Thanks, Mom. And thank Dad too." It was odd that my father wasn't seeing me off—strange that he wasn't checking my headlights and turn signals one last time. "Where is he?"

She looked at me through the window. "Sweetheart, you know your father isn't good at goodbyes."

He couldn't bear to see the Dodge go. I felt guilty that I was taking the car away from him. And then I felt a pang of guilt that I, too, was leaving him.

My mother pressed her palms over the rolled-down glass of the door. "Paige, your dad worries about the long trip, the car— all the variables, as he says, on the open road." Despite her slender frame, I felt the solid anchoring weight of her presence. "But I worry about other things more."

I waited to hear what the other things were, but she didn't say. She opened her mouth but closed it again and stepped back from the car. "Remember to polish that good dresser of your Aunt Eleanor's. Lemon polish only."

"I will, Mom." I found this odd—the bureau had been in the basement collecting dust. I hadn't known it was so important to her. I'd really have to be careful with it.

We said our goodbyes. I put the car in drive. Before I lifted my foot from the brake, my mother was at the passenger window again.

"Paige, if you see Vivian, tell her we love her."

She walked away before I could answer her, but I wouldn't have known what to say anyway. My sister was in California, not Massachusetts. The last time I'd seen her was the fall after I'd visited her in Boston, when she had brought her boyfriend home to New Jersey. In the morning after their first night at our parents' house, I was in my room at my desk when I heard a sound like a hawk's call and realized it was Vivian's voice, high-pitched as if she were crying out or yelling. No one yelled or cried in our house, ever—and it frightened me. I heard the back door slam.

Through the window, I saw Vivian jump into the passenger seat of her boyfriend's car. They drove away. For the rest of the decade, she barely contacted my parents or me. I was sure that the fight she had with my parents must have had something to do with that boyfriend. Years ago, though, I'd made myself stop thinking about it.

In the rearview mirror, as I steered down the driveway, I saw my mother wave and then clasp her hand over her mouth. Again I felt guilty—I was leaving my mom too. As I turned onto the main road, though, I tried to put my feelings aside. I had to concentrate on driving.

I set out for Boston. Two stapled pages of directions were taped to the dashboard. My hands gripped the wheel so tightly that my palms were red when I pulled over at a rest area north of the Tappan Zee Bridge. After Hartford, Connecticut, I left Interstate 84 to eat lunch and to call my dad from a payphone, as I had promised. It took me forty minutes to find my way back to the highway. Throughout the 365-mile trip, I kept glancing at the speedometer, careful to drive no faster than 49 miles per hour. At one point on Route 86 my heart leapt into my throat when I glanced down and saw the speedometer needle at 51, but I instantly eased my foot off the gas and brought the needle lower. My cat yowled for seven hours.

Finally, just south of Boston, I left the Mass Pike at the exit Annie had told me to take. At the two landmarks that she had specified—a Merit gas station and a market whose huge hand-painted sign advertised frogs' legs, I turned left off of Cambridge Street. Two blocks farther, I spotted the three-story pale green house at 349 North Harvard. Annie was standing in the yard in the light of the setting sun. I had called her the night before and had told her when to expect me, but I was late. I hoped she hadn't been waiting for hours, but she looked as if she had. Her hands were stuffed into the pockets of a long cardigan, and her eyes were fixed at the point where my car would likely appear. She smiled—she must have seen me behind the wheel, or maybe she recognized the old Dodge. She pushed her big glasses higher on her nose, lifted one hand, and waved her fingers in greeting.

As a child I had adored her. She had always made me laugh. She could do tricks, like rolling her eyeballs back into her head so that only the whites of her eyes showed. And her singing voice—she made her living as a music teacher—had an astounding range that allowed her to suddenly drop from a primly angelic high note to a preposterously low one: one of the silly things she did that had made me, as a six-year-old, admire her so.

Annie directed me to park on a side street. I hadn't seen her since she'd moved out of state when she and Vivian were high school freshmen, but she looked exactly as I remembered. At twenty-eight, still self-conscious of her height, she slouched as she had when she was younger. Everything about her was high—her forehead, her cheekbones, her arched brows over her large-lidded eyes. Her dark brown hair flipped upward in curls from behind two flat tortoise-shell clips and also from elsewhere on her head, so she looked as if she were sprouting wings. Beautiful in an unconventional way, she had the slow awkward grace of a camel.

When I got out of the car, Annie gave me a hug and then stepped back, holding my hands. "Look at you—you're all grown up! And your hair is curly!"

"I wear it a little longer now than when I was a kid," I said.

"Well, it's still that same nice chestnut brown." Her smile spread slowly across her face. "You look pretty."

I thought it was kind of Annie to say, though I didn't believe her.

Annie grasped the lamp and a suitcase, and I picked up the cat carrier. I followed her to her third-floor apartment. When I freed my cat, she ran past Annie's big tabby and, with a quick hiss, fled in a black blur into the hall closet.

"She'll be all right in there for now," said Annie.

We had lugged almost everything—including that unwieldy dresser of my Aunt Eleanor's—up the stairs and into my room when, before I even knew I was crying, tears began to run down my face. Even though I was happy to see Annie again, I missed everything familiar in my life. Dusk fell, and so did my spirits. How could I stay in this city where I'd never lived before and where I knew no one but Annie?

"Annie, I'm sorry, but I think I want to go home." I couldn't believe I was saying this after driving hundreds of miles, but my dad had been right—it had not been sensible to move such a great distance away.

Annie crinkled her brows in empathy. "Are you sure?"

I nodded, feeling defeated.

"Well, okay, if that's what you want, Paige. I understand." She lifted a book-filled milk crate and started downstairs with it. I grabbed a suitcase and followed her.

We carried about half of my possessions to the car. As I was placing the brass lamp that my mother had given me back onto the floor of the front seat, I hesitated. My mother, I imagined, was as torn about my moving as my father was—and as torn as I, obviously, was as well. I had envisioned that lamp on my desk in my new apartment—a place where I might make decisions about my life.

It was dark now. Annie was heading across the lawn to go to the apartment for more of my things. I was still holding the lamp.

"Annie," I called to her.

She stopped.

"I want to stay."

She returned to the car, smiling. "Okay, Paige. That's good." She didn't make fun of me or complain. She took the lamp and walked with it into the darkness toward the lighted front porch of the house: my new home.

* * *

My room was between Annie's room and the kitchen. We arranged an extra bed of Annie's, Aunt Eleanor's dresser, and a bookcase around the wood-floored room. I pushed the little desk to where it would catch the outside light. I unwrapped the brass lamp and placed it on the desk.

When I woke the next day in my first apartment, I saw the sky from my bed. The western-facing window was open. Through the screen, I smelled hot butter on a grill—someone cooking eggs in an apartment below? A catbird cried, just like at home, but then I heard the roar of an engine. I threw back the covers and rushed to the window in time to see a yellow and white bus passing the house, traveling along North Harvard Street and leaving a trail of exhaust. Smelling the acrid fumes reminded me of that moment long ago waiting for the trolley. I was living in a city for the first time. I felt alive and a little frightened but excited about my new life, whatever it might be.

* * *

Whatever this new life might be, a job had to be part of it. Now that I'd made my choice—I was sure I wasn't going to re-pack the car and return to New Jersey—I decided I'd try for an office job in downtown Boston.

I knew nothing about offices. I didn't even own a suit. I'd always been industrious in high school and in college, though, so I figured the suit didn't matter as much as diligence and a professional attitude.

I bought a *Boston Globe* at the frog legs' market, combed through the Help Wanted ads, and circled a few jobs I thought I had a chance of getting. I had to make more money than I'd ever made before. My half of the rent was $159 a month.

I had three interviews on three consecutive days; I drove the Dodge to each one. Storrow Drive each time was a nightmare. I was carefully driving at forty-nine miles per hour, but every car on the road seemed to tailgate me like an Imperial Star Fighter, swinging left and then right before flying past within inches of my driver's side mirror. Every now and then I'd catch a glimpse of the green Esplanade and the Charles River, but I was too nervous about driving to enjoy the view.

On Wednesday, at an interview in an office near Boston Common, I sat across the desk from a man in a worn three-piece suit who puffed a cigar as he recounted what my duties would be as his secretary. One of the duties would be to take his shoes to be shined once a week. He placed the burning cigar in an ashtray. Leaning forward, he folded his hands and set his solemn, lens-enlarged eyes on me. "Basically what we deal with here," he said through a haze of smoke, "are *nuts* and *screws*."

I tried to model his solemnity. "Oooooh." I dragged out the vowel. "How interesting." I left as quickly as I could.

Back in the apartment, I found Annie sitting cross-legged on her bed, her hand dipping into a box of Oreos. She was working half-days and seemed to spend a lot of time eating cookies. I supposed she could tell from my face that I hadn't found the job of my dreams.

"No luck?"

I let my attaché case—as old as the Dodge, and also from my dad—drop to the quilt and reached into the cookie box. "No."

Annie lifted a pad of paper from the bed. "Your dad called. He wanted me to remind you of three things."

"Oh, no. I'm sure I've done something wrong with the car already." I sighed. "What did he say?"

Annie read from the paper. "One. Check oil. Two. Check distributor cap." She glanced at me. "He says he showed you how to do that. And three. Don't drive the car over fifty miles per hour."

"I'm not going to."

Annie tore off the sheet of paper from the pad and handed it to me. "And he told me one more thing that I didn't have to write down."

"What was that?"

"He loves you and he misses you."

I felt a rush of warmth. It was nice to hear that my dad had said that. I realized I'd never been away before so that he could miss me. Maybe he missed me more than he missed the Dodge.

"So, did you meet any cute men today?" Annie asked.

A cute man was the last thing I needed. "That's not what I'm here for," I told Annie. "I'm not here to meet men. I just want a job. I want to pay my half of the rent."

"I understand, Paige." She reached for another cookie.

* * *

On Thursday, at an insurance agency in South Boston, the receptionist gave me a typing test. She placed a three-page contract on a stand by a typewriter and told me I had five minutes to replicate it. Three minutes or so after the start bell, I moved my eyes from the contract to the sheet in the typewriter: I hadn't typed a single recognizable word. My fingers had been on the wrong keys. I walked out to ask the receptionist if I might begin the test again, but she wasn't at her desk. I returned to the room, sat down, and continued typing as fast as I could. When the bell rang, I winced at the typed sheet. At least this time I'd typed several real words. The receptionist strode in and pulled the paper from the typewriter. I slipped out of my chair. I didn't wait for her to speak. "Thank you for your time," I said, and left.

When I arrived at the apartment, Annie was staring out the kitchen door, which opened onto the wooden deck and fire escape. She looked like a dog at a fence.

"You okay, Annie?"

"Paige, would you please get that apple that rolled out onto the deck?"

"Sure, but why can't..."

"I'm sort of afraid of heights."

I was surprised. Annie always seemed so calm. I had thought she was fearless. I walked past her onto the wooden platform, dipped to retrieve the apple from where it lay near the edge of the three-story drop, and walked inside again.

"Thanks so much, Paige." She shuddered as I handed it to her. "Vivian tried to help me get over my fear. At least now I can stand here at the sink with that deck door open."

It was the first time Annie had mentioned my sister. Part of me wanted to ask if she knew what had happened with Vivian, but part of me didn't want to know. I didn't ask. "Maybe we could work on that some more. When I was a kid I taught my gerbil to climb a ladder."

"Thanks, Paige. It's worth a shot." Running cold water over the apple's striated red and green surface, she squinted at me, in anticipation of bad news. "So, no luck again today, I guess?" Her big glasses slid down her nose.

"No." My cat padded into the kitchen to greet me. "I don't know, Annie. I don't seem particularly qualified to do anything." I wondered whether that cigar-smoking man might have offered me the position if I had shown more enthusiasm about nuts and screws. I picked up the cat and pulled the deck door shut.

"Your cat was scratching her claws on that nice dresser of yours today."

"Oh, no," I sighed, chagrined. "That's the one thing that my mother was worried about—that I'd damage that dresser! And now it's probably ruined."

Annie set the apple on a wooden cutting board. "Well, it's just a dresser, Paige. I'm sure your mother worries about other things more."

How odd—my mother had made a similar comment. I thought she had been worried about the furniture, but maybe she'd been concerned about something else? Maybe it was me my mother was worried about? On occasion my parents spoke cryptically. Like the time when I was thirteen and my father said, "Paige, you've reached an age when you might want to learn certain facts of life. There's a book with a black cover in the upstairs den that you could read if you're so inclined." For years I didn't look for the book. I was sure my parents would be more likely to approve of me if I wasn't so inclined. And after Vivian left I wanted to *prove* to them that I wasn't so inclined. I never went on dates. I never talked about boys or young men.

Annie sliced the apple in quarters. Her face brightened. "Well, did you meet any cute guys today?"

Had Annie read my mind? "No, I didn't—and I don't want to. Look at all the trouble it caused when Vivian met a cute guy."

She handed me a slice of the apple. "Okay, Paige."

* * *

My third interview was on Friday, for a proofreading position at a law firm near the waterfront. I had been an English major in college, so it seemed kind of logical—the proofreading, I mean, not the waterfront.

I first met with Sally, the word-processing department manager, who was, as she said, a transplant from the Cornhusker State, so as we chatted I kept picturing stalks of corn being dug up from one field and planted in another.

"We'll have to give you a test," said Sally.

My heart began to pound—this would be my third test in a week.

She handed me three pages of double-spaced type.

"Mark anything you think is a typo. You have ten minutes. You can stay here in my office." She handed me a pencil and checked her watch. "Okay, go." She walked out the door.

I hated tests. "M-E-M-O-R-A-N-D-I-U-M" was written across the top of the first page.

Paige, I told myself. Concentrate. I circled the "-I" and wrote, "Remove."

As I began to read, I relaxed. The page was filled with typos. My pencil flew—circling words, crossing out letters, and writing correct spellings in the margin. The first three letters of one word were italic and the last three were boldface. I circled the word and wrote, "All italic or all bold or neither?" A blank space appeared in the middle of a sentence on the second page. I wrote, "Close this space." The margins on the third page were justified, unlike the margins on the first and second pages. I marked that too. This was fun, like picking off aliens in the Space Invaders game on the amusement pier back home.

Sally returned to the office. "All done?"

"Yes," I said, surprised that I actually was. What a difference from the typing test yesterday!

Wobbling in her red high heels, Sally led me through a carpeted hallway lined with portraits and seascapes to the office of the personnel manager, Mary Lacey, a pleasant woman who seemed to be around forty. Mary Lacey took my résumé from Sally, shook my hand, and offered me a seat.

The opposite wall of the office was all glass—I could see only the tops of other buildings and a powder blue sky. Mary Lacey, neat in her pressed pink suit, sat down behind the austere desk and scanned my meager résumé, all the while fingering one of her small gold drop earrings. The yellow morning sun hit the white stone facade of the tall building across the street; a shaft of light angled from the east across the gray carpet and fell on Mary Lacey's short auburn hair. The sounds of the street below were muted, as if the outside world didn't exist.

"A degree in English! Perfect!" She fluffed her chiffon scarf. "So, what books have you been reading?"

"Well, last week I finished *As I Lay Dying* by Faulkner."

"Faulkner's always an upbeat choice—ha, ha," she laughed. "You're young. One day when you're older like me, you suddenly won't be able to read anything depressing anymore."

I knew I would never get tired of depressing books, but I didn't say that to Mary Lacey. We talked about other authors, Boston, and proofreading until a knock sounded on the door and Sally appeared with my test in hand. She gave Mary Lacey a thumbs-up sign and left.

Mary Lacey said she thought I'd be a good fit at the firm and asked if I could begin working on Monday.

I said yes. I had a job!

"Wonderful! Welcome to Stover and Baird." She reached across the desk to shake my hand, stood, and gestured toward the hallway. "We'll do the paperwork on Monday. For now I'll just introduce you to the other proofreaders." With a wink, she opened the door. I liked her. I liked this place.

We walked down an undecorated hall, past the word-processing department and past the mailroom to the proofreaders' office. The office was about the same size as Mary Lacey's, but instead of one big window, there was none; instead of one big orderly desk, there were four cluttered smaller ones, in pairs, each pair pushed together and facing each other on either side of the room. Books, stacks of paper, and tea canisters stuffed with pencils and pens were scattered on every surface. At the farthest desk, seated behind a vase filled with several rulers fanned like flower stems, was a young woman with olive skin, glossed lips, and dark narrow brows. She had been smoothing her hair with a curling iron, which she quickly dropped into the open desk drawer as soon as we walked in. Her hair on the unstyled side stuck out horizontally.

Mary Lacey pretended not to notice. "Paige, these are two of your fellow proofreaders, Stephanie and Mason. This is Paige."

As we greeted each other, I wondered — where was this other person, Mason? Then I saw him — he was unfolding himself from a contorted position on the floor.

He cleared his throat. "Pardon me. Just trying to adjust my back." He took a step toward me and extended his hand. Tall and skinny, he had a dough-white face and small, black recessed eyes that reminded me of raisins. His head was capped with a thick tuft of cinnamon-colored hair.

Stephanie and Mason. I said their names to myself. I'd be seeing them every day.

Mary Lacey glanced around the office. "Where is Declan?" she asked. A line appeared on her smooth forehead.

"Sorry — am I late for my scene?" said a melodic male voice behind me.

I turned around to the doorway to see a startlingly handsome young man. He was short, but his slim gray suit fit him perfectly; a folded *Boston Globe* was tucked under his arm, and he carried a small paper bag. He laughed, apparently at what he'd just said, and then he quickly bit his lip and lowered his eyes — sapphire blue and long-lashed. His smile deepened his vertical dimples. He had an angular jaw and blond wavy hair. And, of course, for a brief moment in time, those ominous words, sizzling with phosphorescence, pulsed above his head: STAY AWAY.

I had no intention of getting close to Declan.

* * *

"Hi, Annie," I called out when I walked in the door that afternoon. Annie was playing the upright piano in the hall, her big tabby cat standing on her lap so that she had to keep tilting her head first left and then right to see the sheet music around the cat's meandering tail. At the end of a measure, she stopped playing and looked at me.

"You got a job," she announced.

She must have guessed it from the expression on my face. I explained how well I had done on the test and how, maybe, I was even cut out for proofreading.

"I'll be able to pay half the rent, Annie. I'll be able to stay in Boston."

"I'm so happy for you, Paige."

"I'm happy too." As soon as I felt happiness, though, doubt clenched me, as it often would when I wanted so badly for something to work out. "What if I can't do the job? What if I fail?"

Annie shrugged her shoulders and waved a hand at me. "So maybe you make a mistake now and then. So what? That doesn't mean you've failed. Everybody makes mistakes."

That made sense. Her words calmed me. "Thanks." My cat appeared in the doorway of my room. I reached down to pet her.

"So, I guess you didn't meet any cute guys today."

I thought of Declan—his sapphire eyes and his dimpled smile. "No," I said.

Annie looked at me, her fingers poised over the piano keys. "That's okay. Like you said, that's not what you're looking for."

"That's right." I scooped my cat into my arms. "I'm certainly not looking for anything like that."

"You know, if you ever did meet somebody you thought was cute, we could talk about it."

I didn't know what to say.

Her smile implied that she knew me better than I knew myself. I was glad she didn't ask me any more questions. She turned back to the piano and began playing at the next measure.

In my room I dug through one of my unpacked boxes. I pulled out the book with the black cover that my dad had mentioned when I was thirteen and that I'd taken from the upstairs den a few days ago, before I'd left my parents' house. I wasn't ready to look at it yet, but I placed it on the middle shelf of my bookcase within easy reach.

The piano had been silent awhile when Annie appeared at my door. She was holding a small package wrapped in blue tissue paper and tied with a shiny blue ribbon.

"It's from your sister."

I felt a jolt of excitement—my sister! I reached for the package but quickly withdrew my hand. Annie knew what had caused the rift between Vivian and my parents. I finally felt I needed to know too.

"Why did my parents and Vivian have that fight? What did she do wrong?"

Annie smiled kindly, as if she felt sorry for me. "Oh, Paige, your sister didn't do anything wrong. Your parents didn't do anything wrong either. Things just happen. Vivian needed some distance."

From what? From me? "How did she know I was moving here?"

Annie exhaled. "She was the one who suggested I call you."

I looked at the package. The shape of the ribbon looked so familiar—it was crimped and askew, the way Vivian always tied a bow.

"When Vivian left, you were a child," said Annie. "Now that you're an adult, you might see what happened between her and your parents differently."

I reached out again and took the box.

Annie handed me a slip of paper with a phone number on it. "She wants to talk to you. You can use the telephone in the kitchen any time you want."

"Thanks." My voice was trembling.

I placed the package and the slip of paper on the shelf next to the book with the black cover.

Annie returned to the piano. I sat at my desk, my lamp unlit, looking out the window as the sun descended behind the maples that lined the yard. I left my desk and lay on my bed, my mind racing with thoughts about Vivian, the new job, and the people I'd met at the office, lingering a moment on Declan. Exhausted, I fell asleep.

I slept deeply and dreamed of the fizzling letters encircling Declan's blond head. Although the headlines were still cautioning STAY AWAY, after every few flashes the words transmuted as if polarized and, instead of warning, beckoned: COME TO ME.

I woke with a start, disturbed. I walked down the hall to talk to Annie, but her door was closed and it was quiet inside, so I thought she must already be asleep. I returned to my room and stood in front of the bookshelf. The black book would still have to wait, but I picked up the pretty blue package and untied the ribbon. I opened the box, pulled aside the white tissue paper, and saw a carved wooden sailboat. Its halyard leaned forward, and the burnished pine mainsail curved out as if in a full wind. A wooden wave curled over the boat's bow.

The carved ketch brought back a memory I often pushed away. The boat was just like the one that Vivian and her boy-friend, Thomas—I remembered his name—had taken me sailing in when I visited Boston. As he held the tiller and steered us out onto the Charles, Thomas told me how an oyster forms a pearl and how a cuttlefish can change color to match its environment. I loved the sound of his voice. The shadow from the sail fluttered across his face, and his gentle eyes squinted against the bright sunlight. I remembered hoping that someday I'd find a boyfriend like him. Vivian leaned against the other side of the boat, her arms outstretched, her hands cupping the boat's rim. Her long blonde hair blew in the breeze as she smiled at us. I'd never seen her look so happy.

The gift from my sister was beautiful. It was perfect.

I gripped the boat and felt a fierce anguish at her abandoning me all those years ago.

I looked at the clock on my desk—it was eleven, but it was eight in the evening in California.

When I first heard Vivian's voice I burst into tears, and I didn't even care that crying was something my family never did.

"Paige, is that you?"

I gulped air, catching my breath. "Yes."

"Oh, Paige, I'm so happy to hear you. I've wanted to talk to you for so long—"

I couldn't help but blurt out my pain. "Why did you leave me? How could you abandon me like that?" Hurt and enraged, I barely knew my own voice—it reminded me of Vivian's high-pitched, birdlike cry that night she fought with Mom and Dad before she and Thomas fled.

"I *did* abandon you," said Vivian. "And I'm so, so sorry. I understand your anger and you have every right to be angry."

She sounded steady and strong. I felt her strength fighting to calm me, but I wasn't letting it yet. "Why did you leave?" I asked again.

"I left because I was trying to save myself. It was the only thing I could do." She told me how she had felt swallowed up

19

by the family, afraid to try anything new, afraid of love, always striving to be perfect—and how, in leaving and staying away, she finally gave herself permission to live her own life.

As when Annie said it was okay to make a mistake, her words reached me. I was still angry and hurt, but I was beginning to understand her.

And then I talked, and she listened. Though bruised and aching and raw, I felt loved, and somehow because of the rawness, the love felt all the more real.

She sighed—her version of Dad's "Ah, yes."

"What?" I asked her.

"I was never as strong as you, Paige."

"Strong! Me? I don't know what you mean."

"You're there in Boston, aren't you? You made your decision, and you got there of your own accord."

"Well, and the Dodge," I said. But maybe she had a point. "You were strong enough to leave too."

"Yes, but maybe not in the optimal way." She told me how Mom and Dad had disapproved of her relationship with Thomas because, according to them, she was too young to be so seriously involved with a man. They said she would ruin her life—and she didn't know how to explain to them that she would be fine. And she was fine. It had been hard, she said, but now she was more than fine. She had worked her way through college in California—she'd majored in marine biology—and she and Thomas had become research technicians at a marine lab. Her job was making the world a better place. And she was still living with Thomas. Though they sometimes had their differences, they loved, encouraged, and supported each other. She was living her dream.

I was so happy for her, and I told her so. I told her about my new job and about how much I liked Annie and Boston. She said she was happy for me.

There was a lull in the conversation for a moment or two—a comfortable silence between sisters. I took a breath. "I met a cute guy today, Vivian," I said.

In the pause before she spoke I could almost hear her surprise. "That's wonderful!"

I felt my heart tighten. "I don't think it's wonderful. I think he's trouble." I twisted the phone cord while I waited for her response.

"Maybe he's trouble and maybe he isn't," said Vivian. "Feeling attracted to someone can be scary. Anything can be scary at first."

Her words were like balm. She didn't reject my fear—she accepted it.

"And trouble isn't always a bad thing, either. Sometimes we

have to get into a little trouble to start living. Life can be messy."
She laughed. "I should know!"

I laughed too. It was good to laugh with my sister.

"On the other hand," she said, "maybe your intuition is
speaking to you, and you really do need to listen to it. You don't
know yet. But you don't have to rush into anything. And just remember—from now on, I'll be here for you."

I was so happy I had my sister back.

I remembered what Mom had asked me to tell Vivian if I talked to her.

"Mom and Dad love you, Viv."

And then it was Vivian's turn to cry. "I'll call them soon,
Paige. I promise."

As we said our goodbyes, I saw the sky getting lighter outside. We had talked all night.

I made myself coffee and a fried egg sandwich. I ate at the
table in front of the open window, feeling the breeze that moved
the branches of the maples.

I had ventured out on my own and found my sister. My parents loved me. I had a new home. And I even had a job. I was so
glad I'd decided to unpack the car again that first night here. I was
so glad I'd stayed.

I went outside and slipped into the old Dodge. The Polara felt
solid and strong as I drove it down North Harvard, turned left
onto Cambridge Street, and crossed the Charles. It was early Saturday morning, and there was no traffic. I steered onto Memorial
Drive, along the water's north edge.

The wide river reflected the pink sky of sunrise. The sails of a
dozen boats were bright against the dark silhouette of Boston on
the far shore. That long-ago day in the sailboat, I had loved seeing
Vivian so happy. I believed now that I could be that happy too.

The morning felt fresh and electrically charged as I propelled
the Polara forward. I rolled down the windows, and the reedy
river air rushed in. I glanced at the speedometer and caught my
breath when I saw that it read fifty-one miles per hour. I exhaled
and pressed my foot to the gas, gently urging the needle up higher—fifty-two, fifty-four, fifty-six. The car didn't explode. The engine didn't spontaneously combust. And neither did I.

I eased the car down to fifty and patted the dashboard. My
dad wasn't the only one who loved this Dodge.

And my sister wasn't the only one finding her own road. I
would find my own road too. And I wouldn't let fear stop me.
Capital letters might dance on the heads of angels and devils
alike, but, in time, I would learn to tell the difference.

DOYLE'S DINER

Ray Morrison

Back in 1962, Providence, North Carolina, was no different than most of America's small towns. Main Street comprised a simple lineup that included a movie theater, barbershop, police station, and dime store. The Esso station could be found on the western end of the main drag, but at the eastern boundary of the town proper, where the line of commercial buildings gave way abruptly to the wide fields of the county's many tobacco farms, stood Doyle's Diner, a familiar gathering place of Providence's residents for several decades. Billy Doyle, the owner and cook, was the son of the man who'd built the diner back when Billy was still a baby crawling around the unfinished wooden floors of the two rooms his parents rented in a large boarding house that once stood where the movie theater was eventually built. For most of Billy's childhood, his mother was the diner's sole waitress.

No one on either side of Billy's family had ever attended college, so it was much to his parents' pride that while still in high school, Billy had been on track to attend the University of North Carolina on a basketball scholarship. At six feet, seven inches, he was the tallest boy in school—the tallest person, it was suspected, in all of Randolph County. In truth, Billy was not particularly interested in sports, but he and his family knew his height was a way to parlay his mediocre academic scores into a college offer. Just under a month after Billy's seventeenth birthday, on a frigid, rainy December night, Billy's parents left him studying at home in order to make the forty-minute drive to Winston-Salem, the nearest city, to do some Christmas shopping. Less than a mile from their home, their car hit a dark patch of ice and sailed into the trunk of a honey locust tree in the front yard of their nearest neighbor's house. Billy's parents were killed instantly. Billy abandoned his dream of college and took ownership of Doyle's Diner, where he presided over the grill for the next forty-six years in what he considered his filial duty and homage to his father's legacy.

In those early days, the people of Providence rallied around Billy. Many of the town's women volunteered to help out at the diner. By the time he was nineteen, however, Billy had figured out (in his mind, at least) all he needed to know to run the business and he made it clear he didn't want charity. Billy's first order of business was to hire a waitress and a dishwasher. For the latter, he turned to one of his former basketball teammates, a burly kid named Delmar who was the first post-segregation black student to attend Randolph High School. Delmar lived a hardscrabble existence with his parents and four siblings on a small farm just outside town.

Much harder for Billy was his search for a full-time waitress, as there were few girls in Providence at that time who were not married and raising a family. One girl, though, did come by the diner when word got out that Billy was hiring. Her name was Virginia Denby. Like Delmar, Billy knew Virginia from school. She'd been in most of his classes and her father had been his English teacher. Mr. Denby had earned the reputation of being the hardest teacher at the school and gave Billy the only D he'd ever received. Billy hated Mr. Denby, so he viewed rejecting his daughter's request for a job as a chance for a small retribution against his former teacher. When Billy told Virginia he wouldn't hire her, she didn't argue or beg; she simply nodded and rose from the stool at the counter, picked up her pocketbook, and left. As Billy watched her walking away through the glass door of the diner, he noticed her shoulders hitch and saw her pull a handkerchief from her bag to wipe her eyes. The sight of Virginia crying because of his pettiness caught Billy off guard and occupied his thoughts for the rest of that day. The following morning, after a mostly sleepless night, Billy sent Delmar to the Denbys' house to tell Virginia that the waitressing job was hers if she still wanted it.

So Virginia came to the diner to wait tables, but within a year she was helping with the accounting and had taken over ordering supplies. In contrast to Billy, who was reserved and terse, Virginia was an outgoing girl, talkative and friendly. She wasn't what most people would have called beautiful—she was stout and had poor eyesight that forced her to wear thick-lensed glasses—but Billy thought her face was quite pretty. Months after she'd started at the diner, Billy would sometimes hear teenage boys sitting at the counter making fun of her appearance when she was out of earshot. This angered him, and he knew it was because, to his surprise, he'd fallen in love with her. And, he soon learned, she with him.

One sultry summer evening after locking up the diner, Billy said goodnight to Delmar and walked two blocks along Main before turning north onto Church Street. A trickle of sweat that Billy knew was from more than just the heat slid down his temple. He was on his way to the Denby house to ask Mr. Denby's permission to marry Virginia, who'd left work early to scout out her father's mood. She and Billy had prearranged a signal: Virginia would turn on the porch light if she felt it was safe to proceed. If the light was out, it meant her father was in an ill temper and it would be best to wait for another day to approach him about their marrying.

Billy had changed into a clean white shirt before leaving the diner, but he could feel the dampness spreading under both arms as he turned the corner onto Gilbert Avenue, half a block from the Denby residence. In the trees above him, the trill of cicadas matched the rhythm of Billy's heartbeat. Although sunset was more than an hour away and the town was still bathed in the waning sunlight, the light glowing above the Denbys' porch was distinctly visible when Billy was two houses away.

Despite his trepidation, Billy did not hesitate when he reached the house. He took one long, deep breath and pressed the pearl-buttoned doorbell. Half a minute later, Billy looked down through the screen door at Mr. Denby, who, with a puzzled expression, peered over a pair of wire-rimmed reading glasses.

"Good evening, sir," Billy began. "Sorry to intrude, but I was hoping I could speak with you. It'll only take a few minutes."

Virginia's father looked up at the tall boy he'd nearly flunked several years before, and Billy noticed the tiniest narrowing of the man's eyes. After several moments, Mr. Denby pushed open the screen door and stepped back to let Billy enter. Mr. Denby led them to left of the foyer and into a room that was evidently the man's private study. The wall directly opposite the door was entirely composed of shelves overfilled with books; many of the volumes were packed in sideways above rows of others. A haze of cigarette smoke hovered near the ceiling. Mr. Denby made his way to a large upholstered chair, removed a newspaper, and indicated with a wave of his hand that Billy should sit. The older man then stepped behind a large desk and took a seat himself.

"What can I do for you, Mr. Doyle?" Denby said.

"It's about Virginia," Billy said, wiping a cool slick of perspiration from his palms on the legs of his trousers.

"Is she causing some kind of trouble at work?"

"No, sir. Nothing like that."

"I see then," Virginia's father said, the slightest hint of a smile rising on the corners of his mouth.

At that moment, Billy could see that Mr. Denby did indeed understand why he was there. And likely always had.

Billy proceeded to tell Mr. Denby how in love he and his daughter were and that Billy would be honored if Mr. Denby would allow them to marry. It was a nice, short speech, Billy thought, and he'd even managed to keep his voice mostly steady during it. Virginia's father explained to Billy how he'd always hoped his daughter would settle down with a man of letters or a professional, such as a doctor or dentist. Yet, he conceded, Billy struck him as an honest, hardworking young man and seemed to be genuine in his profession of love for his daughter, who, Mr. Denby admitted, was not the most desirable girl in Providence. Billy started to dispute that assertion, but then decided against it, knowing the less he said the better.

So Virginia and Billy were married the following spring at the True Believers Baptist Church, two blocks from the bride's home. Billy's only family, an uncle who lived in Iowa, could not travel to North Carolina due to ongoing problems with gout. So the wedding was a Denby affair. The newlyweds honeymooned for three days in the mountains near Asheville, driving the two hours from Providence in Virginia's father's Pontiac. It was the first time since he'd taken ownership of the diner that Billy had closed it for more than a day. Upon returning to Providence, the couple moved into their new home (Billy's wedding gift to his bride): a two-story Craftsman-style house at the western edge of town, as far away as Billy was able to find from his in-laws' place. He'd used most of his savings for the down payment and secretly fretted about making the mortgage payments. But as long as business remained at its current level, Billy figured they would manage.

The following spring, on the same day that Billy and Virginia celebrated their first wedding anniversary, the state of North Carolina announced plans to begin construction on a stretch of interstate highway that would pass just south of Providence. It was rumored, and later confirmed, that an exit would be built for the town. This was welcome news, for it meant an increase in business for all the merchants in town, especially the diner and gas station. Billy secretly allowed himself to worry less about their finances. And two years later, when the new segment of I-40 opened, his hopes were realized. Doyle's Diner was busy all day long as cross-state travelers interrupted their journeys to rest and get a meal. Things were so good, in fact, that Billy and Virginia were forced to hire a part-time employee, the teenage daughter of the projectionist from the town's movie theater, to help Delmar and Billy in the kitchen or to assist Virginia during the busiest times. Billy often told Virginia that he worried all their good fortune would come crashing down around them one day, to which Virginia would shake her head and kiss his cheek.

"You are such a worrywart," she'd say.

"Why should we be so lucky when others have such a hard time?"

"It's God's will," she'd always answer.

Then came the miscarriages. Billy did not hear any more from his wife about God's will. Having children was the one topic the normally talkative Virginia never spoke about. Billy would some-times walk into their bedroom to find his wife lying face down across the bed or sitting at her vanity, her cheeks damp from cry-ing. At these times, he would back out of the room as quietly as possible and wait downstairs for her to appear. She would look at Billy, her eyes dry but still red, and give him a taut smile. He'd tried to reassure her that things weren't so bad.

"We have so much to be thankful for. So much more than lots of people in town," Billy said.

She'd look past him, nodding indifferently, saying yes, she knew that was true, but Billy knew she didn't mean it.

The girl who worked on weekends, the projectionist's daugh-ter, was named Nancy. She was, certainly to Billy's mind, an ex-traordinary beauty. She had soft waves of deep auburn hair that seemed to shift color when she turned her head, and bright hazel eyes that were difficult not to stare at (for men at least). Much to Billy's chagrin, whenever Nancy worked at Doyle's Diner, there were always men flirting with the girl or making passes at her. It was also common for a half dozen boys to be loitering on the stools, nursing bottles of Cheerwine and unsuccessfully trying to hide their furtive leers. Billy, who was only about five years older than most of these boys, felt protective of Nancy and would come out from the kitchen every so often to warn the boys to be gentle-men while in his establishment. Both the boys and Nancy would giggle when he did this. Virginia would smile at her husband and then turn to give the boys a quick wink to let them know Billy's bark was infinitely worse than his bite.

After closing time on the weekends that Nancy worked, Billy would insist on walking her home. Her family lived just south of town in an isolated, rundown neighborhood that was situated be-hind the row of businesses on Main Street. Separating the movie theater and the five and dime was an alleyway that provided a shortcut to the cluster of streets where Nancy and her parents lived. On most nights when Billy would escort her home, they would walk in silence until turning into the alley where, the awk-ward silence becoming too much for her, Nancy would attempt to draw the taciturn fry cook into conversation.

"Have you ever met anyone taller than you?" Nancy asked one night.

"Not yet."

Billy told Nancy that it wasn't always an advantage being so much taller than most people. Buying clothes that fit was difficult, especially shoes. He'd have to drive to Winston-Salem or even Greensboro if he needed anything.

"Well, there has got to be more pluses than minuses to being tall."

"At a parade, I guess," Billy said after a moment, feeling the need to say something in reply.

"You think I'm pretty, don't you?" she asked one night, catching Billy off guard during their walk to her house.

He said that he did and quickly added that everyone he knew did as well.

"Prettier than your wife?"

He looked down at her and her eyes held his. Billy felt his cheeks burn.

"A husband can never think there's anyone prettier than his wife," Billy said.

He was pleased with his response and hoped that would be the end of the conversation, but she reached over and slid her tiny hand inside his, squeezing lightly.

"Your secret's safe with me," she said before pulling her hand away.

Billy started to say something else, felt he should, but he just looked at her smiling at him and in that instant his silence betrayed his feelings.

When they reached Nancy's house that night, Billy stopped on the sidewalk to watch her until she disappeared through her front door, which was their routine. But this time, Nancy walked around in front of him and, standing on tiptoe, kissed him lightly on his lips before skipping along the walkway and up the front steps of the house. Then, just before pushing open the door, Nancy turned and gave a dramatic curtsy and waved. Despite the shock of the unexpected kiss, this caused Billy to smile.

A couple months later, on the Saturday before Thanksgiving, the weather turned unseasonably frigid and carried the rare threat of snow. The diner was busier than usual with flocks of people coming in to escape the cold. Billy bustled about the kitchen preparing orders. Behind him, Delmar whistled amid the clatter of the freshly rinsed dishes he was stacking next to the sink. From the dining area, Billy could hear the comforting din of dozens of conversations interspersed with Virginia's voice periodically shouting out orders. Every now and then, when Billy saw that Virginia wasn't looking, he'd peek out through the pass-through to watch Nancy clearing plates and refilling coffee cups, recalling how soft her hand felt against his own rough palm. And how soft her lips felt when she'd surprised him with a kiss.

A group of five boys Billy had never seen before were crowded into one of the corner booths, smoking, laughing loudly, and horsing around. Several of the boys wore lettermen jackets from a high school in the adjoining county. Billy noticed whenever Nancy came near, they'd ask her to bring them a new straw or spoon or another order of fries or a refill of their Pepsi Colas. One of these boys, a tall boy with a thick neck and slicked hair, would try to pull her into the booth when she brought whatever they'd asked for. She would implore them to stop, warning them she'd get in trouble if they didn't, and pushing away from their grasps, but she remained smiling all the while. When she came into the kitchen to bring some dirty dishes to Delmar, Billy informed her that he was going to kick the boys out.

"They're just fooling around," Nancy said. "They don't mean any harm."

Billy told Nancy to just steer clear of them since it was getting late and they'd be closing soon. When the boys' final order of French fries was ready, Billy carried it over to their table himself.

"Here you go, fellas," Billy said. "Enjoy the fries. And, by the way... don't let me catch you in here ever again."

"Yeah? What're you gonna do about it?" the thick-necked boy asked.

"Do us all a favor and let's not find out, OK? Now eat up and get out of my diner."

After the diner closed and they were all cleaning up, Nancy went to clear the booth where the boys had been sitting and noticed that one of them had written "FUCK YOU DOYLE" on the tabletop with the squeeze bottle of ketchup. She wiped up the mess and never mentioned it to Billy.

A couple weeks later, on their walk from the diner to her house, Nancy and Billy didn't talk, both of them seemingly lost in their own thoughts. Several times Billy noticed Nancy looking up at him, appearing upset and on the verge of saying something, but then she'd look away. That evening Billy watched Nancy hurry inside the house with no more than a mumbled goodnight. She didn't curtsy or wave or look back, but Billy had waved even after she'd shut the door. Billy stood with his hands stuffed in his trouser pockets, watching the house for several minutes before heading back toward his own house and his waiting wife.

At five-thirty the following morning, as Billy and Virginia were preparing the diner for the Sunday breakfast crowd, there was a loud knock on the diner's front door. Through the glass, Billy saw Walt Castle, one of Providence's three police officers. Billy noticed an unusually serious expression on the typically jovial policeman's face. Puffs of steam pulsed from Walt's nostrils in the frigid morning air. After Billy let him in and offered him a cup of coffee, Walt explained that Nancy's father had called the police station an hour earlier to report that Nancy was missing. She hadn't come home after work the previous night, the father had said, so Walt was starting his investigation at the last place she had been seen.

Billy explained how he'd walked Nancy home and watched her go into the house. When Walt asked if she'd seemed worried or troubled in any way, Billy thought about how quiet she had been and how she had rushed into the house without saying anything other than a muttered goodnight, but he answered that she seemed pretty normal to him. Walt wrote notes on a small pad with a stubby pencil.

"So you were the last person to see her alive," Walt said.

"She's dead?" Billy asked, an icy feeling seizing his gut.

"Poor choice of words. We don't know that. But you *were* the last person to see her, right?"

"I don't know. I suppose so."

"Oh, her poor parents," Virginia said, coming up beside Billy.

Walt nodded and wrote something else on his notepad. Billy wondered if he was writing "poor parents." Then the policeman asked if either Billy or Virginia could think of anything else that might help him find the missing girl. The Doyles shook their heads in unison. Walt drained his coffee cup, thanked them and turned to leave. Just then, Billy remembered the rowdy group of boys in the corner booth. He told Walt about them, describing as many as he could remember, especially the boy with the slicked hair who'd grabbed Nancy. Virginia occasionally corrected some details. Billy indicated that they wore high school lettermen jackets from the adjacent county and added that he thought they'd been drinking beer. When Walt finished his notes and left, Billy relocked the door behind him even though it was only fifteen minutes until the diner opened for business.

"Why did you say that? About those boys drinking?" Virginia asked when Walt was pulling away in his patrol car.

"Boys that age, it's very possible," he said. "Heck, even likely. You know that."

The truth was he wasn't sure why he'd said it, but even as Virginia headed back to the kitchen, Billy stood there, picturing Nancy curtsying and waving goodbye.

The Sunday after-church crowd was twice as large as usual; the whole town, it seemed, had gathered at Doyle's Diner to discuss the news of the missing girl, which had spread like a contagion. The prevailing theory was that she'd run off with a boy, but there were plenty who suspected foul play by the antisocial projectionist or his wife. Billy considered the latter just the nonsensical ranting of mean-spirited people and the former unlikely. As pretty as she was, Nancy never talked about boys, and she didn't have a steady boyfriend.

Walt Castle dropped by the diner twice more during the week following Nancy's disappearance in order to clarify some points in Billy's initial statement. Walt told him that he'd checked out the boys from Davidson County; all had solid alibis for where they'd been after leaving the diner. The last public sighting of the girl, the policeman said, was by a couple who, while waiting outside the movie theater for friends, had seen Billy and Nancy turn into the alley.

"Technically, *I* made the last sighting," Billy said, a bit more testily than he'd intended.

Walt looked at him and Billy could see that the policeman was someone who didn't like to be corrected.

"Well, if you'll excuse me, I'm kind of busy," Billy said, even though there was only one customer in the diner.

After Walt Castle left, Billy was sullen for the rest of the day. He asked Delmar to please stop his incessant whistling, and once when Virginia leaned through the pass-through window to ask if an order was ready, he snapped at her—something he'd never done before.

"You're acting meaner than a sore-tailed cat, Billy Doyle," she said at home that night. She was packing up some fried chicken and a pecan pie to take over to Nancy's family. "What's eating at you?"

"Walt Castle thinks I might have something to do with Nancy going missing."

"That's nonsense. He thinks no such thing."

"Is it? You didn't see how he looked at me today. And why does he keep wasting time coming around to talk to me instead of being out there looking for that poor girl?"

"He's probably hit a dead end," she said. "The police must be under a lot of pressure."

He conceded that might be true, but Billy couldn't shake the feeling he was a suspect.

"Come with me to deliver this food," Virginia said. "The walk'll do you good."

They hadn't saved enough money for a car yet, so the Doyles walked arm in arm through the crisp autumn evening. When they came to Main Street, both of them stopped to look up at the darkened marquee of the movie theater, which had been closed ever since Nancy's disappearance. Billy started to walk toward the west end of the block, but his wife pulled him in the opposite direction.

"Where're you going?" she said. "Let's cut through the alleyway. It's faster."

Billy hesitated.

"What's wrong?" Virginia asked.

"Nothing. Just hadn't thought about cutting through the alley is all."

Of course, Billy *had* thought about the alley. He just didn't want to be reminded of all the times he and Nancy passed through it together, especially their last time. Or how nice it felt the time she'd held his hand and kissed him. When Billy and Virginia crossed through the alley and emerged two blocks from the projectionist's house, Billy wondered if he should have told Virginia about what had happened that night. He was right, he concluded, to keep it to himself. He glanced down at his wife, who was staring at him with an odd look on her face.

"Is something bothering you, Billy?" she asked.

"No. I'm fine. Why do you say that?"

"You look distressed all of a sudden. And you've been acting strange ever since we left the house."

"I'm okay. Let's hurry now. It's getting chilly."

When they reached Nancy's house, Billy stood to the side of the door and held the basket containing the chicken and the pie while Virginia opened the screen door and knocked. For a moment, he thought no one was going to answer and actually hoped that was so, but then the heavy oak door swung open, its hinges squeaking softly.

The projectionist was a short, stooped man with the pale skin of someone who spends the majority of the time in the dark. Like most of Providence's citizens, Billy did not know the reclusive man well—rarely did Billy and Virginia go to the movies and Nancy's father had been in the diner only once—but it seemed to Billy the man had aged considerably in the past week. The projectionist looked at them in turn with an expression Billy found unreadable.

"Yes?"

"We hope we're not disturbing you and your wife," Virginia said. "We know that these have been difficult days for you both and we wanted to bring you a little something, just to help out."

31

She gestured toward Billy, who took his cue to hand the basket to the man.

"Just some chicken, and a pie for dessert," Virginia added. "It must be hard for your wife to think about cooking."

The projectionist looked at Virginia and said nothing, his blank expression unchanged. He turned toward her husband, looking first at the food basket and then up at Billy's face. Being short, he had to bend his neck back a good ways to do this. And then Billy saw a shift in the man's eyes, like a sudden recognition, and his brows began to furrow.

"You're the diner fella, ain't you?" the projectionist said.

"Yes, sir. My name's Billy Doyle."

"You was with my baby girl when she went missin'?"

"No, sir. I walked her home to make sure she was safe and—"

"Don't you lie to me! I seen you two kissing."

Billy experienced a sudden sensation as though all the air had been squeezed from his body. He stared at the older man, unable to speak. Billy peeked at Virginia. She was looking right at him, her eyes wide and her mouth dropped open.

"You got some kind of nerve showing your face around here," the projectionist shouted, a mizzle of spit spraying out with the words. "I told Walt Castle that you ought to be drug into the police station and beaten until you tell what you done to my girl."

The projectionist's face, neck, and cheeks flushed deep red and his eyes widened, his pupils dilating like a feral animal. He took a step toward Billy, who lifted his arm to ward off a blow, but instead the man slapped the basket out of Billy's hands, sending its contents bouncing and rolling across the chipped, uneven boards of the porch.

"Get the hell out of here! If I see you again, I'll shoot you as sure as you're standing here."

"Sir, please," Virginia started, "surely there's some kind of mistake..." but the man turned toward her and when she saw the fury in his eyes, she flinched.

"Get off my property before I call the police. And take your pissant peace offering with you."

Billy and Virginia gathered up the dirt-flecked pieces of fried chicken and scooped globs of spilled pecan pie into the basket and hurried off the porch. Billy wrapped his arm around his wife, pulling her tight against him, and they walked home in silence. Tears ran down Virginia's face, but she made no move to wipe them away.

Once home, Billy poured them each a small glass of brandy from a dusty bottle he kept hidden on the back of the pantry's top shelf. Virginia rarely drank alcohol, but she accepted the glass readily when Billy proffered it. When she stopped crying, Billy came over to the sofa and sat down beside her.

"Why would he say that, Billy? About you kissing his daughter?"

Billy felt heat rise in his neck and cheeks. He leaned toward the small coffee table where the bottle of brandy was and refilled his glass so his wife couldn't see his face. He drank most of what he had just poured in one big swallow and sat back. He turned toward Virginia, who was waiting for him to explain. He'd never lied to his wife, never needed to; Billy realized he was, at that moment, at an important crossroad in his marriage.

"I don't know," he said at last. "He must be mistaking me for someone else he saw kissing Nancy."

Virginia held her husband's eyes for what seemed like an eternity to him, then took a sip from her glass.

"That explains one thing," Billy said. "Now we know why Walt Castle keeps coming back to the diner. Nancy's father has been putting foolish ideas into his head."

Again Virginia studied Billy's eyes. At last, she leaned forward and poured herself another glass of brandy, filling it to the point of nearly overflowing.

While it had been their routine ever since getting married to walk to the diner together in the early-morning hours no matter the weather—when the streets of Providence were hushed and tranquil—the following morning Virginia told Billy to go on ahead to work, that she had a couple errands to run and would meet him before opening. Billy was surprised by his wife's statement. She'd never mentioned any errands to him and he suspected there truly weren't any, but he didn't argue the point. He knew she was still upset about the events of the prior evening. But over the next several days, Virginia made other excuses to avoid walking to work with Billy and it quickly became evident they'd begun a new routine. After a month, Billy stopped asking Virginia each morning if she was coming with him. And while Billy Doyle was no master of subtlety, he understood that ever since Nancy's father had said he'd seen Billy kissing his daughter, his marriage was, for the first time, in real danger.

Billy would tell himself that he hadn't done anything wrong. Many times he would stand sweating over the griddle at the diner, trying to infuse in himself a sense of outrage at being misjudged. But this thought was usually supplanted by guilt-ridden memories of how soft Nancy's hand felt in his, or how warm her lips had been when she'd kissed him. Billy knew he had nothing to do with the girl's disappearance, so he mostly found himself wishing Nancy would simply show up. Not so much for everyone to know she was safe, but so that she could clear things up for his wife.

But five months later, Nancy's whereabouts still remained unknown. Initially, the girl's disappearance had incited a flurry of interest from newspapers as far away as Charlotte and Richmond, but as spring approached, the matter once again became Providence's own private mystery. And the uneasiness surrounding the case had seeped deep into the town's collective psyche. Rumors spread about Billy and Nancy having "had a thing" and that was why she had to go away. Billy noticed that certain regulars no longer patronized the diner, and Delmar confirmed that some members of his church's congregation had been whispering about it when they thought Delmar was out of earshot.

Even with the loss of some local customers, business at the diner continued to be brisk thanks to the increased traffic on the new interstate highway. Without Nancy to help, Virginia was forced to handle all the waitressing duties by herself. Billy was uncomfortable with the idea of replacing the girl, almost to the point of superstition. Besides, the days seemed easier when he and his wife didn't have time to think about anything but work. They never spoke about Nancy or about their visit to the projectionist's house, but the girl's aura seemed to pervade their lives like an invisible and disquieting fog that never lifted. Worst of all, Billy secretly despaired that his wife had stopped loving him.

Then one bright May morning, as the breakfast rush subsided, Walt Castle walked in the diner and asked Billy and Virginia if they'd heard the news.

"What news would that be?" Virginia asked coolly as she wiped toast crumbs off the countertop with a damp cloth.

"Nancy's back in town."

"When? How?" Billy asked, leaning across the pass-through.

Several of the lingering patrons, most of them locals, turned to listen to what the policeman had to say.

"I'm not at liberty to divulge details," Walt said, "but it turns out she's been in Raleigh all this time. At a hospital a good part of it."

"Oh, my," Virginia said. "What happened?"

Walt looked about the diner and kicked lightly at something on the floor with the toe of one shiny Brogue, and Billy surmised the policeman had regretted saying as much as he had.

"Well," Walt said, pausing momentarily as if to weigh his words carefully, "a good bit of it was written about in the Raleigh papers, so it's not exactly a secret. There was a nurse arrested. Nancy was not the first by a long shot, from what I hear. Poor girl. Apparently they found Nancy just in time, before she bled to death."

Billy looked at Virginia, who had put her hand up to her mouth in surprise and he saw that she understood something he did not. But he sensed it was not the time to ask about it. After a couple minutes of awkward silence, Walt said goodbye and left. An animated murmur rose from the booths of customers, more than a few of whom stole looks at Billy.

As they went about the business of the day, first preparing for lunch and then dinner, Billy and Virginia said nothing to each other about Walt Castle's visit or the news he'd brought. Billy pondered what had happened to Nancy, but a big part of him understood he didn't want to know. Now and then, as he scraped charred bits of burgers and grease off the griddle, or lowered baskets of French fries into the sizzling fryer, he thought of the last time he'd seen the girl. She had seemed distracted and upset, obviously wanting to tell him something. He should have spoken first and encouraged her to open up to him. Would that have changed anything? All day, he desperately wanted to talk with Virginia about it, but he waited for her to bring it up first. She never did.

Within a few weeks of the news of Nancy's return, the projectionist moved his family up north and Billy never heard of them again. More details had emerged about Nancy's disappearance. The nurse who'd been arrested hanged herself in her prison cell the night before her trial was set to begin, and there was new information about a traveling salesman almost twenty years older than Nancy who the police were actively searching for. The amount of tawdry buzz that pervaded Providence during those days had not been seen before or since.

Eventually Billy hired another waitress, a widow friend of Virginia's who'd lost her husband suddenly to a heart attack at the age of forty-eight, and life at Doyle's Diner returned to a monotonous, comforting routine.

One evening at home, Billy wandered into their bedroom to find Virginia smoothing the corner of a bedsheet she'd just put on. Not long after they'd learned about Nancy's return and her problem, Virginia had gotten into the habit of changing the sheets every night before they retired, something Billy found odd and disquieting. He had learned to stop questioning, though, because Virginia's answer to why she did it was always that she simply felt like it. Without speaking, he walked over and took hold of one edge of the spread and helped her align it. They had not been intimate in months and Billy yearned to hold his wife in bed. When they'd finished with the bed linen, Virginia folded down the sheet in preparation for retiring, then walked into the bathroom. Billy heard the water running into the bathtub as she readied her bath. He called her name.

She didn't answer. Billy hoped it was only because of the noise from the rushing water. A brief sense of desperation flickered inside him like a nervous tickle in his midsection. The water stopped. "Virginia," he said, and waited.

She appeared at the bathroom door, clutching her robe closed with her hands.

"Do you love me?" he asked.

"Oh, for God's sake, William Doyle. You ask the stupidest questions." She let one hand go from the front of her robe and reached up to remove the bobby pins from her hair bun. She shook her head once, letting strands of hair fall over her shoulders, and disappeared back into the bathroom. After a minute, Billy could hear the soft splash as she slid into the water.

Although she was out of view, Billy nodded. He often felt stupid around her, but not just when he asked her questions. And, more importantly, he realized, he didn't feel *just* stupid; he felt guilty. How could he ever tell Virginia of the nugget of shame he felt whenever he thought about Nancy? The shame that he knew had nothing to do with what happened to the girl, but rather with the pleasantness he felt whenever he recalled that night she had kissed him. He pushed that thought to the back of his mind and convinced himself, as he always did, that it was a frivolous and innocent memory. After all, it truly was. To think otherwise would be ludicrous.

Billy undressed and climbed into bed to wait for his wife to join him. After she did, he turned onto his side and reached over, placing his hand on her arm. To his surprise, she didn't pull it away. Billy wanted to say something then, something healing or clever, but his mind could not fix on anything.

"I heard there's a new Italian restaurant in Winston-Salem," he said at last. "Would you like to go this Saturday night? We haven't dressed up and gone out in a long time."

Virginia craned her head back to look at him before placing her free hand on top of his own, which still rested on her arm.

"That would be lovely," she said, and smiled.

It was the first smile he'd seen on his wife's face in a very long while, and it filled Billy Doyle with hope.

BRIDAL BOUQUET

John Engell

Somewhere along highway 15/501 near Sanford there's a brick Baptist church. A sturdy, unadorned oblong box topped by a squat white steeple. The sort of church that doesn't appear to celebrate God or proclaim human vanity. The sort of church no one notices, especially late-afternoon travelers returning to Chapel Hill from the beach, educated travelers who've trained their eyes to pick out the few buildings, the few remaining old farm houses and barns that momentarily transform the Piedmont heat and haze and monotony and plainness into beauty. At least I'd never noticed. Not until our last trip down that way.

My husband was driving, as always. As always, I was sitting in the front passenger seat, as always. I was reading *North of Boston*. Half New England, half afternoon nap, zero North Carolina. "Home Burial" woke me up. I'd read it years before, in college, with faint annoyance shading to fear. Now the talk brought me to the edge of tears. The failure of actions and of words seemed complete, and cruel, as if Frost, for all his sympathy, were taking cool pride in dissecting the misery of a wife and a husband. Misery matters, Frost seemed to be saying, but it changes nothing. It lends no dignity to sufferers, only unending loneliness and pain. Catharsis is impossible in such a world. My still-born tears were worthless.

I looked up in a watery daze and saw the church. I saw everything at once and quite clearly, as if a sea had parted to reveal a temple on the shore. Around the entrance beneath the squat white steeple stood a knot of a hundred people. I knew at once I was watching the end of a southern Saturday June wedding. As we drove past, the bride threw her bouquet into the air, a beautiful arching toss. She probably pitches for the local girls softball team. The bouquet rose ten or twelve feet from her hand, a perfect rainbow of color. It sailed above the people assembled below her at the foot of the concrete stoop and fell into the hands of a bridesmaid. I guessed she was a bridesmaid, though I never saw her buried in the crowd. I only saw her hands, broad and maternal and strong, reach up toward the bride, the steeple, and the cloudless sky and make the catch, an assertive, fluid grab, the motion of a sturdy left fielder. Blond or brunette, tall or short, lovely or plain, she caught the bouquet and pulled it down through the sea of heads to her bosom. We sped on, leaving the church and wedding party behind.

"Did you see that?" I asked my husband.

"What?" His eyes were on the road.

"That wedding. The bride threw the bouquet. One of the bridesmaids caught it."

My husband's head turned toward me for an instant. He stared, his flat, quizzical brown eyes focused just above my head.

Of course he hadn't seen the church or the wedding party or the bouquet. What man would, especially when he was driving?

* * *

Her name is Amy. I know she's the bridesmaid who caught the bouquet.

Amy lives on a farm a few miles outside of town with her father, mother, two younger brothers, and two younger sisters. After the reception in the church hall, after the ritual tossings of bouquet and rice, after the departure of the bride and groom, Amy and her family drive home. Amy sits in the middle bench of their van with her sisters, one on either side. The bouquet is tucked in the crook of Amy's round arm. It perfumes the van. At home in the kitchen, Amy runs six inches of water into a tall green glass vase, slides the stems into the vase, rearranges the flowers, then walks to her room and sets the bouquet on the vanity near her bed and in front of the mirror so she can see two bouquets. Amy has a streak of sensuality in her blood, a gift from some unknown relative, but later she says her prayers, kneeling, her elbows propped on the mattress, her hands folded below her chin. She's dressed in a white nightgown with lace at the throat and wrists.

"Lord," Amy prays, "protect me and my family and make us happy."

The images of her mind are firm and linear.

"Bless all my relatives and friends, especially Julie now she's married, and bless this world you've given us, that it may blossom and grow."

She looks at the two bouquets, the one on the vanity, the one in the mirror.

"Amen," she says.

Amy turns off the lights and slips between the warm sheets. She stares at the dark outline of the bouquet, trying to see its reflection, and cannot sleep. It's unusual for her, not being able to sleep. But she knows what to do. She rises, jerks the nightgown over her head, pulls on a green t-shirt and jeans, and hurries on silent bare feet from the house. Her thoughts become more color-ful and chaotic.

She walks past the family burial plot through the knee-high corn down to the willow trees whispering by the creek. The new moon is rising. She stands beside the creek, its banks covered with vines, saplings, brambles. Beyond the willows a sycamore waves its leaves, crackling softly in the faint breeze.

Lying by the creek, Amy sees the bouquet arch through the air. Her hands reach up. It falls softly. She pulls the sweet smell to her breast. Her mind enters the bouquet. She nestles among the stems, the blooms. Their softness brushes her cheeks, her breasts, her thighs. Great bursts of green, yellow, orange, red, and pur-ple fill her eyes. She breathes the fragrance. It puffs her lungs. She hears the petals rustle her ears. Fingers of night breeze move among the flowers. Dew falls.

* * *

One winter over twenty-five years ago when I was a sopho-more at Smith, I walked through the snow with my best friend, Liz Rowlandson. She wore only khaki-colored cutoffs and a white short-sleeved blouse, open to expose her cleavage, and a pair of hiking boots. Her arms and legs were long and fluid. Her fine, corn silk hair was done up in a bun behind her head. Her light, seagull-blue eyes squinted against the arctic glare.

"What do you want to do when you grow up?" she asked.

I might have said, 'Go to law school; practice law in Philadel-phia; have a string of unsatisfactory affairs; marry a career-driven biochemist and move with him to Chapel Hill, North Carolina; mother two bright, competitive, annoying, selfish boys; practice more law.' But I only laughed and said, "I am grown up."

"I want to discover why Pythagoras was right," said Liz. "No one knows. Even Stroud doesn't know."

"Yes she does," I said.

"No she doesn't. None of our teachers knows anything essen-tial." Essential has always been Liz's favorite word.

"Aren't you cold?" I asked.

"Then, after I find out, I want to go to the moon."

"It's cold there," I said.

"I like being cold," said Liz. "Except when I'm warm."

Liz teaches drama at the American School in Oslo. She mar-ried an international banker. They have three teenage girls whom I've met only once.

* * *

I sense the coming dawn and see Amy waking beside the creek. She sits up to watch the horizon light. Her back is soaked with dew. Standing, she raises her arms above her head and curls her fists up and back. She yawns, her chest gulping air, then laughs, the muscles and tendons in her upper back cracking with expansion and contraction. She smiles toward the promise of the sun then hurries to the house, tiptoes inside to her room, takes off her t-shirt and jeans, and climbs naked into bed. When she wakes again, the sun streams in her bedroom window, its probing light touching the vase of brilliant flowers, radiating rainbow-like into the mirror. Amy reaches out with her right hand and rearranges the blooms. She dresses quickly. When she returns from the bathroom, she sits in front of her vanity and combs her long, thick, dark hair. Fifty strokes on the left, fifty on the right. She applies lipstick and eyeliner and a touch of rouge and blush. In her eyes she sees happiness alloyed with a faint fear she cannot place. She wonders who she is, and who she will become. The face staring back at her is lovely, but it seems older than nineteen. Twenty-five, thirty perhaps. A woman. A strong, kind woman with long, thick, dark hair and dark eyes and a full, sober mouth. A mine of emotion and love and hope. A stranger who may become a friend. She smiles and the face smiles back.

* * *

"When will we get home?" asked Luke. "I'm bored."

"Don't say you're bored," said my husband. He might have added—Boredom is a sign of failure—one of his core beliefs.

"We'll be home in a half hour," I said, lying.

"Let's play a game," said Paul.

"Twenty questions," said Luke. "I'll go first."

"No, me," said Paul.

"Me," said Luke.

"Let your little brother go first, Luke," I said.

"Mom!"

"Do as I say."

"Who am I," said Paul.

 "Are you a man?" asked Luke.

"Yes."

After a pause, Luke said, "Your turn, Mom."

"Living?"

"Yes."

"A living man," said my husband. "American?"

"Yes."

"President Obama," said Luke.

"No."

"An athlete?" I asked.

"No. That's six," said Paul.

"Five," said Luke.

"Someone you know?" I asked.

"It's not your turn, Mom. You just went," said Paul.

"Someone you know?" asked my husband.

A pause.

"Someone you know?"

Another pause. Finally, "Yes."

"Someone in this car?" asked Luke.

"That's not fair."

"Yes it is."

"No it's not."

"Come on. Someone in this car?"

"Yes."

"That's only six," said Luke.

"Seven," said Paul.

"Your brother?" I asked.

"No."

"Me," said my husband.

Silence.

"Me?"

Ominous silence.

"That was easy," said Luke.

"No it wasn't. You cheated."

"Did not."

"Yes you did."

"He did not cheat, Paul," said my husband. He might have added—Stand by your choices, no matter how foolish they may seem—another of his core beliefs.

"He knew."

"He couldn't have known," I said.

"He asked if it was someone in the car."

"Because it was easy," said Luke. "We only had to ask seven questions."

"Eight."

"Seven."

"Eight."

"It was still easy."

"Was not."

"Cry baby. You're always such a little cry baby."

"Am not."

"Cry baby. Cry baby."

"Boys," said my husband, "there'll be no yelling in this car." He might have added—Yelling is unseemly—a third of his core beliefs.

"Just be quiet, boys," I said.

"He always cheats."

"Do not."

"Yes you do."

"No I don't."

"Cheater."

"Cry baby."

"Cheater."

"Shut up," I yelled. I might have added—Or I will go stark, raving mad—my core fear.

Uneasy silence.

"It's my turn," said Luke.

"There'll be no more game," said my husband. "And no more yelling."

"Mom yelled," said Luke.

"And you two are in time out for ten minutes or until we get through Pittsboro, whichever comes last," said my husband. In the car time out means no talking.

"But Dad!" in unison.

"No buts. Or there'll be no computer when you get home."

"Dad!" in unison.

"Be quiet."

Silence. Merciful silence.

* * *

When I was in college, I ran track. I wasn't very fast, but I had a long steady stride and fairly good wind. During my junior year the coach converted me from the 400, which I'd run without much success, even in high school, to the 1,500. I never won a race, but once in a while I finished third. The first time I came in third, we beat our arch-rival Holyoke by a single point. At the end of the day Coach Condon took me aside, put his hand on my shoulder, smiled down into my face, and said, "You won that meet for us, Laura. You're not one of our best athletes. I didn't expect you to place. But you've worked hard and improved and today your one point was the difference."

"Thanks," I said.

"Everyone can contribute," he said.

"That's some compliment," said Liz when I repeated Coach Condon's words.

"I think so," I said without conviction.

"Coaches are always discovering lessons," said Liz. "If there isn't one lying around, they dig it up from some bullshit pile."

I defended Coach Condon.

"That's all right, Laura," said Liz, smiling her arch smile. "You can moon over the guy. He's cute. They don't call him Condom Condon for nothing. Just don't believe a fucking word he says."

"You're a smart ass," I said.

"If you were a smart ass, you'd have won instead of coming in third."

"You're no good at sports," I said. "You're envious."

"I like non-competitive games. That way I never feel envy. You can't lose playing my sort of game."

"You can lose at anything," I said.

"Only if you're competitive."

"Thanks, Coach," I said.

* * *

I see Amy taking orders at the McDonalds in Sanford. Since graduating from high school a year ago, she's been trying to decide what to do. Fall semester senior year, her guidance counselor had urged her to apply to Chapel Hill. She'd been so scared by the idea that she'd had trouble sleeping nights for nearly a week until one morning she decided not to apply anywhere and wait until she could think things through. But what with helping her mother keep house and cook meals and tend the garden and oversee the four younger kids and on top of that twenty hours a week at McDonalds, Amy hasn't had much time to think, so she hasn't decided anything. Plus there's the softball team in summer and the girls' basketball rec league in winter and Sunday school teaching year round and working with the youth fellowship director planning and running parties and field trips for the primary classes. Sometimes, Amy wonders why she needs to make a decision. She already has too much to do and she likes it all, except working at McDonalds, and her job there brings in steady money year round, which is important to the family.

Then that Monday at work she meets a young man. She thinks he looks like a quarterback, tall, thick-chested, heavy-armed, a thatch of unruly blond hair framing a handsome face. She watches him stand in line and can tell he's trying not to get caught watching her. When finally he's at the front of the line he smiles while he orders a quarter-pounder value meal upgraded with giant fries and a giant Coke. After he's done saying the words she smiles back. He waits a few seconds then says his name is Lyle and asks Amy her name and after she tells him he says he's noticed her before— though for some reason she can't remember seeing him. Then he asks if she'd like to go out Friday night to the movies. She hesitates, then says yes. He writes her cell phone number on a napkin and says if it's all right he'll call her that evening around eight to make sure things are set for Friday. She says all right then wonders all day if he was just fooling around with her or if he'll call. He does, exactly at eight. In the McDonalds Lyle seemed pretty forward, but over the phone he sounds shy, his voice slow and faltering as if he's embarrassed or hasn't had many dates, which Amy finds hard to believe since he's so good looking. She gives him directions to the farm and discovers he lives nearly twenty miles away in another district, which explains why they never met in high school. Lyle says he'll pick her up around six and they can eat at the fish camp before the movie. She says she doesn't like fish and he says they have barbecue, too, and she says she likes barbeque so it's OK. After hanging up, Amy rearranges the bouquet. The flowers are still fresh, no hint of decay fringing their petals. She studies her face in the mirror beside the flowers and laughs with pleasure.

* * *

We drove through Pittsboro, half circling the county courthouse and the statue of the Confederate soldier. The boys were silent, knowing their father meant business.

"I like this town," said my husband. "It looks like a good place for a family."

"You say that every time we drive through Pittsboro. Maybe we ought to move out of Chapel Hill. I bet there aren't so many yuppies in Pittsboro."

"The schools are probably terrible."

"With the money we saved on housing we could send the boys to private school."

"Where?"

"I don't know."

"This is North Carolina, Laura. We're five hundred miles from a first-rate prep school."

* * *

The non-competitive Liz graduated Summa Cum Laude in mathematics and music. She started graduate school at MIT but quit after the first year. She said she hated the other students and her professors and Cambridge. Long before she quit, I visited her once in late October, riding the train up from Philadelphia where I was a first semester law student at Penn.

Liz was already living with Jeffrey, her future husband. He was a few years older and was finishing his M.B.A. at Harvard. I thought them mismatched, both preppies, but opposite types — Liz non-conformist, ironic, and clever, Jeffrey conformist, earnest, and literal. At least he seemed accommodating, something of a surprise given his career goals. He also liked to cook, which surprised me even more, and made a luscious mushroom lasagna the first night I was there, serving it with an excellent salad, superbly dressed, and an expensive Chianti, and finishing with a perfect crème brule.

The next morning — one of those perfect New England Indian Summer mornings — Liz took me to Salem, where I'd never been, and showed me the Custom House. It seemed much as Hawthorne had described it, cavernous, somnolent, lost in the past. Instead of housing a few old men sleeping in chairs, it was inhabited by two national park rangers, who whispered their knowledge as if it had occult significance, and a handful of cowed, middle-aged female tourists who hardly spoke but whose steps resounded on the uncarpeted wood floors and through the high-ceilinged, denuded rooms.

Standing at a huge window on the second floor looking over the empty harbor, I asked Liz about Jeffrey.

"He's a great lover," she said.

"Really?" I was incredulous.

"First rate. All that sublimated Puritan passion. And he's a fucking good cook as you noticed last night."

"But he's so different."

"From what?"

"You."

"I'd be bored with two of me around."

"You never bore me."

"That's because we're so different."

I wanted to say — No, we're not — but Liz was right, as usual.

"Is the attic open?" I asked.

"There isn't any attic," said Liz. "Hawthorne invented the attic so he could find the scarlet letter there. It was the only part of 'The Custom House' nobody minded. The stuff where he told the truth about his fellow Salemites gave them apoplexy. But as long as he made the story up, even Hester's adultery, they loved him. Fucking idiots."

We took the train back to Boston and the subway to Cambridge. When we arrived at the apartment, Jeffrey wasn't there. Liz poured two huge Wild Turkeys and we sat in the kitchen, our bare feet on the table.

"Jeffrey and I are going to get married," she said. "I'm planning to quit school and raise kids."

"I don't believe it."

"It's true."

"But why?"

"That way I'll learn something essential."

"What?'

"Who knows. That's the beauty of it. No one knows."

"But is it worth finding out?"

"Fucking yes. But I'm sure I won't. No one does. The essential is inscrutable. Besides, Jeffrey will be stinking rich."

"Liz!"

"Shock does not become you." Liz poured Wild Turkey down her elegant throat.

"Gold digging doesn't become anyone."

"I suppose you'll marry a pauper."

"I'll marry a man I love, if I marry anyone."

Liz made vomiting sounds. They were so realistic and so prolonged that after a few moments I thought she was going to throw up. But when I stood and offered to get her a glass of water, she laughed and laughed until tears rolled down her cheeks. Then she stopped laughing very suddenly and looked up at me with what I thought might be rage.

"Don't give me that shit about love and marriage," she said. "Not until you fall in love and get married."

* * *

I watch Amy and Lyle go out every Friday evening for a month. Then they go out Saturday evenings as well. Lyle waits to kiss her until the fourth date and when he does she's surprised at his strange tenderness. He's big and strong and works at the local brick factory where her friend Julie, who just got married, is a secretary. Lyle knows Julie's husband, who also works at the factory, but he's not like Bill or the other boys she's met. He's shy at odd moments. He always pays for their dinners and movie tickets, but she does the ordering and buying because Lyle seems uncomfortable talking to strangers. Sometimes, for no reason she can guess, he seems suddenly uncomfortable talking to her. Once in a while he even reminds Amy of her father who has a peaceful, almost sad voice, and who seldom leaves the farm except to buy things at McMartin Hardware or to attend church with his family.

One Saturday night after they've seen a movie, Lyle stops his red pickup at the edge of the long dirt drive up to the farm and turns on the overhead light.

"I have something to give you," he says, almost whispering.

She smiles. He hasn't given her any presents.

"I don't know if you'll want it."

"Yes I will, Lyle."

"Oh, I don't know."

After a silence he produces a tiny blue felt box and shoves it toward her in his left hand. As soon as she sees the box, Amy knows what's inside, and it makes her afraid. But she opens it anyway.

"It's an engagement ring," says Lyle.

"Oh."

"Can we get engaged?"

"Yes," she says, hardly knowing how or why.

"We don't have to."

"Do you want to?"

"Yes," he says.

"Me, too."

He takes the ring out of its blue felt box and gently slips the ring on her finger. It fits. He holds her large hand in both of his. Gently, he spreads her fingers out straight then strokes the back of her hand.

"I like your hands," he says. "They're beautiful."

She unbuckles her shoulder harness and nestles against his warm, strong side.

"I love you," he says.

"I love you." Amy doesn't know if this is true but she feels happy.

"Will you come to church with us tomorrow?" she asks.

"Sure."

"We leave at ten o'clock."

* * *

I didn't catch the bridal bouquet at Liz's wedding. She threw it toward me, as planned, but David, my new boyfriend, who was six foot five, a former Princeton basketball player, reached up, snapped his long, narrow right hand, and lowered the flowers to my chest.

47

"For you," he said, his gaze proprietary.

"Thanks."

Later that year David asked me to marry him. I thought about it for two days, then said no. He went off to New York to marry someone else and have two or three long, narrow kids and be a rich proctologist. My husband happened along many affairs and many years later. The first wedding I attended with him was ours, and when I threw the bouquet my younger sister, Janet, who'd been married for five years, caught it and handed it to my mother, who'd been divorced for twenty years. I watched my father who was standing in another part of the crowd with his second wife. He studied this transaction through his ironic, drink-softened eyes and laughed his ironic, drink-softened laugh. He and my mother hadn't been on speaking terms since I was eleven. Each of them told and retold nasty stories about the other. Janet and I hated these stories. They weren't sordid, exactly, but they were cruel and self-serving and, worse yet, we suspected they were mostly true. Whenever I was forced to listen to my mother or my father, these stories made me faintly nauseous. When Janet and I were alone together, we tried to speak of Mom and Dad and their endless anger and hatred with something approaching good-humored distance, while silently hoping that our lives would be entirely different from theirs.

* * *

Amy and Lyle are married in the Baptist church on a lovely Saturday in October. I imagine highway 15/501 rolling under the wheels of our car as we head north to Chapel Hill. I imagine my husband is driving again, the boys are fighting again, but this time I'm reading "Questions of Travel," struggling with the elegiac rhythms and intimations of Bishop's exquisite visions. As we pass the church, I look up and see Amy arch the bridal bouquet into the air, a perfect rainbow of color. A pair of strong, competent hands reaches skyward, grasps the stems, and pulls the flowers into the crowd. I roll down my window. I hear shouts and laughter and feel the cool air whip my hair and my face.

"There," I say. "The bouquet."

"What bouquet?" asks my husband.

* * *

Amy and Lyle drive to Gatlinburg. I watch them check into a honeymoon motel. Their room has a huge, heart-shaped bed covered with red sheets and a red blanket. The bed is squeezed between the kitchenette and the sliding glass doors that open on to the six by eight back deck which faces on a creek. Beyond the creek a thickly wooded hill, blue in the evening light, rises above the motel. They sit on the two red plastic deck chairs, holding hands and listening to the water and watching the stars come out. Neither of them says a word. Amy is excited and scared as hell. She's not quite a virgin, but she's never been to bed with Lyle. After a while, they go inside, close the glass doors, pull the frayed white drapes, and undress in the dark. He kisses her, touches her, makes love to her gently. When they've been in bed for about an hour, Amy cries. Lyle holds her, silently. After she's done crying, Lyle laughs and she laughs too. In the early morning Amy cooks sausage, scrambled eggs, and instant grits on the electric, two-burner stove top. Lyle makes coffee. The room fills with breakfast smells. They eat in bed, red, heart-shaped plastic trays holding white, heart-shaped plastic plates decorated with smaller red hearts, balanced on their stomachs. Lyle eats quickly, ravenously. Amy tries to finish, but she can't.

"You look beautiful," says Lyle.

Amy sets her tray on the floor beside the bed then turns and smiles at Lyle. After a few seconds, Lyle sets his tray on the floor on the other side of the bed. He sits up higher and gently pulls Amy's white nightgown over her head. Her small, high breasts rise to meet his warm hands.

"This is happiness," he says.

"Yes," she says. "It's real happiness, Lyle."

* * *

"You boys wash up," said my husband.

"Can we play on the computer, Dad?" In unison.

"After you wash up." He turned to me. "I'll finish unloading the car."

"I'll get dinner."

He went out the front door into the falling night, his back slumped forward as if he were still driving.

"Use soap," I yelled up the narrow stairs.

"We will Mom," yelled Luke, his voice coming from above, his tone bordering on contempt.

I stabbed four chicken-apple sausages with a fork, put them on a plate for the microwave, and ripped open a bag of unsalted corn chips. There wasn't any lettuce, so I peeled and rinsed four old carrots.

"Where's the cooler?" asked my husband, standing in the kitchen door with a suitcase dangling from each hand.

"In the trunk."

"No it isn't."

"It isn't in the trunk?"

"That's what I said, Laura."

"I heard you."

"We forgot the cooler," he said. "It's gone."

"I guess it is."

"The rental agency can't mail us a cooler."

"Maybe they can."

"The cleaning crew will steal it."

"Probably."

"Now can we play on the computer?" asked Luke, his hands dripping soapy water on the kitchen floor.

"No, you may not," said my husband.

"Let them play on the computer. They haven't played on it for a week."

"All right. Play on the computer."

"Ten minutes," I said, "Dinner will be ready soon."

"Ten minutes!" said Luke.

"You can play for a half hour after we eat."

When Luke had disappeared, my husband said, "You know we'll have to buy a new cooler."

"I suppose so."

"Every vacation we leave something behind."

"Are you accusing me?"

"No, of course not." He paused. "But I distinctly remember asking you if we had packed everything."

He turned and stomped out of the kitchen. He returned less than five minutes later and said, "Sorry I got worked up about that stupid cooler."

"I know you are," I said. "You're always sorry."

"But we leave a trail of things wherever we go."

"We can't remember everything," I said.

"We should at least try."

"Wash up," I said. "Dinner's almost ready."

My husband was right. The country was littered with things we had lost.

* * *

Liz's latest email from Oslo tells of her three girls, ages sixteen, fifteen, and fourteen, who are trilingual, "disturbingly clever," and "even more disturbingly lovely." She describes her job teaching drama at the American School where she continues to direct "loud musicals" and "witless comedies" and where the students "learn nothing essential from me." She relates a story about Jeffrey's latest infidelity with a young Norwegian beauty, "of whom there seems to be an infinite and ready supply." She insists we must visit them in Oslo, or come next July to their summer house on Mount Desert Island "to drink, bullshit, and laugh." She urges me to avoid chronic boredom, calling it "the bane of our class of post-modern women." She rails against "insipid Norwegian culture," the "deadening sameness" of the people, the "tortured, unacknowledged alcoholic neurosis" of the "maddeningly handsome, emotionally frigid" men. Reaching into the lexicon of our college days, she calls Oslo "a fucking gorgeous dump," a "shit-hole of unsurpassed whiteness," a "mecca for all of us who hope to freeze off our noses, our tits, our clits." She asks if I love my husband.

* * *

I watch Amy and me walk past the family burial plot, through the field of stubble corn, down to the creek. The late October waning moon shines faintly on our bare heads, our bare arms. The last cicadas drone their fall dirge. The air smells of harvest. We lie on the grass, pressing our backs to the earth. We reach our hands toward the stars, watching them wink between our open fingers, listening to the creek purl, feeling the dew soak our buttocks, tasting the crisp breeze.

"I'm happy," says Amy.

Tears trail into my ears, filling and cooling them.

* * *

Somewhere in Chapel Hill two boys sleep, a man snores, a woman—a woman like me but perhaps not me—sits before her mirror brushing her long, thick, black and grey hair, fifty strokes on the left, fifty on the right. When she stops, she looks into the flowering of fine, dark eyes, and sees for once, then, just once, some truth, or hint of truth, there, beneath the surface, behind the reflection. Something small. Something ancient. Something white.

HOLIDAY

Gregg Cusick

Cal Mabe stood on the fourth-from-top rung of the exten-
sion ladder, thirty-five feet over the lushly sodded lawn.
He guessed that were he to fall he might bounce softly the
way he did in his youth in the barn when he'd jump from the rafters into a huge mound of unbaled straw. Mabe dipped his brush
into the bucket and continued stroking the white paint along the
soffit beneath the roof's edge. A well-built 1940s colonial, the
three-story house boasted vented soffits all around, a rare feature
of conscientious craftsmanship that few but Mabe even noticed.
As he brushed the new paint onto the underside, he heard a voice
from below.

"Leave it, Mabe!" It was Dabney, the owner of the small, not
quite a year-old company. He stood on the front flagstone walk
looking up, his palm shading the brim of his paint-splattered
Yankees cap. "That soffit don't need it, man. That's a holiday," he
yelled up rather angrily.

A holiday was a painters' term for an area that they didn't
to worry about painting—the undersides of shelves or the wall
behind the refrigerator, the tops of doors—and some workers
lived for them. Mabe hesitated, scowling in the sun, looking up
at the roof overhang which, he had to admit, that if the new
paint hadn't been shiny wet he would not have known where
he'd just brushed.

Mabe started cutting-in the side trim until Dabney went back
to work, and then he quickly but carefully finished painting the
soffit. Each time he dipped his brush into the can he looked off
in the distance. From this height, he could see down the street
to a small park, a lush grassy oval surrounded by mature oaks
and sweet-gums. He wished he were on the park bench he could
make out, painting the verdant landscape before him. Mabe was a
person who daydreamed in bright color—the scene he envisioned
was filled him with longing, in deep reds, but also a calmness, the
greens of leaves and mosses. He thought of his wife, Daphne, just
now at the end of her teaching day. He thought of the longing
she'd voiced, again, that morning.

* * *

Over cereal—hers hot, his cold—she'd been quiet and he could feel, moody. Her eyes moved over the newspaper while he worked the crossword. She lifted her spoon toward her lips and then set it back down into her bowl, even though it had a bite of oatmeal on it. "You said you were going to think on things," she'd told him.

Mabe looked up from the puzzle, his own cereal spoon in midair. "I did," he said. "I have." He ate the spoonful of Cheerios.

"Well?" she said.

Mabe chewed slowly, swallowed. "Well, for one, we don't have the money."

"We've talked about that. We've got the money. We'd just have to alter our spending habits a little."

"My job's secure—Dabney's got plenty of work lined up," Mabe said. "But it's not very lucrative. There'd be new expenses."

"Tell me something, like what you're afraid of," Daphne asked. "You said you'd given it a lot of thought." She waited.

He looked at his sogging cereal. Her oatmeal completely abandoned. "What are *you* afraid of?" he asked back.

"I'm scared I can't love."

"You love me."

"But another. You know what I mean."

When they had first started seeing each other, Daphne had confessed that she had some sort of irrational fear related to the story of the mythic figure of her same name. Mabe told her how beautiful she was, and she reminded him the story. How Apollo made fun of Eros, and so Eros had shot Apollo and the nymph Daphne with love arrows—Apollo's made him fall forever in love with her; Daphne's made her never to love him. So when Apollo lustfully pursued her, Daphne begged her father, the river god Peneus, to save her. He did, by turning her into a beautiful tree, the laurel.

So Mabe's Daphne explained that she feared she was, like the mythic nymph, somehow not capable of deep feeling. They had been married now a dozen years. But the fear still surfaced in her at times. Like that morning.

"I think another person. A small, dependent person. I'd *have* to be capable of love, don't you think?"

He didn't answer, away somewhere with his own concerns.

"I'm afraid, too," he said. "I don't know that I want to handle it, Daph. We got it so good just now."

Mabe reached over to put his hand over hers, the hand that still held her spoon. He then rose from the table, dumped his soggy cereal into the sink. He brushed his teeth, kissed her, and headed to work.

At day's end he stood on the ladder as the rest of the crew packed it in and he climbed down to do the same. Walking to his truck, Mabe saw Dabney and Pete, Dabney's old frat buddy, watching him. When Mabe looked over and gave a wave, the two glanced away.

* * *

The next day, Tuesday, Dabney and Mabe and the other three members of the crew moved inside the big colonial. The home-owners — a British-transplant couple with jobs in sales of pharmaceuticals and software, childless — were away at the shore, drinking Mai Tais at a beach Mabe had never been called Emerald Isle. The words, the place, conjured in Mabe's mind the island of the Cyclopes in Homer. If he and Daphne had a child — he envisioned a little girl — he would tell her the dramatic story of Odysseus, just as Mabe's father had told him. How the hero blinded the one-eyed Polyphemus and escaped his cave tied to the belly of a sheep. And how the gloating, then livid Odysseus nearly had his ship sunk by the boulders flung by the Cyclops. But at work, Mabe mostly continued to think of his conversation with Daphne the night before. Daphne had been quiet at breakfast, not exactly hurt or angry-seeming, but subdued.

Since virtually every surface of this house was to be painted, Danny assigned them partners. Mabe had been teamed for months with Enrique, a good-natured hardworking father of four. But Tuesday Danny put Mabe with Pete, a fast, sloppy painter. Pete and Dabney had been fraternity brothers back at Clemson. When Dabney married, Pete kept partying. But when working together, they could still relive the Tennessee game sophomore year, a story everyone had heard, which ran like a joke involving a cheerleader, a fat guy, and a goat in a bar. Mabe much preferred working with Enrique, and while he found Pete likable enough, he had little in common with him. To start, Mabe had twenty years on Pete, and their work styles were a hundred-eighty degrees apart. And Mabe could never figure out what Dabney was thinking. Perhaps that his buddy Pete might learn something from the careful Mabe.

But that didn't seem to be the case. When Pete and Mabe set about painting a huge den, Mabe first laying dropcloths over every surface. Pete frowned. "Jesus, Cal, let me know when we can start work." He stepped out the French doors onto a stone patio to smoke a cigarette.

When Pete returned, they got going, Mabe cutting in and planning on moving to the trim when he finished, Pete quickly and somewhat messily rolling ceiling, then walls. Dabney stopped in midmorning to check progress. He was dressed un-painterly in white slacks and a pink knit shirt; he looked to Mabe like he belonged on the fairway at Augusta.

"Looks good, fellas." Dabney's practiced eye scanned the entire room, careful to miss the drips. The partly still wet, partly shiny walls looked terrible, spotty, but would be acceptable once fully dry. "Whew, Pete, you're really knocking it out, huh?" Danny added. "I'll swing back later after I do a couple of estimates."

Mabe offered no comment and had no idea whether this was true. Frankly he didn't care. Continuing the trim-work, he was much more preoccupied with his situation at home, his conversation with Daphne. With each upstroke of the brush, he constructed arguments and counterpoints to her proposal to grow their family. Each downstroke was her words smoothing his objections, quietly asserting they could afford a child, how he needn't fear anything, and that she wanted to love another in addition to Mabe. He thought of his own family, too, his sad mother, his distant father, his cold and successful younger brother. And Mabe worried that Daphne was angry at him, felt he was not considering seriously the issue of a child. One thing he sometimes loved, sometimes hated about painting was that a person had time to think.

Mabe frowned over the window molding. Part of him wished he could be fast and carefree, or even careless, like Pete. That he could just relax and let go of the, what, perfectionism? No, it wasn't quite that. Or Daphne, who wasn't bothered if dishes piled up in the sink, who could pass litter without pulling the car over and picking it up (or worrying if she didn't). Daphne would probably hit it off well with Pete, Mabe thought morosely. Pete was probably good with kids, too. Mabe bet they loved him. He probably did card tricks and could twist animals from balloons, giraffes and dachshunds. Mabe felt his depression descending, covering him like a dropcloth.

The rest of the day went much the same as the morning. While Pete blazed through two more rooms, Mabe spent the afternoon still in the den, painting the trim of the doors and many-mullioned windows. He'd be at it again tomorrow, he knew. At the end of the afternoon, Pete joined Mabe to help with trim. It was as if they'd been running on a track, and Pete had lapped him.

* * *

Back at their little ranch house that itself could use a paint job, Mabe needed a drink. Really needed it, he thought. Daphne had been home and left a note that she was going to her yoga class and the grocery, that he should get himself dinner. He patted Chiron distractedly—their big, shaggy mixed breed bore no resemblance to the wise centaur of myth—and headed straight for the refrigerator and a cold Pabst. He downed the first in five long slugs.

Working on his second beer, Mabe continued thinking of his father and his brother, who had been visiting his mind much while he painted that afternoon. Mabe had been nine when his brother, Freddie, was born. A surprise, since Mabe's parents had not planned on having more children. His father, Jacob, had always been a drinker, himself the son of solid Irish drinking stock. But Mabe's parents had been tight in the close sense, too, and engaged parents. That is, until Freddie.

Mabe's younger brother incited some change in Jacob and Maura, something Mabe noticed even at nine. His father's drinking increased; there were no heroic tales of gods for Freddie. While his mother began battling depression, although it was years before doctors diagnosed it as such. (She called it a fog; what Mabe, the painter, sometimes called a tarp.) While his parents never fought, openly or not (as far as Mabe could ever tell), the feeling of the home had changed somehow, like it was being lit, and even heated, by a thirty-watt bulb.

In this dim light, Freddie was kept (and soon kept himself) at a distance from his brother and his parents. He wasn't given chores, as Mabe had been, and steered clear of the barn Mabe had loved. Freddie had read much of Adam Smith and *Gray's Anatomy* by age twelve, but he had no friends. He'd won scholarships to Columbia and Harvard med school. But he never shook the nickname given him in middle school French class, "froidy," for his lack of human warmth. Now thirty, Freddie was an eminent anesthesiologist up in Richmond, had married and now lived in an oak-filled neighborhood of stately homes much like the one Mabe was currently painting. He visited his parents only rarely, his brother even less. At the holidays mostly, and he never stayed long.

Mabe popped open another beer and stood at the kitchen sink, feeling his father's need to inebriate himself and his mother's fog of depression. He looked out the window at their muddy back yard that he'd started but never finished landscaping. Chiron, a shaggy brown and white part-Airedale—who looked nothing like horse *or* man and was as wisdom-free as any canine—looked up from the overgrown garden. To the dog, Mabe said aloud: "With my genes, any kid of ours would be a depressed alcoholic." Chiron went back to sniffing the dried stalks of last year's tomato plants. "She'd be obsessive-compulsive, or screwed up like Freddie." Chiron ignored him. "But at least she'd know her mythology." Mabe twice rinsed and neatly flattened the beer cans and carried them to the recycling tub on the back deck. He was drinking fast enough to require almost constant rinsing and crushing.

"How was work," Mabe asked without energy when Daphne came home. He was still at the kitchen sink. "How was yoga?"

"Okay" was her only response.

Then she kissed him, patted Chiron in the same distracted way he had when he came home, and went to their bedroom to read. Mabe made a note to himself to talk to her about his thoughts, his fears, but he opened another Pabst instead. He waited until the bedside light went out before crawling in beside her.

* * *

The next morning, back at the oversized colonial, Mabe was again partnered with Pete. Dabney gave the crew their marching orders and disappeared as he often did. Never very talkative on the job—although he and Enrique, a fine, careful painter, used to joke around and discuss stories they'd heard on NPR—Mabe battled a vicious headache and painted quietly. Pete continued his speed-rolling through room after room, and it was all Mabe could do to get the surfaces prepped and cut in before Pete blew past with the wide swaths of beige and olive and canary yellow and even magenta. When the rest of the crew headed to Hera's Deli in town for lunch, Mabe stayed behind painting catch-up. He broke for ten minutes to eat a cheese sandwich he'd brought, and then was back at it, this time in one of the smaller bedrooms, yellow with white trim, for a child's room.

Mabe opened the door to a small closet. Inside the empty space was a clothes bar and above it a white-primed plywood shelf. He stared up into the dusky light of the closet ceiling. With the rest of the crew gone, the house was completely silent. He would have to get a stepladder to reach, to brush the upper edges and cut in and then to roll the ceiling that no one else would ever see. Like the day before, Mabe thought of the barn of his youth, his place of refuge.

Mabe watched the room's light angling into the closet and thought of the shards of sun that came through the cracks in the barn's pine siding. How the hay dust swirled in the spotlights of sun. He smelled the sweet warmth of the place. He thought again of leaping from the huge hand-hewn crossbeams into the piled straw.

Mabe set his paint can on the shelf, the underside of which, he noted, had been hastily and sloppily primed decades ago, never painted. Perhaps never noticed. He went to the hall, where he picked up the stepladder and carried it back to the closet opening. He took a step up and looked at the closet ceiling again, sighed. He couldn't just let it go, neither the ceiling nor the underside of the shelf. Or could he?

His mind dipped and stroked on. Could he try to have a child like Daphne wanted? Despite the risks, and what seemed so irresponsible, should they bring a child into this messy world, with its careless paint jobs, its drips and missed spots? He could try to control, to paint, carefully and neatly this tiny space; he could try, but he couldn't control much, not at all, really. He could coat the holidays, the ceiling and underside of the shelf. Or he could force himself not to paint the places. His brother could go on to greater success as a doctor but might never outgrow his coldness; their parents would die, sooner than later, he knew. And what he couldn't control or know was blended—like a complex paint formula—in the fear and excitement of the leap from the barn rafters. Mabe stepped down and took the ladder in one hand, his bucket in the other, and backed up. He used the toe of his paint-dappled sneaker and edged the closet door closed.

When the crew returned from lunch, Mabe had left the yellow room. He was trim-painting window moldings in the large magenta guest room when Pete got back to work. He nodded at Mabe, perhaps acknowledging Mabe's progress, and filled his roller pan. It was all Mabe could do to keep his brush moving steadily over the moldings and mullions and sills.

What a feeling! Mabe wanted to scream. He'd made the decision, he felt, without yielding to Daphne's influence—the answer came from somewhere inside himself. He wanted a child! He'd climbed up and crawled out and knelt on the rough-hewn beam high in the barn. And despite the fear, and after some hesitation, he'd leapt.

Yet even excitedly looking forward to getting home to Daphne, Mabe had trouble finishing and getting cleaned up by five. The rest of the crew had left when he headed across the lush lawn to his truck. Dabney came out the front door and trotted toward him.

"Hey, Cal. I want to talk to you for a sec." Dabney was winded by the thirty-foot jog. Mabe looked down to his tasseled loafers and up to his flushed face, his cheeks pink as a newborn hamster Mabe had had as a kid. "I wanted to say I appreciate all your hard work."

"Well I thank you for that, Dabney," Mabe said genuinely, feeling something like surprise to hear his efforts acknowledged by the boss, especially one who'd said as little to him as Dabney had over time. Mabe turned toward his truck, but Dabney continued, his voice steady. "Which is why it's a hard decision for me to take you off the crew."

Mabe wasn't sure he'd heard this right. In his ears there was a slight whirring, like the box fan that blew hot air into his attic bedroom growing up. Sometimes when he heard this sound, Mabe worried about his health, had even asked Daphne if she thought it could be a brain tumor. She'd laughed.

"See, Cal," Dabney went on, "I view you as a quality painter, but what I need is *quantity*. I got to do what's best for my business—to be profitable we've just got to complete more jobs. I'm sorry." Dabney did his best to look genuine and regretful. Because he was trying, Mabe would think later, he was unconvincing. Mabe's mouth opened slightly but he didn't say anything.

"Oh, kay," Mabe finally got out. He extended his right hand, a gesture he'd be angry at himself for later. Fucking nice guy— Mabe felt somehow he was condoning the boss's action, was even complicit. Dabney shook it, a hint of surprise on his face.

"I'm sorry," Dabney said again, like a mourner at the funeral of someone he never liked. Mabe walked stiffly to his old pickup, feeling nothing. He opened the door and climbed in. Directed the key into the ignition, started the truck, and pulled away. Dabney went back inside the house, as if he owned it.

Mabe headed north of town where the narrow US 101 wound gently through farmland. He stopped at Poseidon's Gas & Bait near the lake, and bought a six-pack of Pabst. By the time he had drained two and circled twenty miles or so back to town, Mabe remembered what had put him in such a good mood that afternoon. After a quick stop at the roadside where he picked a bunch of wild daisies, he turned toward home.

To get there, he had to pass the entry gates of the Parkwood neighborhood where he worked that day, just a few blocks from the stately, near-painted colonial. In front of which that frat-boy prick Dabney had cold-cocked him, had given him the pink slip. The sun was falling fast but still circular, not yet sliced by the horizon. Mabe couldn't help but drive by the scene.

In his mind, he'd pull up and the homeowners would be in

their front yard with Dabney. They'd be screaming at him: You sloppy, unprofessional son of a bitch! You irresponsible lorrie full of shit! The wife would be picking up Pete's cigarette butts and throwing them at Dabney, and he'd be cringing like they'd hurt if they hit him. The husband would gesture wildly at the soffit that Mabe had painted—you'll see it all in the lawsuit—you might want to find yourself a barrister! You're finished in this hamlet! At the end of the scene, Dabney would sheepishly stretch his hand out to the man and his wife. The couple would just look at Dabney and laugh, incredulous.

But when Mabe eased his truck to the curb, all was quiet at the Parkwood colonial. No front yard altercations, not a soul in sight. He popped the top on another, now not-so-chilled Pabst, and pulled a Camel from the glovebox, a long-opened pack he kept on hand for just such an occasion. He lit it and inhaled deeply. The warmth of the day stayed on the manicured lawn, while Mabe sat smoking in the cool maple shade of the street. He felt unexpected relief, realizing that he wouldn't have to work for Dabney again, not tomorrow morning, or ever. He leaned back against the headrest.

* * *

Mabe woke, dried-sweat cold, and realized where he was. Beside him on the seat sat wilted daisies. The dashboard clock read 8:19. He rolled up the windows, started the truck, and headed for home. On the way, his mind replayed the day, flipping through the scenes like the windblown calendar pages in old movies. At the end of the show, Mabe remembered what he'd been so excited about in the afternoon, before Dabney fired him. But his resolve, at least his sureness, had dwindled. He didn't have any odds on whether he could still pull it off. His confidence waned. He was hardly Odysseus returning home to Ithaca and his Penelope.

Pulling into the driveway, Mabe saw the bedroom light go out. The porch and kitchen remained lit, and he could see into what looked like an empty house. Chiron trotted to him when he stepped inside, a slobbery tennis ball in his mouth. Mabe quietly moved through the house, drawing curtains, turning out the lights. Then he stepped into the bedroom.

"Hey, Daph," he said softly. "Can we talk?"

She murmured in a way he loved, but he knew she wasn't asleep or even close. "You can turn on the light," she said.

He did, and sat on the bed beside her. Daphne sat up, her eyes red but taking no time to adjust to the lack of darkness. "Remember what you said when I was telling you about Pete and his sloppy painting?" he asked her. "Remember when I told you I was scared to have a kid because I could pass on my craziness, my depression, all my faults."

"That's two questions," she said. "Can I start with the second?"

"Sorry. Sure."

"Okay, well you never did tell me why you were scared."

"Maybe I couldn't tell you until I wasn't scared anymore. You know how I said about depression, that in that fog you can't see? A part of me knows it, that I can't see clearly. Like being blinded by rage, or jealousy, we know, the myths are full of it. Blindnesses anyway." Mabe took a breath, tried to figure what he'd planned to say, what he needed to say. "When I start to come out of the fog, I start to see things differently. I know I will, but I can't at the time, in the fog, see them. Only a little part of me knows I will. It's a voice I can hear but can't act on. I'm not saying this well, but you know."

"Thank you for trying," Daphne said.

Mabe got the feeling she understood, knew his words before he said them. The feeling didn't bother him at all. He was grateful for it.

"So the first," Daphne reminded, "Pete's painting."

"Forget it now," Mabe touched her neck just below the ear. Ran his index and middle fingers down and across her shoulder, a carpenter feeling the smooth finished edge. And looped the fingers under the strap of her camisole. While in his mind he could hear her softly repeat, remind as if she were sure he knew, what Chiron should have told him, that the world is full of drips and missed spots.

FACES

Maria Stephanie Bolanos

Haunting eyes on the front page of the Sunday paper stared back at Angelo so darkly that they stole his breath. He removed his glasses, raised the photo close to his face, studied every angle, every eerie contour. An icy uneasiness prickled his neck, and he shivered despite the humid July afternoon, thick with the fragrance of star jasmine.

Viking Orbiter I Photographs Mysterious Face on Mars, declared the headline. Angelo mused over the article, learned that the orbiter, launched months earlier to explore the surface of Mars, had captured a humanlike face etched into the landscape. The news had swept across the globe, sending schoolchildren and scientists into a flurry of speculation.

The photo was stark white with gray smudges—a depression here suggested a mouth, a ridge there represented a nose, two craters hinted at eyes. To Angelo, the image was both riveting and repugnant. By turns, it resembled a motherless child, or a soul separated from a kindred spirit, or the head of a pagan god, fierce and unforgiving.

Angelo's wife sat across the patio table in the shade of a palm tree. She bent over a copy of *The Great Big Book of Crossword Puzzles* from The Dollar Tree, tapping her cheek with the eraser tip of her pencil. This morning she had gleefully ascended to the rank of intermediate puzzle-solver, having conquered the beginners' section in only three days.

"They've found a face on Mars," said Angelo. The thin trickle of his words faded into the hot afternoon.

She looked up, narrow-eyed. "What?"

"A face on Mars." He handed her the front page. Her eyes, quick and analytical, scanned the paper. She snorted, tossed it back.

"Some people will believe almost anything," she said. "That's not a face at all."

For once, he did not immediately relent. "But it *is* a face. Look again."

She peered at him over her reading glasses, a look of cool assessment quickly morphing into contempt. "It's a trick of light and shadow. Nothing more, nothing less."

With that, she returned to the puzzle, murmuring to herself: "Hmmm. A six-letter word meaning 'fanciful notion'. Starts with

W…" She shot up in her seat. *"Whimsy!"* Pumping her fists into the air like an Olympian, she stooped over the page and slowly filled in the squares, naming each letter under her breath.

He sighed. It was no use. As always, she had sucked the life out of the most promising moments, choosing to abide firmly in the here-and-now, refusing to venture into the sweeping sphere of possibility. Angelo looked away, accepted his reality with a certain serenity—that whimsy was just a word to her. That for the rest of their lives, he would see what she could not.

He turned back to the photo, raised it to eye-level, its lure irresistible. The face beckoned him, drew him gently beyond the realm of cold tangibility. Gradually, he forgot the row of palms shading their garden, the lapping swimming pool, the sights and sounds of an ordinary day. His surroundings turned hazy, faded into a blinding whiteness, earthly bonds slipping away. His body drifted, suspended by humming stars, arms and legs weightless, his face peering directly into those dark, disquieting eyes a galaxy away.

Its expression had shifted again, the lips kind and comforting, the smile of a loyal, longtime friend. A warm whisper whirled inside his ear. *She cannot see, and it matters not at all.*

In an instant, he swooped back to earth, his lips slipping into the same secret smile.

THE ROSE

Martin McCaw

Sparrow saw the three men as soon as he left 8 Wing's gate. They huddled together in the breezeway, facing each other. He recognized the lifers' club president and his enforcer. Sparrow's cellmates. When he drew closer, he saw the shoes of a fourth man, quivering an inch above the concrete.

Sparrow ran. He slowed to a walk where the concrete ended, though his pulse still hammered in his ears. What he'd seen shouldn't have surprised him. Blood Alley was covered with a roof, the only walkway that couldn't be seen from a guards' tower.

He glanced over his shoulders every few seconds. That's how he'd stayed alive in the housing project. His dealer used to say he acted like a bag lady. Sparrow had seen bag ladies pick through garbage cans, their eyes darting around like a bird's, on the lookout for cops and rival scavengers. He'd been too puny and too scared to be trusted with anything bigger than nickel bags of weed, except for the one time he'd delivered crack—to an undercover cop, it turned out.

He hurried up the stairs to the education floor. No one would stick him in the basic education lab, the only place in the prison where you'd see blacks and white supremacists in the same room.

Next to the wall, the Chicanos clustered around two small tables. He chose an empty table next to the Black Muslims. He felt safe around them. The Black Muslims were sworn to nonviolence and didn't deal drugs. Behind him the teacher was explaining a math problem in a voice so loud it jarred his nerves. The old guy had hearing aids, but he still asked Sparrow to repeat everything he said.

What was this? A woman with long blonde hair was chalking something on the blackboard. Only the title was visible, "Prayer of Saint Francis." She frowned as she wrote, her lips puckered, like Suzie used to look when she drew a picture. He didn't like to think about Suzie. Ma blamed him, but what happened wasn't his fault. He'd tried to keep her away from drugs. After she got addicted he'd kept her supplied so she wouldn't use the dangerous stuff, heroin cut with quinine. He'd shown her exactly how much she could safely inject.

The woman finished writing and stepped aside, still frowning as she surveyed what she'd printed.

Where there is hatred, let me sow love,
Where there is despair, hope,
Where there is sadness, joy.
Let me not so much seek
To be loved as to love;
For it is in giving that we receive;
It is in dying to self that we are born to eternal life.

She turned and smiled at him. A jolt of electricity surged through him. She was beautiful.

She pulled a chair close and sat by him. "I left out some of the lines. What do you think of it?"

He couldn't make his mouth work.

The old teacher erased the poem's title. "You can't promote religion," he said. Sparrow flinched. Macintosh spoke in the same exasperated voice whenever he marked one of his answers wrong.

"Are you studying for your GED?" the woman said.

He nodded.

She thumbed through his English workbook until she reached the page he'd been working on. He stiffened as she silently read his responses to the sample questions.

"These are really good," the woman said. "I'll make one suggestion." She tapped the paper with a fingernail. "Put a period here instead of a comma. Otherwise you've got a run-on sentence."

He squinted at the sentence, baffled.

"Let's try something." She took his pencil and enlarged the comma to a huge period. "Read what comes before the period."

"The boy took out his sling shot."

"Now read what comes after the period," she said.

"He aimed it at the rat."

"Do you have two sentences now? Do they each make sense?"

"Yeah."

"That means you're not supposed to separate them with a comma." She smiled again. "Don't ask me why. I didn't make up the rules."

He felt his lips move.

"You're the first person I've seen smile in the whole prison," she said. "There must be a sign posted somewhere, 'No smiling.'"

He heard a strange sound leave his throat, rusty and creaky. He hadn't laughed since Suzie was little.

"Now let's try something else." She crossed out the period and the word "he." She handed the pencil back to him. "Can you think of a word you can put between the two sentence parts? A word that will make them one sentence?"

His armpits moistened. He couldn't think straight with her sitting beside him. Wait! He printed a word above the crossed-out period. "The boy took out his slingshot and aimed it at the rat," he said.

"Brilliant." She beamed at him. "You've just licked one of the toughest problems in English grammar. Some people never figure it out."

She'd called him brilliant! Nobody ever gave him a compliment. Suzie once said, "You're smart, Gerald," but she'd only been five years old.

For the next two hours the woman worked with other students—he'd switched chairs so he could watch her. She smiled at everyone, but she'd given him the biggest smile.

On his way back to 8 Wing, his shoes crunched on frozen snow and the wind numbed his cheeks, but he felt warm inside, even when he passed the reddish-brown stain on the breezeway. The two lifers were waiting for him in their cell. "We got some things for you to wash," Trigg said. He pulled some wadded-up shirts from under his bunk.

Sparrow turned on the washbasin's faucet. "Not there," Trigg said. He motioned toward the toilet. The cell was ten by twelve feet, and two tiers of bunk beds took up most of the space. Trigg, the lifers' president, owned the cell. Sparrow had agreed to keep the cell clean. He also paid Trigg fifty dollars a month rent, all Ma could squeeze from her wages as a motel maid. He felt lucky. Other frail young guys paid rent with their bodies.

Bloodstains spotted the shirts. He'd seen Trigg's shank, a scrap from the metal shop that the lifer had sharpened into a double-edged blade. He flushed the toilet, waited for it to fill, and scrubbed the shirts. He dug his fingernails into the bar of soap so it wouldn't slip out of his hand. When the water turned pink, he flushed the toilet.

He draped the wet shirts over his cot and took his razor to the sink. He couldn't show up in class tomorrow with a scruffy beard.

* * *

The two teachers were arguing at the far end of the classroom. They had their backs to him, and thin books with brightly-illustrated covers were heaped on a table between them.

"Their reading levels are so low," the woman said.

"They're not children," Macintosh said.

"That's the problem."

"What do you mean?"

"Most of our students grew up in horrible homes," Ms. Dodd said. "They never had a childhood."

"So you want to give them one?"

"As much as I can. They don't know what it feels like to be happy."

The old teacher picked up a book. *"Pokey Puppy."* He snorted. "How will you keep track of the books?"

"I'll give them away."

"You can't."

"Why not? I bought them." She saw Sparrow. "You're first. Come and choose a book."

He spread the books apart. *Squeaky and the Cheese.* Suzie's book. His eyes watered. He took the book to a table and turned the pages, but the words blurred.

The woman sat down across from him. "I noticed you chose that book without looking at the others. May I ask why?"

"I used to read it to my little sister."

"What a nice coincidence. How old is she now?"

"She died." He lowered his head so she couldn't see his eyes.

"I'm so sorry." She patted his wrist and stood up.

Had she seen his tears? Had anyone else? The worst thing you can do is show weakness. He looked around the room. The other inmates were absorbed in the children's books. Some moved their lips as they read, some smiled. He heard his breath hiss through his lips, like a balloon going limp.

During the next week he watched Ms. Dodd while he pretended to read. When she smiled at another inmate, he could tell she was just being polite. He knew she wanted to spend more time with him, but whenever she sat down, students lined up three deep, waiting to ask her trumped-up questions.

On Friday she asked him to come to her office after class. Uh-oh. He'd spent more time watching her than studying.

Macintosh didn't look up from his desk when Sparrow entered their office. "Some students aren't making much headway," the woman said when he sat down. "They need more individual help than we can give them."

His stomach cramped. "I'll work harder," he said.

"You're an excellent student. That's why I'd like you to be a tutor."

An excellent student! "What's a tutor?"

"It's like being a teacher. You would help Mr. Alvarez. He wants to learn English."

Alvarez must be one of the mules who sneaked across the Mexican border looking for orchard work. In return for packing drugs, they got bus tickets to the Yakima valley, where narcs arrested them at the depot. Why would they want to learn English? After they served their time they'd get deported.

"I don't know any Spanish," he said.

"Neither do I. Here's what you'd do." She opened a workbook. Illustrations covered each page, with the name of the object printed beneath the drawing. "You point to a picture and say the word. Then you ask him to repeat it."

The Chicanos were the lifers' main rivals in the drug business. What if word got back to his cellmates? "Couldn't I help someone else?"

Her pupils shrank. "I'd like you to help Mister Alvarez."

He swallowed and said, "Okay."

At first Alvarez acted as uneasy as Sparrow felt, but on the second day they both relaxed. On day three, after Alvarez repeated "dog," Sparrow drew a bone next to the animal's mouth, printed two more words, and said, "Dog eats bone." He pointed to his mouth and pretended to chew.

"Dog eats bone," Alvarez said. Grinning, he got up and showed the open workbook to three Chicanos at another table. "Dog eats bone," he said.

"Ingenious," the woman said behind Sparrow.

By the end of the fourth week Alvarez had gone through two workbooks, and Sparrow had filled several pages of a pencil tablet with three-word sentences. The children's books had disappeared into inmates' cells, so Ms. Dodd brought a second batch to be used in the classroom. He began reading the easiest books to Alvarez. Whenever the Chicano repeated a sentence correctly, Sparrow said, "Good." Ms. Dodd had confided that a key teacher's trick was never to criticize, but instead to compliment a student when he got something right.

He couldn't recall ever feeling this happy. Other students were helping each other, and the classroom's atmosphere had changed. Before the woman had arrived, some inmates spent the whole three hours talking to each other. Macintosh would caution them, but as soon as he turned away they would resume their chatter. Now the lab had a waiting list, and the slackers had been dropped.

One February afternoon, Alvarez greeted Sparrow with a broad smile and said, "Good morning, teacher."

He was a teacher! Ma would be proud of him. He wanted to write her, but Trigg had taken his allotment of stamps.

Three stanzas of a song were printed on the blackboard. It was titled "The Rose." He recognized the words. He'd heard the song on the lifers' radio.

"How can love be a flower?" he asked Ms. Dodd.

"The song is about us." She waved her arm, taking in the whole room. "We're the seeds of love. Love starts with us."

The song is about us. Love starts with us. She was in love with him!

He felt giddy. She would tell him her first name so he could put her on his visiting list. He'd never had a visitor. Ma lived too far away. Ms. Dodd would come Mondays, Wednesdays, and Thursdays, five to eight-thirty. He worked the numbers in his head. Ten and a half hours every week they would sit in the visiting room across from each other, talking about the things they'd do after he got paroled. The seven years would zip by. Maybe she'd bring him a little weed tucked under her bra. They would get married in the chapel, and next August the prison planned to start conjugal visits. Two trailers were already stationed between 5 Wing and the hospital.

Tomorrow was Valentine's Day. He'd make her a valentine. What could he use for paper? His pencil tablet wouldn't do.

Snowflakes caressed his cheeks as he hustled to the prison library. He'd never ventured between the stacks—too dangerous—but this was an emergency. He pulled out books until he found one with a red end paper. He ripped it out, wincing when he heard it crackle. He took a white end paper from another book.

Back in his cell, he tore the red paper into a misshapen heart. How could he stick it onto the white paper? He dug through the wastebasket until he found a hardened lump of Trigg's chewing gum. He wanted to wash it off under the faucet, but the washbasin was full of water and a plastic bag that contained fermenting apples, and he didn't dare mess with the lifers' pruno. He chewed the gum and stuck it onto the white paper. Then he pressed the lopsided heart into the gum. On each side of the heart he printed "I love you."

When Ms. Dodd sat at his table the next day, he slid the valentine from between the pages of his tablet and handed it to her, upside down. He held his breath as she turned it over.

She smiled at him, her eyes shining. "It's beautiful. Thank you very much."

He wanted to whoop for joy. She showed the card to Macintosh, who shook his head. The old guy was jealous.

He still felt light-headed when he sat down alongside Alvarez. They started on a new workbook that had longer sentences and no illustrations. He read the sentences aloud, but Alvarez couldn't understand them. When the buzzer sounded, Sparrow realized he should have been drawing pictures. He would tomorrow, he promised himself.

He waited on the stairs' landing for five minutes. The teachers always left their office door open, a safety precaution so passing guards could look inside. He crept close to the door.

"The heart feels lumpy," the woman said. "I wonder what he used for glue. Yuck! It's chewing gum. I think tobacco flakes are embedded in it."

"You act too friendly around them." The man's voice was hoarse from talking too loud.

"He thinks you're in love with him."

"Five students gave me homemade valentines. The cards are sweet, but I'm not in love with any inmate."

Sparrow stumbled down the stairs, unable to make sense of what he'd heard. She loved him. *The song is about us. We're the seeds of love. Love starts with us.* Those were her exact words.

It wasn't until he heard the deafening din of 8 Wing, men yelling and rattling their bars, gates clanking and toilets flushing, that the truth sank in. He was a loser, a scrawny punk afraid of his own shadow. How could she love him? He'd created a fantasy world in his mind. She'd done him a favor, shocked him back to reality.

For two days he lay on his bunk. He left the cell only for chow. On the third morning he remembered how puzzled Alvarez had looked as he mouthed the words in his new workbook.

He brushed his teeth but didn't shave. When he reached the classroom he went straight to Alvarez's table. Instead of reading a sentence aloud from the workbook, he circled one and opened his student's tablet. He drew a boy with his arm extended over his head and a girl with her arms held out straight in front of her. He clutched an imaginary ball and made a throwing motion.

Alvarez looked from the picture to the sentence. "The boy threw the ball to the girl," he said.

"Perfecto," Sparrow said, and the Chicano's face brightened.

A radiant feeling welled up inside Sparrow and spread outward, enveloping Alvarez. Two months ago his student couldn't read a single English word.

"You're so creative," the woman said. He hadn't seen her approach the table.

He hunched his shoulders. He couldn't trust anything she said. When she went to another table, he straightened up. Strangely, he felt free.

The buzzer shrieked. How could three hours go by so fast?

Alvarez stood up and smiled at him. "Goodbye, teacher," he said.

"Goodbye, Mr. Alvarez," Sparrow said.

Ms. Dodd was standing by the door. "You're doing a wonderful job," she told him.

He looked straight ahead as he silently passed, and he sensed that her smile faltered. At the bottom of the stairs he waited until Alvarez was ten yards ahead before he walked on.

He rounded the corner of the metal shop and entered the covered breezeway. Near 8 Wing's gate, his two cellmates lounged against the wall, alongside an inmate with tattoos on his neck. He tensed but kept walking. They couldn't be waiting for him, could they?

The three men sprang away from the wall and pounced on Alvarez. Sparrow saw the glint of Trigg's shank.

Run! Get away! He ran, his legs pumping and his elbows swinging. But something was wrong. He was running in the wrong direction, toward the men instead of away from them. He saw the lifers' startled faces as he launched himself at them. He clawed Trigg's eye and heard a scream. An elbow clamped him around the throat. He bit a tattooed wrist but couldn't break free. He glimpsed Alvarez running away. He heard a grating sound, like a saw going back and forth, sawing wood. Then it was over.

* * *

The roof had been torn down, so the tower guard could see the length of the breezeway. The woman knelt among gray weeds near the concrete. She swiped the back of her hand across her forehead. Barely above freezing and she was sweating. How did she get clearance for that trowel? He picked up his binoculars. The stick she held was a spindly thing, brown and jagged, obviously dead. The teacher didn't know much about gardening.

* * *

In the predawn light of a warm June morning, the guard saw a splash of red at the edge of the breezeway. Another stabbing, he thought, until he focused his binoculars on the rose.

BOURBON MOON

Lawrence Buentello

Ed Ashley turned abruptly, regarded the long path he'd just traveled, and turned again.

The stars hung in the cypress trees like glittering celestial fruit; a bewildering number of the trees surrounded him like the silhouettes of stooped old men, and whispered, as old men do, as the wind moved through their boughs.

He stood uncertainly on the path, inhaling the musk of the Gulf waters. The thought occurred to him that, if he could locate the position of the moon in the sky, he might be able to determine his location relative to the casino he'd just left. Unfortunately, he had no idea where the moon was hiding. He was drunk, fantastically drunk, and only possessed a partial understanding of his perceptual limitations. He'd been walking a long time, and in an unknown direction; all he knew was that he wanted to be as far away from the blackjack table—the one that had taken his last five-dollar chip—as possible.

Though not so far that he found himself inside a Mississippi alligator.

He squinted, brushed at the mosquitoes on his neck and shrugged.

Then suddenly, as the humid ambience of Gulfport spun around him, the moon appeared in the south through the trees and he felt redeemed. Still, the moon seemed to have no interest in its role as heavenly savior, and he realized he was no closer to learning his location.

Selfish moon, he thought as he continued walking.

After a while the sky seemed to funnel down into his eyes and expand incomprehensibly in his mind. The tapered clouds, the mourning lilt of the cypress branches, and the selfish, reticent moon created an impression of reality only several rounds of good bourbon could refine. Then he lost the moon in the trees again, lost the stars, and lost his reason for wanting to find the moon in the first place. These losses were only of secondary importance, since he'd already lost all hope for his life in the previous hour.

Finally he noticed a light flickering through the trees some distance away, and it wasn't the moon. It might have been a streetlight; but it seemed too low in the trees. Still, it was a light, and toward this light he decided his direction was best taken.

He measured every step—he wasn't a masterful drunk, but had enough practical experience—and managed to walk a fairly straight line.

When he looked up from his shoes he realized the light was attached to the doorframe of a thoroughly dilapidated house, a frail, wooden frame affair of three stories receding into the greedy armature of the cypress branches. On the door hung a large white cross, quite Protestant in design, but very large; above the doorway, painted on a long whitewashed board, hung the legend: The Church of the Giver of Life.

Ashley smiled at the thought of reaching such a sanctuary and placed one shoe on the first step leading to the porch. Then he felt a familiar hollowness in his stomach, casually realized the implication of the sensation, and turned to vomit into the grass.

When he finished retching he sat on the step, rubbed his mouth on his shoulder, then cradled his head in his hands and began to cry softly. He was tired, anciently, grievously weary, but that was the last thought he had for some time.

* * *

When Ed Ashley woke he was no longer sitting on the wooden step, but reclining quite uncomfortably on a cot in a dark room.

His first thought was that the local police had found him and dragged him off to the county lockup to sleep off his drunk. But when he raised his miserable head he realized he wasn't in the county jail, but in a small room with a small window without bars. His viciously throbbing temples kept him from wondering how he'd managed to find a room while unconscious.

He sat up and slung his legs over the side of the cot. His shoes, still on his feet, hit the floor noisily. Sounds echo well in old houses, he thought, and then remembered the same type of sound echoing through his grandfather's house in Montgomery. A faint nostalgia invaded his physical discomfort, but then fell away in the presence of the overwhelming pain in his head.

He rose and moved to the door, peering around the threshold. A long hallway presented several closed doors to him, and in the distance the railing of a stairway.

A faint smell in the air of cooking grease immediately turned his stomach; he also heard soft scratching sounds he couldn't immediately identify. Perhaps some swamp denizen was making inroads in the crawlspaces. He thought he must be in the old house—The Church of the Giver of Life—but he couldn't be certain without going downstairs.

He ignored the scent of regurgitated bourbon on his shirt, tucked in its tails, smoothed down his hair and walked to the stairs.

His weight caused the treads to moan loudly, so he was certain his presence would surprise no one. Still, when he reached the first floor he was met by an empty hallway. The scratching intensified, and he decided to follow it, ultimately entering a small room lit only by a guttering candle. An odd figure sat at a table on which the candle stood in a brass holder, writing furiously on loose sheets of paper with what appeared to be a quill pen. The writer dipped the quill into an ink well at regular intervals before once again scratching his thoughts upon the parchment.

The person seemed anachronistic, dressed ostensibly in a monk's robe, two pale hands protruding from the sleeves and two sandaled feet from the hem. A lowered hood prevented Ashley from identifying the sex of the figure, though by the shape of the body he knew it must be a man.

He found himself in the quandary of needing to interrupt the man's scribbling, but also not wanting to exhibit bad manners. Still, he knew his lineage possessed fewer Southern gentry and more of the proletariat, so he cleared his throat loudly, immediately regretting the effect of the sound on his temples.

The figure raised its head, then turned to face him.

As the hood fell back Ashley could see it was a man, perhaps a little older than himself, with rich red hair and beard. The man wore rimless glasses on his nose, and held the quill guiltily, as if interrupted in an impure act.

"I'm sorry to bother you—" Ashley began.

The man with the red beard quickly set down the quill and rose from his chair, standing in place with an awkward expression—perhaps pleasure, perhaps pain. If the man was a Gulfport local he was certainly atypical.

"No need to apologize," the man finally said, and then smiled. "I'm glad you're awake. I worried for your health."

"If I don't worry about it, then no one else should. And I don't."

The man raised his eyebrows. "I'm sorry?"

"It's just a little humor. Don't mind me, I'm sure my one-liners are as bad as the pain in my head."

The man gestured to a chair by the table, the arms of his robe fluttering as if he were semaphoring. "Please, come and sit."

Ashley, uncertain of how to respond in such a bizarre situation, decided to honor the memory of his mother, who always told him to show people his best manners. His best manners were nothing to brag about, but from time to time he assumed the role of Southern gentleman, just to keep his hand in the myth.

He sat at the table, glancing at the paper on which the man had been writing, though the hand was fairly illegible.

"I'm Ed Ashley," he said. "I owe you thanks, if you're the one who pulled me off your porch."

"Please, don't thank me," the man said. "It was God's will."

Ashley ignored an impulse to respond sarcastically and simply nodded.

"I'm Brother Anselm," the man continued. "I am the founder of The Church of the Giver of Life. Of course, we used to be The House of the Lord, but ever since the messiah arrived I decided to post a more suitable title."

Ashley sat blinking as he tried to process the statement. "I'm sorry, did you say something about the messiah?"

Brother Anselm nodded enthusiastically. "Yes, the *messiah* himself. He's upstairs in his room, resting."

If he hadn't been overly familiar with consciousness, Ashley might have thought he was dreaming. "*Which* messiah?"

"The only one that counts, of course."

Ashley attempted to change the subject. "How many other people live in this house, brother?"

"Only myself, at the moment. And yourself, of course. And the messiah. At one time two other brothers belonged to the order, Brother Peter and Brother Stan. Unfortunately, Brother Peter left to grow medicinal marijuana and Brother Stan left to pursue his CPA license. God bless them in their journey through life. But I'm actively recruiting, I assure you."

"I see." Ashley began rising from his chair. "Well, it was nice chatting with you—"

"No, no!" Brother Anselm said. "Please, sit. I understand how this must strike you, but I'm not crazy. Besides, you still need rest. You're in no condition to travel."

Ashley couldn't argue with that logic, but he also didn't want to find himself embroiled in some lunatic cult. Still, he sat back down, if only to keep the man from reacting violently. "You don't really believe the messiah is sleeping upstairs, do you?"

Brother Anselm raised a finger and shook it steadily. "That is the heart of the problem, and the reason for your presence. God sent you to mediate this dilemma."

Ashley dearly wished to tell him that it was only the light from a bourbon moon that guided him to the house; but that might not reflect well on his own character, so he only said, "How so?"

Brother Anselm leaned in over the table, as if disclosing a great secret. "Not two weeks ago a man came to my door claiming to be the messiah. Now, I'm only a simple man of God ministering to the pathetic and downtrodden cast-offs from the terrible sin-makers of the casinos, not a biblical scholar, so I really didn't know whether to take this statement seriously. But the man persists, claiming he has been sent to Earth for the Second Coming."

"And you believe him?"

"Well, to be truthful about the matter, I'm not certain what to believe. He seems sincere, and he's very persuasive. All this time I've been waiting for a sign, some kind of divine revelation to let me know whether or not to believe him. But that was before you arrived."

Ashley rubbed his chin a moment. "What does my arrival have to do with it?"

"You're the sign, of course. You were sent here to assist me in determining the messiah's divinity."

Ashley smiled broadly and shook his head. "Brother, I'm afraid you have me all wrong. God didn't send me. For all the gambling and drinking I've been doing, I'm sure He'd consider me to be the worst sort of judge of human character imaginable."

"It's not a *human* character I must define, Mr. Ashley."

"Now, I'm not one to challenge God's will, but I wouldn't have the first idea of how to prove anyone's divinity. I'll tell you what I am, though." Ashley raised his arms and began enumerating on his fingers. "The first thing I am is a failure. I failed to keep my job, my woman, and my sobriety. The second thing I am is fiscally irresponsible. I spent my last five dollars at the blackjack table and now I don't even have enough money for a bus ticket home to Alabama. But there's no reason for me to go back to Alabama, because I don't have the money I planned to win gambling in Mississippi to get my woman back. The third thing I am is a bad judge of character, especially my own. No, I'd be the very worst person in the world to answer your questions for you."

"God works in mysterious ways," Brother Anselm said, unfazed. "He made you a loser so you could come to us and do His will."

Ashley frowned at the statement a while before asking, "What is His will, exactly?"

"Mysterious, to be certain. Such is the nature of miracles."

Ashley sat contemplating the hooded man before him, wondering why he always seemed to find himself in strange situations. Oddities seemed attracted to him, like a moth to a flame. But there was no profit in playing along, and so there was no reason to stay. "I'm sorry, Brother," he said, "and I don't want to seem ungrateful, but this is just not for me. I no more believe you're boarding the messiah than the next president of the United States or a man from Mars. I can't help you."

He began to rise again, but Brother Anselm raised his hand. "I don't expect you to gamble your good name on my account alone. I have a proposition for you."

Ashley, uncertain, finally sat down again. "What kind of proposition?"

"The best kind. You see, I'm not an uneducated man, or a foolish man. I know the nature of human beings, which helps me in my work. If you help me determine the true character of the man upstairs you'll profit whether or not you find him to be the true messiah."

"How?"

"It's obvious, given the manner of your arrival. I will task him to perform a miracle for you, free you of your sinning ways, relieve your spirit and return your happiness. If he can achieve these things for a loser like you then he surely has the will of God with him."

Once again, Ashley had to force himself to keep from responding unkindly. "And if he doesn't perform this miracle?"

"Then I will have my answer, and you will be rewarded. I'll buy your bus ticket to Alabama. Does that sound fair?"

"Well—"

"And while you're here, you'll receive free meals and a room. Does that sound like a fair proposition to you?"

"Do you have anything to drink?"

"Oh, lord no!" Brother Anselm laughed, though Ashley found nothing funny in the remark. "Your sobriety will be one aspect of the miracle. Don't you find this to be a divine convergence?"

Ashley sighed. Free room and board, and meals, was something he could very much use right now. And his head hurt so badly that all he really wanted to do was lie down in a dark place and close his eyes. What harm could it do to indulge the Brother for a couple of days? By then he could pull himself together and leave on his own terms.

The only thing that bothered him was the thought of staying in the same house with a man who considered himself the messiah.

Still, one of his great uncles believed he was the reincarnation of General Lee, so who was he to cast stones?

"All right," he said. "But I'll hold you to your word."

Brother Anselm laughed. "I swear to God that I'll uphold my word."

"In that case, I'm going back upstairs to sleep."

Brother Anselm, humming happily, resumed his writing, which was, Ashley was later told, a 'chronicle of my experiences with the new messiah', while Ashley walked slowly up the stairs to sleep off the rest of his misery.

* * *

The next morning Ashley's head seemed less a cauldron, though he wished he had just a little shot of whiskey to take the edge off—the scent of frying bacon smelled much better now, and he ate a decent breakfast prepared by Brother Anselm in the house's small kitchen. He ate at a table by the kitchen sink, marveling at how similar the accoutrements seemed to those of a couple of old shotgun houses he'd visited in New Orleans. The piquant Gulf breeze accented the memory, as did the relentless attack of mosquitoes.

In payment for his breakfast Brother Anselm told Ashley that he would like to introduce him to the messiah.

"Don't worry," Brother Anselm said, holding Ashley by the arm as they walked to the stairs, "he's quite a docile messiah. You'll feel comforted in his presence."

Ashley, now dead sober and regretting his agreement with the brother, gazed up the staircase and wondered what oddities waited in its shadows. Could he simply break free of Brother Anselm's grasp and make a run for the road? No, that seemed hardly gentlemanly, and besides, he still hadn't determined what he might do in order to get back to Montgomery. Hitchhiking was always a possibility, but he knew the local police were always watching for vagrants and thieves; the casinos seemed to attract them like vultures to road kill.

The loudly creaking stairs announced their arrival on the third floor. For some reason the brother kept the hallway darkened, which didn't fill Ashley's heart with assurance. When he remarked on this, Brother Anselm replied that the messiah preferred the darkness, claiming that only in darkness can human beings see the brightest light.

"Profound," Ashley muttered as they approached the messiah's room.

The brother knocked, and a quiet voice replied. Brother Anselm opened the door.

Ashley didn't really know what he'd expected to see—a towering figure in purple robes adorned by a shimmering golden aura, perhaps—in actuality, what he saw was a small, thin man of about thirty, dressed in white kimono and sandals, sitting on the edge of a single bed. His face was clean shaven, no beard, not even a moustache, though his black hair was slightly disheveled. He held a plastic rosary in his hands, and smiled palely when they stepped into the room. The only light came from the sunlight seeping through the thick red curtains of a solitary window.

"Good morning," Brother Anselm said, bowing slightly. "I hate to disturb your prayers, but I have someone I would like you to meet."

The man gazed up at Ashley, nodding.

Ashley smiled weakly, wondering how one behaved in the presence of a messiah. Or *the* messiah—he wasn't actually certain of the proper way to address divinity.

"I have foreseen this visitation," the man said in a high, almost effeminate voice. He possessed as strong a Southern accent as Ashley, which meant he was no East Coast liberal gone bad in the head. "All things happen for a reason."

"So I've heard," Ashley said. "My name is Ed Ashley. I'm glad to meet you." Ashley extended his hand, but the man didn't move to take it. Ashley lowered his hand, assuming messiahs had their own sense of cordiality.

"Mr. Ashley comes to us by way of the casino," Brother Anselm said. "He is a grievous sinner, I'm afraid, filled with Satan's influence. Gambling and drink have corrupted his soul and sent him on a dark, dark path in life."

Ashley glanced at the brother a moment, uncertain if he should be offended, or if this was only hyperbole to assist Anselm in his quest.

"Yes," the man said, "I know him to be a sinner, a grievous sinner, reeking of demonic influence. But there is always the hope of salvation for the penitent."

"That is why I've brought this man to you," Brother Anselm said, nudging Ashley farther into the room. "He is in need of guidance, of a spiritual nature, of course."

"Of course," the man said. He gestured toward a chair in a corner of the room.

Brother Anselm retrieved the chair, setting it near the bed. Then he ushered Ashley into it, patting him on the back firmly. "I'll leave you to your counsel," he said, backing out through the doorway. He pulled the door closed as Ashley watched, but thankfully turned no key.

Ashley sat in the chair, leaning forward, his hands on his knees. The man stared back at him, smiling gently.

"So," Ashley said, because he could think of nothing else to say, "I hear you're the messiah. Is that correct?"

"Yes, it is," the man said with great sincerity.

Ashley nodded, bit his lip a moment, and then said, "Do you mean to say you're Jesus Christ come back to Earth?"

The man laughed, a high, unnerving laugh. "No, I'm not Jesus Christ. He was incarnated on Earth and died two thousand years ago. I am the physical incarnation of the savior in this time, come to Earth in this body."

"I don't understand. I thought there was only one Christ."

"Yes. And no. There *was* only one Jesus Christ, but he came in that guise as an emissary of God to save humanity from eternal damnation by original sin. God chose to manifest himself in the body of the one called Jesus in the time of the Roman occupation of Jerusalem."

"And now God is manifesting Himself in the body of—you."

"Yes, now you've got it."

"Well, Jesus of Nazareth lived two thousand years ago, whatever you believe," Ashley said, finding wit enough to test the man, if only through his spotty religious education. "He was the son of Joseph and Mary. He had a life and identity, aside from *messiah*. What's your identity?"

"Yes, I understand what you mean. I've not yet fulfilled my purpose on Earth, and so still retain my physical identity."

"So what is your real name?"

"My Earthly name?"

"Sure, let's call it that."

"Ernie."

"*Ernie?*"

"Yes. But if it makes you feel any better, you may call me Lord."

Ashley couldn't be offended; he couldn't even be righteously outraged at this seeming blasphemy, since the blasphemer was obviously crazy. Bless me in your name, Christ Ernie—no, it just didn't seem very *reverent*. But he'd made a bargain with Brother Anselm and felt he had to carry it through.

He cleared his throat. "Tell me, Ernie, when did you discover you were the messiah?"

"I've always known."

"Well, when did you decide it was time to assume your role as messiah?"

"About three months ago," the man said, now manipulating the rosary in a careful way. "Life has a way of telling you that your Earthly pursuits are done and your spiritual pursuits have begun."

"I see."

"Also, I turned thirty. It just seemed like the right time."

"What were you in your previous life?"

"Nobody."

"I don't understand."

"Mr. Ashley, you're not here to learn about my mission. You're here to unburden your soul upon me, so that I may offer guidance. So, please, tell me about yourself."

Brother Anselm had been correct; the man had a peaceful, almost soothing persona, bereft of any aggression or tension. Ashley sat back in his chair and felt it would do no harm to talk about himself, something he was fond of doing, anyway, at the blackjack table. Certainly there wasn't anything he could tell the man that he hadn't already disgorged on his fellow gamblers.

Laid off from his job with the city, Ed Ashley broke the news to his fiancé, Elizabeth, with the expectation that she would understand his plight, and comfort him in his time of need. Instead, she told him she had no intention of marrying a man who couldn't keep a regular job, who had no savings in the bank and no prospects for the future. He had broken her heart one too many times, lost one too many jobs, and if he intended for her to support him in marriage he was sadly mistaken.

She seemed decided on the matter, though they'd been seeing each other for five years and he knew her penchant for histrionics.

Reconciliation, he felt, was only a matter of economics. Though he never did have much luck gambling, he thought if he could win big at the casinos in Mississippi he could buy back her affection, as least until he found another job, as she seemed to him to be the type of woman whose affection was best measured in carats. Perhaps this was a purely calculated move on his part, preying on her coldly pragmatic heart, but he still loved her and wanted to marry her. So he read a couple of books on blackjack to sharpen his skills, bought a bus ticket to Gulfport, and traveled to the casino in a grand mythic journey to win back his love.

And lost every penny he had in his pockets, which, in truth, wasn't so great a loss if measured in dollar bills.

"My daddy always referred to me as a footnote in life," Ashley said. "A good man, but luckless. He was fond of telling me that I'd spend my old age divorced and alone, drinking beer at a neighborhood bar until my liver burned a hole in my gut and left me dead—dead, nameless, heirless, and without any accomplishments to speak of. Yeah, my father was a grand old man. Of course he didn't leave me anything when he died, since he was about as successful as his son, except for passing on his priceless wisdom."

"I'm sorry for you," the man said. "You have a good heart, but have received poor guidance. So many in life suffer the same condition."

"I thank you for your sympathy. But I drink too much from time to time. I guess that makes me a sinner, along with the gambling."

"That you're a sinner goes without saying, but your sins are not unredeemable."

"Let me ask you something," Ashley said, sensing his opportunity to fulfill his part of the bargain. "You're the messiah, right?"

"Yes."

"Then you have the powers of the messiah, right?"

"Oh, yes."

"You can heal the sick, turn water into wine, that sort of thing?"

"It is in my power to do so, yes."

"And do you believe I am sick in my soul?"

"Oh, *yes*, you're disgustingly sick in your soul, no question."

"Then you have the power to heal me, to set me on the straight path, so to speak?"

The man raised his hands and laughed. "Yes, certainly."

Ashley ignored the absence of a joke. "Well, then, can you cure me now? Lay on the hands, so to speak?"

"No."

"No? Why not?"

"Well, my son, if you are hungry, and I give you the fruit of the tree, and you eat of it, will you always have it?"

Ashley sat back again and put a hand to his chin. "Is that a riddle?"

"Will you always have it?"

"Evidently not."

"No, you wouldn't, for the fruit would be gone and soon you would be hungry again."

"So you're saying I should horde fruit?"

"No, it's just an analogy. Find the root and you will find the tree whereon the fruit grows."

"Can you phrase that in practical terms?"

"Of course," the man said, reaching out to pat Ashley on the knee, "I'm used to ministering to the ignorant. I simply mean that before I can heal you, you must contemplate your life and discover your greatest sin. Once you know this, and tell me of it, and tell me why it is your greatest sin, then I may heal you by forgiving you."

"But until then?"

"Until then, I'll pray for you that you are strong enough to fulfill this spiritual task. Come back to me when you are ready."

The man pressed his hands around the rosary and said nothing more.

Sensing their conversation had concluded, Ashley nodded, rose from his chair and walked to the door. He opened the door and stepped into the hallway, feeling the man's gaze on his back and wondering why it disturbed him so much.

* * *

Ashley found Brother Anselm behind the house bent over a hoe in a rich black plot of soil. Nothing seemed to be growing in the soil, which made Ashley wonder why the brother worked so furiously at his chore.

Brother Anselm straightened against his implement, his face and beard glistening with sweat. Certainly the robe he wore gave him no relief from the heat of the day, or his labor.

"Are you planting a garden?" Ashley asked, momentarily forgetting why he'd sought out the brother.

"No, no," Brother Anselm said. "Just turning the soil."

Ashley scratched his chin. "Wouldn't it be more productive to actually plant something? That way you'd know the fruits of your labor."

Brother Anselm laughed, enjoying the joke. "No, you misinterpret my intent. I labor to know the fruits of deprivation. Ascetics no longer encourage self-flagellation, so we have to have some means of suffering for our bread."

"Why don't you just bake bread? I tried that once, and it was work enough."

"Buying bread is so much easier. Besides, I have a bread maker in the cupboard, so it really wouldn't be much of a strain."

"So you turn the soil instead."

"Yes. To tell you the truth, I actually tried growing a few things out here, but this climate is so unpredictable, and I never was much of a farmer. So I come outside and spread around the dirt until I break a sweat and then go back inside and call it good."

Ashley decided to change the subject, as he wasn't any nearer to understanding Brother Anselm's motivation for nonproductive gardening as he was to solving any other great riddle of the universe.

He recounted his 'counseling' session with the messiah, including the proviso that he must contemplate his life's greatest sin before any spiritual healing could be affected. He was hesitant to declare the man an outright lunatic, but he was hoping the brother might draw that conclusion for himself.

Instead, Brother Anselm said, "I suppose you'd better go to your room and begin your meditations."

"On what?" Ashley said.

"On your greatest sin, of course. The sooner you comply with the messiah's request, the sooner we'll know if he can actually heal you."

"To tell you the truth, I'm a very mediocre sinner. I'm not sure I even have a particularly impressive sin to contemplate."

Brother Anselm chuckled, stabbing at the ground with his hoe. "We all have one or two impressive sins about us. Please, if you would be so kind. Find the sin of which he speaks."

Ashley wiped the sweat from his forehead, glancing up at the poorly clouded sky. It was a long walk back to the casino. "If you say so."

"Good, good. And when you're finished, there'll be pork chops for supper."

* * *

Ed Ashley lay in bed meditating.

He'd drawn the curtains to darken the room—which helped keep out the oppressive heat—and lay staring at the ceiling, which he could barely see, reviewing his life, his good decisions, his bad decisions, his obvious sins and his subtle sins—but he couldn't summon to mind one single, definable sin that might be considered the root of all his problems. He was a Southern man, to be certain, and if he thought about it in just the right way he could assume the burden of all the sins of the past, slavery, racism, intolerance—but these were social trespasses, not personal ones. He found it difficult feeling as if he were better than any other man—considering the man he knew himself to be. He and his grandfather didn't share the same beliefs; the old man fairly dripped venom at the mention of the 14th Amendment. Ashley only held a ghost of such beliefs, and grudgingly felt that, after observing for many years how most people behaved, old Darwin may just have been right about a few things. The rest was posturing, and to tell the truth he'd rather be fishing on the Alabama River than attending political rallies. No, his education had ended after high school—though he had always read books as a means of maintaining his self-concept as a man of fine Southern literary heritage—and his life thereafter had been supported by a series of forgettable jobs that adequately funded his perfectly mundane habits. He didn't attend church regularly, it was true, and perhaps that could be considered a major sin, but failure to attend services didn't affect his religious beliefs, which were Protestant, functional, and usually only contemplated in times of need.

In his life he'd lied any number of ways, cheated on his taxes a couple of times, disappointed his father, disappointed his mother, borrowed a hundred dollars from his sister, Fran, never paid her back, drank more than his share of beer and assorted spirits, gambled on occasion, caught more than his limit of largemouth bass, slept through many a graveyard shift, and a dozen other menial offenses; but he couldn't think of one obvious, egregious sin that might serve as a lightning rod for corruption.

Instead of contemplating his lack of evil ambition any longer, he closed his eyes instead, only coming awake when his sleeping mind alerted him to the smell of cooking pork chops.

* * *

Over dinner, attended by only himself and Brother Anselm, since the messiah took all his meals in his room, Ashley reported his lack of progress in locating his own particular heart of darkness through meditation.

"I'm still working on it, though," Ashley said as he cut determinedly into the slightly overcooked entrée. "I'm sure I'll have it before long."

Brother Anselm set down his fork and stroked his beard. "So nothing obvious is presenting itself to you?"

"I've never been to prison, if that's what you mean." Ashley worked to free some gristle from the bone. He stared at his fork dubiously. "And I don't think I've seriously broken any of the commandments. Not seriously."

"If you haven't found this great sin by morning, then report your difficulties to the messiah. This may be part of the process."

Ashley set down his own fork, having reached the limit of his ability to forestall his conscience for free room and board. "Listen, I don't mean to disillusion you or anything," he said, "but I think you should prepare yourself for disappointment. I'm certain it would be nice to be at the forefront of the Second Coming, but I'm just as sure that a lot of people over the years have believed themselves to be some reincarnation of Christ. There may even be a name for it, you know, some psychiatric condition."

"I know what you mean." Brother Anselm sighed. "It's so difficult to know, though, right? Sooner or later the real messiah is bound to show. Then how would we know?"

"I'd expect more pyrotechnics. You know, fire and brimstone, the wrath of God, that sort of thing."

"One would think."

"Anyway," Ashley said, picking up his fork, "it's something to think about."

Brother Anselm nodded sagely as he reached for more bread.

* * *

The long, muggy Gulfport night did nothing to bring forth any one sin greater than the others, so when Ashley rose in the morning, cleaned himself in the bathroom and climbed the stairs to inquire at the door of the messiah, he had nothing better to offer his divine counselor than his own mediocrity.

The man seemed as if he was already waiting to receive him, and as Ashley sat in the chair before the bed he saw a bewildering humility in the man's eyes. No, it wasn't humility, but a sadness born from something other than the bearing of human sin.

"Have you contemplated your sins, Mr. Ashley?" the man asked, fingering his rosary.

Ashley nodded, and simply held his hands together, since he possessed no object of worship with which to fidget.

"And what did you discover?"

"I'll be honest with you, Ernie. I didn't discover much."

"What do you mean?"

Ashley raised his hands and shrugged. "I thought over my life, my habits, my sins, but I just couldn't define one special sin that might have influenced the downward spiral of my life. I'm sorry to disappoint you, but I don't really think I have one."

"What do you mean?"

"It's like this," Ashley said, hoping to be as honest about the matter as possible, "I know I'm a sinner. I know I've committed sins, but they've all been ordinary, everyday sins, common sins. I've never murdered anyone, I've never outright stolen from anyone, hell, I've never even been in a fistfight. Now, that's hard for a Southern man to admit to, but it's the truth. I've always preferred to talk my way out of difficult situations. I'm not fond of violence. Sure, I drink now and then, gamble occasionally, tell a white lie or two to make things go a little easier in my life—but I'm basically a boring, ordinary man, there's nothing special about me, not even my sins."

The man seemed to absorb this information carefully, his mouth pressed in interest. Then a small, candescent smile appeared on his lips, and he laughed again in his strange, high voice. "That's it, then, Mr. Ashley!" He waved the rosary in a decidedly unreligious way. "You've found your greatest sin without even realizing it."

Ashley sat back in his chair, running his tongue over the molars in the back of his mouth. "How so?"

"Don't you see?" The man leaned forward, his face bright with some version of joy Ashley hadn't seen before. "Your greatest sin is the greatest sin of so many others. Your greatest sin is your *mediocrity.*"

"Beg pardon?"

The man gesticulated wildly as he spoke. "Mediocrity! The absence of a commitment to something greater than your basest desires. That's the greatest sin of most of humanity. We live our lives day to day, committing only small sins in our pursuit of muted happiness. We don't engage the world, we don't pursue greater truths, more exhilarating experiences, we don't pursue greater beauty and elegance. And why don't we?"

Ashley shrugged.

"Because we're afraid to! Our fear keeps us anonymous, unambitious, and lazy. We're afraid to seek salvation, just as we're afraid to seek corruption. We are non-entities, Mr. Ashley, and that is our greatest sin!"

"*Our* greatest sin?"

The man's smile waned, then faded altogether. He stared at Ashley with small, unfocused eyes. "I'm afraid so," he said, in a much quieter voice. "That is the cross I bear, and the sin I will take with me after the Resurrection."

Ashley recognized the quality of the man's tone; it was the same tone he'd heard in the casinos from all those inexpert gamblers who were searching for just one grand win at the table of life. Suddenly he didn't want to be in the man's room anymore, or in The Church of the Giver of Life, or even in Mississippi.

"Tell me, Ernie, what was your life like before you became the messiah?"

The man smiled again, a shy, embarrassed smile. "I wasn't anybody." He clutched his rosary nervously. "I wasn't anybody at all. I was one of the mediocre, a great, great sinner. You see, I had to know the worst sins of the people of the world before I could come to forgive them. I will bear their sins with me to Heaven when I go, and they will be saved from themselves. No, I wasn't anyone you would notice, or care to be around. But that was my share of human life. To be honest with you, I'll be much happier when I can relinquish this burden unto my Father."

"When will that be, exactly?"

"I don't really know. You see, I came to Brother Anselm to seek a place for meditation and solace. I must prepare my mind and spirit for the trials to come. And when I am ready—I don't know when that will be—then I will go among the people of the world and begin my holy ministry."

"I see," Ashley said, understanding more than he actually wanted to. He didn't want to interrogate the man any further on his plans, so he deftly changed the subject. "I don't mean to be rude, but you said that if I discovered my greatest sin you would heal me of it. Is that something you still intend to do?"

"It is already given unto you," the man said, smiling weakly. "Go, and sin no more."

In the dark room, as he sat staring into the eyes of the man who believed himself to be the messiah, a terrible feeling fell over Ashley, as if a cold breeze had slipped down his shirt and gripped his spine. No, he thought, it couldn't be that. But it could be; it could be that he was staring into a strange kind of mirror, of himself, perhaps, in a different incarnation. The man was nearer his own age, and about as masterful at life as him. And he suddenly knew why his great uncle believed himself to be General Lee, and why, after a long life of indescribable insignificance, a man could suddenly believe himself to be the messiah.

He knew there were a thousand things that he could say to this, but he didn't have the heart to say them to the man sitting on the bed, nervously working his beads.

"Thank you, Ernie," he said as he rose from his chair.

The man smiled then, more sincerely, just before Ashley left the room.

* * *

Ashley passed over dinner that evening. In fact, after visiting the messiah, he walked down to his room, closed the door and remained isolated within its shadows for the rest of the day.

Certainly Brother Anselm awaited his pronouncement of Ernie's pedigree, but his feelings on the matter were more than conflicted. The man, of course, was delusional. He was a nondescript nobody who finally found a means of achieving relevance, a grandiose version of relevance to be certain, but he was ultimately dismissible. If he'd assumed the mantle of great artist, or wise philosopher, or sensual lover, he might have actually convinced a few people of his legitimacy. But no one, aside from Brother Anselm, perhaps, would ever believe he was the Son of God.

Well, if you're going to dream, Ashley thought, dream big.

But that was the problem; he saw too much of himself in Ernie, a man without dreams who gathered every undeveloped ambition all at once in his life and created one gigantic, impossible reality that made up for all his previous failures. That was no way for a man to spend his days. Poor Ernie would eventually be committed, or ridiculed so intensely that he would return to his previous incarnation and live out his life as a cipher.

But should he really tell this to Brother Anselm? What harm would it do to let them both have their fantasies?

And what of Ed Ashley?

Would he ever see Elizabeth again? Or was the question moot? The reality of the matter was that he didn't need a fiancé right now; he needed a sense of himself, some self-respect, enough to keep him from declaring himself messiah, or General Lee, or some other impossible historical reincarnation. But how simple was that to acquire? Could one just assume it as a fact?

Yes, he was conflicted, and miserable.

After a while he dozed, and fell into a bizarre dream: he was standing at the bottom of a hill staring up at a sky painted gray with storm clouds dense with imminent rain. A flash of lightning turned his attention to the apex of the hill, on which a large crucifix stood throwing its shadow on the world; and tied to the armature of the cross, in bloody rags that suggested gore beneath, the unmistakable body of poor Ernie, raised high above the people gathered below. His mouth opened once against the pain of his impending death, but no sounds came, only a thin line of blood spilled down his chin. All at once inside the dream, inside his mind as he experienced the martyrdom of the man, Ashley heard a voice, and it spoke the same words over and over again—

I am dying for your sins—

Ashley woke in the darkness of his room, his clothes heavy with sweat, his face slick and a muted curse lodged in his throat.

When his mind relocated his senses, he lay back down staring at the ceiling. I won't lose myself that way, he thought, I won't, I swear it. And the first step to doing so would be to face life on its own terms.

The next morning he would report everything to Brother Anselm. He wouldn't commit the sin of lying to the brother just to spare the man's feelings. As disappointing as unmasking a false messiah might prove to be, he would tell the truth and sin no more.

* * *

Ashley gazed up from his plate of scrambled eggs and found Brother Anselm staring at him expectantly.

He didn't want to disappoint the man on an empty stomach, so he thought it best to consume three eggs, four pieces of toast, and eight slices of bacon to compensate for his unintentional fasting. The brother sensed this was important to him, and so let him gorge himself in silence.

But now the man's stare insisted Ashley address the requirements of their compact, so Ashley set down his fork, wiped his mouth on a napkin and cleared his throat. He'd rehearsed his speech the previous night, and again that morning in the bathroom mirror as he shaved the stubble from his face. He had no qualms about its content, only about it effects, which might include Anselm's angry eviction of him from the premises.

But he forged on, because he felt it imperative that he be honest with the man.

"I'm sorry to tell you this, brother," he said, "but I don't think our friend upstairs is any holier than you or me."

Anselm's lips compressed into a frown. "Oh, dear. Are you certain?"

"I'm afraid so." Ashley recounted the events of his second meeting with the messiah, emphasizing the fact that he'd received no healing, only a great deal of sleight of hand. He included his observations of Ernie's character flaws, which echoed eerily of his own. "I'm still the same man you found on your front steps. A common sinner, unhealed and unhumbled."

"Are you sure?"

"Positive."

Brother Anselm sighed as he sat back in his chair. His red beard glowed faintly in the morning sunlight. He wore the emotional stigma of a man who had gambled on his future notoriety and lost. Ashley could certainly sympathize.

"Then it is as I feared," Anselm said. "I was only trying to fulfill my spiritual mission on Earth, you know."

"Sure." Ashley tried to remain positive. "If the man had been the messiah you would have been derelict in your duties if you cast him out. You had to be sure."

"That's true, Mr. Ashley. But I'm glad you came along to clear up the matter for me."

"I'm glad to do my part."

"And I will keep my word. Since you were kind enough to assist me, I in turn will assist you. But I'm afraid I can't do more than a bus ticket for you."

"That's more than enough. In fact, it's exactly what I need."

"And after I deliver you to your conveyance, I'll have to address the gentleman upstairs. I'm not quite sure how I'll handle the matter."

"I believe you'll find a compassionate solution."

Brother Anselm nodded, and rose to bring them both more coffee.

When he returned to the table with the coffee pot he asked Ashley, "What will you do now with your life, Mr. Ashley? Will you resume your gambling ways? Your drinking, too?"

"Lord, no," Ashley said. "I've learned my lesson. I'm going back to Montgomery and find a job, maybe even a new girlfriend. Sadly, I think my old one may be a little too materialistic to participate in a meaningful relationship. No, sir, I have no intention of ending up like our friend upstairs."

This declaration struck Brother Anselm visibly. His mouth open, he set down the coffee pot and resumed his chair. "Do you mean to say you intend to change your ways?"

"Well, yes. I'm not an evil man, brother. I've just been a little lax in my life. No, my experiences here have given me a new perspective on myself."

"Don't you see the irony? You're speaking of personal redemption."

Ashley sipped his coffee, then reconsidered. "No, that's not quite accurate. I meant—"

"It's true, isn't it?" Anselm's smile had returned, burning through his fiery beard. "You're healed, body and spirit?"

Ashley set down his cup, sorry for giving the brother the wrong idea.

"No, no, no. That's not what I meant. I meant that *seeing* how a man can be deluded—"

"The Lord works in mysterious ways!" Brother Anselm proclaimed. "It *is* a miracle!"

Ashley sat dumbfounded. He couldn't understand how the man could make the leap from object lesson to divine miracle. There was nothing miraculous about his decision to bring back order to his life, only the fear of concluding his life as a lonely, delusional failure.

"You may not see it, Mr. Ashley, but it's plain for me to see. You've been healed!"

"Really, I don't feel any differently—"

Brother Anselm clapped his hands together triumphantly, casting a wayward glance above him, ostensibly to the room on the third floor that held the man who had performed the miracle in question. "I myself feel redeemed!"

"You're still going to buy me a bus ticket to Montgomery, aren't you?"

"Yes, yes, of course! It's the least I can do to repay you for sponsoring the greatest moment of my life!"

Ashley said no more. In fact, something inside him told him that it would be a sin to try to argue Anselm from his convictions. The brother wasn't searching for proof of the man's mortality; he was desperately trying to prove the man's divinity, and now he'd found a way. Nothing Ashley said would change his mind. Ashley was absolutely certain of this.

So he simply shrugged and bit off another piece of bacon.

Still, he had to wonder—if the brother kept his word, and if he made it back to Montgomery to salvage the ruins of his life, would his circumstances change because *he* had changed? And if so, what had changed in him?

This was all very complex, and too much to think about in the moment; so Ashley simply accepted the circumstances, ignored the implications, and concentrated on finishing his breakfast. Which, he had to admit, would have tasted better christened by a little Irish coffee.

THE TRACTOR

Mark S. Jackson

The two old men trudged up the small hill as the sun began to rise beyond the eastern horizon, the sky awash with pink and purple hues. Behind them a young group of children led a team of horses tied to a strangely shaped harness. Their goal was the large shed at the top of the hill, and soon they arrived at their destination.

A guard stepped forward from the shadows near the shed to greet them.

"Good morning, Elder Johannsen. Elder Brennon." The young man who addressed them held a Remington 870 in his hands, sawed off to the stock, with a bandolier of reloads across his chest. Another young man, with the same weapon, stood quietly behind him. All the young men in the village shared this duty, and all of them hoped no one was desperate enough to try to break in to the shed, past armed guards. But it had happened, on more than one occasion. Blood had been spilled on the ground they stood on.

"Good morning, Kyle," replied Elder Brennon. "Quiet night?"

"Yes, sir."

"Good." He looked over at Elder Johannsen. "I reckon we should get started, then."

The two aldermen each fished out a necklace from under their shirts. At the end of each necklace was a pair of keys, which fit one of four locks on the door to the shed. Elder Johannsen waited patiently while Brennon unlocked the two padlocks that fit his keys. When the other Elder was done, he stepped up to the two remaining locks, and soon the door was unlocked, for the first time since the prior year's harvest.

Inside, an aging John Deere 6000 series tractor rested, it's green and yellow paint greyed by age. The tractor was famous throughout the region, as it was the only one that still ran, all these years after the Fall. Old Man Harrington had been a survivalist, and instead of stocking up on dry rations and guns and ammo, he had invested quite a bit of his family wealth in infrastructure. The Tractor and its store of spare parts were but one example. Thousands of gallons of diesel were stored in nearby underground tanks, along with stirrers and freshening agents to keep the fuel from turning to sludge. A smithy sat not far from the shed, along with all the tools necessary to work iron and steel. The Old Man had not built a mill, but he *had* imported all the parts necessary to build one, including a gigantic millstone. Within a year after the Fall, and for almost a decade after, their village was the only one in the region that could make bread, at least in ample amounts.

The winter that year had been mild, and while every best effort had been made to keep the date and time accurate since the Fall, the simple truth was this: they were not sure if it was late February or early March. But the early crops needed to be planted, and they hoped that if there were a late frost, it would not harm the seeds.

But it was the tractor that gave the village its power base throughout the region. A full-sized John Deere, it could plow just over one hundred acres per day during the planting season, and harvest just as much in the summer and fall. Other villages and communes used horses and mules, and some of the poorer ones had been forced to resort to human power.

And while there was still plenty of fuel in the underground tank, the tractor was never driven anywhere if a team of horses could pull it to its destination instead. After the shed was unlocked, four of the children grabbed hand-pumps from off the wall, and began the arduous process of pumping up the tires. One of the older children backed the team of horses up to the opening, and hooked the strangely shaped harness around axles of the tractor. Once the tires had sufficient air, the team of horses eased the tractor from its resting place and down the gradual slope, while the other children checked the ground ahead for any sharp objects. Its tires were heavily patched, and no effort would be spared to protect them, as the village was down to their last set of spares.

Not long after, the tractor was in place, at the edge of the first field, the horses were unhitched and led back to their barn. A team of men arrived with fuel cans, full of fresh diesel from of the underground tanks, and proceeded to fill up the tanks. Another arrived with the external starter, used to replace the nonexistent battery. Once everything checked out, Elder Johannsen gingerly climbed into the seat, adjusted his hat, and inserted the last surviving key into the ignition. He eased out the choke, gave the engine a little gas, and signaled to the starter crew, who began to furiously pump the generator that would deliver the spark to the ignition. Then he turned the key.

Nothing happened.

* * *

It did not take long to discover the problem. One of the village's biggest ongoing problems was vermin, and it became quickly evident that during the winter some rats had gotten into the shed, and promptly invaded the electrical system of the tractor and chewed through some of the wiring. Several of the cables would have to be completely replaced. The only problem, of course, was that they did not have any spare ignition cables, which meant they would have to trade for them.

Which meant dealing with the Denton clan.

They were the only ones that had spare parts for anything, and they kept a tight grip on them. The truth was they were worth their weight in gold, and the village elders would have to pay whatever price the Dentons asked. There were still over eight hundred acres of beans and corn to be planted.

They sent a rider over to the Dentons'; it would take him the better part of a day to get there by horseback. A letter, requesting a meeting to barter at the small township between the two villages, was sent with the rider. The Elders would not have to wait on a response; the Dentons would be there at noon, along with the part, if they had it, and with their demands.

* * *

The two old men did not speak as the wagon pulled out of the village compound. Elder Johannsen had the reins; Elder Brennon sat next to him, a double-barreled shotgun in the crook of his arms. The back of the wagon was full of foodstuffs—jams, jellies, hams, flour, and cornmeal.

Behind them, ten of the village men rode, two with shotguns, several with handguns, and few carrying crossbows. They expected no trouble, but since the Fall trouble seemed to find them on a fairly consistent basis. Most had learned the hard way to always be wary, and that Trust was the rarest of currencies.

"You know it won't be enough," said Elder Brennon, after they had cleared the last ridge.

"You're probably right," replied Elder Johannsen. He held the reigns limp in his hand. The horses knew the road, and what speed was expected; he did not have to drive them.

"Bah," spat Elder Brennon. "Probably. You know good and well what they will want."

"You never know. They might need some of these things, this time."

"Of course they *need* them. They've got bellies to feed. Too many, if you ask me." Elder Brennon was quiet for a time, and then continued. "We should have burned them out years ago when we had the chance."

"I don't disagree. But the simple fact is we don't know where they keep their parts stash. We would have to resort to certain means to get the truth, and even then that might not be enough. And the idea of...well, that doesn't sit well with me."

"And what we're about to do...that sits well with you?"

Elder Johannsen did not reply. He clucked at the horses, but they didn't need the encouragement. He clucked because he could think of nothing to say.

* * *

It was midday when they arrived in Coventry. The small town was no more than a sparse collection of farmsteads and workshops, centered on a well at a crossroads. There was a bit of a market, and a permanent building that had been erected some years before, and was considered neutral ground by all the surrounding areas. If one needed to barter, one went to Coventry. But one certainly didn't go alone.

The Elders left the horses and wagons with half of their escort, and went inside the building. The rest of the escort followed them in, and placed themselves strategically around the interior of the sparse building, with good angles to see out the windows and cover the interior of the room. The Elders sat at the lone table in the room, and brought out a bottle of whiskey, made from their own still.

They did not have long to wait. The sound of approaching horses could be easily heard from inside the building. It was not long before Darby and Ed Denton entered the room, followed by two armed boys, each carrying a shotgun almost as long as themselves.

But the Elders did not notice, for in Darby's right hand was a box, clearly marked "Wiring Harness—John Deere—x567-BV". Which was the exact part they needed. They had looked it up in the parts manual before they left.

"Hello Darby, Ed," Elder Johanssen said, trying hard not to stare at the box Darby Denton carelessly tossed on the table. The Elder did reach out and moved the box over to one side, to get a better look. It was still sealed. Nearly one hundred years after the Fall, here was a spare part for his tractor, the tractor that helped keep his kith and kin alive, and the container the part arrived in was *sealed*.

"Well, well, well," said Ed, smiling the lunatic smile the Elders knew and loathed. "If it ain't the high and mighty come to ask us for our help. Again." He was missing most of his teeth, and the few that remained were yellowed and stained.

"We are here to trade, no more," replied Johanssen.

"Well, call it what you will," said Darby, "but you need what we have, and we don't need anything you have out in that wagon."

"Bah," spat Elder Brennon, his grey beard bristling in outrage. "There's enough food in that wagon to feed a large family for a year. And it's better food than anything you manage to grow, Darby Denton."

"Well, that might be true, but it doesn't mean we don't have food." Darby patted his expanding waistline. Both Elders knew the old men in the Denton clan ate well while everyone else suffered. It was clearly evident in the gaunt faces of the two boys standing guard.

"So, let's cut to the chase, Ed," said Elder Johanssen. "What do you want for that wiring harness?"

For the first time, Darby and Ed stopped smiling and exchanged a look. Ed reached out and grabbed the box, and placed it square in the middle of the table, formally offering it for trade.

"Two."

"Out of the question," was the immediate reply from Elder Brennon. He got up to leave; Elder Johanssen reached out and grabbed the fraying sleeve of his jacket, and gently tugged him back down.

"Two wagons? Done." Elder Johanssen said, and stood up to formally shake on it.

This time it was Ed Denton who laughed, long and hard. It took a while for him to comport himself.

"Oh, Rick, you know how to make a man laugh," he said, still chuckling. "You know we aren't talking about wagons filled with corn and ham hocks."

Neither of the men replied. Elder Brennon refused to look across the table, instead preferring to intensely study the design of the window nearest the door. Elder Johanssen calmly met the eye of Ed, then Darby.

"One. No wagon. And we get the wiring harness, and all the chocolate you have that will fit that engine." Elder Johannsen knew the Darby brothers hoarded the confection like gold.

Ed shook his head. "One. No chocolate. And we get to pick."

"The chocolate isn't negotiable." He paused. "You do not get to pick."

Ed and Darby did not respond. They glanced at each other, and Ed started to say something, but Elder Johanssen cut him off.

"You don't get to pick. That is our final offer."
Ed nodded without glancing at his brother. "Done."
"Done."

* * *

"You could have offered more food. Hell, even weapons!" Elder Brennon was still fuming as they trundled back home in the wagon, the food still packed in behind them. He had been ranting at Elder Johanssen since the trade party left. They would return tomorrow to pick up the wiring harness and the belts.

"It would not have mattered," Elder Johanssen replied. "Tom, they would have turned down ten wagons stuffed to the brim with corn, and seed stock, and flour. And they don't need weapons, everyone knows they all walk around armed to the teeth, that's why nobody bothers them."

Elder Brennon was quiet for a while.

"You knew, didn't you?" he asked, breaking the silence.

"Yes."

"Then why load up the wagon? Why go to all the trouble?"

"For the others. They didn't know. Some might have guessed before we left, if we hadn't. Could have made things difficult."

"You think it's not going to be difficult when we get back, and break the news?"

"They already know. I had Martha tell everyone after we left."

"I...how did you *know?*"

"Because, Elder Tom Brennon, if I was in their shoes, and had that much leverage, I would have asked for the exact same thing." He paused and spat over the edge of the wagon before continuing. "They are *dying* Tom, and they know it, but they are too proud to ask for our help. Too proud to ask for anyone's help."

* * *

In the end, it had to be Carrie. Her parents had died young, so she had almost no family to speak of. She was still young, and not too badly deformed. The shrinking gene pools meant more and more bad babies, and her IQ somewhere south of sixty. No one expected her to live more than a few years longer; most of the afflicted had congenital heart defects in addition to their mental impairments.

But her cycle was regular, meaning she could carry a child to term. The Dentons might get one or two babies out of her before her heart gave out.

She had a soft touch with animals, and spent most of her days tending the livestock. She could do the same for the Denton clan. What she did at night for them...well, Elder Richard Johanssen did not care to think about that too much. He hoped they would be kind, considering her condition, but somehow he doubted it.

The wiring harness fit perfectly, and the tractor started on the second crank. Elder Johanssen started plowing the northern fields first, spreading corn seeds into the furrows of rich, dark earth.

He had insisted on the chocolate for the children's sake, as most of them had rarely had the delicacy. He hoped it would help to calm them from the distress of losing a friend. All had liked Carrie.

Elder Johannsen had made a lot of hard choices in his life. The Fall had made sure of that, and he had over a thousand souls to feed. One less now, but that couldn't be helped.

But there would be no chocolate for him, no soothing candy to take his mind from the evil he had committed. As he turned the tractor, and started on the second row, he wondered what, if anything, might calm him and soothe his frayed nerves, might offer him some level of succor and comfort.

He doubted anything ever could.

ANTHEM
Bruce Watson

Scott's career, which would end with an awkward plea, began on the day he discovered the hill he would soon call "my country." Friends later told him the overlook was a "great make out spot," but except for that one night with Kathi, he always went there alone. He found it toward dusk just hours after he hit those three long ones against Tustin. Back home, the phone had been ringing and ringing. The Old Man was shouting about his Major League Son, the three homers, the scouts calling, and his mother was nagging about homework. When her teacher's voice began scraping his ears, when the phone kept up and his father would not stop, Scott had to get out. Piling into the Old Man's pickup, he cranked up KFWB—Patti Page again—and rattled along the edge of the groves. A dirt road rose behind a row of eucalyptus, and he skidded onto the gravel, then climbed above the flat land. The tired Ford clattered and fish-tailed, but just as he considered turning back, he came around a rise and there, stretching below him, was the entire county. He mouthed a single word.

The setting sun had left the horizon glowing like a ripe peach. A warm Santa Ana had blown the Southland clean. Scott stepped to the edge of the bluff. A gust almost took his cap but he barely noticed. Big and broad-shouldered, he stood like some benevolent king on a throne of scrub and sage grass. To his left was Catalina, rising like a humpback whale above a shimmering strip of ocean. To his right was Mt. Baldy, its rounded summit holding a final finger of snow. A paradise, he thought. And below him were the groves, lush green and flecked with orange.

His look of triumph turned to a smile as Scott thought about the Tustin game. Three homers, the first soaring, the second a streak barely clearing the chain link fence, the third sending a cluster of boys chasing it across the parking lot. Teammates pounded him in the locker room, snapping towels at his meaty whiteness. His father went crazy with pride, driving him from the house to find this throne, this darkness spreading across "my country."

"Well," he said aloud. "At least I'm good at one thing."

Once a week for the rest of that spring, Scott came to the hill. Then in June, after signing with the Giants, he headed for Fresno in the California League. But that fall, and for several Octobers after his mother left, he rumbled up the dirt road again. If Kathi asked where he was going, he said, "Out" and in those first years, the answer was good enough.

During the fall after Scott reached the Texas League, he noticed his country changing. The plush carpet of groves was becoming a patchwork mottled by red tile roofs. The change started at an Eisenhower pace, just a few subdivisions added each summer while Scott hammered fastballs on the dirt diamonds of Texas. For those first few autumns, he could stand on his hill and pretend — that he was already in the bigs, that his mother was still in the house, that the Old Man was still young. Following his first season in the Coast League, dusk still brought just a sprinkling of lights below, but by the fall when JFK was killed, sundown saw his kingdom lit up like a pinball machine. "Might as well be L.A.," he told himself. Disgusted, he spun the pickup in the dirt. The following Octobers, in the wake of his best seasons — '64 (.323, 29 homers), '65 even better, and '66 when he was called up to the bigs in September — he did not visit the hill.

Then it began. Midway through '68, when he failed to make the Coast League All-Star team, he came home for the break and drove up the dirt road for the first time since Kennedy died. He was shocked, appalled, but could not turn away. His mounting dread was not just for his country but for the game.

It was only July, but they were saying baseball was tired, dated, dull compared to football. "They" meant not just sportswriters, but newscasters, front pages, even the Old Man. Scott's father had been his coach, idol, encyclopedia of the game's lore. Tall and skinny, tight-lipped and jumpy, the Old Man had played Class D ball in the early '30s before hitchhiking west to work in the groves. Because he had hit baseballs over painted wooden fences, the Old Man saw the game as sacred. So when Scott came home from Phoenix that July, he was stunned by his father's question. Was baseball still the national pastime?

"Sure," Scott stammered. "Sure it is."

"Glad to hear it," the Old Man said. "I thought, maybe these days...sex."

All that summer, a season of riot and war, the Phoenix Giants rose for the national anthem. Caps over hearts, the players stood straight as tenpins. Veterans mouthed the words. Younger teammates chewed gum, making fun of the "old men" for singing along.

"...and the hommme of the...bra-aaave."

Then as if the nation was still the same rawboned country that had nurtured Scott Fairly and his Old Man, the umpire shouted "Play Ball!" And the game, like an aging athlete going through the motions, began. Scott knew those motions as if they were his birthright. Almost thirty years had passed since his father had handed him his first bat. The heavy stick waved, wobbled, and clunked into his forehead. Tears and wails for "Mommm!" but minutes later, the bat was back in his hands, and had been ever since. The rules the Old Man taught him remained his rules; the game's timing was his pulse. The aching wait for the pitch, the split second decision. The umpire barking "Steeee-rike." Another wait, another second, and this time the ball streaking off his bat, arcing like water from a drinking fountain. Thirty years, his life so far, and as his mother and his ex-wife so often told him, the one thing he was good at.

Other star athletes doubled as quarterbacks, guards, or sprinters, but Scott Fairly played baseball, just baseball. Too sluggish for speed sports, too gentle for the crunch of contact, he embodied baseball's patience. Standing 6' 3," weighing a rounded 240, Scott did not look like an athlete, but from Little League on, coaches stopped to watch him hit. When he stepped to the plate in high school, boys gathered beyond the fence, pounding their gloves. Scott thanked God for his talent, but he also thanked the Old Man, who had thrown him thousands of pitches.

The Old Man had once been just "The Man," named for the legend on the team he had loved since his Iowa boyhood. Even Scott's mother called her husband "The Man," or sometimes "Stan the Man."

"Might as well call him that," Doris Fairly said with a shrug. "Might help him grow up some."

Later, Scott's mother was often asked the grounds for her divorce. She gave the same answer — "baseball." Her estrangement started the day Scott ran to her with a lump on his forehead from the meat end of a bat. She had picked him up, only to have him yanked from her lap. The distance had widened each summer morning as father and son huddled around the *LA Times* to read the Cardinals' box score. Scott's mother, a wisp of a woman with silver-rimmed glasses and hair in a bun, sat across the table doing a crossword. Even before Scott entered Little League, she hated the game as much as she hated the scarlet cap her husband wore from breakfast until bedtime. The cap suggested her classroom of second graders, especially the ones who gave her trouble. She still thought her husband handsome, even funny, but she could not understand a grown man who thought a boy's game was the only thing a boy needed to learn. Her bitterness deepened on the afternoon Scott came home clutching one hand, his face red, wincing.

"Bat hit it," he said.

Stan the Man burst in. "Told him to play first! No catchers in this family!" When the hand turned purple, The Man drove to the doctor, bringing Scott home with a cast and a promise to become a first baseman. Doris Fairly was not included in either decision.

"You're loons," she often said. "The both of you."

And then came the fall after the war. School had started, but over his wife's protest, Stan Fairly sent an excuse note to junior high. The note read: "PENNANT RACE!" Leaving at dawn, Scott and The Man drove winding two-lanes all the way to Pomona to pick up Route 66, then headed out past the last groves in Redlands, across the desert and on and on, through Arizona and New Mexico and into what his father called "Okie country." The miles unfolded, the country flat and brown, the flatbeds and pickups passing. Billboards for Nehi soda and "Blatz—Milwaukee's Finest" reminded his father of the Gashouse Gang. Pepper Martin— "I ever tell you how he once hopped a freight to spring training?" And Ol' Diz. "Know what he used to say? 'It ain't braggin' if you can do it.' Hah!"

Scott and his father finally reached Sportsman's Park on the dingy north side of St. Louis. There amidst the steel awnings and Erector set light towers, they watched the Cards' tie the Dodgers for first, then win the playoff opener. In a dim motel room, they listened to the second game from Brooklyn. The Cards won but what Scott would remember was how frail his father looked. Back home, Stan wore starched work shirts, but when the Cards clinched he leapt around the motel in baggy BVDs. Ribs showing, he was thin, scrawny even, with pencil arms and a patch of red skin on his sunken chest. For the first time Scott saw his father not as his coach or idol but as a man, a victim of time.

Watching "our Cards" play the Red Sox in the Series, Scott could not stop staring at Ted Williams. Teddy Ballgame, his father called him. Tall and thin, Williams carried himself like royalty even after striking out. Scott's mother sat at home, doing her crosswords. When her husband and son came back bristling with stories—"Slaughter scored from first on a single!"—she waited for Scott to mention something else he might have seen. The bluffs of New Mexico? The Great Plains? The Rockies from a distance? But all he could talk about was the game. Maybe The Man was right, she began to think. Maybe baseball was all the boy was good for. Often, infuriated by a report card or his refusal to read, she told Scott as much. She hated herself later.

From that trip until Scott signed with the Giants, Doris Fairly lived for the hope that when her son was gone, her husband would talk to her. She gave Stan a year, then moved in with her sister. She later met and married a short, plump man from Anaheim. She did not care that he was Jewish, though Stan made much of it—"My ex-wife married this Jew." She cared only that he made a good living as an accountant, had three daughters, all grown, and preferred bridge to baseball.

"She never understood us," his father said when Scott came home after his second season in Fresno. Searching for some sign of regret, Scott saw only pursed lips and blue eyes pinched at the corners. For twenty years his parents had shared a bed, fought, made up, roamed the county side-by-side in the pickup. But all his father said was, "I ever tell you how she nagged me to stop wearing this cap?"

Later, when Kathi left him, Scott remembered that conversation. "Guess I stink at marriage, too," he thought. He considered telling his father that Kathi had never understood him either, but being misunderstood was a cliché by then. He finally broke the news when The Man drove down to watch him play in San Diego.

"Keep your mind on the game," his father said. "That's all you're good at."

Kathi had been with Scott since high school, when he first noticed her in the stands. Curly brown hair and Pepsodent smile, she was the only cheerleader who came to baseball games. He could spot her from the on-deck circle, even from first, and whenever he looked she was looking back. Asking her out was as easy as stepping to the plate. Talking was tougher but they did not talk much on that night when he took her to his hill. The few lights glittered below. Kathi often asked to go "park" again but being there with her made him resentful. That was *his* country below. He suggested other places to park. The county had no shortage of dark roads in those days.

They married two years later, once he saw that she was good at the only skill required of a baseball wife—waiting. She moved with him to Texas, which she hated, then Tacoma which she loved. But Scott was on the road half of each summer and she found the other wives boring. The game was all Scott talked about, and their exhausting, waning efforts at making a child failed. Each autumn brought them back to Orange County, where Kathi had friends, where Scott spent days with the Old Man in the groves, nights with him in the empty house.

"He's lonely," Scott said when Kathi complained.

And nothing, not even her habitual flirting, could disturb

Scott's placid façade. After three years in love and seven more of faking, Kathi needed little excuse to end it. The excuse came when the Tacoma Giants moved to Phoenix.

"It's no big deal," Scott said as they sat on his father's porch. "It's still AAA. I'll still be starting." Kathi stared at the peeling paint.

"Hey, I know, Kath. But it's no big deal."

She had been a cheerleader all her life, first for her father and three brothers, then for high school teams, finally for her husband. But she had been in Phoenix once, she told Scott. It was 96 degrees. At midnight. Brown and ugly. "People shouldn't live in that sauna," she said. So his marriage ended with his wife calling him "a loser." He moved back in with his father and they talked about the game. Its pace, its motions were all that Scott loved, and by '68, that was the problem.

Because the country he viewed from the hill was not his anymore. Gazing down, Scott saw just a few patches of green in a sprawl of red tile and asphalt. Catalina might have been to his left, Baldy to his right, but both were hidden behind a smudged sky. No breeze blew his cap, no pride filled his chest. He did not know how much longer he could play the game but he knew he would never come to his hill again.

The changes sped up just as Scott noticed himself slowing. Deeper aches each morning, hamstrings that would not stay stretched, back as stiff as a bench. Sitting out the second game of double headers, he wondered what he would be doing in a few years. Coaching? Selling used cars? Still alone? The question left Scott with a nagging unease. He tried talking to teammates about it. He asked an outfielder from Indiana, a shortstop from Alabama, and two starting pitchers fresh out of USC. "Is it just me or is this country getting weird?" The outfielder shrugged, the pitchers told him to stop reading the papers and the shortstop said, "Damn right it's weird. You got your niggers takin' over."

The war that framed his childhood was two decades distant now. The shortstop from Alabama, Scott reminded himself, was not even born when they dropped the bomb. Folks his father's age still talked about the war, yet each evening the news described a different war, with battlefields no one could pronounce. And each evening's war was followed by raw, random violence. Eight nurses stabbed in Chicago. Some nut case gunning down people from a tower in Texas. These things never happened before, did they? Next came the riots. Smoke rising over Detroit. Newark. D.C....The riots tightened tensions; the Negroes on the team no longer talked to players like him. And now everyone was asking about the game. Wasn't it time for a new national pastime, one not based on waiting, waiting as Kathi once blurted out, "for someone to *throw* the damn ball!"

In the bigs, they were calling it "The Year of the Pitcher." Almost no one hit .300 anymore and fans were staying away. On the night in Spokane when the Giants played before a crowd of 723, Scott's manager, a former Yankee, told the team what Yogi Berra said—"If the fans don't want to come out to the ballpark, no one's going to stop them." But it wasn't funny when the game that made your heart soar seemed as washed up as a 33-year-old minor leaguer with five at bats in the bigs.

He had just a season or two left. His legs told him that. His back agreed. But when Scott came down from the hill that July, it was still the Year of the Pitcher. How much easier to use that name than "The Year of Assassinations" or "The Year More Cities Burned." By August, the Giants were slogging along just over .500. Still, September held out hope.

For the last two Septembers, Scott had been called up to Candlestick. Pinch-hitting was all they gave him, but during that first year, he made his Major League debut against Koufax. Ninth inning. Two out, bases empty. Giants down 3-1 and Franks sends Scott Fairly to bat for the pitcher. Shoulders solid but arms trembling, Scott swung at the first pitch. The ball made a terrifying *zzzi-pfff* and exploded into the catcher's mitt. "Steee-rike!" He took the next one, a wise choice since he never saw it. The third was moving faster than any car, plane, or bottle rocket he had ever seen. And the game was over. Other players, even Mays, ribbed him in the locker room, welcoming him to the club. A coach explained that by "club," they had not meant the San Francisco Giants. So one day he could tell his grandsons, if he ever had them, that he had faced Koufax. But what would he tell them about what he had seen the following September when called up again?

One afternoon on his way to Candlestick, he took a detour. He had heard what was going on in Golden Gate Park that summer, kids flocking to the city, bringing their drugs and their weird music. He figured on a quick drive along the park, maybe check out the girls, then head to the game, but a red light put him beside a parade of the strangest creatures he had ever seen. Skinny, shirtless men with hair to their shoulders. Girls in tank tops, their bare backs painted with flowers and butterflies. Drums, bells, tambourines. Bubbles drifting. A funny smell in the air.

Back in Phoenix, they had warned him. He remembered the term "Summer of Love" but with Kathi gone, it seemed a bad joke. When he was called up, coaches kidded him about "steering clear of all that LSD," and two players asked how many "hippie chicks" he figured on fucking. "Be sure to wear some flowers in your hair," a rookie told him. None of it fazed Scott. He was going to "Frisco" again, he told the Old Man, and this time he would start a game or two. So what was this about flowers? Now, sitting in his car jostled by chanting, shirtless kids, he gripped the wheel.

Did anyone remember when girls wore blouses? When men sported crewcuts, as he still did? The more Scott watched, the tighter his grip. When the parade passed into the park, he drove through the wispy fog, cursing. He tried to leave his anger in the clubhouse, yet the Summer of Divorce made that tougher. Planted on the bench, he was relieved when not called on to pinch hit. He showered, muttering how glad he was that the Old Man had not been with him that afternoon.

Again that year, Scott went 0 for September. A sacrifice fly earned him his only real stat in the bigs. One RBI. He was called up again in '68 but sat out the month on the bench. By that October he was back working in the groves, what was left of them.

"Won't be long now," the Old Man said a week after Scott returned home.

"Long till what?" His father turned, sat, started in.

Scott had never been good at math, and he felt dumber than usual as his father began with numbers. "Ten million orange trees." Back when he arrived from Iowa, the groves stretched from north of LA to the edge of the desert. "Ten *million* trees, each acre clearing a thousand bucks a year. Just figure. And profits even higher after the war." His father fell silent and Scott thought he was finished, but he was only revving up. "Then that goddamn Walt Disney came! Plowed up a dozen groves and built his goddamn kiddie park! Put his goddamned castle on TV, and the whole goddamned country discovered what I knew all along! That this place is a paradise. Was."

Paradise. The Old Man let the word linger. "Thousand bucks an acre. But the bulldozers had their numbers. Plow up an acre, build a crappy stucco house, sell it for 20 or 30 grand. But why one? Why not five, six, seven shitboxes crammed on an acre? Multiply by all those acres and you got yourself a new Gold Rush. And not even a workaholic running a 600-acre orchard can keep oranges in Orange County."

The Old Man stood. "Won't be long now," he said. He shuffled off to bed leaving Scott feeling stupid and alone.

The following morning, Scott piled into the pickup. He found the dirt road behind the eucalyptus but it was paved now and lined with beige houses. "The bastards," was all he could say. He turned around in a driveway being hosed down by a chubby woman in shorts and an Angels T-shirt.

That winter, most of Scott's work was just listening to the Old Man talk about his heyday. Sunkist Days, his father called them, but beer turned nostalgia to bitterness. "The Depression, when you were born, was the shits. Couldn't give away the fruit. Then there was the strike, when they rounded up the wetbacks, shipped 'em back across the border. Broke the strike, all so's they could keep paying 25 cents an hour." Scott knew where these stories led. To what "tight-asses" the growers were, holed up in their Pasadena mansions. To how you could grow up in Orange County and be too scared to pick an orange. To the story everyone knew, of the Mexican kid who stopped on his bike to pick one and was blown away by a shotgun the owner had rigged.

"Tight asses."

In November, the Old Man was relieved to see Nixon win. The country would be "back on track soon," he said, yet he had no time to celebrate. Two days after the election, he was up on a ladder. Soft soil gave way, the ladder toppled and the Old Man hit the ground hard. Scott was out buying fertilizer and his father lay for an hour, crumpled, his scarlet cap upended in the dirt. Alert all the way to the hospital, Stan Fairly hung on for a week but died on Thanksgiving. Ranchers from as far off as Redlands, thin, graying men with skin like old suitcases, gathered in silence. First their groves. Then their livelihoods. Now the men themselves.

Scott spent the rest of the winter alone in the house. Any moment he expected the Old Man to step out of the kitchen. Each morning behind the sports pages, the ache deepened. His grief mounted until one rainy evening in January when he went to the attic. Spotting a photo of his father in a baseball uniform, he sank to his knees and sobbed. He was okay after that. His coach, his idol, his baseball encyclopedia, was gone. To pay last respects, Scott drove one sunny afternoon to what remained of the groves the Old Man had managed. Walking through the few rows rimmed by houses, he fingered the green fruit and considered picking one but remembered the Mexican kid. As he walked to the pickup, a sweet smell summoned afternoons an age ago when his father had let him race through the grove, running his hands along the leaves.

With the Old Man gone, Scott saw the seasons ahead. The last groves would sell for more money than his father had made in a decade. No one could believe the wealth pouring into the county now, all for stucco and asphalt. The last crop would go, and by the time the bulldozers came Scott would be back in Phoenix.

It was a slow season, each game dragging. By mid-August, the Giants were barely over .500. Players were snapping at each other, and Scott was counting the days until his September call-up.

"Can't miss, right?" he told coaches. "They need me up there."

The team was in Eugene when the call came. The big club wanted five players, including both USC pitchers and the shortstop from Alabama, but not Scott Fairly. He got the news in the manager's office.

"Tough luck, old buddy."

Scott heard one word—"old." Thinking of how The Man would have taken it, Scott pursed his lips and walked out. Eugene. It would happen here, he thought. A Podunk town just added to the Coast League. Scott's Fresno team had played here back when Ike was president. Now, a full decade and five big league at bats later, here he was again. Hearing every click of his cleats, he stalked out of the clubhouse. Once in the dugout, he sneered at the rinky-dink stadium. The place seated 5,000 at most but twenty minutes to game time, it echoed like a funeral parlor. The empty bleachers mocked him. The tiny scoreboard seemed quaint to locals, but to a veteran who had played in windswept Candlestick, in spacious Dodger Stadium, its painted letters read "LOSER!" He was Scott Fairly, goddamn it! Hit .625 in high school, been a Coast League All-Star. Faced Koufax, had an RBI in the majors. And here he was about to play another goddamn game in another goddamn Podunk town at the goddamn end of his goddamn LOSER career.

A few minutes later, Scott stood for the national anthem. He had just taken off his cap when a voice washed over him.

"Ohh-oh sayyy can you seeeee…"

He took a deep breath, but "dawn's early light" made his hair stand on end. "What so proudly we hailed" stirred him more deeply than anything since Kathi had left. The words were the same, the tune unchanged, but the voice soaring over the outfield and nestling in his chest suggested that the singer knew him, knew his country, and was immensely proud of both.

"…and the rockets red gla-aaare,"

With every instinct come alive, Scott searched the field. Usually these anthem singers were easy to spot—in centerfield or at a microphone behind the plate. But where was this girl?

"…the bombs bursting in airrrrr…"

He finally spotted her in front of the home dugout. Another spasm gripped him. His eyes weren't what they had been in high school but her trim figure, red skirt, and blonde hair reminded him of a girl he'd known in Fresno and had often wished he had married instead of Kathi. Even from the dugout, he could feel the warmth. By the time "home of the... braaa-ve" was drowned in a smattering of applause, Scott had forgotten the call-up. Feeling as empty as when his mother disappeared, he watched the girl set the microphone back in the stand and tiptoe across the grass.

"Hot chick," the second baseman said. The shortstop stroked a bat. As the red skirt passed through a gate held open by an usher, Scott made a promise.

"I stink at marriage," he reminded himself. This was just a girl, he said, just the national anthem. Yet she seemed to know his country, not the free-for-all it had become but the nation the Old Man taught him to love. The country where men sported crewcuts, where you could see Catalina from a hill forty miles away. She sang of the country that won the war, kept the peace, and what was so wrong with that? He would meet this girl, Scott promised himself. He would find her and find out how she knew so much about him and his country.

Scott was hitting clean-up but the first three batters grounded out. Grateful to leave the on-deck circle, he got his glove. He needed time to flush that voice from his head. When he came to bat in the second, he managed to concentrate but flied out. For the rest of the game, she was all he thought about. In the two years since the Summer of Divorce, he had a few "slam, bam, thank you ma'ams" as the players had begun to say. One in Indianapolis, with freckles like a farmer's daughter, even on her breasts. One in Denver who wore him out, leaving him hitless for a week. One in Portland, whom he called when the team returned but got no answer. Each made him feel younger and less alone, but none cared about baseball, none were even born when they dropped the bomb. That made for a sweet body, but the soul? The heart?

After the game in Eugene, his drinking buddies went to a bar but Scott went back to Motel 6. He did not turn on the TV, just sat swigging beer. He kept thinking of her—skirt, hair, slim wrist and hand on the mike. When he awoke the next day, he called the general manager of the Eugene Emeralds, posing as a reporter.

"Hey, who was that fox doing the national anthem last night?" he asked. "Wanna interview her. Incredible voice."

"Hot chick, eh?" the general manager said. He promised to get the name and call back. Scott left the motel number but the phone never rang. The Giants had an afternoon game and when players rose for the anthem, teammates were startled to see Scott Fairly hurry to the end of the dugout. It wasn't her, just some Italian crooner. The Giants won 6-1, Scott went hitless, and his career, his life, and his country stunk like fresh asphalt as the team bus headed for Portland. Scott rode alone in the back.

Three games in Portland, three in Spokane, then there would be the cramped, thousand mile ride back to Phoenix. A two week homestand in Sauna Stadium, and his dream would be over. Scott had no idea what he would do in the offseason, let alone for the rest of his life. He had never cared what he did so long as he could keep playing.

"That's your problem," Kathi often told him in those final years when identifying his problem had been her national pastime. "You're so goddamned placid. So happy just to play. Fresno, Tacoma, Phoenix—it's all the same to you. To get to the majors, buddy, you gotta *want it*." Scott told his father what Kathi said. "When your wife starts telling you how to play the game," the Old Man said, "it's time."

The Giants took two of three in Portland and Scott continued to drink in his room. Random thoughts sent him careening through his career, his marriage, his parents' lives. All seemed so pointless. What he needed was a hill, standing above it all, overlooking his life as it stretched to the horizon. For a few beers each night, he tried not to think of the anthem singer, but as the longnecked bottles lined up like chimneys, he thought only of her. She was back in Eugene, a three hour drive. But then the Giants moved on to Spokane, and the distance made his shoulders slump.

The Giants split the first two in Spokane. Scott managed two hits but forgot to tag up at third on a fly. Coaches barked—"Get your goddamn head in the game!" By the series finale, he had made up his mind. He would not go back to Phoenix. Fourteen years after the Old Man called him his Major League Son, Scott Fairly had this much to be proud of—191 minor league homeruns, a .282 average, assorted girls and beer bottles left in towns from Fresno to Indianapolis, and one RBI in the bigs. The list of things he no longer understood—women, the popularity of football, why Indianapolis had ever been in the Pacific Coast League—was now longer than the list of things he never claimed to understand—math, reading, the cost of a stucco shitbox. Time had plowed over common sense, decency, and the last orange groves. There was nothing for him in Phoenix. He would play his final game, then board a different bus. He told no one of his plan. His suitcase sat with the rest in the clubhouse. He would shower, slip away, catch a cab. He'd leave a note in his roomie's locker and be gone while the rest were snapping towels.

Scott knew how Ted Williams had gone out—a towering homerun at Fenway in his last at bat—but how had Stan the Man finished? The Old Man would know but Scott was on his own when he stepped to the plate one last time. The Giants trailed 2-1 in the top of the ninth. Two on, two out. The first pitch was far outside. The next was grooved but he lined it foul. The third was in the dirt but the fourth came in as big and fat as they made them back in high school. Was there anything sweeter? Watching the ball streak, then soar, Scott felt like Teddy Ballgame. But as he jogged toward first, the ball caromed off the centerfield wall. A triple would do. Puffing around second, he headed for third. Each step made him feel ancient. He was out by ten feet. Back in the dugout, teammates kidded him as he got his glove. Three quick outs ended his career.

The kidding continued in the showers but talk of "Did you see that Scott..." soon turned to "Hey, where is the old guy?" No one could believe the news. The manager shouted at Scott's roommate but when the Giants' bus pulled out, Scott was at the Greyhound ticket counter. He reached Eugene at ten the next morning. She had been closer than he imagined.

Leaving his bag in a locker, Scott walked the streets. If Kathi could see him now, he thought. Or his mother. Neither ever had the slightest faith in him. Kathi would have been surprised to see how quickly he was walking. Their differing paces had turned strolling or shopping into games of hurry up and wait. "Will you *ever* get a *move on*?" He never figured out what the rush was. Now he strode the streets of Eugene, working up a sweat even though the sky was battleship gray. Hustling past bookstores, searching cafes, he scoured the city for a girl he had never met but felt as if he had known all his life. She must have grown up near L.A., he thought. Half the people here did.

After lunch, Scott found a pay phone, called information, and dialed the Emeralds' general manager.

"Oh yeah. I was gonna get back but I lost your damn number."

Starting a new life, Scott dropped the pretense of being a reporter.

"She was hot, all right," the GM said, "But Jesus, Fairly. You oughta be on a ball field, not chasin' some skirt."

"Just give me the name."

Denise Higgins. Scott hung up and walked on, turning the name over. Denise. Denise. There was a song once. Oh, with your eyes so blue...Swept along by the song, the name, he kept walking. By late afternoon, his feet ached and his legs were stiff. He picked up his bag and checked into a motel. It was a long night but at least the Giants never called.

For the next week, Scott roamed the city. He visited the university's music department. Denise. Figuring her for a waitressing job, he questioned restaurant managers. Denise Higgins. On Sunday, he went to the ballpark. Same rinky-dink stadium but maybe she'd sing the anthem again. She didn't. Watching the game, Scott felt like a spy. He knew half the players, had hammered both starting pitchers, could still do it if he wanted. But here he was in the stands with 700 strangers. Kathi was right. Baseball was goddamned slow. He left in the fifth inning.

The following morning, the city teemed. Hundreds, maybe a thousand young people streamed along University Street. Beat up beetles and VW vans, their drivers honking, waving, clogged downtown. Several vans had peace signs, and the beetles had bumper stickers. STOP THE WAR...DON'T CALIFORNICATE OREGON...The stringbean girls and shaggy men reminded Scott of that afternoon in Golden Gate Park. He wanted to grab each hand outstretched in a V and snap off the fingers. Then remembered why he had come to Eugene.

When the idea of searching the newspaper finally occurred to him, Scott felt dumber than usual. Why hadn't he thought of it before? Opening the entertainment section, he skimmed past movies and found "night spots." The first five listed trios or quartets, but at the bottom was a club he recognized from passing it on University. LIVE AT 9 P.M. — DENISE HIGGINS.

Scott arrived at seven. Taking a table near the stage, he ordered a beer, then another. He tapped the formica with his motel key, eyeing the mike stand, the piano, the glittered poster with her name. Smoke billowed as strangers filled the tables. Some frowned at the hulking man with the crewcut. Scott did not notice.

Towards 9 p.m., he began to worry. What the hell was he doing here? Scott Fairly, first baseman. Born in the Depression. First memory — Pearl Harbor, the Old Man running in the house that Sunday morning. Graduated high school in 1953. 19-fifty-*three*! Before Elvis, even! As he sat in the smoke and clatter, Scott took himself back to the groves, the smell of orange blossoms, how the long rows made you feel like you owned all ten million trees. By the time the singer stepped onstage, Scott knew he had made a mistake.

An old guy started at the piano, a jazz number. Denise lifted the microphone and Scott just stared. Clear hazel eyes, soft cheeks, blonde hair falling around her forehead. Mistake? From her first words, Scott felt her melt through him. After each song, he clapped a few times, yet inside he was shouting as if in the bleachers, giving standing O's to this girl who knew him so well.

He ordered another beer. He sat alone, empty, full, lost in his life, adrift in America, knowing nothing about women, wanting to know everything about her.

Shortly before 1:00 a.m., when the place was nearly empty, Denise turned to him. Suddenly there were no lights, no clinking glasses, just her singing. To him. The song stretched on for minutes, hours, then closed with a sigh. The next tune was upbeat, then the stage went dark. Scott stood. As beefy as a bouncer, he stumbled toward the piano. Denise was stepping away from the mike. He towered above her. She craned her neck, then backtracked but Scott sensed her fear and sat in the nearest chair.

"Please," he said, pulling up an empty chair. "I just wanna ask..."

With a worried smile, she sat. Scott was silent. There were times at first base when a ball scurried out of your glove and you scrambled after it. Pick it up! Pick it up! Pick up the goddamn...

"Didn't I see you?" he finally asked. "The national anthem? At Emeralds' stadium?"

She smiled, his shyness assuring her he was no threat.

"Yeah, that was me. Week or so ago. Why?"

"I just wanted to—I was one of the players. For Phoenix."

"Oh, you play... baseball?"

"I did. I just retired. Anyway, I wanted to... meet you. I loved the way you sang, the way you sing, I mean."

Scott bought her a beer and they talked. She was from Corvallis, had only been to California once, hated it. The only baseball she had seen was the game she watched after singing that evening. She found it "like watching grass grow," but she had questions. Why did the players spit so much? Why were the coaches so fat? And what were they doing when they rubbed their chests and touched their caps? Scott measured his answers and Denise, ignoring every flare sent up by the late night and awkward approach, listened. He wasn't so bad, this ballplayer. A little old, maybe, and not exactly her type, but he was kind of sweet. Scott, worried he would bore her with baseball, asked about the national anthem.

"Oh, I just got that gig for fun," she said. "A friend knew a guy who knew a guy in the front office. Tell you the truth, I don't think I'd sung it since fifth grade. It's impossible to get right. You practically have to stand on tiptoe to reach 'rockets' red glare'."

"But you *sang* it," Scott said. "You sang it like it means something. Like the country means something. Not like all these kids on the street with their—"

Whether it was the hour, the end of his career, or her face, Scott never knew. But for the next few minutes, he unleashed all the dismay of the last few years. What they had done to his country. What happened to the groves and to the Old Man. What he had seen in Golden Gate Park and what he saw on the news every night. What was happening to everyone? Why was everything so—he mouthed an "f" but caught it—messed up?

She searched his face, then lowered hers. She considered telling him how thoroughly she disagreed, but what would be the point? His rant snuffed out any flicker of interest, yet he still seemed kind, honest, no threat. She was startled to meet someone a decade older yet somehow so much younger. Rather than another angry man, he seemed like a boy, a bewildered boy. She did not know how anyone could pass thirty and be so innocent, but she hadn't bothered with boys since she was a girl.

"Sorry," Scott said as they stood. The bartender was at the door, holding it open. "Guess I get worked up."

"That's all right. Everyone's uptight these days. It's—I don't know—the war and all. Look, it's been nice..."

On the sidewalk, he felt as awkward as his mother always made him feel. Denise thanked him for the beer. He asked what she was doing the next night. Singing. And the next. Same. And—

"It's late. I have a day job."

"Where?"

"You're nice," she said, and stuck out her hand. They shook, she turned, and Scott made the long walk back to his motel room. The following evening, he considered going back to her club but he knew something about women now. He stayed another night in Eugene, then caught a Greyhound. The bus passed through San Francisco. The Giants were in town and he could have watched the teammates they had called up instead of him, maybe even visit the clubhouse. He did not leave the station.

Back at the Old Man's house, Scott called his mother and told her about the end of his career. To his surprise, she said she was sorry, that she always knew how much the game meant to him and that she was proud. How many home runs? That many? And was it true what the Old Man said? That he had played in San Francisco? And had a what? An RBI? They did not talk for the rest of the winter. Scott spent the rainy months fixing up the house, putting it on the market. By spring, it was sold and he was living in an apartment in Anaheim, looking for coaching jobs.

One night that summer, going around the TV dial to find a game, Scott stumbled on the news. There were fewer riots now, but the war went on, students protesting, some shot. Scott drank a beer, then another. He was almost asleep when the news showed a clip from a new movie about that rock festival in upstate New York the previous August. A sea of people, mud, long hair, mobs and mobs of strung-out kids like the ones in Golden Gate Park. And suddenly out of this mess rose something that sounded like the national anthem. But it was scorching, electric, raging. On-stage was a guitarist, a Negro with that big hair his teammates had started to wear, and a getup that looked like a Davy Crockett jacket bleached white. Scott leaned closer to the TV. He could barely believe it but he could swear this guy was stroking his guitar, running one hand up and down the neck, as if...And he was playing—no, he was torturing the national anthem.

The clip ran for thirty seconds. As the anthem screeched, Scott paced the carpet, plugging his ears. A dull rage filled his chest, his shoulders, his aching head. Finally, he lifted a chair and sent it crashing into the TV.

THUNDER ROLLING DOWN THE MOUNTAIN

Keith Madsen

The thing about having only one leg is that it's much easier to mount a horse. You might not think so, but six inches of stump doesn't take a hell of a lot of clearance to swing it over a saddle. At least that's what I've always found.

So there I sat astride my favorite steed, a golden Palomino. She stood steady, gazing out at the horizon with me, waiting for just the right nudge from me to send her galloping in whatever direction I would choose. But there was no need to choose quickly. We could saunter off to the north, where the great river *Wimahl* runs; we could trek to the west and the ocean white men call Pacific, or we could head directly east to the mountain the Salish people called *Wy'east*, named after the brave warrior who fought *Klickitat* for the heart of the beautiful maiden *Loowit*.

Of course, I have always been called by the spirit of the mountain myself. To ascend a mountain is to be drawn by the Great Spirit to his own tipi, to be granted the freedom to see all that a god sees, and to understand how the land which is my home connects to all that is beyond it.

I was getting ready to head east, when a voice surprised me from down below.

"Where do you think you're goin', Chief?" A white man's police officer. He had other officers with him, while I was accompanied only by a squaw. I would have to be careful.

"To the east, to the mountain you call Mount Hood. I go in peace and mean you no harm."

"Really? What's your name, Chief?"

"Roy."

"Gotta last name, Roy?"

"Just Roy."

"Well look, Roy—that horse ain't takin' ya to Mount Hood, or any other place outside of this park, for that matter."

White men never understand the power of a Nez Perce on his favorite horse. I smiled.

"This is a golden Palomino, a Quarter Horse bred for speed. Should I call upon her to do so, she could turn and be gone out of your sight before you could even remember where you left your car."

The officer shook his head. "Yeah, I don't think so, Roy. First of all, that isn't a Palomino; it's a gilded statue of a European war horse. And second, if you look over your shoulder, the squaw sculpted to ride that horse is Joan of Arc, the world's most famous female warrior, and she's lookin' a little pissed right now that you've hijacked her horse."

Little did he know that Nez Perce squaws always looked pissed. I wondered if I should expose his ignorance and make him lose face with his other officers.

"You see, Roy," he said, speaking a little arrogantly for someone probably twenty-five feet below me, "that's a pretty famous statue of a pretty famous lady. Teenage girl who led an army to free the French people from an oppressive invader. The statue is dedicated to those who lost their lives in World War I."

"Against an oppressive invader?" I said, mostly to myself. *Perhaps she could be more helpful than I had previously known.*

"Roy, I'm sorry," the officer continued, interrupting my thoughts, "but you've got to get down from there. And, if you don't mind my asking, how in the hell did you ever get up there in the first place?"

I noticed that the earth-bound are always searching for the secrets of those called into the sky. Still, he seemed to have a good soul. I lifted the rope near the noose-end of the lariat I had used to snare this steed. "My people are raised around horses, officer."

"So you lassoed the head of Joan's horse, and you—what?— pulled yourself up by your arm strength alone?"

I nodded. "In a wheelchair, all you've got is your arms."

"Nice," he said. "Still, you've got to get down from the statue, Roy. You're distracting the drivers passing by."

So again the call to surrender to the white man. I scanned the horizon. I scarcely could view the trees without my eyes being pulled away toward the droppings of white culture—including the traffic he had spoken about. Even the steed on which I rode was made as a tribute to a white woman who had never even seen this land, and given in honor of a white man's war fought on the other side of the world.

"Tell me, officer," I said, "had Joan of Arc fought with the French alongside my people against the English invaders of this land, would they have given her a statue?"

I could see in the officer's eyes that my question had gotten past his ears to his soul. His eyes had softened. His jaw had lost the rigidity of one standing for the law. No quick answer came.

Four birds left their branches in the nearby trees and found new places to rest their spirits before the officer raised his eyes toward me and spoke again. "It's not always fair, is it, Chief?—life, that is. Sometimes you're just screwed, and it makes no difference what you do."

I nodded.

"Would it help for me to mention they have a statue of Chief Joseph downtown near Portland State?"

"I know that," I said quietly, "but they gave him no horse."

"True," he said, walking up a little closer. "Probably afraid he would be like you and ride it off through the streets of Portland."

"Yeah, he would."

The officer took hold of the handles of my wheelchair and turned it around toward me. He looked up at me again.

"Still, I got to tell you once more to get down from there, Roy," he said. "I know it ain't fair, but it's my job, and I like my job."

I looked back up at the birds in the trees. It seemed they had stopped singing in order to see how our little drama would play out. But I bet they knew, just like I knew.

I lifted my hands to the heavens. "Hear me, my chiefs! I am tired; my heart is sick and sad. From where the sun now stands, I will fight no more forever." Then I swung my stump over the saddle and dismounted. Yeah, super dramatic. Über-Nez Perce. It would have probably been more so had I not forgotten to grab my rope—and that I was still over twenty feet off the ground.

* * *

I have to admit that when you live your life on the street, it's kind of nice spending a little time in the hospital. Warm blankets.

But it's also true that when you live your life on the street they don't let you stay very long, and so as I wheeled my way from the front entrance of Providence Medical Center, my head still throbbed, and my formerly good leg felt sore and unsteady whenever I put weight on it. They say that if I hadn't grabbed for Joan of Arc's leg on the way down, I probably would have broken that other leg. Even as it was, the impact caused sprains and threw me off balance, so I hit my head on the concrete base of the statue. Thus my throbbing head.

When I reached the sidewalk I noticed the police car parked on Glisan. The officer who climbed out of the driver's side door I had seen before.

"Don't tell me, officer. Now I've taken Joan of Arc's wheelchair. I'll give it back. I would hate for her to head into battle without it."

"Glad to see you're feeling better, Roy. By the way, I'm Officer Warner."

He held out his right hand, and I took it. "Wonderful. You have a last name and I have a first name. Together we could be a whole person."

"Okay, then," he said, "I'm Officer Karl Warner."

I smiled and let go of his hand. "Still just Roy."

"Where are you heading this morning, Roy?"

I shrugged. "Not back to the statue, if that's what you're worried about."

He sat down on a nearby bench. "You know, Roy, if you would drop the cynicism just a little bit, I might be able to be your friend. I want to make sure you're going to be okay."

I looked into his eyes. He had a good soul. "I'll be okay."

"But you have to stop drinkin' and climbin' up on statues."

"Friends don't let friends drink and climb."

He laughed. "That's right."

"Except I wasn't drunk," I said. "If you really want to be my friend, you need to know my spirit. I do not surrender my spirit to drink."

He cocked his head to one side and looked at me with narrowed eyes. "I gotta say, Roy, you seemed a little out of touch up there on the statue."

"I don't drink." I spoke quietly, so he could hear the power of the truth. "I'm hooked on something even more dangerous."

"And that would be—"

"I still dream," I said. "You should try it. It's hallucinogenic."

"So I've heard. Just don't let your dreams lure you into high places, or else next time your dreamer could be splattered all over the concrete."

A honk came from Officer Warner's police car, where his partner looked flustered.

"I guess I gotta go," said the police officer. "Where are you headin'?"

"Downtown. Pioneer Square I guess."

"Is that where you hang out?"

"Most of the time. It's what we Indians do—lurk around pioneers and look dangerous."

"Need a ride?"

I thought of some guys I knew who might give me a hard time if they saw me getting out of a police car downtown. "Maybe you can give me a ride over to the MAX line."

"Sure."

I wheeled over to the car. He opened the rear door, and I maneuvered into the seat. Officer Warner folded up my chair and tossed it into the trunk. As I fastened the seatbelt, I noticed Warner's partner didn't look too pleased.

"We haulin' in the Injun," he said as Karl Warner slipped into the driver's seat, "or are we just startin' a friendly taxi service?"

"Don't get all bent out of shape, Wilson," Karl said. "It's good community relations. We're taking him over to the MAX line."

"You got money for the MAX line, Tonto?"

My eyes did not feel comfortable looking at the man called Wilson, so I looked out at the traffic as I responded to his words. "If I were Tonto, I would have a horse."

Wilson turned around and glared at me. "Then how about if I just call you Sitting Bull-Shit?"

I let him wait a little while for his answer.

"Did ya hear me, Sitting Bull-Shit? Or are ya deaf as well as dumb?"

"He's not our prisoner, Wilson, so stop trying to brow-beat him." Officer Warner looked at me in the rearview mirror and smiled. "Besides I happen to know that Roy here is Nez Perce, while Sitting Bull was Lakota Sioux and Tonto was Potawatomi— unless, of course you're talkin' about Jay Silverheels, who was a Mohawk from Canada."

Wilson now turned his glare toward his partner. "God, you're a walkin' Injun encyclopedia, aren't ya? Of course, I wasn't talkin' to you, I was talkin' to your soul mate, Sitting Bull-Shit back there."

It appeared that Officer Warner was about ready to lose his temper, so I intervened. "Actually, I kind of like 'Sitting Bull-Shit.' It suits my spirit. Nothing is more healing to the spirit than a little fittingly-applied bullshit. So, I accept. And, yes, I have money for the MAX line."

"Well, hallelujah, now I can sleep at night." Wilson diverted his attention to the neighborhoods we were passing.

"You know, Roy," Karl Warner continued, "I'll tell you a secret. The reason I know so much about various tribes is that when I was a teenager, I always wished I was an Indian. Studied all about 'em."

"Really?" Having wished throughout my teen years for the opposite, this was intriguing.

"Not surprising to me," said Wilson, still looking out his window. "Anything but a regular American. Me, when I was a teen, I wanted to get laid. That's what's called 'normal', Warner."

"Yeah, I was anything but normal in my teen years," said Warner as he turned the car into the little parking lot by the MAX station. "I always felt like an outsider. Probably still applies. I identified. Indian making his way alone through the wilderness, fighting all the battles more civilized people were afraid to fight. And, yeah, Wilson, you cow terd, I wanted to get laid too, but I thought the girls would think my Indian self was hot."

The car stopped and I opened the door. "Let me know how that works out for you, Officer Warner. Because it sure as hell didn't work well for me."

Karl Warner got out of the car and went back to the trunk, where he pulled out my wheelchair, unfolded it, and put it, brake set, in front of me.

"I'm not sure you're going to be able to do this, Roy," he said, "but ya gotta keep your battles off of public property now. It will only get you arrested, and there goes your freedom."

"Public property, huh?"

"Yes."

I looked into his eyes. I never tired of looking into kind eyes, even though there was much these eyes did not yet see. "Isn't that property which belongs to us all?"

I love it when I ask questions people can't answer.

* * *

Coming back downtown was like a crash-landing. Instead of soaring into the air from horseback, I was suddenly having to look up at everything: the tall buildings rising overhead, the lights which told me to "walk" or "don't walk" (as if I could), and even the people standing in line for a free meal at the First Baptist Church.

At least they knew me at the church. They called me Roy, and they smiled.

After receiving my food plate, I pulled my wheelchair in next to a man I had seen many times, a man who called himself the Peacemaker. One of the church volunteers carried my plate and sat it in front of me. The shame of it all quickly came and jolted my spirit. I was Nez Perce, a tribe which, along with the Salish, were the most ancient residents of this land. Yet I depended on whites not only to provide my food, but even to carry it to my table.

"Enjoy your meal, Roy," the volunteer said. I didn't know her name, but I thanked her.

"Hey, Roy," said the Peacemaker. "I haven't seen you around much. What have you been doing with yourself?"

The Peacemaker had a salt and pepper beard which seemed just a few hours older than a five o'clock shadow. It was well-trimmed. I had always wanted to be able to grow a nice beard, but that was not a gift the Great Spirit had given to the Nez Perce. I always thought it would be a nice way to hide scars and moles, among the other imperfections on my face.

I took a bite of the chicken casserole. "Nez Perce are naturally nomadic. I have been reminding myself that the world is bigger than Pioneer Square."

The Peacemaker nodded.

"So, why do you call yourself 'the Peacemaker'?" I asked before savoring another bite of the casserole. "Among my people, a man must earn such a name."

I'm not sure why I asked the question. On the street you learn that a person's name is given as an expression of trust. It is one thing you can own and control, in a world where there is so little where that applies. I glanced over at the man in between bites, and he seemed deep in thought as to whether he was going to grant me this gift. He was halfway through his meal when he looked in my direction.

"I believe sometimes a name is not what you have earned from your past, but something you want to shape your future. Do you think your people might agree?"

I grunted. Again, I'm not sure why. I remember as a child an old man who grunted at stories told around the campfire. With him it seemed profound.

"You see, Roy," he continued, "there is so much conflict in the world. In my past I was a big part of that conflict. I wanted what I wanted, and the needs of others didn't matter. It destroyed my life. I had a wife once. A son. A home. I kept fighting battles which were all of my own choosing, and I lost. Now, no more."

I glanced across the table, and noticed two other men who seemed to have frozen in place, their loaded forks in front of them, their eyes vacant.

"On the street I've noticed that about everyone is fighting a battle, and most of them are losing. I figure they all need a Peacemaker. Someone to help them put a halt to all of the conflict inside of them. I mean, look where we are." He motioned toward the walls of the church dining area. "'Blessed are the peacemakers, for they shall see God.'" Then he added, "Jesus also said, 'Blessed are the meek, for they shall inherit the earth.' Maybe that is what would bring you peace, you know."

"When my people made peace with the white man," I said, speaking quietly but not meekly, "they lost the earth; they didn't inherit it."

The Peacemaker looked into my eyes. "Maybe the one you need to make peace with is not the white man."

He would not release my eyes for what seemed like hours, but was probably just several seconds. When he finally did, I quickly finished my meal.

"How did you lose your leg, Roy?" The question came from a man across the table. Maybe he thought he was changing the subject.

"In battle," I said. Then I wheeled my chair around and left the table.

* * *

It is amazing how fast you can go in a wheelchair when you are fleeing the truth. Eight blocks separate the church from Pioneer Square, and I had traveled that distance before another thought even entered my head.

When people asked about my leg, I normally did not tell the truth. *Why had I done so this time?* "In battle" normally was a lie. I had an elaborate story of how I had fought in the first Gulf War, helping to continue the tradition of the Code Talkers, Native Americans who fought in World War II. I was helping to decipher codes, and generals depended on my knowledge and insight. We were attacked, and a grenade exploded nearby when I was carrying a buddy to safety. I saved him but lost my leg.

That wasn't really the battle. Maybe Warner's partner was right. Chief Sitting Bull-Shit was a good name for me.

I had told the truth when I told Officer Warner I do not surrender my spirit to drink. Of course, I didn't say I never had. There was a time when drinking alcohol was my only refuge in the battle with myself. When you drink enough, all the stuff you don't want to think about is just purged from your mind. For me there came a night when I had drunk an adequate amount of this spiritual anesthetic, and I found myself on the west side of the city where the MAX train travels faster between stops. All I could see was that I had left my jacket on the other side of the rails, and I thought I was fast enough to beat the approaching train.

When I awoke in the hospital they told me I was lucky I survived at all. I wasn't so sure. Still, I went into rehab and now I don't drink.

When you are Nez Perce, scouting your way, living off a paltry disability check and wheeling your way through downtown Portland; and you have given up drink, you are an unarmed warrior.

So it was as an unarmed warrior I now surveyed the urban valley ahead of me. The mountains surrounding this valley were skyscrapers made by human hands, and the valley itself was a two-block square sunken plaza of brick, concrete and tile called Pioneer Square. Store clerks and corporate executives gathered there for lunch alongside the homeless, students on break, and shoppers escaping from the nearby shopping mall. It was a nice summer day, and so there was a band playing below, and people were relaxing and reading on the steps.

I wondered what they all would think if a screaming Indian would suddenly descend upon them, thumping down the steps in his wheeled, aluminum horse? *Yeah, they would probably just call the cops. Probably Officer Warren again, and I would be embarrassed.*

My battle really wasn't with these people anyway. I remembered something Officer Warren had said, and I turned my wheelchair back toward Eleventh Avenue. I boarded the free trolley to Portland State University, disembarked, and wheeled my way over to Jackson Street.

There it was, a bronze statue of Chief Joseph. I slowly wheeled my way up right in front of the commemorative piece. Already I could feel in my spirit this was the place I needed to be. I had seen it before, but I had shied away from it. Why? Perhaps it had been shame. Shame to come before such a father of my people and show him what I had become.

It was indeed true that the statue portrayed the great chief without a horse, but this did not seem to take away from his dignity and power. The statue was of bronze and was about ten feet high. He had a blanket draped over his left arm and a walking stick in his right, but his eyes were what drew my attention. The eyes were attentive and wise, the eyes of a man who let nothing pass before him unexamined, the eyes of a man who took charge of his world.

The eyes shifted and now looked at me. I know, that does not make sense when you are looking at a statue, but it was true nonetheless. They looked at me and penetrated to my spirit.

"Why do you come before me, my son?"

The lips had not moved, but I had most certainly heard the voice.

"I don't know who I am or where I belong, O father of my people."

His eyes were on me. I could feel his sorrow.

"So much has changed since you walked this land," I said.

"Yes, we were contented to let things remain as the Great Spirit Chief made them. They were not, and would change the rivers and mountains if they did not suit them."

"What should I do?"

"Reclaim the land."

"I have no weapons! And they are mostly good people."

He was patient with my confusion. *"The earth is the mother of all people, and all people should have equal rights upon it. I did not say 'wage war.'"*

I felt ashamed that I had misunderstood, and I hung my head. "The man Jesus said, 'Blessed are the meek, for they shall inherit the earth.' But I do not understand how that can be."

"This Jesus is from the Great Spirit. He speaks the truth. When I was a child I learned from the Christian missionaries. They taught some good things."

"But then you lost the land where your father was buried. So did it really help that you were meek and a peacemaker?"

"'Blessed are the meek, for they shall inherit the earth. Blessed are the peacemakers for they shall see God.' Yes, that is what I believe."

"But unless I go back to our little reservation, all I have is this wheelchair, and occasionally a place under a bridge."

"No one said anything about inheriting the bridges — or tall concrete buildings, or houses where one can hide from the Great Spirit."

"Inherit the earth?"

"Inherit the earth. Reclaim it. Yes."

"But I am not a wise and powerful leader. I am just Roy, a man with one leg, who rides on and speaks to statues."

"Then you need a new name. I grant you mine."

"Chief Joseph?"

"No, not my Christian name. My Nez Perce name, Hinmaton-Yalaktit. Thunder-rolling-down-the-mountain."

"I could never be worthy of such a name!"

As I looked, the face of the statue was no longer looking at me, and his spirit no longer spoke. His eyes once again focused on his own horizon, a horizon which I could not see.

What I could see was the face of the Peacemaker, standing perhaps fifteen feet behind me. He said nothing; he only smiled.

I whirled around in my chair. I did not know where I was going; I simply knew I must go.

"Inherit the earth."

The words echoed over and over in my mind. They echoed as I raced past the buildings which housed the classrooms of Portland State University. They echoed as I sped through intersections, ignoring lights and dodging cars. They echoed as I rolled past the taller buildings of downtown Portland to the MAX station at Pioneer Square. When the Blue line came heading east I got on it right away. I didn't even stop to think about it.

"Inherit the earth."

The words now whispered in my head, timed to the clickety-clacking of the train on the rails as it picked up speed.

"Inherit the earth. Inherit the earth. Inherit the earth."

We sped past asphalt-laden interstate highway, mini-malls, houses, apartments, and townhouses, all of which began to look the same after a while; but very little earth.

When the train came to the end of the line in Gresham, I got off and sped down the sidewalk, as if my wheelchair knew where I was going, even if I didn't. I reached Highway 26 heading east, and turned in that direction. I wondered what people thought as I wheeled past, head down, determined to go somewhere, no longer sitting in a concrete and tile square, waiting for nothing.

My arms were burning from the strain. I wondered how long I could go on. As the vision came to my mind of where I was going, I wondered even more. It would take days.

I was now out beyond the residential and commercial fringe of the city and was rolling down a hill past tall Sitka Spruce, trees which lifted my eyes to the heavens. I smelled their sweetness and relished the wind rushing past, caressing me; the same wind which made the tree branches flutter and sway. Deer grazing by the road ran off into the forest—perhaps to tell their friends of the return of the Nez Perce to this land.

As I came to the bottom of a hill I saw the Sandy River to my right. The embankment leading down to it was not too steep, so I pulled my chair off to the side of the road, braked it, then scrambled and slid my way down to the river itself.

The water was definitely chilly! I took off all of my clothes except my undershorts, and crawled my way in until the water swept up over my back. I shivered with delight. The life of the river washed over me and infused my soul with its energy. I looked up and saw an eagle flying high above me, a sign which my people have always seen as a messenger from the Great Spirit, a sign that brought honor and courage.

I cupped my hands, drew from the water, brought it up to my lips and drank deeply. Then I did it again. I know, I was supposed to think of the dangers of *giardia*, but at that moment I was no longer a 21st Century man, withdrawing from the dangers of an untreated world; but rather I was immersing myself in the life of the earth. While I had not even considered the need to bring food and water on my venture, what I thirsted for was not just water, but *that* water, water fresh from the mountains, water supplied by the earth, my mother.

When I pulled myself out of the water I became aware of my hunger, and that hunger drew me to a bush of salmonberries, and I ate my fill.

After I had dressed and crawled my way back up the embankment, I should have been exhausted, but I was the opposite. I felt like I had been reborn.

That evening, before the sun went down and I stopped to sleep on the pine needles of the forest, I got my first view of what I now knew was my destination. Capped with snow, even in summer, and majestically rising over the surrounding hills, stood the mountain I would claim as *Wy'east,* and not Mount Hood. I still wasn't sure of how I would do it. To ascend such a mountain in a wheelchair, straining with all my might for each foot of ascent gained. But the eagle would fly high above me to give me courage, and the God who made the mountain, and spoke from within the mountain, would draw me with his power. I would go to the top and see God. I would look down from near the summit and see the distant valleys where my people and the Salish people once roamed, and when I was done, I would roll down as if on the wings of the eagle, and I would shout out to the wind,

"Thunder once again rolls down the mountain!"

INTERVENTION

Richard Hawley

Eric looked dead ahead into his mother's eyes and said, "Do you know how much I hate you?"

I can't picture Mrs. Everett's response because I was preoccupied, although very uncomfortably, with Eric. He held his skinny body so tight he shook a little, and when he told his mother he hated her, his eyes welled with tears.

This was almost unbearable for me. In fact it had started feeling unbearable from the moment the Everetts and I sat down with the counselor to discuss how Eric's intervention would work. The counselor, a stringy, pale man of about thirty, told us to call him Mark. He wore blue jeans and a crew neck sweater with no shirt. There was something vacant in his expression, and his speech somehow managed to be both flat and insistent. I noted at once that he didn't use language very well—the point, he told us, was "to get real honest with each other"—and I wondered if the Everetts, already on edge, would dismiss him, and thus the whole process, before we started.

"I'm an addict," Mark said, "a recovering addict, and you need to know that. All the counselors here are recovering, and we think that's real important in working with these kids, because you get a lot of denial and dishonesty from kids when they're using, and we can deal with that. We can work through that, because we've been there. We know the tricks. I used them all myself. The kids need to know that it's over, they can't bullshit anybody anymore."

"How is Eric doing?" Mrs. Everett asked. This was the second day he had been in the treatment center since they had, with the cooperation of Juvenile Court, checked him in. According to plan, no one in the family had spoken to him since.

"He's about the way you would expect at this point." Mark, whether intentionally or not, gave no hint of reassurance. "He's not being real honest with us right now. He's mad at you for sending him to treatment." Mark looked at Mrs. Everett almost aggressively. "You're going to see that Eric's a very angry kid."

"He's probably scared out of his mind," Sarah Everett said. Sarah, Eric's older sister, had flown home from Dartmouth to participate in the intervention. "Can I smoke?" she asked suddenly. "I'm sorry, but this feels like a prison. I can't believe we are doing this."

"Sarah," Mrs. Everett said softly, "you haven't been home."

My attention at that point was drawn to Nora Everett, Eric's little sister, who, wide-eyed and still, sat close to her mother.

"I can't believe we are doing this," Sarah said again.

Mark gave us our instructions. In a minute Eric would join us. He would be wearing only pajamas, the required dress of new referrals. As he made—if he made—progress through the individual counseling sessions and group sessions, he would gradually be given more privileges: socks and slippers, T.V. time, access to the snack bar. When he had completed his Drug History, and when it was approved, he would be able to wear street clothes.

"My god," Sarah said. "It *is* a prison."

"Sarah—" said Mrs. Everett.

"It isn't a prison," Mark said, looking levelly at Sarah Everett. "It's a system. It's no fun, but it's a system that works."

Mark told us that we should arrange ourselves in a circle. When Eric came in, he would sit in the center of the circle. Each of us in turn was to tell Eric our own personal experience of his drinking or drug use and the behavior related to it, like lying or causing trouble or failing to keep commitments, and then to tell Eric as plainly as possible how it hurt us or inconvenienced us, how it made us feel.

"This is very important," Mark said. "You've got to keep it specific, very objective. Don't say, 'Eric, you've been lying.' Say 'On such and such a day, you said you were staying for the night at X's house, and then I learned that you weren't there.' Say that, say what happened to you, and the important thing is that you tell him how what he did made you feel. He needs to hear, 'When you stayed out all night' or 'when that money was missing, I was really scared' or 'I didn't think I could ever trust you again' or 'I cried.' Remember, right now he doesn't need to hear what you think of him. He needs to hear what's been happening to you because of his using and how you feel about that."

Eric, we were told, was not to answer anything we said, not even to deny it. His job, Mark said, was to listen until we had all spoken. Then, when we were finished, Mark would ask Eric if he had anything to say to us. If he did, we were supposed to listen but not to respond.

I remember thinking, as Eric came in, that I was grateful for the highly specific regimen. By adhering to the protocols, it might, I hoped, just be possible to bear the sickening uneasiness in the room.

I did not want to do this. The agency had asked the Everetts if there was anybody from school or church who knew enough about Eric's using to participate. I taught Eric English and was also his assigned faculty advisor, and as it happened, I did know something about the problem.

Half-thoughts swam around in my head as I tried to think of what I could say that was "objective." How could I put it? Mainly I thought about Eric seated at his desk, with no books or the wrong books. Slumped at his desk, he appeared both idle and agitated. I pictured his eyes, bright and moist, that look of staring without seeing.

In my office, he would look away. "I don't know," he would say. "I was unprepared." He didn't know why. He didn't know if he would prepare tomorrow.

Actually I knew more than that. There were things I could say. I could tell about moving up and down the rows of seated students, pausing behind Eric, a faint sweet musk hovering about his head and shoulders. Pot or incense, probably pot. It was in his hair, in his clothes.

"Are you high?" I asked him one day in my office after class. "You look like you're high." I told him I was sorry I had to ask, but I was worried about him. I told him I thought I smelled pot on his clothes. He tensed a little and somehow absented himself behind his bright eyes. He didn't answer.

"Are you? Are you high?"

"No, I'm not."

"Can you tell me why you smell like pot?"

"No," he said. "I didn't think I did."

Eric was going to wait me out. I couldn't think of anything else to say. "Is there something you want to tell me, Eric?"

For just an instant he seemed to look at me. The light overhead flashed in his eye, and he looked angry. "No, there really isn't."

All I got from Eric Everett was unease. He seemed to have read nothing from *The Great Gatsby* and was flatly unresponsive to questions I asked him in class. He wrote short, empty essays that barely touched the relevant passages of text. Yet, he conveyed nothing like weariness or boredom. There was an almost sickening tension emanating from his chair. What would I say, how could I say this in the session?

Mrs. Everett started. Her voice was wavering and soft, far back in her throat. Eric glared at her as she spoke. She had experienced quite a bit of Eric's drug use and its effects. More than once she had found little bags and canisters of marijuana behind the sweaters on his closet shelf. There was the redolent clay pipe under the driver's seat of his car. She had picked up the phone in the kitchen and heard bits of talk, plans. She had phoned the families of the boys with whom he said he was sleeping over and learned that he wasn't there. She had met him at the door in the morning. She had told him that, except for school, he was confined to the house for a week. She had stood between the counter and the kitchen door, trying, physically, to keep him in. She had felt, for the first time, the rough grip of his hands on her shoulders as he thrust her away from the door. "You are *hurting* me," she cried out. When he pushed past her, she almost fell. She had called after him, "Eric Everett, don't you dare leave this house!" Her ears had rung when her son said, "Oh, *fuck* you" and slammed the door.

When she finished, Eric inclined forward. That's when he said, "Do you know how much I hate you?"

"You don't talk," Mark said, with surprising force. "You just listen. If you can't do that, you can go back to your room, and we'll do this another time. You understand me?"

Eric's father told a story about Eric flying into rage when he was told he couldn't use the car after his mother found the pot pipe under seat. Mr. Everett had placed the little clay pipe on the table in front of Eric. "So where did this come from?" Eric said he didn't know.

Eric's father asked for the car keys. Eric said it was his car. Eric's father demanded the keys. Eric said, "This is such bullshit," then got up from the table and left the house. Eric's father called after him that if he didn't come back to the table immediately he was no longer welcome in the house.

"Did he come back?" Mark asked.

"No, he did not," said Mr. Everett.

"And what happened?

Mr. Everett looked confused.

"What happened after that? Did Eric come back home?"

"Yes, he did. Eventually."

"And did you make him leave the house?"

"No."

"What did you do when he came home?"

"We were—very angry with him."

"What did you do? What did you say?"

Mr. Everett could not remember what he had done or said.

"So," Mark said, "You told Eric that if he left the house, he couldn't come back. Then he came back home, and you were very angry, but you let him come back and you can't remember if you said anything to him. Is that what happened?"

"Yes, that's what happened." Now Mr. Everett was irritated.

I wished Mark would stop. Mr. Everett was uncomfortable. A long-limbed, handsome man, he seemed suddenly diminished and weak. I could not imagine him now, despite his size, standing up to his son, either to keep him inside or outside the house. The discomfort of the session was coming to feel like terror. I could see it in little Nora Everett's eyes as she listened to her father. Nothing he said seemed to touch the silent figure of her brother, hugging himself tightly. Without exactly saying it, Mark seemed to confirm an obvious, terrible fact: *you people are all so ineffectual.* I wished he would stop. I wished I had never agreed to come.

Sara Everett did not help. She began by asking Eric directly, "Are you all right?"

Eric made an angry silent gesture toward the counselor.

"He's not supposed to talk," Mark said.

Sara said she didn't agree with any of this. All she knew, she said, was it drove her crazy that every time she came home or called home her parents were obsessed with Eric and drugs. She said her brother needed to learn to use some sense and that her mother had to get over her obsession. "You are, mother," she said. "You are obsessed."

"What do you think your mother's obsessed about?" Mark asked.

"I wasn't talking to you. I was talking to her."

"What do you think your mother's obsessed about?"

"About pot—about control. I mean, listening in on the phone?"

Little Nora Everett was almost too upset to speak. Mark talked to her softly and waited. Finally, she said that her brother scared her now. All the yelling and the crying scared her.

I made a fairly complete account of Eric's flatness and lack of effort in class. I told about his smelling of pot and about our session in my office. I said it was frustrating to work around a student so disengaged and unreachable. Then I said to Eric, with more feeling that I had intended, that I really liked him, that I wished him only good things, that if he was sick, I wanted him to be well. I almost said—but I couldn't make it sound sensible— *Eric, you're lost. You've lost connection, and you haven't a clue about how to get back. You're lost, lost and falling.*

After that all I could think about was Ellis.

I had forgotten Ellis, buried him. In college and for a year or two afterward, Ellis was the most vivid presence in my life. Crazy Ellis. In recollection he was like a bright parrot on a grey day.

Ellis would do anything, say anything. "Let's play a game," Ellis would say to people he had only just met. "Let's play Nazi and Jew—really, really. It'll be fun, really. Let's go. I'll be the Jew. You start."

I met Ellis in the dorm library at four in the morning. I was studying all night for an exam, and looked up blearily and saw that I was not alone. I started.

"You are very serious," Ellis said. He was a compact, tightly wired boy. A thick crown of shiny black hair grew out stiffly from the block of his skull. He would always complain about his hair "It won't lie down! Even if it's three feet long, it's like a fucking crew cut."

That first night—morning—may have been my best time with Ellis. Not too long after greeting each other, we began, I can't remember why, singing songs from musicals. "I don't believe it," Ellis said, "another guy who knows *Oliver*."

Ellis liked the plaintive little ballad Oliver sings: "Where is Love?" Improbably, given his beet red face and the impression he conveyed of an Apache brave about to do something physically menacing, Ellis managed to suggest a lost waif as he cast his eyes up toward the fluorescent lights and sang:

"Where-ere-ere-ere-ere is love? Is it somewhere up above?"

Abruptly, he stopped singing. "The bridge of this song is very hard. It goes all over the place."

Miraculously, I knew it. It was tricky, but I knew it.

"Amazing! What are the odds that there would be a guy who knows the bridge to "Where is Love?"

The odds, I am sure, were long. It was so good, such a relief, to sing, or at least fumble, through the scores of "West Side Story," "Mame," "Gypsy," "Stop the World, I Want to Get Off" as the tooth yellow light of the dorm library melded weirdly into sunrise and then daylight.

Ellis's general effect on me was to wear me out, but his friendship went deep. He is one of two or three people who have felt as if they came into my life for a reason. In Ellis's case, I can't name the reason, but it seemed urgent.

He had a way of describing other people with such intensity that I longed to know them, felt somehow cheated by not having been present in the loony anecdotes Ellis recounted.

Over the course of the year we shared a dorm room, I listened in the dark for hours to his stories about his father, who at the time was approaching seventy-five, a retired T.V. producer who as a young man had been an eye witness to the dawn of live television. There were stories about Jimmy Durante, Lucy and Desi,

Ed Sullivan, Donald O'Connor. Ellis's mother, a startling bird-like character who stood well under five feet, had lived in a convent for two years before choosing the world. By the time I finally met his parents at their summer place on the Jersey shore, I was almost too much in awe of them to speak.

But as much as I liked him, Ellis was unnerving. Some of his whims and gestures were not very nice. He could scare people away. I remember returning with him to our room in the middle of the night, both of us worse for drink, and even in that impaired condition wishing he wouldn't urinate under the doors of people he didn't like.

His betting really wore on me. He would bet on anything. He had a sure sense of what I was unlikely to resist. "I'll give you fifty bucks"—I never had any money then—"fifty bucks if you can eat three more of those cheeseburgers." Or six more beers. Or scream out something unthinkable in the library.

I was surprised, although I don't know why, when he was asked to leave the college. He rarely did any work, and he cut most of his classes, even the theatre classes he said he liked. I knew his absences spoiled assigned scenes and, once, a whole one-act play.

For two or three years after that, Ellis would show up on campus without warning for dramatic, disruptive visits of uncertain duration. Without writing or calling, he always managed to find out where I was. The summer after I graduated, when I was tending bar in a lodge on the Canadian side of Glacier National Park, I was honestly not surprised to see him moving toward me one evening, bent low under the weight of an enormous back pack. The first thing he said when he sat down at the bar was, "Give me something for free." Then he said, "Where the fuck are the northern lights?"

I have no good reason to believe Ellis is dead, but I'm sure he is. When I decided to get married, I tried hard to locate him through friends and through his parents, but after his father died, his mother's address changed, and I lost touch.

The last time I saw him was about a year and a half after the Glacier National Park visit (which cost me my job). Some friends and I had driven up to the college for a ski weekend. On a whim, we decided to have supper at the College Diner, a grim little eatery in the middle of town. Throughout our undergraduate experience the College Diner was nearly legendary for its owner's undisguised loathing for the very few college students who, whether desperate or uninformed, stopped in to try it.

A half dozen of us entered the College Diner in a spirit of bemused superiority. Thinking back, there may have been a deeper appropriateness to our assembling in that unwelcoming, drearily lit place. Ours had not been an era of undergraduate ebullience. The post-college twenties for me, and I think for most of us, were a bewilderingly anxious, often gloomy time.

Not long after burgers and pitchers of beer were placed grudgingly before us, Ellis walked in, followed by a terrific draft of cold air from the street. Scraping a chair into our midst where there really was no room, he settled in. "God, I always loved this place," he said.

Ellis was wired. He dodged our greeting, and casual inquiries and launched into a long and, I'll have to say, hair-raising account of enlisting in the National Guard and then trying to get out on psychiatric grounds. I wanted the story to be funny, funny and outrageous in the old manner of Ellis at his best, but it was not funny.

Apparently Ellis had been asked to leave his parents' house after aimless months of hanging around and supposedly looking for work. "I guess I wore out my welcome. Which is too bad, because I was having a really good time, I was playing a lot of hoops with these kids in the church lot. I was getting to be fantastic. We had these good games, all afternoon, every night till it got dark. I mean those were great kids. We actually had a little *league* going. But my mother and father couldn't get into it. They've never really encouraged me athletically. They said I had to go. Imagine that, my own mother and father." Ellis's father had finally suggested the National Guard.

"Hey, I said, I can endure anything for five months. Five months and then some summer camp for a few years, and then it's bingo! They pay you for life. Anyway, I thought they did, but it was terrible. A lot of guys who are good with cars. A lot of guys who get sexually aroused by raising their trucks way high over huge wheels and vrooming around the A & W lot. They didn't like me—I mean they really didn't like me. A guy says to me, and really, he means it, 'Hey, asshole, you're an asshole.' Imagine insulting me like that, on my first day."

Even allowing for the familiar hyperbole of Ellis's narratives, it was easy to picture him as an impossible reservist, badly disrupting his barracks if not the entire training program. "I couldn't make my fucking bed," Ellis told us, now on his feet and gesturing. "I'd do these tight little corners just like everybody else, and Sergeant Mingus—Sergeant *Mingus*—would come up and say, 'What the hell is *this*, ratshit?' He was ripped, totally furious, and I had done my very best. He never let me explain my approach. He hated me. They all hated me."

One morning, Ellis said, Sergeant Mingus called him a "crazy fuck," and this had given him an idea. "I decided to go crazy—at night. They wouldn't be able to stand it at night." Ellis said he waited until the barracks was dark and absolutely quiet, and then he would scream as hard as he could. We all remembered this from the dorm. I wanted it to be funny, for all of us to laugh, but something unspeakable seemed to be evolving in Ellis's story. I could feel it in the air of the diner.

"At first they beat the shit out of me," Ellis said, "but I had to keep going. I had to get out, or they were going to off me. I was screaming like a maniac"—Ellis opened his cavernous mouth and did a strangled, muted version of his nocturnal screams—"I was hyperventilating, I was wetting the bed."

Ellis said he was relieved when the medical and psychological tests started. "I had them, I knew had them. One guy told me he had never seen a psychological profile like mine. I loved it. I told him we were all precious and unique. Didn't he know that every snowflake is different. I kept hyperventilating like a bastard." Ellis hyperventilated for us, his eyes fixed and wild. The rasping in his lungs was deep and awful.

"Then," Ellis began pacing around the table, "Then, I had my big final session. The fucking exit interview with the base psychiatrist, Major Treat. I walked in and sat down, and Major Treat just looks at me. He says nothing, not even hello. So I say, 'What's up?' Major Treat says nothing. I say, 'What? What? *What?*'" It occurred to me that Ellis was shouting in the restaurant.

"Nothing. Major Treat sits back at his desk and looks at me for forty-five minutes. Forever. I try staring back at him like Charles Manson. I'm going nuts. My sphincter is like a BB. I'm sweating like a bastard. Finally, finally Major Treat sits up and says, Mr. Berry we have spent a lot of time testing you and observing you. You have disrupted your unit since you arrived on base. You have behaved bizarrely, screaming in the night, talking nonsense. This is what I think.'" Ellis paused, his eyes on the linoleum.

"Mr. Berry I think you're faking. I think you want to be discharged from the service, and I think you've decided to do anything to get out. That's what I think, Mr. Berry. I think you're faking."

Not just our table, but everyone in the College Diner was listening to Ellis's story.

"He had me," Ellis almost whispered, "The guy had me. And then it really started to happen. I was paralyzed. I couldn't breathe. My lungs were like cement. I couldn't breathe, and then I exploded"—Ellis's lungs rasped and screamed as he inhaled—"I started hyperventilating like a lunatic, really hyperventilating. I was a madman, I was all over the place until somebody gave me a shot in the ass and then the big black adios."

Ellis sat down and let his head flop over the back of his chair. For a full minute nobody in the diner spoke.

Ellis did not look well. His normally livid complexion was mottled and pale. It could have been the cold. When I caught his eye, he looked as if he might possibly cry, although I had never seen him cry. Ellis looked lost.

Someone said, "So did you get out?"

Without changing his expression, Ellis said, "Am I here?"

That was the last story I ever heard from Ellis, but it was not the most memorable story. Ellis told me the most memorable story a few weeks after we met, when he decided for some reason that he wanted me to know him. He had been telling me hilarious stories about his parochial grammar school, Our Lady of Lourdes. Throughout my childhood Catholics telling about their distinctive practices always made me long to been born Catholic. Ellis was, by his own account, alternately the bane and the darling of the nuns. This was easy to imagine.

"But then," Ellis said, "I started cheating. We had a math test every Friday. There were always twenty questions, multiple choice, and I was, you know, going along. I was getting eighteens and seventeens, maybe a *sixteen,* then eighteens and seventeens, and then all of a sudden we were multiplying and dividing fractions, and it was really hard, and I couldn't fucking do it, and I started getting sixes and eights. I started getting *fours.* I couldn't believe it. I was in junior high and I realized I was already really stupid. It drove me berserk.

"So I started cheating on the tests. I slid my desk up behind Jimmy McVickers, who was like Newton, and I would circle the answers he circled, except for maybe one or two. I kept doing it, even though it made my heart pound so hard I could hear it. Every time I would say to myself, holy shit, I'm cheating. I was cheating Sister Mary Therese. I was cheating the nuns."

"And then I got caught." There was deep sadness in Ellis's face. "I got nailed. McVickers told on me, and on the next test Sister Mary Therese was watching. I was all over McVickers' answer sheet, and she nailed me. She said, 'Ellis Berry!' and I went '*Aaah!* I felt like I was being electrocuted, and she told me to stand up, tear up my answer sheet, and throw it in the waste basket. She and I would visit Sister Louise Gregory after the class was over.

"That was it for me. They called my parents. You have to know that my parents could not even imagine cheating, anything dishonest. I could have smashed somebody in the head with a bat, I could have sexually molested little kids, and they would have tried to understand, but cheating was..." Ellis looked miserable.

"My father kept saying, 'Tell me again exactly what Ellis did.' Sister Mary Therese would tell him again, and my father would say to me, 'Is that what you did? Did you look on this boy's examination sheet and write down his answers?' And I said, 'yes. I did it. I did it, I did it. I'm sorry.' My father kept asking, 'And how many times did you do this? Come up behind this boy and copy his answer?' He wouldn't let go of it. 'Fifteen times,' I said. "I did it about fifteen times."

"My father couldn't get it. 'You did this fifteen times?' I kept saying yeah, I did it, I did it, I did it, I'm sorry, I'm sorry, I'm sorry. My mother was crying the whole time, and then for about three years after that, every time she looked at me. My father still couldn't put it together. 'Ellis,' he said to me, 'Why didn't you do the problems yourself?'

"I was in total disgrace. I was a cheater. Every kid in school knew. All the nuns knew. My parents knew. Every Friday afternoon for the rest of the year I had to go to the Nun's Residence and wait outside Sister Mary Therese's door, until she showed up with a make-up test for one of the ones I cheated on. There was nothing in the hall except one little school desk. I would wait there by myself until she came out of her room with the test. As soon as I got started, she would go back into her room. *And,*" Ellis said loudly and unnaturally, "And then I realized. They were the exact same tests she had given me before. And they were just as hard. On about the third one I realized I couldn't do one problem. O.K., I said, this is it. I looked down the hall, made sure there was nobody around and I took my book out of my bag and looked up how to do the problems. I cheated. I was cheating again, in the Nun's Residence. Yes, I said. Here we go. After that, I brought along the answers already filled out. On the last Friday, Sister Mary Therese looked at me and said. 'You've done a good job, Ellis. You made a mistake, but now you've learned your lesson.'"

Ellis stopped talking. I was not used to silences from him. I could have commented or asked him about a lot of things, but I could tell he didn't want me to. "I'm a cheater," he said.

A week after Eric's intervention, the Everetts and I assembled again at the treatment center for his Amends session. Probably because the first session had been so tense and draining and, more deeply, because we had been through something intimate and strange and awful together, the atmosphere in the office as we waited for Eric to come in was positively affectionate. Sara Everett had lost her edge. She was teasing and tickling Nora, and she was, for some reason, especially warm to me.

The counselor Mark was a reassuring figure this time, and it was easy to give him our confidence. He told us Eric had had a very hard, very good week. He was starting to get real honest. The format for the Amends, he explained, was to form a circle again with Eric in the middle. This time he was to do the talking. First, he would summarize his drug history, which had been approved by the staff the evening before. Then he would address each of us individually, telling us how he had been dishonest, how he had failed to keep commitments, how he had been hurtful. Then, if he wanted to, he would apologize. "You should get ready for an emotional session," Mark said. "I think you're going to see some tears."

It was an emotional session.

Eric entered the room wearing pajamas, a robe cinched tight around his waist, and slippers. His hair was unwashed and spikey and his face looked sallow, but he was very different from the clenched and agitated boy who left us the previous week. It was as if some terrible current in him had been switched off. Even before he spoke, he seemed mercifully at rest.

Eric said, "Hello again." and smiled sheepishly. His mother wept.

"Mother," said Sara Everett, "We haven't even started!"

Then we all laughed.

Eric's drug history was staggering. I have since learned that this is common: families full of doubt and guilt commit an unmanageable child to drug treatment and then learn the involvement was far deeper, more extensive, more longstanding than they had imagined on their darkest day. In Eric's case he had bought, used, and intermittently sold marijuana, LSD, powder cocaine, quaaludes, and something he was told was Ecstasy, which had made him temporarily delusional. He had on occasion exchanged family valuables—a watch, a clock- radio, jewelry, sometimes stolen money—for drugs, and he had sold some of his supply to others. He had stolen an expensive scales from the science lab at school, and he had also shoplifted hash pipes, a coke spoon, some beaded bracelets and compact discs from stores. He had twice taken friends' cars without asking and he had frequently driven while he was, as he said, "out of my mind." Eric consulted a small spiral notebook as he spoke. "I think that's it," he said.

"And do you still have drugs in your possession?" Mark asked.

"Oh yeah," Eric said, seeming relieved. "I do. Or did. There's a little bit of coke in an aspirin bottle in my medicine chest at home, and three's a baggie of marijuana under the spare tire of my car."

"Now," Mark said, "Is there anything you would like to say to your family and to your teacher?"

Eric looked directly at each of us as he spoke, only occasionally dropping his gaze to his notebook. He was neither reticent nor overly effusive. He was most visibly upset about having cursed his mother and having handled her roughly. He seemed to want to make a complete account.

By the time he got around to me, he had already confessed such consequential indulgences and misbehaviors that I thought there was little purpose to add any instances of school-related activity, but doing so was clearly part of the process, and I thought it might be somehow good for Eric. He *was* high in class, he told me. He was often too buzzed to prepare. He had lied to me, he said, and he was very sorry.

"I think that's it," he said to Mark.

"Is there anything else you want to tell these people?"

Eric looked around the circle. His eyes met his little sister's, and then he quickly looked away.

"Only," he said, and then his voice broke, "I'm really sorry."

"Do you folks want to say anything to Eric before you go?" Mark asked.

My throat was constricted, and I could not speak. I wondered if anybody could. Mrs. Everett said, "Can we touch him?"

"Of course you can," Mark said, "He's yours."

Mrs. Everett, and then all the Everetts surged forward to hold Eric tightly to themselves. They made an awkward, beautiful configuration, Mrs. Everett clasping her arms around her son's neck, Mr. Everett to one side, his arm curled around Eric's skull, Sara standing behind, leaning her head into the back of her brother's neck as if listening, Nora nestled against her mother's hip, an arm extended blindly into the huddle of her family.

There was no room for me, and of course I was not family, but I too was drawn to Eric and to the sobbing, swaying cluster of Everetts as they held him fast, saying, *Eric, I love you. Eric, we love you.*

It was Sara Everett who saw I didn't know what to do. She smiled and extended an arm to me. I dropped one arm around her waist and reached in for Eric.

I reached in for him, and this time I found him.

SHINING STAR

Nim Stevens

Once upon a time, in the little town of Hollywood, Joe the beggar trudged into the hills. The summer was hot and dusty and the authorities had redoubled their efforts to make the streets pleasant for tourists. The bums were chased from under the bridge but Joe had found a new hidey hole in the shadow of the Hollywood sign.

He sat in his grass filled hollow, the sweet smell of wild rye filling his head as the blue sky transformed into the soft yellow haze of city night.

He lay back, ignoring his hunger and thirst and brought out his secret treasure. The diamond, or maybe cubic zirconium, was waiting for him the very day he'd arrived in this magic town. It twinkled up at him from the center of Judy Garland's hand print outside the famous Chinese Restaurant. Welcome home, Joe, what took you so long?

He watched the light shine through the diamond until it disappeared in darkness. As he stared into the gloom a star fell burning through the night. He gasped, but before he could re-cover another star shattered past, then another. Three of them. He laughed out loud, then shushed himself, looking warily into the dark for hidden listeners.

"I wish I had a little bottle," he muttered. "That would make this perfect."

He heard a chink in the rocks above his head, then a half pint of Mad Dog rolled into his lap. Powerful but sweet, it was a sip-ping wine. Joe sipped, recalling it was also kosher and a devout glow entered him with the alcohol. What a night.

The morning started bad. They were watching the garbage now, and the old man spent a second day without food. Kindly vol-unteers enticed the vagrants with tasty sandwiches, tempting them to shelter, but Joe saw through their ruse. He would not be caged.

At day's end his luck changed: he found a takeaway container abandoned at a bus stop. He filled his bottle at a fountain in a children's park but had to run when parents spotted him. They pulled their cell phones. He escaped away to scuffle up the slip-pery grass to his haven. His to-go box contained a barely touched chicken dinner.

He would have been the happiest of men if the chicken had not lodged in a tooth, restarting an ache he'd hoped would not return. He pulled his diamond out to shine in the last of the day, sucking water over his teeth to soothe the cavity.

A star shot across the horizon. As he watched another followed and another still. He drew a breath in awe. A second night of triple meteors. His chest expanded with the wonder of life and tears came to his eyes at nature's beauty.

"I just wish I didn't hurt so bad," he said.

Joe felt his mouth rearrange itself, the teeth shifting like docked boats in a swell. The pain was gone. Cautiously he probed, fearful of restarting his toothache but unable to quell his curiosity. His tongue discovered a full set of smooth neat teeth. Each tooth was solidly inserted in healthy gums and bone, a mouth he hadn't felt since his teens.

He blubbered, he bawled. He could not contain his joy and his chest was wracked with deep breaths of delight. After blowing his nose onto a filthy shirt sleeve, he fell asleep, his face wet with happy tears.

There is a special hour each day, when the night cops make their tired way home and the day cops pray for a crime to divert them from the endless round-up of the dispossessed. Joe chose this hour to rush the donut shop.

He'd avoided sweets since the toothaches began, though these rubbish bins contained a certain and delicious source of calories. Piled in fresh clean sacks, the day-old donuts were all his. He stuffed his coat and mouth with maple bars and apple fritters and cream puffs. He even found a coffee on a windowsill, still hot and laced with sugar and cream.

Charged with carbohydrates he hid in a doorway looking out at the marquees. Improbably muscular men and impossibly luscious women stared down in a changing light show of movie hits.

Clouds cooled the sun and Joe pretended his day away, imagining his leading roles. He swept the heroines off their feet, smiling with his perfect teeth. The sugar took a long time to wear off.

Day's end brought clearing skies and he returned to his bed of straw. His diamond glittered as he ate his final donut. His full belly creaked.

Long ago a planet exploded, and every year Earth approached its debris field to capture some hapless dust to spark for Joe's entertainment. He laid back in sweet melancholy, waiting for the show. Slowly and majestically it happened again, one, two, and three stars blazing out as they crashed toward the planet.

Joe's head felt full. He could barely breathe yet his voice, when it came, was rich and resonant.

"I wish I was a star."

His body rose from the ground, head over heels, arms spread wide. A ringing in his ears became angelic choirs. Rapture filled him. The city and then the planet receded and still Joe ascended. He was bliss, he was ecstasy.

The spark of sun on space rock intruded and he remembered why he'd come. Asteroids surrounded him and his purpose hardened. He was ready for his audition.

He curled forward and pushed off into a dive. He flew down, down, back to the planet he loved, his hair flaming. A blue light enveloped him as he expanded; his shining presence filled the California hills.

All over town they looked up. All over town their jaws dropped. Some were fast enough to catch it on their cell phones. Observatories were googled and it was verified. It only took a moment but Joe winked out, content. He was the biggest star of the season. He had arrived.

PARTY ON THE POINT

John Engell

When I open the door, Bobby Joe Mills is standing under the bug light, a yellow ghost. He pulls off a black leather driving glove and sticks out a hand.

"Hi," he says, "I'm back."

We shake and he follows me into the family room. It's late. Ruth is upstairs asleep. I'm shocked. But somehow I'm not surprised.

"You didn't expect me," he says. He pulls off his other glove and sits in my rocking chair.

"You been gone thirty years."

"Twenty-eight," he says.

"You never wrote."

"Wrote?"

"To say hello. Let me know where you were. A postcard. An email."

"Shit. I knew I'd be back."

"You want a drink?"

"Bourbon."

"Don't have bourbon."

He gives me a strange look.

"I have wine. Red or white or rose."

"Red," he says.

In the kitchen I open a bottle and pour two glasses, both very full. I hear my rocking chair click, click, click.

"Thanks," says Bobby Joe.

"Where you been?" I sit on the sofa.

"New York, Chicago, Seattle, Silicon Valley, Hong Kong, Singapore, Bangkok, Bangalore, Sumatra."

"Sumatra?"

"I assisted tsunami victims."

"You work for the Red Cross?"

"Yeah," he says. "The Red Cross."

He may be ten pounds heavier or he may not, and he has a splotch, like a birthmark, on the left side of his nose. Otherwise he's amazingly the same. Broad shoulders, trim waist, coal black hair. We're both over fifty but he looks ten years younger than me, maybe twenty in the dim light.

"What's been happening?" he says.

"Not much."

"I hear you and Ruth have kids." He smiles.

"Two."

"Girls?"

"Yes. Girls."

"They must be big."

"Rachel's a sophomore at Chapel Hill. Rebecca's a lawyer."

"A lawyer."

"Works for the D. A. in Durham."

"Girls take after you?"

"More like Ruth."

"I bet they're gorgeous."

I sip my wine.

"Insurance business flourishing?" Bobby Joe smiles again. His smile is still half way to a sneer, or maybe it's the other way around, but now one of his lower front teeth is chipped and along with the splotch it makes his angular features look slightly lopsided and slightly sinister.

"Business is fine," I say.

"You haven't moved."

"We like it here."

"It's a damn small house." He stares around the family room which is a mess, as usual.

"Big enough for us."

"Old, too."

"Ruth likes old houses."

"Remember the day we trashed old man McAlpin's place." Bobby Joe leans forward. "He and his blond bimbo wife'd gone on a fucking cruise or something. You and me and Elmer jimmied the back door and we trashed it. Big fucking place. Regular mansion. Living room the size of this house. We did the bedrooms first. Sawed one leg off each bed. Broke all the cups in the kitchen cabinets. Just the cups. I carved the dining room table, dug a couple of skulls into the maple while you threw a gallon of red paint all over the living room walls and Elmer brushed it on with a broom. Then we closed the drains in the bathroom sinks and tubs and turned on the hot water and left it running. Wanted his house to float down Main Street. Kept wishing we could see the bastard's face when he got home."

"But we didn't."

"How old were we? Fourteen? Fifteen?"

"Seventeen," I say.

"Shit. That old." He finishes his wine. "Anyone rich was a shit to us. We were the one and only original hard ass radical gang of three. Dan, Elmer, Bobby Joe. Liberty, equality, fraternity."

"We were small town punks. McAlpin hadn't done a thing to me."

"He fired my daddy's ass."

"I'd forgot."

"Fucking right he did."

For the first time Bobby Joe laughs and in spite of the chipped tooth it makes him look even younger.

After a minute he says, "Now you sell insurance, I work for the Red Cross."

"That's what happens."

"I wonder what else'll happen," says Bobby Joe. He puts his wine glass down and stands up to leave.

* * *

Sometimes we feel nothing we've ever done matters. One summer day when I was about ten, my momma came in the front door, wiping sweat out of her eyes with a Kleenex, a gust of hot wind chasing her heels. She walked right on by me, chucked a bag of groceries on the kitchen table, turned, her right eyelid twitching, her face puffed with heat, and said, "That is the last bag of groceries I ever buy." Then she walked out the front door.

It wasn't. She bought a thousand more bags of groceries before she died, some in the summer heat, some on cool autumn days, the leaves red and gold, the sky brittle blue.

Years later, when I was home from Chapel Hill for Christmas break, my daddy had the last of his fits. You could never forecast them, but the cause was always trivial. He couldn't get a screw to screw or he couldn't fold the first section of the paper without tearing it or he forgot to return the library books on time. Things like that. His fits didn't happen often—two or three a year maybe—and they lasted just a few minutes, but he'd go completely crazy. I don't remember what set him off that night. Maybe I didn't know. Suddenly he was on his knees, screaming and blubbering, "God damn it to hell. What have I done? I'm nothing. A worm. A loathsome worm. The vileness of the universe. Scum. Pure scum." Then he keeled over on his stomach, splayed against the hardwood floor. "Oh Lord, Lord Jesus Christ, sweet Jesus Christ. Help me Jesus." He went on and on, the most horrible blasphemies and pathetic pleadings you ever heard. I disappeared into my room and closed the door and sat on the bed wondering if I'd ever have fits like my daddy's.

* * *

The next morning Amy waits until I settle behind my desk and start working then bounces in, all pert and breathless, and says, "You hear the news?"

"What news?" I lean back and try to look curious.

"Bobby Joe Mills's back in town."

"You're too young to remember him."

As usual Amy ignores me.

"He's stayin' down to the Holiday Inn but they say he's gonna buy a house and settle," she says.

"That's hard to believe, Amy."

"Gloria Pilcher told me and she knows Bobby Joe's momma real good."

"Really well, Amy." Once in a while I correct Amy's grammar. She doesn't mind. But she doesn't care, either.

"Says he come back rich and he's gonna buy a mansion in southeast Charlotte or out to the lake and live."

"He has to live somewhere."

"Where's he been all these years? That's what I wanna know. Gloria says even his momma don't know, and a mother oughta know."

"Yes, she should."

"I bet he's been doin' somethin' illegal. I bet he's been runnin' drugs."

"Bobby Joe wouldn't run drugs." He might take them but he wouldn't run them.

"How do you know?" Amy pulls up and smoothes her hair. "Everybody says he was no good."

"He and I went to school together for twelve years, Amy."

"Then you know he was no good." Her bony shoulders arch.

"He wouldn't run drugs."

"Thirty years is a long time. He might of changed. He might be worse."

"I sell insurance, Amy. I know most people change once. When they die."

"So what's he been doin'?"

"Any appointments this morning?"

"Miz Sims called. Wants to talk to you about her policy. Says it's not worth the paper it's written on." Amy winks.

"What time?"

"Ten."

"Anything else?"

"That's all boss." When Amy says boss I know she's in a particularly good mood.

"I'm going over to the Anchor. If anyone comes in tell them your boss had to go out and he'll be back at ten."

* * *

Elmer's alone behind the counter and I can see by the tilt of his mouth that he's primed. He has my coffee mug full and waiting before I sit. His thick arms fold on the red formica.

"He's back."

"I know. He came to see me last night. Says he's been working for the Red Cross."

Elmer laughs his huge laugh. Then he straightens, walks to the old-fashioned coffee urn, and pours himself a mug. He walks back and sits across from me. His square, thin-lipped face expands.

"Talk is Bobby Joe's been up to no good."

"That a fact?" I smile then sip heat.

"Talk is he's been in with drug runners down to the coast bring the stuff in by fancy yachts and sell it to niggers and injins and white gutter trash or send it up north to New York City."

"You believe it, Elmer?"

"Don't know."

"We knew Bobby Joe."

"We sure did." Elmer chuckles.

"Sounds screwy to me."

"Me, too."

"What you think?"

Elmer sends his eyes around the Anchor looking for something. His big face gets even bigger.

"He was always one for the women."

"Yes, he was."

"Always had a girl or two or three hangin' around."

"Mostly three."

"Liked girls much as he liked liquor."

"Maybe more."

"Well," says Elmer, "I bet Bobby Joe had himself a sugar baby."

"A sugar baby?"

Elmer chuckles again and hugs his mug with both hands.

"You know. A rich one took him round the world first class."

"Took him to Sumatra?"

"Where's Sumatra?"

"Indonesia."

"Yeah?"

"In the Indian Ocean."

"Who says he went to Sumatra?"

"He does."

"Maybe his sugar baby has family in Sumatra."

Elmer's sense of humor still surprises me.

"Amy told me he's going to buy a house."

"Guess Amy knows. Bobby Joe walked into Jimmy Knotts's agency a half hour ago. Saw him myself. He was wearin' a real bright shirt had big red and gold flowers on it. The kind you buy in Hawaii."

"Any girls hanging around."

"Not that I could see."

Sonny Cashion shuffles in and sits at his regular booth. Elmer pours his mug then freshens mine and his own.

"Bet he gets himself one of them fancy new condos out to the lake."

"Bobby Joe wouldn't buy a condo," I say.

"Why not?"

"Likes his privacy."

"Then he'll buy a house on the point."

"If he's got the money, Elmer."

* * *

My grandpa owned a two hundred acre farm on the Catawba River about five miles west of town right in the middle of what's now the lake. My mother hated her father's hard-shell Baptist ways, so we only visited the first Saturday of each month for dinner. I was tiny back then but I remember. Those Saturdays on the farm are about the only memories I have of the years before I was six. My big brother and I never had to eat with the old folks in the dining room. We would have disturbed Grandpa. So Grandma fed us fried chicken, butter beans, rice, pan gravy, and ambrosia at the kitchen table. Then we ran the place. The house sat on a hill and looked west across the river toward the mountains. It was a small hill, but in a few places you could see across the bottom-land to the Catawba peeking through the trees that grew along its banks. You couldn't see the mountains. They were too far away, pretty near a hundred miles. But Momma had told us they were there and promised we'd drive up some day which we never did. The cows, gold and white, grazed in one pasture. There was a corn field, too, and a small peach orchard and what must have been a full acre vegetable garden. But mostly my brother and I played on the side of the hill below the farmhouse. It was covered in high grass with morning glories, goldenrod, and ragweed in the fall. At that age I had bad hay fever. From early August to late

October my eyes got so wet and glazed that everything looked unreal. The land swam up on me in strange, bleary shapes like I was staring at the world from under water. I sneezed and blew snot all over the grass. My brother laughed, called me snot-nose, and chased me down the hill. When he caught me, which he always did being so much bigger, we rolled over and over, laughing and gathering grass stains and cow shit.

Duke Power Company built the Cowans Ford Dam to last, but they didn't bother to clear most of the land upriver before the deluge. No reason to, they claimed. Farm houses, barns, fences, telephone poles, one little crossroads town just got covered. They even left some of the family plots. After a while the water worked on the soil and bodies popped up—the recent ones. A boy from Charlotte in a motorboat hit a body. He almost died but they cut off one of his legs and he didn't. My grandpa died in 1963 and was buried in the family plot the year before they filled the lake.

* * *

That afternoon Amy sticks her head through my door, looks at me with this odd expression, stutters something I can't understand, and disappears. After about two seconds Bobby Joe walks in. He's wearing the Hawaiian shirt, Bermuda shorts, and sandals, and even in the daylight he looks about thirty-five.

He sits in the chair across my desk and says, "Guess you heard. I bought a house on the point. Paid cash. Nine-hundred-forty-nine thousand cash."

"You need a life insurance policy, Bobby Joe?"

His face gets a look I have never seen before, a hard blank mask, and for a moment I think I have made a big mistake.

"I'm gonna give a party," he says, suddenly smiling, or sneering. "What kind of party?"

"A party like nothing that ever happened around here before."

"Sounds good."

"I'll let you know. You and Ruth, you're invited, not your girls, they happen to be in town. I'll send you the invitation."

"I'll be there," I say.

"You better be, man."

* * *

For six months I don't see Bobby Joe. I don't even hear from him. Spring heats toward summer. Rachel comes home from Chapel Hill to live with Mom and Dad and earn some money giving swim lessons at the Y. Rebecca plans to take a vacation from prosecuting murderers and rapists and go with us to our mountain cabin next to the stream above Mars Hill. I start closing the office on Fridays so I can drive up Thursday evening for long weekends. Rebecca visits in early August, Rachel quits the Y until next summer, and the four of us spend two peaceful weeks at the cabin listening to the wind in the trees and the burbling of the creek out back and taking hikes. We pack up and close the cabin and drive home and Rachel and Rebecca leave. Ruth goes back to work. The house feels empty. I return to the five-day-a-week tedium of my office. The air cools and the leaves start to change and it's fall and no invitation, not a single word from Bobby Joe.

But right through all the changes people talked and talked about his place on the point. It's about all they did. None of the talkers had been in the house, of course, though I know lots went to gawk at the outside. Said it was the biggest place on the point, the finest place right at the very end on the most beautiful lot. And what with the recession no one was buying even the smaller places, let alone with cash. The talkers told stories about Sodom, drug city, the devil's breeding ground. Bobby Joe's reputation had followed him all those years he'd been away and had come back with him, too. Even those who had moved to town since he'd left or were too young to remember him joined in, and their opinions were always bad and always gleeful. It made folks feel alive to talk about Bobby Joe and his place.

Amy focused on bathrooms. She claimed there were five, six, once she said seven, and every one had a marble-topped sink, a Jacuzzi, and floor-to-ceiling mirrors on every wall. What went on in the Jacuzzis surrounded by all those mirrors, Amy never specified. Her imagination was active, but it scrubbed things clean like a bar of Ivory soap.

Then one morning in mid-September Bobby Joe's invitation comes in the mail—not one of these e-vite things on my computer but an old-fashioned invitation printed on the kind of paper reserved these days for weddings. As soon as I read it and see the date, I tell Amy I'll be at the Anchor for an hour.

Before Elmer has my cup on the counter I say, "Bobby Joe's giving a party three weeks from Saturday. Ruth and I are invited. Bet you're invited, too."

"Just got the thing."

"You going?"

"Hell no. I don't belong on the point. Not like it is now."

"Ruth won't go either."

"But I guess you will."

"I guess."

"Why?"

I don't answer because I don't know why.

After a time Elmer says, "People claim it's quite a place. Big and bad. Real bad."

"What do they know?"

"Nothin'. They make it all up. That's the fun of it. Course they might be right."

"They might."

"Bobby Joe was wild."

"So were we. Look at us now." I finger my tie.

"He was wilder. Sometimes I thought he was crazy."

"He had a streak."

"He could be mean."

"He could."

"And violent."

We sip.

Finally Elmer says, "R. D. went out there last week. Had to fix a toilet. Darn thing ran all the time. Started to flood the bathroom."

"Which bathroom?"

"How the hell would I know. Some bathroom. Some toilet. They're all the same."

"Not on the point."

"R. D. says the place smells like Calvin Klein lives there."

"How does R. D. know about Calvin Klein?"

"R. D. knows a lot about smells."

"Did he fix it?"

"Fix what?"

"The toilet."

"Didn't say. Suppose he must of. Did say there's a picture of a naked woman over the toilet."

"Was she doing anything?"

"Didn't say that either. Just said she was naked. Maybe she's Bobby Joe's sugar baby."

"Sure you won't go?"

"No way."

"I wonder who else'll be there."

"Don't know. But if you've gotta piss, watch out for that naked woman."

* * *

Folks were right about one thing. It wasn't a place on the point. It was *the* place, the place at the end, the very end, the place surrounded by water on three sides. A huge ranch—six maybe seven thousand square feet—spreading out to invite the three and four and five thousand square foot places behind it to be envious. A smart place with a fine new lawn and lots of trees, old and young, spaced just right and around a thousand feet of lake front footage, maybe more. Everything trim and neat and proper. A nice place, a grand place, a manicured estate about as sinister, about as bad as Ruth's pet collie.

I drive all the way to the end of the point, turn around in Bobby Joe's driveway, and crawl back by parked cars, twenty-five, maybe thirty sitting single file along both sides of the street. Lots of Mercedes and Beemers. Two Escalades, one Acura, one Lexus, three Hummers, a Porsche convertible, a vintage Mustang. Southeast Charlotte cars. A single Beemer has a Florida plate. The rest are North Carolina. I pull over about four houses down at the front of the right hand file, lock my twelve-year-old Camry, and walk back, thinking about smoking a cigarette. On my way out I stopped at the Quik Pik and bought my first pack in more than twenty years, but at the moment I imagine Ruth's reaction and feel too guilty to light up.

The front door is wide open. I press my nose against the screen door and see down a long, dark hallway to what must be a room on the lake end of the house. Framed by the hallway door like a painting sits a dark-haired woman in a red dress. She's looking straight toward me but I can tell she doesn't know I'm there. A gray-haired man in a brown sports jacket and green slacks walks through my line of vision. There's hardly any noise, just a subdued murmur of voices and some soft music I can't quite make out. I open the screen door and walk down the hall past closed doors. The room is huge and has a cathedral ceiling with exposed beams. The far wall is all glass, giant floor to ceiling windows, about ten huge panes facing the lake. The light is dim but I can see the furniture is exotic, sofas and chairs and lamps, tables and statues, all of it beautiful stuff made of strange woods I can't name, stuff from places like China and Thailand and India, maybe Sumatra for all I know. The kind of stuff you see in a museum or a palace.

There are maybe thirty-five or forty people in the room, one for every fifty square feet, and after a good look I realize I don't know a single one of them. With a couple of exceptions, they're at least forty or forty-five, most of the men older, and they're dressed for a formal cocktail party. I have on a denim work shirt and jeans. No one pays me any attention, like I'm the gardener or something. They sit or stand in small groups and drink and eat and talk in subdued voices. The dark-haired woman in the red dress looks up at a man who's standing next to her and laughs merrily, her head tilted back, her neck long, liquid, very white.

I stand there for a while, frozen. I hear Ella Fitzgerald singing "I let a tear fall in the river." My eyes go unfocused. I feel my muscles and my spine relax. Then I come out of my trance and see the bar and walk over. There's a bartender, a light-skinned black boy who can't be a day older than twenty-two, the only black person in the room. He's dressed in a white jacket, a white shirt, and a red bow tie.

"What will you have, sir?" he says.

"Bourbon on the rocks."

He tongs four cubes into a short, thick glass and pours me about three shots of Jack Daniels.

"Where's Bobby Joe?"

"Who, sir?"

"Bobby Joe."

"Bobby Joe who, sir?"

"Bobby Joe Mills. Our host."

He smiles. His teeth are white and large and beautiful. "Mr. Mills is around somewhere, sir. He was here just a few minutes ago. Maybe he stepped out on the veranda."

"The veranda?"

"The deck, sir." He motions toward the wall of windows.

"Thanks." I hand him a dollar bill.

"Thank you, sir." He smiles again and I can almost swear his voice is condescending.

I search around for a while and finally find the door, which looks like another window, then stand on the deck by the surrounding rail. By day the lake is ugly, rimmed with red clay and fancy houses, a huge, flat, dirty looking bathtub covered with motorboats and jet skis and oil slick. Ever since they filled the lake I've hated it by day. But at night in the cool clear autumn air it's transformed. I am at the very tip of the point on Bobby Joe's horseshoe-shaped deck. The water laps under the deck almost up to the front edge of the house and extends off to the west, as far as I can see, glittering faint and empty and quiet under a calm and starry sky.

"Hello, Dan."

I feel a hand on my shoulder, and when I turn Bobby Joe bends his face, shining and clean, toward mine. He smells like bourbon but he's wearing a tight-cut blue blazer, a button-down white shirt, and a broad red tie.

I step back.

"Glad you could come. Where's Ruth?"

155

"She had to stay home."

"I knew she wouldn't come."

"She would have liked to," I lie.

"You can tell her all about it."

"This is beautiful."

"I want you to meet some friends." Bobby Joe keeps his hand on my shoulder and guides me back away from the rail a few steps to where two men and a woman stand in the shadows. "Buzz and Eleanor Strickland, Link Dagenhart, this is my old comrade in arms, Dan Stutts."

They nod shadowed heads. Now that I'm close, I see that each of them is dressed in about five thousand dollars.

"Buzz," says the woman, her voice low-country insouciant, "I'd like one more Campari. Just a tiny squirt of soda."

As if on cue the three disappear. Bobby Joe's hand guides me again and we stand looking at the lake.

"Why didn't you tell me this was a formal party?"

"It ain't formal, man."

"Then what is it?"

"A gathering of a few friends."

"You're friends with these people?"

"In a way."

"Who the hell are they?"

"Business people."

"What business?"

"Tech, mostly. Bankers. Lawyers. Couple of the old mill owners."

"How do you know them?"

"I've saved these people more in twenty-eight years than all of them will make before they die."

"That's saying a lot."

"Damn right."

Another woman, an exquisite blond wearing a plain black dress, glides up to Bobby Joe and puts her hand on his shoulder.

"Bobby Joe, dear," she says, her face radiant with pleasure, "I'm afraid Doug and I have to be going. We promised the Kuyk-endalls we'd stop by their party. It will be pure dullness,"—she laughs lightly—"absolutely deadly, but we must keep our word. You know how it is."

"Glad you could come," says Bobby Joe and kisses her on the mouth.

She turns and glides away but stops in the door, framed by backlighting. "You have a lovely place," she says. "I must talk to you about your decorator." And she's gone.

"That woman," says Bobby Joe, "is the smartest, meanest bitch in the world."

"She in tech or banking?"

"I have to talk to someone," says Bobby Joe. "Can I get you another drink?"

"No, thanks." I'm still holding my full glass.

"That bourbon?" says Bobby Joe.

"Yeah."

He disappears and I turn to face the lake. Ella's voice slides into the dark, headed west to an invisible shore and the invisible mountains. "I want the waiter with the water," she sings. I hitch up my jeans and pat my stomach. It's cool and getting cooler. I gulp about half my bourbon. Immediately my gut feels furnace-warm. I open the pack of cigarettes, Marlboro extra light, strike a match, take a breath, and am suddenly, pleasantly dizzy. Someone taps my shoulder. I turn on a second glass of bourbon, nose high, only a few inches away, aromatic.

"Your drink, sir," says the black bartender. I take the glass in my right hand, the one not holding my first bourbon.

"I'm Dan. What's your name?"

"Jacob," he says.

"What kind of party is this, Jacob?"

"A very nice one, sir."

"You know any of these people?"

"I know about some of them."

"You do parties in Charlotte?"

"Yes, sir."

"And these people, they're rich, well-respected types? Business types?"

"Yes sir." He pauses and leans toward me, suddenly. He smiles, or maybe sneers, and his teeth sparkle in the night. "There's money in that room. Enough money to make half the black folk in North Carolina rich."

And then he's gone.

I sit on a deck chair. I sit there for a long while, drowsy and dizzy and alone. Occasionally I sip my first bourbon until it's gone. I set the glass on the deck and start on the second. I listen to music. Bessie Smith, Cleo Lane, Billie Holliday crooning "I cover the waterfront."

Finally the dark-haired woman in the red dress walks by and stands against the railing, looking out over the water. She's draped a thin black sweater over her elegant shoulders. Her head is tilted just slightly to the left. She moves her right arm, straightens her head, and drinks from a tall glass. I'm less than six feet away and I can hear her sigh.

"Nice night," I say.

She does a tiny hop, like she's spooked for a second, and turns to search out the voice.

"I'm here."

"I see," she says, looking down at me, her face blank with reserve, or maybe contempt.

"Nice night," I say again.

"Yes," she says.

"A little chilly."

"Yes."

"You live in Charlotte?"

"Raleigh," she says, clutching the black sweater to her throat with her long left hand.

"You cold?"

"Yes."

"Maybe you ought to go inside."

"Yes," she says and disappears, like everyone else at this party.

I sip my second bourbon until it's gone. I crunch an ice cube until it's gone, too. Then I just sit, getting drowsy again, watching the stars fall ever so slowly toward the western water. And then I'm asleep.

* * *

Someone shakes me. I open my eyes and it's Bobby Joe with a bottle of bourbon in his right hand. His blazer and tie have disappeared, the collar button on his shirt is open, and he's wearing a black leather jacket.

"Drink up," he says and pours my second glass full. He sits in the deck chair next to mine. "Aren't you cold?"

"No."

"It must be forty fucking degrees out here."

"Sorry I fell asleep. I want to talk to some of these people."

"They're gone."

"All of them?"

"Yeah." He sounds tired.

"What time is it?"

"These people come early, go early. They've got money to make. Even now. Even with the fucking market gone bust they make money. That's what they were born to do."

Bobby Joe props his feet on the rail. I light a second cigarette.

"Who's that bartender?"

"Jacob?"

"Yeah, Jacob."

"He's a smart black boy. Got himself a scholarship to David-son College. Studied philosophy. Now he's saving up to go to law school."

"How'd you meet him?"

"Remember that Yankee bitch I kissed? She introduced us. Says she's Jacob's sponsor."

"What does that mean?"

"Not much, I bet."

"Who are these people, Bobby Joe?"

"I told you. I worked for them."

"No more?"

"I'm retired, man. But some of them still pay me. They're my 401K."

"So what did you do?"

"First I helped the mill owners. Made sure they weren't both-ered by the protection goons. Lots of protection goons in Asia." He stops and drinks from the bottle. "That's where they moved the mills," he says.

"Yeah," I say.

"Then the tech crowd heard about my work. I saved their ass-es. Kept the foreigner fuckers from stealing their secrets."

"What secrets?"

"Tech secrets. Shit like that."

"How'd you do it?"

"Various ways."

"Did you kill people?"

"No."

"Beat them up?"

"Some people got killed. I never killed a soul."

"Did you try?"

Bobby Joe takes his feet off the rail and looks at me for a cou-ple of seconds.

"I don't try to do things," he says. "I do them."

I let his words float out across the lake. Then I say, "So you're a big time thug."

He laughs, leans near me, and tops off my drink. Then he sits back, looks out over the lake, and says, "I'm a Development Analyst. These people are straight. They make money like water makes oceans."

"You never ran drugs?"

"Shit no. I never ran anything 'cept my mouth."

Bobby Joe laughs. I laugh with him and gulp bourbon.

"That's what Elmer and I thought," I say.

"Elmer looks old. He didn't used to look old."

* * *

Over thirty years ago before most of the houses were built around the lake Bobby Joe and Elmer and I came out here to drink. We'd park at the crotch of the point and walk fifty, one-hundred, two-hundred yards and settle in beside the shore. We'd build a fire, smoke cigarettes, talk, and empty three or four six packs. A few times Bobby Joe brought a girl or two or three along. The only one I remember is Betty. She was a tall, round, dark-haired girl. Everything about her was round. Bobby Joe drove me and Elmer to her place and he said "Hello, ma'am, nice to meet you, ma'am" to her momma before we drove off. When the fire got high and we were all pretty drunk Bobby Joe kissed Betty and fondled her, and after some more kisses and fondles Betty danced around in the firelight, stripping her shoes, then her socks, then her skirt and her blouse and her bra. She never took off her white panties. I think she did her dance two, maybe three different nights. I don't remember how often. It all seems like one dance and there was never any music. Betty had a sweet smile, wide and simple and shy. Every time she took something off and threw it toward the lake, she smiled more. Eventually her smile swallowed up her insteps and her ankles and her calves and her thighs and hips and belly and breasts and neck until all I saw was her smile. She had dimples. In the firelight they cast tiny shadows up her plump cheeks, cute shadows. I always wanted to pinch her cheeks, but I never did.

* * *

I hear Bobby Joe's voice.

"So this guy gets up off the floor and wipes the blood from his nose with the back of his hand and I say, 'Let's talk,' and I'll be goddamned if he doesn't talk. Fucker talked and talked and talked. Shitty English. But he talked."

"About what?" I say.

"About everything. The whole goddamn operation. Gave me everything I wanted. Gave me stuff I didn't know existed. Afterwards it was all downhill, or uphill, depending on how you look at it. That guy made my reputation."

I don't have any idea what Bobby Joe's talking about, so I stare at the lake and drink a tiny sip of bourbon. Betty Carter finishes "By the Bend of the River" and starts "When It's Sleepy Time Down South."

"How's your momma?"

"She's fine," says Bobby Joe. "Says you're a fine insurance agent. Take care of her every need from first to last."

"I try."

"Says your girls take after you."

"I guess they do."

"Says Ruth's the best goddamn teacher in the county."

"She is."

"Course Momma doesn't say goddamn. Never said goddamn in her life."

"I guess not."

"I love that woman," says Bobby Joe. "Doesn't know a thing, ignorant as a cow, silly as a sheep. But I love her. And I revere my daddy's memory. He was a good man."

"Yes he was," I say.

"But what the fuck was he? A red neck good for nothing nice guy lazy cussing drunk let every rich shit mill owner walk all over him and his family. That sort of guy." Bobby Joe laughs again. "Scrawny as a chicken."

"He was scrawny."

"Your daddy was scrawny too."

"Yes he was."

For a long time we don't talk. Then Bobby Joe falls asleep. I take the bourbon bottle out of his hand and set it on the deck. I pour myself another drink. The music stops. Except for the gentle lap of tiny waves under the deck it's suddenly, perfectly quiet. I stare across the lake and at that moment the water brightens, brightens everywhere except along the shore where I'm standing. I turn around and through the tops of the trees see the moon rising. It's waning but it's not far beyond full and it's harvest gold. I turn again and stare across the lake, straight off the point, on toward the other side. Far, far away a bass jumps high and full out of the still water. The lake beads up, up, up into starlight and moonlight. The beads fall to darkness.

* * *

Times were the lake wasn't here and Grandpa said to Grandma, "Mother, serve these boys their dinner. They need sustenance from the Lord for the Sabbath. They must not want." Then he touched my momma on the head. "Esther," he said, "I thank you for the gift of these boys who will walk in the ways of the Lord. They will be his anointed. They will be baptized in his name and will dedicate their lives to his teachings. They will bring a new Christian age of belief and order out of this heathen chaos. They will be my inheritance."

He had a beautiful face, my grandpa, rippling, awful. Sweet, horrible emotions moved across his face. It changed and changed.

"Let us pray," he said.

We prayed then my brother and I ate.

"Go," he said.

We went, my brother and I, running down the hill facing the western mountains we never saw, falling over grass, over morning glories and goldenrod and ragweed and cow shit toward the sunset.

* * *

"You see this lake?" Bobby Joe's awake.

"Yes."

"It brings back memories."

"We used to come out here to drink before they built these houses."

"Yeah."

"I had fun."

"Yeah."

"Didn't you?"

"Sure," says Bobby Joe. "I had my first fuck just over there." He motions to his left.

"Betty?"

"Hell no. That was years later. Somebody you never met."

"How come you never told me about it?"

"Didn't I?"

"What happened?"

"What the hell you think happened."

"Don't know," I say.

"In and out."

"Oh," I say. "In and out."

We stop talking again. I stare at the water, my mind blank.

"I saved six people," Bobby Joe says.

"In Sumatra?"

"How the hell do you know?"

"You worked for the Red Cross, remember?"

"Shit. The Red Cross. I was there and they needed help so I helped. You know anything about it?"

"About what?"

"The tsunami, you dumb shit."

"The big one?"

"Yeah, the big one."

"It was three, four years ago."

"Seven years this Christmas." Bobby Joe stops then says, "I'm gonna get my file." He stands up and walks inside and in less than thirty seconds comes back out of the glass door with a file folder around two inches thick. He stands beside me and opens it and starts to look through the stack of paper.

"Big file," I say.

"Big flood," he says.

After a minute or two Bobby Joe pulls a couple sheets from the folder and holds them about two feet from my eyes. In the moonlight I can see he's showing me something he printed from the *New York Times* website. He holds the sheets of paper in front of my eyes long enough for me to read a headline: "From Heart of Indonesia's Disaster, a Cry for Help." Then he steps away from me and positions himself so the moonlight streams over his left shoulder and lights up the paper.

"Get this," he says. "'On Saturday the President of Indonesia flew in briefly and the examination finally began. It was a picture of grief and devastation beyond that of any other in the dozen countries hit. Apart from a few sturdy mosques and buildings, there is simply nothing left under the mountains of black mud and debris. The people the President met wept as they spoke. After his convoy snaked through streets of crumpled buildings, the president admitted that assistance was slow in coming and asked the world for help. In Indonesia alone, at least 100,000 people have died, most here in Aceh Province. The president acknowledged that his government had been slow in organizing and dispatching aid. Bloated bodies remain uncollected in the city of Banda Aceh, and there was no sign of any ability to clear the huge amounts of debris and black mud in this isolated town.'"

Bobby Joe stops and looks at me then says, "Fucking slow is right. I was there for three weeks after the waves and except for a few army guys and a handful from the Red Cross there wasn't a sign of help. Fucking President. He hated Aceh province. Thought they were all rebels. Probably wished another half million had died. Probably thanked Allah for the destruction. Like Allah cared." He picks up the bourbon bottle and sits on the deck rail. "I pulled ten bodies out of the goddamn water and the mud for every one I saved."

"But you saved six."

"Dozens of corpses. Came out stiff as surf boards or slipped through my fingers like seaweed." He pauses. "More like shit."

"The other six didn't."

"No."

"Who were they?"

"How the hell should I know?" He pauses again. "Two women—one young, one old—one guy who looked old but was probably thirty, and three kids. Every one of them so caked with mud you could hardly tell they were human. Every one of them half dead. There was this little girl, maybe seven or eight. After this gook and me scraped some of the mud off her we realized she was fastened to a goddamn big piece of wood. Couldn't get her loose. Almost decided to cut her fingers and her legs off to get that goddamn thing away from her. But finally I rolled her on her back in the bottom of the boat and used my foot and both hands and pried it off her chest. She was straddled to it like it was a fucking life raft. I got it off her and threw it overboard. She looked at me and didn't blink. She looked and looked and looked. I never saw a human being look so long without blinking. Then she closed her eyes and went to sleep. She fucking went to sleep. Right there in the bottom of the boat. She was naked. She was naked and she weighed maybe thirty-five, forty pounds."

"You saved her."

"Yeah," he says. "I saved her."

"You're a hero."

"Yeah," he says, "a fucking hero."

We stop talking again but Bobby Joe doesn't fall asleep. He stands holding the file folder and looking at the lake.

After a long time he drops the folder on the deck and says, "I hate rich people. They're all bastards."

"You're rich."

"Yes," he says, "I am."

"This is a nice place."

"Sure," he says. "I like it here by the water. Last night I sat out here all night. Sat here for hours and hours and hours of dark and then for a time not so dark and then the sun came up behind my back. Lit up the whole goddamn lake. Stretched my shadow out there about five hundred feet." He points out across the water.

"It's peaceful," I say.

Bobby Joe picks the bourbon bottle up by its neck, throws his head back, and drinks. I can hear it glug down his throat. He puts the bottle on the railing and walks closer to where I'm sitting. He looks down into my eyes and his eyes expand. They become saucers, great flying saucers.

"Look out there," he says, not turning.

"What?"

"Look out there." Now he turns and points across the water west toward the invisible shore.

I stand and stare. Starlight and moonlight reflect and ripple off the lake.

"You see it?"

"What?"

"You see it?"

"No."

"Come on, Dan. Look."

I look for a long time. "I see water," I say.

"Yeah," he says. "Water." Then, after a time, he says, "Get the hell outta here, Dan. I'm tired."

I don't move.

"It's nothing," he says. "I'm just tired." He looks at me and smiles. As far as I can tell it's not half sneer, just a smile, as exhausted and hopeless as the smile of a dying man.

"You all right?"

"Yeah," he says. "I'm all right."

"Get some sleep."

"I don't sleep much. I never slept much. Now I don't sleep hardly at all. Just cat naps."

"You look like you've always slept eight hours a night. You've hardly aged a day."

"Yeah," he says. "I'm blessed."

"See you," I say and shake his hand. It's cool and hard and strong like the hand of a young man.

"When you gonna let me see Ruth and the girls?"

"Maybe we could have you over for dinner some time during the holidays when Rachel's home from Chapel Hill and Rebecca's got time off."

"Sure," he says, "over the holidays." He turns away from me to face the lake.

"I mean it, Bobby Joe."

"Good night, Dan," he says, his left hand curled around the neck of the bourbon bottle, his eyes pointed over the water.

Before I leave the empty house I manage to find a bathroom. There's no marble-topped sink, no Jacuzzi, no floor to ceiling mirrors. Just a bathroom like the one at home, only newer, and bigger. I get ready to pee and there, over the toilet, hangs a naked woman, a Picasso print stroked with four curving, liquid lines.

A LITTLE OFF THE TOP

Mathieu Cailler

Shaker stood in the barbershop alone. He was new in town, and the other barber, the owner of the shop, had given him the late shift—from two to nine p.m. He didn't understand why she stayed open so late in this small coastal town where the homes went dark after dinnertime, but he had work and that was all that mattered.

It was quarter after eight, but since night arrived early these November days, Shaker thought it seemed much later. No one would show up for a haircut at this time. No one had yesterday or the day before, so he started cleaning up. He dunked his combs in the blue Barbacide, organized his brushes, and filled his spray bottle. Then he clicked off the red-white-and-blue barbershop pole.

He plopped down on his chair and placed his feet against the metal footrest. There wasn't a more comfortable chair in the world, and Shaker didn't understand why the manufacturer hadn't made designs for homes and offices.

Rain was falling now. Since he had arrived in Point Reyes, it had rained almost every day. The big surprise was when it was clear. He clicked on the TV and watched a college football game, Fresno State versus USC. He didn't care who won. To him they were all winners: all that fame and dream ahead of them and they weren't even old enough to buy beer.

The handle turned and the door squeaked open. A man took a step inside. He was small, wearing a heavy coat, scarf, and a black fedora with the brim pulled low.

"Oh," Shaker said. "Um, we're closed."

"Why are you still here then?" the man said in a smoker's voice.

"Just cleaning up."

The man entered and closed the door behind him. He worked his arms free from his coat and secured it to the rack by the entrance. Then he tossed his fedora onto a chair in the waiting area. The man was short and old, maybe eighty, with a round face. He wore a thin gray mustache and tortoise-shell glasses that sat on the bridge of his nose. Wiry hairs sprouted from his ears, too.

"You're in my seat," the old man said.

Shaker sighed, got off the chair, and went to press power on the remote control.

"Leave it on," the man said.

"All right," Shaker said. "Have a seat."

The man had trouble getting into the chair, but eventually settled in. Once seated, Shaker pumped the pedal and raised the old man into the air. He then secured a neck strip to the man's nape and draped a barber's cape around his torso.

"I love these chairs," the man said.

"I know, right?" Shaker misted the man's hair with the spray bottle. The man's hair provided little coverage on the top of his head, but the sides and back were thick and wavy. "So what can I do for you today?"

The man coughed, then said, "Cut the back and sides short. And only a little off the top. Trying to grow it out."

Shaker continued to spray and the old man shut his eyes and let the droplets greet his face.

"Always feels nice," the man said.

Shaker glanced at his watch. It was twenty till nine. He reached for his scissors and comb and began at the back of the man's head.

"Who do you like?" the man asked, pointing to the TV.

"Fresno, I guess."

"They're good this year."

"Yeah?"

"Yes."

A car outside drove too fast down the road, and the tires sloshed on the wet pavement.

"Never seen you here before. You just move or something?" the man said.

"Yeah, not that long ago," Shaker said, taking a strand of the man's hair between his fingers.

"How do you like it?"

"It's nice. Quiet."

"Yes, too quiet sometimes."

"Yeah. And a little cold for me. I'm from Palm Springs, so even hell's cold."

"Nice out there, though." The man folded his hands and lined his gaze with the entrance. Rain was falling hard now and beads traced the windows and rapped on the roof. "I'm Horace," the man said.

"Shaker."

The two men nodded.

"What kind of a name is Shaker? And for a barber? Dangerous." Horace coughed again. This one lasted a bit.

"You all right?"

"Yes. It's just damp, you know? Are you married?"

"No," Shaker said. He dropped his comb to the floor and pulled a new one from the Barbacide. It was the first time someone had asked him that question since he'd tried to start over, and he pictured Allison on his bed, her hair wild on the pillows, and her shirt hiked up past her belly button.

"What a catch," Horace said. "Did you see that? With one hand!"

"Yes, what a beauty," Shaker said, pulling a comb through Horace's shiny hair. "How about you... you married?"

Horace took his time to answer. He flicked a few wet chunks of his hair off the black barber's cape and they landed on the floor without a sound. "Yes, been happily married for over fifty years. Met her at a funeral of all places. She's home right now making meatloaf. She really makes a terrific meatloaf. You know what she does to make it so good?"

Shaker didn't answer, figuring the question to be rhetorical, but Horace craned his neck and stared at him, wanting a reply.

"What?" Shaker said, swapping his scissors for thinning shears.

"She soaks little pieces of bread in milk for a few hours... then sprinkles them throughout the loaf. Stays moist that way. You like meatloaf?

"Sure. Reminds me of when I was a kid. My mom's was always smothered with ketchup." Shaker thought back to those nights at the table when his father would come home from work as a pilot and talk about the different planes and the nutty air-traffic controllers at La Guardia. He always thought he'd be a hero to someone the way his dad was to him.

"Yeah, never liked ketchup. You need those little pieces of bread."

Shaker nodded and snipped around the arches of Horace's ears. Four times he'd failed the fireman entrance exam. He just wasn't fast or strong enough. The worst part wasn't learning that he hadn't made the cut, but coming home to Allison and her pity-glazed eyes.

"Kids?" Horace asked.

The volume on the TV surged as Fresno State's quarterback fumbled the snap.

"No," Shaker said. "You?"

"Yes, two boys. They're both doctors now. One's in Seattle, the other's outside of Austin." He coughed. Once it cleared, he continued. "Just had my first grandchild, too, a sweet little boy. They named him Horace."

Shaker couldn't picture a little kid named Horace. Would he carry a cane to preschool, or push a walker with tennis balls secured to the ends of its legs? He and Allison had talked about having children. They'd even told a couple people they were "trying," which always seemed like a gross way to describe the process.

Each time Horace spoke about his wife or children or grand-children or famous bread-soaked meatloaf, his voice softened. It was like normal conversation was a pair of grease-soaked cover-alls, while his family was a white-tie affair. When Shaker looked at Horace, he didn't see a man in love. He didn't see his father who brought his mother flowers for no other reason than to cel-ebrate a Tuesday in June. His father had always told Shaker that he'd grow up strong and smart and kind, but he hadn't. And Shaker believed that who you were at forty was who you were at fifty and sixty. The last time—the fourth time—that he had failed the fireman's exam, he'd met another dejected man in the parking lot. They'd sat in the man's car, bitching, puffing weed, and slug-ging beers—a couple of forty-year-old teenagers.

"My sons' wives don't cook like mine, though," Horace said. "Today's women don't know how to cook. No. The only things they can make are reservations. I bet if you open the door, you can smell the meatloaf. I live just up the road. We've been there a long time, but we met during the summer of '48 in Cincinnati, at a ballgame."

"Oh, that's cool." Shaker thought Horace had said that he'd met his wife at a funeral, but he didn't stop him.

"Yes, we were at the ballpark and she was sitting in the same section as me. After the third inning, she hurried up the steps and returned some time later with a bucket of popcorn. You should've seen the size of the bucket. Just as she made it to her row, she tripped and spilled it all, and I rushed over to help her. Oh, was she embarrassed… her face was as red as the uniforms."

USC kicked a field goal and knotted the game up at ten. Shaker reached for the clippers and evened out Horace's neckline while he went on and on about the bright lights of the stadium and what she smelled like that summer night and how her hands were shiny with butter.

"Do you want to see a photo of her?" he asked.

"All right," Shaker said, pulling his clippers away from Hor-ace's head. Horace leaned forward, flung the cape to his side, and eventually yanked his brown wallet from his back pocket. It was thick, crammed with coupons and cards and pieces of yellow pa-per. "Damn, you got a yard sale living in your pants."

"What?" Horace said.

Shaker didn't answer.

Horace spread apart the billfold. Everything but cash seemed to live inside. He searched for the photo, then grabbed it, unfolded it, placed it on his knee, and worked the creases out with his liver-spotted hand. He held it high. "This was taken a few years after we met... at a friend's party in Dallas." The woman in the photo looked familiar—a dirty blond with dark red lipstick. Shaker thought he'd seen her on TV before, advertising an energy drink. The edges of the photo were jagged and the paper shiny, like it had been torn from a magazine. Wouldn't a picture from that time have been in black-and-white? Shaker thought.

"Gorgeous, right?" Horace said, placing the crinkled woman back in his wallet, and the wallet back in his trousers.

"You're a lucky man," Shaker said.

Horace nodded.

The woman in the photo looked nothing like Allison, except for the pale skin. That night, after another unsuccessful try at the station, she'd glared and yelled at Shaker for being high and drunk. She'd called him a loser and told him to just work as a barber. "Stop trying to be *the man*, and just be *a man*," she'd said. Without thinking, he'd grabbed a plate wrapped with tin foil on the dinner table and hurled it her way. He'd felt the relationship die right then, and he turned from the kitchen, with Allison clutching her forehead, and took to the front door.

Horace clapped his hands as Fresno State ran the ball for a first-down. "What a spin," he said. "You always been a barber?"

"Pretty much. And you? What did you do?"

"I was an architect. Ever been to Indianapolis?"

"No."

"Designed a lot of churches out there... a lot of commercial buildings, too."

"And your wife?"

"She took care of the kids. Boys don't grow up to be lawyers without someone working the levers."

Shaker shut off the trimmer and yanked the hair dryer free from its holster. He blew hot air over Horace's head, allowing stray hairs to fly from his scalp. Horace closed his eyes and his lips curved in a smile as the warm stream tickled his brow, crown, neck, and ears.

"Oh, that feels good," Horace said. "It's been so cold."

Shaker remembered shaving alongside Allison, in their bathroom, where she'd swing her hairdryer around wildly, trying to dry and style her thick mane. He, too, had always savored the heat of her stray gusts. It was one of many memories that he'd needed to get through those homeless nights at the park, tucked between rocks, fronds, and a thicket of palo verde.

Shaker shook some talcum powder onto a shaving brush and dusted Horace's neck and ears.

"That's nice," Horace said. "Smells soft, like youth."

Fresno State flung a pass and entered the red zone. Shaker handed Horace a hand mirror and had him hold it up to the right side of his face and angle it so that he could see his neckline in the wall-mounted mirror.

"Clean and tapered," Shaker said.

"Yes, perfect."

"You want some hair tonic?"

"That's all right. At this age, it's best not to call attention to your head. Plus my wife likes it natural."

Shaker ran his fingers though Horace's hair one last time, then unfastened the neck strip, and yanked off the cape. Usually people were eager to jump out of the chair and take off, especially late at night, but Horace stayed put. He scratched at his scalp and crossed his legs. "It's gonna be a close one all the way," he said. "Tit for tat, tit for tat."

The gutter over the entryway was filling up and overflowing, and each time a car drove by, its headlights lit up thick strands of water. "It's good and warm in here," Horace said. Shaker agreed. He remembered the surprising cold of Palm Springs during the winter, and how there were times when he'd trembled with hunger and begged to die and be reunited with his parents, but not long after, a spot opened up at the shelter and he met the owner of the shop's brother, a preacher, while eating supper. "Move up north, son. My sister could use a good barber. It's not too late," he'd said.

Horace removed his glasses and cleaned them with the sleeve of his sweater, then coughed a few times, and Shaker patted his back.

"Okay," Shaker said, "you're all set." He stomped the pedal, brought the chair to its lowest level, extended his arm, and helped Horace down. "It's fifteen bucks."

Horace reached for his wallet and pried open the tough leather. He removed four folded bills—a ten, a five, two singles—and handed them over. A couple scraps of paper fluttered to the floor, but Horace didn't notice and Shaker didn't care to mention it.

"I'll see you soon," Horace said, pushing his glasses up. He plopped on his fedora and grabbed his overcoat. Shaker walked over to the door and held the coat open so that Horace could easily thread his arms through the sleeves.

"Button up," Shaker said. "It's really coming down."

"Yes," Horace said. "I'm just looking forward to that meatloaf."

Shaker nodded and smiled and felt pressure in his chest.

"I'm so hungry for it." Horace opened the door and the rush of rain found their ears. "There… you can almost smell it, right? All those spices." He tilted his head back, shut his eyes, and inhaled through his nose.

Shaker popped his head out the door and did the same. "Yes. It's a beautiful smell."

Horace tipped the bill of his hat, buttoned his coat, and turned up his lapels. He headed off, down the street, through the rain, his body blending with the night one step at a time. In minutes, Shaker thought, Horace would be back at his home, where he'd change into his robe and cook eggs or noodles with his socks pulled up to his shins. Maybe he'd watch a game show or enjoy a movie and fall asleep on his recliner. Or maybe he'd just listen to the rain and wonder when morning would come.

Shaker closed the door, grabbed his broom, and swept Horace's hair into a pile. All white except for those two pieces of paper that had escaped from his wallet. Shaker bent down and picked them up. They were again from a magazine—one a portrait of a redhead with her fingers placed coyly over her mouth, the other an action shot of a boy playing tennis. Shaker studied the photos over and again before sliding them into his pocket. He continued to sweep the floor, the roaring sound of the football crowd echoing through the empty barbershop.

ALL OF IT

Douglas Campbell

B ronson Blaine—his name haunts me to this day. God, how
I hated that guy. I'm forty-eight years old now, high school
thirty years behind me, and my heart still leaps into an
adrenal sprint when I think about the Fairmont County Class
AAA championship baseball game, New Goshen against Dennison, my senior year. I was team captain and the top pitcher
on my team, the New Goshen Rams. I'd made All-County my
junior year, and I went 9-0, with a 1.74 earned run average during my senior season. Even with that kind of success behind me
I went into that championship game feeling like I still had plenty
to prove. Did I have the genuine talent and the poise under pressure that would make me stand out and lift me to the top, no
matter what course my life might take? Or was I a phony, a loser
sure to crumble when the stakes were high? Sounds ridiculous,
I know. But let's face it, that's how you are at eighteen. You see
life in heroic terms, the world as a stage of high drama. And at
that age the line between success and failure is as clearly drawn
and unmistakable as the foul lines that run from home plate to
the outfield fence.

Bronson Blaine was a senior that year too, and he could hit
a baseball, no doubt about it. He led the Fairmont County Interscholastic League with a .485 batting average and 14 home runs,
playing for the Blue Wave of Dennison High. Dennison was the
next town to the south on Old Post Highway, just six miles from
our town of New Goshen, and they were our arch rival. We both
had great teams that year and came into the championship game
with only one loss each. Our only loss came against a mediocre
Ridgefield team, on a fluke, when Diggy Myers, our swift-footed,
hard-hitting centerfielder, got his feet tangled up and fell down
chasing a fly ball with the bases loaded. Dennison's one loss had
come against us, in a 9-7 slugfest. Bronson Blaine hit two doubles
and a triple in that game, but it hadn't been my turn to pitch, a
source of raging frustration to me. I'd been looking forward to
pitching against Bronson since the start of the school year, imagining his at bats and the sequences of pitches I'd use to get him
out. Finally, as the Dennison game drew near, my frustration
spilled over the dam of my better judgment. I went into Coach
McClain's office one evening after practice and begged him to

juggle the sequence of starting pitchers so I could make the start against Dennison.

"Absolutely not," he said.

"Coach, I'm your best pitcher. And Dennison's the best team we're going to play."

He gave me a stare that iced and shriveled my skin. You didn't challenge Coach McClain. The man was a local icon. He'd been coaching New Goshen High School baseball for nearly forty years, and while he'd aged into the wrinkled and white-haired look of a soft-hearted grandfather, he was a tough, relentless coach, baseball practically his religion. He coached us down to the smallest details and wouldn't accept anything less than perfect execution.

"Karl's been pitching well," he said. "He's finally got some confidence. I'm not going to kick him aside and put you in his place. Karl's turn to start. You'll be in left field. End of story."

Karl Olson was a junior, a decent pitcher, but early in the season he'd been hit hard a couple of times.

"It's not about Karl's feelings, is it?" I said. "We want to..."

"Whoa, whoa, whoa." Coach McClain thrust out his arm, his hand raised. "Stop right there, mister. You might be my best pitcher. But I coach this team. Now get out of my office."

It drove me insane standing helplessly out in left field while Bronson Blaine whacked three extra base hits off Karl Olson. My only comfort was that I'd pitched against Bronson during junior year, and I could savor the memory. I got him out that day on a popup to short and a fly ball to center, then struck him out on a filthy curveball over the outside corner at the knees that he swung at and missed by a foot. I'd dominated him, and during that senior year I had more motivation than I could possibly need for my desire to dominate him again. To humiliate him, in fact.

The thing is it wasn't Bronson Blaine's ability to hit a baseball that made me hate him. Heck, I respected him for that. But he took Cassie Rollins away from me, and I loved that girl. I still think about her often, even now, at my age, after all that has come and gone. This has been an especially rough year. A corporate merger back in March left me jobless, with six months severance. My daughter, the youngest of my two children, graduated from college in May and found herself a job a week later. The empty nest she left behind and our rapidly emptying life savings proved to be too much emptiness for my wife and me. Ten days ago our divorce became final. So I have plenty of time on my hands, and the other day I found a photo of Cassie on the Internet, smiling at the grand opening of an environmentally cutting-edge office building in Zanesville, Ohio. Her name is Cassie Kiley now. Her husband James, the architect of the building, was standing next to her, big smiles on their faces that looked genuine.

So somewhere along the line Bronson Blaine too had struck out with Cassie. That brought to mind a poem Cassie had written in high school. Poetry numbered among her many talents, and she always had a poem or two in the annual high school literary publication. The one I remembered had to do with the way things are all tied together and how almost everything is in some way held in check or exploited by something else. I don't remember the whole poem, but I've never forgotten the closing lines:

Broad oaks block the wind and soften the breezes.
Bees steal pollen from the aster.
Only love flows free and goes where it pleases,
because the heart alone has no master.

Cassie looked lovely in that Internet photo, just as she did in high school. She had the kind of hair every woman must envy, blond hair in her case, long, thick, and shiny. When she moved it slid across her back in golden layers. Cute blue-eyed face, full, dark red lips, her upper lip shaped by two graceful arches that met in the middle, precisely centered under her nose. She moved through the world with a light, quick stride, eyebrows slightly raised and a hint of a smile on those perfect lips, a curious and hopeful girl with a sweet, floaty presence, supportive and encouraging to everyone she came in contact with. Smart as could be, and smart about everything, straight A's in English, straight A's in biology. Everyone adored her, not just me. When she walked down the halls between classes she never had to dodge around people like everyone else. The crowd opened up and let her through.

I was a star player in football, basketball, and baseball in high school, and during our sophomore and junior years Cassie and I were a high school celebrity couple, Honor Roll students, good-looking, popular. We got along effortlessly, too. I don't know how we did it, immature as we were, but we could do anything or talk about any subject without getting on each other's nerves or winding up in the stupid arguments kids get into at that age. With the passion and certainty only innocence makes possible, we agreed on solutions to all of the world's intractable problems. War, hunger, pollution. You name it, we solved it. One night we got going on racism, though I don't recall what set us off.

"It drives me insane," Cassie said. "How can you hate people because of the color of their skin? Why are we so afraid of people who are different from us?"

"Ignorance," I said. "We're too isolated from each other. We fear what we don't understand."

Cassie nodded. "Maybe what we need is a huge festival," she said. "An international friendship festival. Where people from all over the world could get together and just get to know each other. All races, all religions. Music, dances, films, poetry readings. What do you think?"

Those were pre-Internet days, before you could find everything from Norwegian folk dancing to Indonesian gamelan music on YouTube. So it sounded like a great idea to me.

"Fabulous," I said. "I'd love to go to one of those."

"It would need to have lots of publicity and be on primetime television," Cassie said. "Like the Olympics. But every year, not every four years. And no sports."

"No sports?" I said. "Really?" It was hard for me to imagine a get together on such a massive scale without some baseball being played. "No harm in a little laid back softball."

"No, no, no. No sports. Cooperation, not competition. We already have the Olympics for sports."

"True," I said. "So this would be like a cultural Olympics."

"Exactly." We were in my old Mercury Capri that night, parked beside Pequot Reservoir. Cassie slid toward me, right up against the parking brake, and put her arms around my neck. "Let's always be kind and thoughtful like this, Lyle. And please, let's always be honest and tell each other everything, okay?"

"We will," I said. "I love it. I love you."

And I did. I loved Cassie, and I loved my life. Every morning I rolled out of bed ready for anything, eager to start the day that awaited me. We lived within walking distance of the high school, and on my way home in the evenings after football or baseball practice, when the trees had leaves on them, I'd run the last three blocks to our house high-fiving the maples, leaping up and slapping the leafy branch ends of the young maple trees that lined the sidewalk. The elation and energy that carried me through my long days seemed bottomless. Honor Roll, sports stardom, Cassie Rollins for my girlfriend—it all seemed to foretell a charmed life, a buoyant journey on a rising river of happiness.

During the summer between my junior and senior years I spent the month of July in Minnesota, working on my Uncle Steve and Aunt Sarah's dairy farm. I'd done that the previous summer too, and I loved the work, mowing hayfields on Steve's big John Deere, stacking the bales in the huge barn, learning to do the carpentry, electrical, and mechanic work required to maintain farm buildings and machinery. It was a whole other kind of sport for me, a very different sort of school. Not that I forgot about my favorite sport. Uncle Steve was a busy man, but together we put in a pitcher's mound and a home plate, with the barn wall for a backstop. Most evenings Steve would make time to be my catcher while I practiced pitching. My curveball and changeup needed refinement and consistency, and I focused on those two pitches over the course of that month. I loved the pleasures of farm life too, all the fresh beef, milk, and garden vegetables I could eat, the annual pig roast with a gathering of Steve and Sarah's neighbors, the ceaseless, ever-changing beauty of the wide Midwestern sky.

I had no idea, while I spent that month farming and pitching and skygazing, that back in Connecticut Cassie and Bronson Blaine had found lifeguarding jobs at the same country club. Toward the end of my month in Minnesota I got a letter from Cassie that seemed a tad cool, but I didn't give it a moment's thought. We were a thousand miles apart, unable to share the day to day thread of little events that ties people's lives together. I fully expected that when we reunited we'd pick up right where we left off.

The first thing I did when I got back to New Goshen was call Cassie, and we made a date for that evening. She was waiting for me outside and gave me a big smile when I wheeled the Capri into her driveway, but I thought the hug was a little brief, considering we'd been apart for a month.

"How about we go to the beach?" Cassie said. "I haven't been there all summer."

"Off we go," I said.

We headed for Sherwin Island in Westham, a beach we'd been to many times. On the drive I told her about my adventures on the farm and she told me about crazy things that had happened at the country club pool. We chatted easily and laughed. Everything seemed fine.

But on the beach, when I went to put my arms around her and kiss her, she pushed a hand into my chest and held me off.

"What's up?" I said.

"Over there," Cassie said, pointing. "Let's go sit on that bench. We need to talk."

I knew then she was going to say something I didn't want to hear. On the way to that bench I felt tense and stiff and kept lurching like a zombie. I just couldn't seem to keep my balance walking in the soft sand.

We sat beside each other, and true to the vow we'd made, Cassie was honest and told me everything: what a caring, gentle, humble person Bronson Blaine was, how they'd fallen in love without meaning to or wanting to. How it was all over between us, and how very, very sorry she was. Cassie did all the talking, because I couldn't. It was too much to take in, too much coming too fast, words, thoughts, feelings. I couldn't latch on to any of it.

Cassie said what she had to say, then waited for me to respond. I still couldn't. "Lyle?" she said finally. "Do you have anything to say?"

"I don't know what to say. I can't believe this is happening."

"I didn't mean for it to happen," Cassie said. "Please believe me. I never, ever meant to hurt you."

"Well, it hurts."

"I'm so sorry, Lyle."

"You've said that."

We sat quietly for a while, listening to the Long Island Sound roll in and hiss across the sand. Cassie was right there beside me, but I'm not sure I've ever felt lonelier. How could it have happened? And why? Bronson Blaine stood six-three or so, maybe two-hundred and thirty pounds, thick and powerful through his chest and shoulders, thighs big enough for two people. Broad face and head, blunt nose, meaty cheeks. Nothing much to look at, in my opinion, certainly not the kind of guy you'd put together with a beauty like Cassie. It just didn't make sense to me, no matter how nice he was.

Finally Cassie said she had to be at work early to open the pool, and needed to get home.

On the ride back to New Goshen it was anger that gave me back my voice. "You betrayed me," I said. "You know that, right?"

"I've hurt you, Lyle. I know that. I didn't intend to, but I have. You have every right to be angry."

"Intentions don't mean a thing," I said. "You knew what you were doing. And you did it anyway. Did you tell Bronson about me?"

"Of course."

"So he knew what he was doing, too. The two of you betrayed me."

"We fell in love," Cassie said. "I don't know how it happened. I didn't want it to happen. But sometimes things happen that you don't expect. You can't always control how you feel."

"Bullshit," I said. "It wouldn't have happened if you hadn't wanted it to."

"Don't get ugly, Lyle. Please."

"It's already ugly, thanks to you and Bronson."

Neither of us said anything the rest of the way. When I pulled up in front of Cassie's house I pulled the parking brake on but left the engine running.

"Good night," I said. "Say hi to Bronson for me."

"Right now I wish I could turn things back the way they were," Cassie said.

"Well, you can't," I said. "But hey, at least you warned me."

"I warned you?"

"'*The heart alone has no master,*'" I said. "Ever heard that?"

"I hate this ugly ending, Lyle. We've been so good together."

"We were better than good," I said. "We were perfect."

She looked straight ahead out the windshield and nodded two or three times. "I'm sorry," she said again. Then she glanced at me. "Good night, Lyle." She opened the door.

"Bye," I said.

I wanted to say something more. Something eloquent and true, something that would stick in Cassie's mind. But the war between anger and grief had me too bewildered, and the words I wanted stayed hidden wherever it is words hide when you need them most. So I kept my silence. Above all I didn't want to say something stupid or pathetic.

The car door closed with a thunk, a sound as eloquent and true as anything I might have said.

For weeks after the shock of that night I felt like I was living inside a tunnel, surrounded by darkness, with a small circle of light up ahead of me I could never reach. I'd been utterly unprepared for the blow Cassie dropped on me, despite that fact that I was a smart kid, attending a good high school where I'd been taught the concept of mutability and read poems about it. I wasn't much good, though, at applying intellectual notions like that to my own life. At that age it's easy to think the hard truths of life are only true for everyone else. Back then I only listened to my heart. Not anymore. The heart has its wisdom, I suppose. But it can make a fool of you.

Now I only listen to the wind.

The night before the championship game I had a hard time falling asleep. I tossed and turned, thinking about how much I had riding on that game. I wanted the self-assurance a great performance would give me. I wanted the residents of New Goshen to read about me in the newspaper and talk about me in glowing terms even when I wasn't there to hear them. I wanted the championship for the team and for the school. And I wanted Cassie and Bronson to see, beyond any doubt, that I was the better man. I wasn't foolish enough to think winning that game would win back Cassie's love. But I wanted to rattle her. I wanted her to think that maybe, just maybe, she'd made the wrong choice. I wanted to infect her happiness with a virus of doubt, a germ of regret. That would be my ultimate victory, and I wanted it.

I wanted all of it.

The game was being played in Norwood, on a neutral field. I was so nervous that several times during the ride there, with the school bus bumping and swaying over the Connecticut back roads, I came right to the brink of throwing up. But the nausea went away immediately once I got out into the fresh air of that beautiful May afternoon and started warming up, starting with some easy jogging and stretching. While I stretched I looked around at the crowd and spotted Cassie sitting over in the Dennison grandstand, gorgeous blond hair shining in the sunlight. She spotted me at the same time, and she smiled and waved.

That surprised me. I smiled and waved back. As I did so something loosened inside me, and I felt a swift, sharp pang, a mix of longing and shame. That surprised me, too. I'd gone the entire school year without speaking to Cassie, not so much as a hello passing in the halls. I'd hardly even looked at her except for a glance now and then when I was sure she wasn't looking at me. I'd cold-shouldered her out of my world, and yet there she was, smiling and waving at me despite the fact that her loyalty lay with Bronson. She'd hurt me, hurt me terribly, and in the dark tunnel of my bitterness I'd lost sight of what a truly good, kind person she was and how much I'd loved her. I wasn't about to let her off the hook, though. I still couldn't understand it. What could possibly have made her choose Bronson over me?

Our catcher, Roger Nordlund, tapped me on the shoulder and plopped a baseball into my right hand. "It's time," he said, and we got down to business. I felt sharp and focused mentally as Roger and I tossed the ball back and forth, and when I'd warmed up enough to start throwing hard I seemed to have great stuff: good pop on the fastball, smooth action on the changeup, sharp bite on the curveball.

Turned out I was right. I was practically untouchable. At the start of the game I retired eleven straight Dennison batters, seven of them by strikeout, including a three-pitch strikeout of Bronson Blaine, Dennison's cleanup hitter, leading off the top of the second. He managed a foul tip on a high fastball, swung and missed at a curveball in the dirt, then swung and missed at a changeup that fooled him so completely he stumbled and practically fell on his face. A humiliating strikeout. Exactly what I wanted.

Dennison's first hit off me came with two outs in the fourth, a swinging bunt down the third base line. That brought up Bronson for the second time. I got two strikes on him with the curve and changeup, my soft stuff. I figured I had him set up to blow a fastball by him, but he caught up to it and hit a missile right back at me that smashed into my chest before I could get my glove up. Luckily the ball dropped down in front of me, and I picked it up and threw him out, ending the inning. It hurt, though. It hit the left side of my chest, and I'm right-handed, so I could still pitch. But it throbbed and ached for the rest of the game. The bruise lasted three weeks.

Unfortunately, we weren't doing much with our bats either. Diggy Myers homered in the second, but that was it, and we came to bat in the bottom of the sixth only leading 1-0. I led off the inning and hit a rocket into the right-center field alley. I took off running as hard as I could, thinking I had a triple for sure. As I rounded first base, Bronson's position, he was standing in the base path, and I had to slow down and dodge sideways to keep from running into him. That delay forced me to stop at second base.

"Interference!" I shouted to the base umpire. "Come on, you saw it. I could have reached third!" Coach McClain saw it, and came out and argued too. The ump wouldn't budge.

It pissed me off, but I didn't have a moment to fret over it. Diggy Myers came up next, and on the first pitch he drilled a scorching line drive into left field. The Dennison leftfielder, Tony Romero, was a good ballplayer with a cannon for an arm, but I'd seen him uncork some wild ones. Sprinting toward third base I glanced out to left just as Romero fielded Diggy's liner on one hop and reared back to throw home. When I reached third, our base coach, Terry Jenks, had his hands held high, screaming "Hold up, hold up, hold up!" And that would have been the sensible thing to do.

But nothing was going to stop me. I blew right through Terry's stop sign and sprinted for the plate, my eyes on the Dennison catcher, looking for some indication of where the throw was going. Whichever way the catcher moved, I'd slide in the opposite direction and try to hook the plate with my foot. If the throw was right on the money my only hope would be to slam into the catcher hard enough to make him drop the ball.

The throw beat me, but just as I'd hoped it was off target, up the first base line. The Dennison catcher caught it and lunged for me as I dropped into my slide and threw up a cloud of dust. My foot touched home plate an instant before the catcher's mitt, with the ball in it, punched me in the face, a blow that flattened me and knocked me numb and senseless. I couldn't feel or hear a thing, but through the dust, from down on my back, I saw the umpire's arms spread wide in the safe call. Then I closed my eyes and lay there, still woozy, unable to think or move.

The game had to be stopped while Coach McClain and a couple of teammates helped me get to my feet and over to our bench. My left cheekbone ached where the catcher had hit me. Coach McClain helped me dust off my uniform, then sat me down and looked me over. "You'll have a black eye," he said. "That was a stupid chance you took, mister. If you'd been thrown out I would have let you have it with both barrels." Then to my astonishment he clapped me on the shoulder and cracked a semblance of a smile. "Good hustle. We needed that run."

The words were barely out of his mouth when we got another run. Diggy Myers had taken second base on the throw to the plate, and with two out our third baseman, Freddy Gomez, who'd had three or four hits all year, blooped a broken bat single into right field. Diggy scored easily, and we went to the top of the seventh, the last inning, leading 3-0.

I took the mound with the New Goshen fans already on their feet, clapping and cheering, sensing the win. Dennison's number two, three, and four hitters were due to bat. That meant that if things went as I wanted them to Bronson would have to slink off the field after making the final out, the one that would send Dennison down to defeat. I hadn't scripted the battering I'd taken, the line drive in the chest and the punch in the face. But I was three outs away from a one-hit shutout, a performance that would come within a hair of exactly the kind of triumph I wanted.

I blew three straight fastballs past the number two hitter for the first out. The New Goshen fans got even louder, and I fired another fastball past the number three hitter. I don't know what happened then. Maybe I was wearing out, maybe my bruises were taking their toll, but suddenly I couldn't throw a strike. I threw a changeup way outside, then bounced a curveball in front of the plate. Two fastballs up high and I'd issued my first walk of the game. And there was Bronson Blaine, Dennison's horse, digging in at the plate.

My control came back as quickly and mysteriously as it had left me. I fired a fastball at the letters that Bronson swung at and missed. Then I threw my best pitch of the game, another fastball that shaved the inside edge of the plate, belt high. Bronson swung at it and made contact, but didn't get the result I'm sure he was hoping for. His bat exploded into three pieces and the ball dribbled into foul territory outside the third base line. Another humiliation. I had to turn around and face center field to hide the smile on my face.

With a new bat Bronson dug in again, the count no balls, two strikes. That's when I remembered the filthy curveball, outside corner at the knees, that I'd struck him out with as a junior. After two good fastballs he was perfectly set up for a pitch that would not only break but change speeds on him.

I rocked into my motion and turned it loose. When the ball was halfway to the plate I knew that just after having thrown my best pitch of the game I'd thrown my worst. I didn't get a hard, tight spin on that curve ball, and it floated toward the middle of the plate in a soft, lazy arc. If ever a pitch had a neon sign on it flashing "hit me, hit me," that one did. And Bronson hit it. He got all of it. The ball landed in a soccer field at least thirty yards beyond the left-center field fence.

That made the score 3-2, and the Dennison fans were up and howling, sensing blood. Somehow though, I pulled myself together. I got the second out on an easy two-hopper to Freddy Gomez at third. Then a lazy fly ball to centerfield dropped into Diggy Myers' glove, and that was it. We were the Fairmont County Class AAA champs.

We came together in the middle of the diamond for our leaping, hugging, high-fiving celebration, but to tell the truth I had to fake it. I couldn't get Bronson's home run out of my mind. I still can't. I'll go to my grave cursed with a high-definition memory of that magnificent home run, its towering trajectory, the ball a soaring dot in the blue May sky, hanging in the air, taunting me, taking forever to travel from the crack of the bat to a silent and distant landing.

In a ceremony in front of the grandstand where the New Goshen fans were sitting, Coach McClain took the microphone and in his raspy bass voice said we'd surprised him and he guessed we weren't such a bad team after all. Then the superintendent of the Fairmont County public schools presented us with the championship trophy, a nice one, a big, heavy, silver-plated bowl mounted on a wooden stand. Coach McClain gave me, as captain, the honor of accepting the trophy and carrying it back to New Goshen High.

After that we headed for the bus, whooping and hollering, all except for me. I didn't have any whoop or holler in me, and I brought up the rear, carrying the trophy. I guess that made it easy for Cassie to find me. Someone called my name off to my right, and when I looked there was Cassie, trotting toward me. She stopped in front of me, a little winded, a mist of fine sweat on her forehead.

"Whew, I'm glad I caught you," she said. "I wanted to tell

you, you guys were great, Lyle. County champs! Congratulations. And look at that trophy. Wow!"

"Thanks," I said. "It feels pretty good."

She leaned toward me, peering and pointing at my swollen cheek. "I bet that doesn't feel too good."

"No big deal," I said. "I'm fine."

"You were fantastic, Lyle. I've never seen pitching like that."

With her standing so close to me I realized how much she'd changed over the course of senior year. By walling her out of my heart I'd completely missed seeing it. Ten months ago, on the night we'd split up, she'd been a pretty girl, but still teenage skinny, a little boney, half child, half woman. Now all trace of the child had vanished. She'd filled out everywhere, arms, legs, butt, breasts, hips. Smooth, clear skin, lavish hair, lively, knowing eyes, a stunning vision of flawless animal health. After having barely looked at her for so long I found myself staring at her.

"Not all that great," I said. "But it's nice of you to say that. I pitched well enough to win, I guess."

"Lyle, come on. Only two hits!"

I laughed. "Yeah. One little hit, one big one."

"Oh, my god," Cassie said. "Isn't Bronson amazing? What a home run that was!"

That stung a little, but she wasn't trying to wound me. Cassie understood baseball pretty well, but not well enough to know it wasn't exactly tactful to rave about a mammoth home run to the pitcher who'd served it up. What stung me more was watching her eyes, flashing with sunlight and love, when she talked about Bronson.

"It was a long one, for sure," I said.

Bronson called her name then from over by the Dennison bus.

"Gotta go," Cassie said. "Great game, Lyle! Congratulations again." She turned and ran toward Bronson.

"Cassie, wait," I called, with no thought of what I was doing, no idea what I wanted to say. I thought I called pretty loud, but she kept running toward Bronson. And I'm glad she did. If she'd stopped and looked back, eyebrows raised, expectant, I would certainly have said something stupid or pathetic. Her ears, eyes and heart were wide open now for someone else. I had to bite down on that sour fact and swallow it once and for all.

She ran to Bronson and practically jumped into his arms and kissed him. No way I could stand there watching that. I climbed on our bus and sat down beside a window. I tried holding that trophy in close on my lap, then out on my thighs, but it was heavy and awkward and I couldn't get comfortable. I kept looking at it, waiting for the surge of pleasure and satisfaction I thought I should feel after our victory in a game that just a few hours ago had seemed so momentous to me. I never did feel that surge though, not then, not later. The trophy hadn't been inscribed yet, but I guessed it would say something like *New Goshen Rams, 1984 Fairmont County Interscholastic League Baseball Champions.* It would wind up on display in the big trophy case at the high school. Students would come and go, and maybe now and then one of them would stop and look at that trophy. Twenty, thirty, fifty years would pass, until no one would recall who the winning pitcher was in that championship game, who hit the home runs, what the final score was. Hardly a soul left alive would remember Coach Keith McClain, Stuart "Diggy" Meyers, or Lyle Simmons.

When the rest of the team had climbed aboard for the trip home the bus backed up and turned around in the parking lot. I swung sideways for a good view out the window, shifting the trophy to keep it from pressing against the bruise on my chest. As we pulled out it looked like all the Dennison players had boarded their bus too. All except Bronson. The bus door was open, waiting, but Bronson and Cassie were still standing out on the asphalt, arms still wrapped around each other. I turned away, closed my eyes, and settled back in my seat.

I had the trophy, a big, silver-plated bowl. But Bronson Blaine had the prize.

ALL OF MY MOTHER'S NAMES

James Goertel

onald Kessler wasn't sure two weeks would be enough
to reconstruct a past which lay buried a world away, but
there was finally nothing and no one to hold him back
from at least trying. With his mother's Alzheimer's finally reliev-
ing her of the pitfalls of her past, Donald no longer felt he was
digging up a corpse she'd left for dead decades before. Donald's
name, much less his father's, meant nothing to her now. On occasion, she even had to be reminded of her own: Katherine. For
now it was just Katherine to the nurses, the doctors, and the at-
tendants at the nursing home. No longer was she saddled *Mrs.*
this or that. Left behind at last was the pocketbook of surnames–
Kessler, Jacovitz, Biddle, Freilinger–she had suffered since giving
up her own five decades before. Now Donald was free to sift the
fragments of his father's life and death during wartime; a father
he could not recall, but whose name he had carried with him for
forty-odd years, unburdened but yet haunted by it.

He had boarded a plane headed for Saigon with just three
clues to the past, the only real clues he had found while clearing out his mother's house after her move to the nursing home:
his father's dog tags, his mother's *Dear John* letter to him, and a
Polaroid of his father and a young Vietnamese woman, his arm
around her, standing in a kitchen, with cardboard party hats
upon their heads, inscribed in pen on the back:

Pham Bao, New Year's 1972

As the plane began to descend, Donald felt himself nodding off and finally gave himself to a few minutes of the darkest
dreaming.

He was no stranger these days to nightmares which sat him
straight up in bedrooms both casually strange and familiar. Lovers, of whom there had been many in the past year, would do
their best to comfort him, to bring him back from his unconscious
wanderings through anxieties, phobias, and fears. Some were old
flames for whom there was only a carnal connection; others were
new conquests on whom his hope for a new, all-consuming love
hung. These dalliances were equally unfair to both parties. He
knew this. For no one could ever replace Michael. Donald was an
old queer now. He knew there was nothing sadder than an old
queer looking for love in all the wrong faces, especially when his

wounded heart had not yet recovered from the death of his soul mate. It was Michael twenty years before who had been the salve for his sense of failure at not having achieved more in the city's theater scene. He hadn't even made it to Off-Broadway, but in Michael's eyes he had always been a star. The light behind those eyes had been extinguished in an instant twelve months before when the driver bringing him home from JFK airport fell asleep at the wheel. Donald and John had been legally married just months before and it fell to Donald to identify the body. That moment had revisited itself upon him several times a week since the accident in nightmares which even a host of prescription sleep aids and anti-anxiety drugs could not seem to quell.

This. This trip. This was another one of his quests. There had been many in his adult life; crusades for truth, for justice, for sanity amidst the insanity of a world both achingly beautiful and numbingly cruel. At one point, Donald had taken in so many stray cats and dogs that even bighearted John had said enough was enough. Of course there were the AIDS marches of the 1980s and the gun control marches of recent memory. Donald fought City Hall on a regular basis, protesting park ordinances here, petitioning on behalf of the homeless there. He had singlehandedly marched for gay marriage rights in no less than half of the states in the lower forty-eight over the past few years. But even with all of these altruistic feats of results-oriented activism under his belt, there was still something missing, something that had always been missing. His father was the missing link between the chubby kid with sexual orientation issues he had been and the fat, but happily gay man he had become. All the other pieces of Donald's life, the good and the bad, were completely knowable. This was the one piece which had eluded him and had mocked from afar his public face which pretended that identity with a capital "I" could and should be carried along with head held high from context to context. This theory of his had yet to be tested in the one context that until now had only existed through photos, hearsay, keepsakes, and anecdotes: the context where he might either find out nothing about the man who had fathered him or where he might find out just enough to change the sense of self he had so carefully constructed to keep at bay just these sort of painful, forced metamorphoses.

The plane was now taxiing toward the gate. Beyond it lay the intricate web of his father's life and death. He pictured his father arriving as a stranger in this strange land. In a sense, Donald was walking in his father's footsteps and for the first time in his life felt a tentative, albeit fragile, kinship with him. Donald looked out the little, oval window past runways and planes to a flat expanse of vegetation that only ended at the horizon where the rising sun announced the east and the arrival of a new day which felt at once familiar and foreign to him.

* * *

1973 began on a bright note in Saigon. The Paris Peace accords were made public before the end of January and the specific details of troop withdrawal, free election guarantees for South Vietnam, and the release of all American POWs by North Vietnam were enough to get all parties to sign despite a lack of finer details concerning a reunification of the country "through peaceful means." The accords Nixon promised would "bring peace with honor." Whether this would be borne out would take some time to know, but in the end Nixon would not be there to either reap the praise or take the blame. The Watergate scandal, which would culminate with his resignation, effectively slammed the door shut on a thirty year political career that had begun with him embracing the post World War II Red-baiting of the Republican right and would end with a self-conscious, made-for-television moment with Tricky Dick and his family smiling and waving one last time from the White House lawn before stepping into a helicopter which lifted them into the skies and up and away from the carnage he had wrought upon the highest office in the country. His peace accords, for the record, were already in shambles by that fateful day in August of 1974. The fall of Saigon was only eight months away along with Operation Frequent Wind, the code name for the city's evacuation, which shepherded nearly 140,000 to safety over two days in April of 1975; a handful of American helicopters alone carrying nearly 6000 South Vietnamese souls to waiting ships and by association to new lives in the United States.

* * *

Choppers. Kenny Kessler knew them well. From setting them down in the scant clearings of a jungleland to skimming their runners just above the treetops to drop his load of napalm, and from bombing runs across the border into Laos. Those runs cost him one career, but paid dividends on another. In South Vietnam Kenny was somebody, especially in Saigon. Back in Nebraska, he had been just another farmer's son with no way out of a life already decided for him by his father. He resisted the role every step of the way except when it came to tinkering with the farm equipment. It was said by locals who knew him well that he could damn near take a tractor apart and put it back together in a dark barn. On his father's farm, as on most family farms, something was always in need of fixing when it came to tractors, plows, tillers, and pickup trucks. This was the only work on the farm Kenny enjoyed. He graduated high school near the bottom of his class, married his high school sweetheart, and resigned himself to a life on the farm toiling beneath his father's long shadow until he could one day call the spread his own. That was until just after his nineteenth birthday when he found himself walking into the Air Force recruiting office in downtown Lincoln. When he walked out, he was signed up and set to head off to boot camp. His bride was unhappy, but resigned herself to a fate she could not know would be as arduous and disheartening as it turned out. Kenny let his father know he would be leaving to make a life for himself and hopefully a future for his young bride. His father was livid and disowned him then and there. But Kenny took it like a man, never once looking back, for he knew he had found his escape. What he didn't know was that Katherine was already pregnant with his child, a child he would never know.

* * *

Donald hailed a cab outside the airport and handed the driver a slip of paper with the Saigon street address his mother had used to send her *Dear John* letter to his father. He had a little book of Vietnamese phrases with him, but there was no need for it. The driver spoke good, if somewhat broken English. The cabbie was about his age–too young perhaps to remember–but Donald tried anyway to ask him what he knew about the war, if he had any memories of it.

"Viet Cong killed my parents," was all Donald could get from him before the cabbie asked, "Where you from?"

After answering, "New York," the cabbie filled the rest of the ride with anecdotes about his cousins who lived in New York, their families, and the restaurants they ran, pausing occasionally to ask if Donald had eaten at this one or that one.

* * *

Donald stepped from the cab into the humidity of a ginger and sewage perfumed rain falling from the gunmetal, fog-whisked sky descending over, and sealing from above, Saigon. Here he was standing in front of the last known address his father had inhabited. A shiver ran through his core and radiated down either arm. The swill in the air, though peppered and pointed here and there by the smell of street cooking above the steady licks of flame conjured from both acetylene and propane, gagged him and without warning he vomited. Spatter hit his trouser legs and the single piece of luggage at his side. It was more a matter of nerves, he decided, pulling a handkerchief from his pocket and wiping at himself and the bag. Before he would have the nerve to knock on the dilapidated door beyond him, he would need a drink and maybe more than one. He grabbed the roller bag and took off down the humanity and bicycle choked street, looking every bit the fat, sweating, hulking American straight from central casting.

After a few sweaty blocks he found a hotel and, walking beyond the registration desk, located the bar. He took a seat on a stool and ordered a double scotch. The thin, bronzed barkeep with a deep scar down the right side of his nose placed it in front of him. He reached into the inside pocket of his suit jacket for his wallet but before he could extract it, a voice came from behind his shoulders.

"Let me get that, Donny."

No one had called him that since childhood and Donald turned to find a tall, fit Caucasian man in his fifties with a crew cut, a long face, and wide, wild blue eyes.

"How do you know my name?"

"I know lots of things about you, Donny. But you prefer to be called Donald, don't you?"

With those words still hanging mid-air, the man extended his right hand which was missing both the pinky and the thumb. Donald did not shake it as the three-fingered man sat upon the open stool next to his.

"Drink up, my friend, or you'll miss your flight."

"I just arrived."

"I know. And if you are smart you will finish your drink and grab a cab to the airport."

Donald, shaken but not showing it, downed the double on the spot, motioned to the bartender for another set up and turned himself toward the man, their knees touching.

"I don't know who you are or what you want, so why don't you kindly fuck off. I'm here on business."

"I'm well aware of your business, Mr. Kessler," the man offered while waving off the bartender, then continuing, "Just as the people I work for were well aware of your father's business. You wouldn't want to end up like him now, would you?"

Donald could feel a trickle of sweat moving down his forehead to the bridge of his nose. He swallowed hard, then stood straight up in one swift, bolting motion from the stool and began screaming, "You fucking pervert! Don't you ever try to touch my fucking cock under the bar. You sick, god damned fuck!"

The entire bar, men in expensive suits, women draped in Versace, Lagerfeld, and Prada, turned to see the scene as Donald continued his tirade, backing away from the three-fingered man until he bumped right into two large men from hotel security. He hid himself behind them and screamed over and over, while pointing out the man, "He touched my junk! He touched my fucking cock!"

As the security muscle moved toward the bar, the three-fingered man raised his arms and waved his hands in a gesture of surrender just before launching himself over the bar and bursting through the double doors leading to the kitchen, the sound of pots and pans, glass and silverware hitting the floor as he made his escape.

* * *

They had been following him the past three weeks. That much Kenny was sure of. Every night when he hit the clubs, there they were, sticking out like sore thumbs in their black suits, white shirts, and skinny black ties, trying to look casual despite the fact that they never removed their sunglasses once inside the dimly lit venues. Just the night before, though, they had changed tactics, the three of them waiting outside the club while Kenny partied inside until dawn before walking out into the morning glare to find them leaning against his Jaguar convertible. Back home they all drove Buicks and Kenny had kept this in mind as he casually thanked them for watching the Jag. Now, there they were again, on the street below his apartment on the third floor of a building which mainly housed cabinet members and local officials of the South Vietnamese government his government had helped install, but who had nothing but contempt for their U.S. puppet masters. But they all loved Kenny because Kenny was the *Good Joe*, as they called him, who could get anything; from top shelf cognac from France to a new Cadillac from Detroit. Kenny knew the men in black were just doing their jobs. Back home the men in black who tailed him were probably regular guys with suburban houses who liked McDonalds and Budweiser, played golf at the public courses, and fucked their formerly skinny wives once a month just so their peckers wouldn't dry up and fall off. To mess with them, Kenny liked to arrange and pay for local prostitutes to approach the car they sat in for hours at a time waiting for Kenny to emerge. Once there the gái mại dâm would expose their breasts and press them against the car windows or hump the bumpers with their panty-less pussies while Kenny watched from the balcony above, sipping ruou and smoking Gitanes. Kenny had come a long way since his days in Nebraska. His life there now seemed like simply a foggy notion that had passed slowly over him for twenty years before being burned off and out of his mind by the flash and thrust of the jet engines which had brought him from an aircraft carrier in the Pacific to a new and eastern dawn in South Vietnam.

The sun setting, he drew the curtain at the window from where he watched those who shadowed him below, threw off his silk robe, and took his young lover, Pham Binh, in his arms, a young man as beautiful as he was dull witted. But Kenny was not interested in conversation; only in the fleeting reprieve from the crushing spells of loneliness he and others like Binh could provide. It was not love between them or any of the others for that was reserved for one and only, the man who was entrusted by the C.I.A. to make sure Kenny was watched 24/7: Mack Dodson.

Everybody Kenny knew who knew Mack just called him *The Colonel*. But none of them really knew what rank he held for sure or whether he was even military at all. Was he C.I.A.? No one could say for certain. But Kenny knew just enough to be star struck, but not enough to know that when Mack was involved in something people tended disappear or end up dead. Mack had been in Vietnam since the French fuck up at Dien Bien Phu in '54. He was only nineteen at the time, but was already working alongside American advisors who wanted to make sure the three to four billion dollars the U.S. had given the French in the previous three years to turn the tide against the Soviet backed Viet Minh in the north was put to good use. Mack liked to kid that the French had spent it on wine and pastries instead of air strikes to keep the "little red rice eaters" out of the south. He'd been in Vietnam ever since, but in "an unofficial capacity" as he let slip to Kenny after a night of too much ruou and not enough sleep. Mack knew more about Vietnam than most of the natives. The truth was Mack was neither military nor C.I.A. He was a new breed, a cold warrior without a country, plucked from the academy for his smarts and groomed neither by the armed forces nor the C.I.A. alone, but in conjunction with advocates, powerbrokers and financiers of the military-industrial complex President Eisenhower had warned of while busy enabling it from 1952 to 1960. Kenny couldn't be sure, but he had a hunch Mack worked for the same people he did.

* * *

Donald composed himself in the lobby as two police officers conferred with the two security guards and the manager of the hotel. The manager then broke away from the group and approached Donald. In perfect English he asked if Donald was okay. Donald nodded. Then the manager asked Donald if he had known the man who had groped him; the police were curious.

"Absolutely not," Donald answered, but this was not entirely true.

In the direct aftermath of the altercation with the three-fingered man, Donald had been struck by a *déjà vu* so powerful it had jogged his memory. He was the same man who had boarded his flight from La Guardia at the last minute, just before the cabin doors had been closed in preparation for take-off. One of the stewardess' had offered to take his suit jacket and hang it up as they normally offered for all first class passengers, but he had demurred and had taken his seat in the last row before the curtain leading to coach. Donald hadn't noticed him after that, but he was sure it was the same man. The manager was still talking as this all ran through Donald's mind, finally coalescing in a question he had to keep himself from saying aloud: *Why am I being followed?*

He knew he had to knock on *that* door. But he couldn't go alone.

He thanked the manager without looking at him, his eyes on one of the security men who had come to his rescue. Donald followed him outside to where he stopped to light a cigarette, leaning back against one of the columns supporting the covered valet area. Donald wasn't sure what a Benjamin would get him, but he thought it worth a shot.

* * *

Donald had killed time by booking a room and showering. He now sat in the hotel bar, off in a corner, nursing another scotch, trying not to look at his watch every five minutes. Another fifteen minutes passed before the security guard, finally off-duty, showed up. Donald handed him two fifty-dollar bills and left a ten on the table.

Neither spoke as they walked the blocks back to the last known address his father was thought to have lived before his death. Donald thought over the few facts he had been able to find out about his father's military service. He had served in the 82nd Airborne from July 1967 until March of 1970 when he was given an honorable discharge, but much of the document detailing this had been heavily blacked out. So much for the *Freedom of Information Act*. Donald had been born in January of 1968 and would have been almost two and half when his father was discharged. Why hadn't his father come home to his wife and son? Had he been ashamed? No. The marriage had fallen apart long before the discharge; his mother's letter saying goodbye from 1971 had made that much clear. *What in the hell could he have been doing here as a civilian from 1970 until his death in '73? And what of his death?* The details were beyond sketchy and the only thing Donald had been able to draw from his mother before her diagnosis had been that it was that his father had been cremated after no one had claimed the body at the morgue. And yet it was the military who had informed the family of his death, who had sent the few personal affects back to Lincoln, Nebraska. It didn't add up, but then again maybe it did. It was hard to think clearly given the heat, the scotch, the humidity, and the pace of the security guard as they walked against the flow of two-wheeled and four-wheeled traffic and what seemed half the population of Southeast Asia.

Fearing a heart attack or a case of heatstroke, Donald unbuttoned yet another button on the crisp dress shirt he had put on after his shower, a garment that was now sweat soaked and stuck to his humid skin. His father's dog tags, though, felt cool against a tiny patch of skin on his barrel chest. He was chasing a ghost, a memory that had never been his in the first place, a name not even marked by a gravestone. He suddenly felt very foolish, very alone, and paranoid enough to begin looking over his shoulder as he walked. He decided then and there that this would be the end of a folly which had taken him halfway around the world in search of a man who had never loved or maybe even wanted him. Maybe *he* was the reason his father had never returned. That was it! It had taken forty-odd years and this fool's errand to see the obvious. He was at once relieved and emotionally overwhelmed for it dawned on him then that *he* had been the cause of his father's death. He could feel himself start to hyperventilate and thought he might pass out just as they came upon an impassable crowd in a wide circle on the sidewalk and spilling into the street.

The large-framed security man slowed but began pushing his way through until he had breached the eye of the throng. Donald pulled up beside him, a dozen or so pedestrians fleshing out the inner circle, some looking up toward a balcony, others down at the ground. The security guard, still wearing his security guard uniform, took control of the scene, kneeling beside the body of an elderly woman who had apparently jumped from the balcony. Sirens that had been nothing more than white noise a block before suddenly took on an intensity of purpose as they came closer and closer. Donald looked to the woman, the balcony and then past the sea of faces and heads to see the door to the apartment building–the same door he had not had the courage to knock on hours before.

The door was ajar, a short, squat traffic cop standing guard and clearly waiting for reinforcements given the throng that continued to gather. Donald pulled a hundred dollar bill from his wallet and moved toward the door, the gawkers parting to let him through but never really looking away from the old woman on the ground. He was past them and at the door where he shoved the Benjamin in front of the traffic cops face, saying, "Let me in. Five minutes." The traffic cop grabbed it, stuffed it in a pocket, and stepped aside. Donald pushed open the door and stepped inside a dingy vestibule with a wall of mail slot boxes numbered 1 to 6 which had names above them written variously in blue, black, and red pen across swatches of masking tape. Donald scanned the swatches above the buzzers, each name as unfamiliar as the one before until number 6:

Pham B.

The door beyond the vestibule was wide open and led into the true first floor. It was dark and dank, a wooden staircase that had seen better days on one side, a hallway with two doorways on the other. Donald's first instinct was to head upstairs to the number 6 apartment, but he was drawn to the doorways on the left and so, almost tiptoeing, moved toward them. As he approached he could see that they were not doorways, but doors which were already open. He looked into the first to see that door had actually been kicked open and off its hinges and lay on the floor, its cheap, golden numeral 1 somewhat cockeyed. He could hear a television, could smell curry and against his own better judgment stepped carefully into the apartment. He looked to the left at the small kitchen occupying that space and then to the right where a threadbare couch and equally threadbare recliner sat separated by a floor lamp and side table even the Salvation Army might reject. Beyond this furniture of last resort, a console TV, circa 1975 at best, flickered with the crickety chat of a daytime drama. Donald, despite his own trepidation, walked into the sitting room making his way to the couch beyond which lay a body on the floor, face down, hair matted with blood which had also pooled on the wood floor. The sirens arrived outside. There was no time. Donald knew that anyone who had been in the building had met a similar fate as the resident in death's still frame before him. He made his way out into the hallway and headed for the back of the

195

building, not stopping to look in the second open doorway. At the back he found what he was looking for: a way out. He hoisted the large framed window on its runners until there was just enough room for him to squeeze through and landed hard when he hit the ground outside. Without looking back he scrambled to his feet and took off down the alley across two intersections before heading back to where the woman lay on the ground. The crowd had somewhat dispersed and the security guard and his one hundred dollars were nowhere to be seen. A few police officers stood over the body now and a few more were on the stoop at the door talking with the traffic cop… and the three-fingered man. Donald panicked at the sight of him and retreated to the opposite side of the street, but knew it would not be wise to linger. He was about to leave when a Vietnamese man in his late fifties came running down the road, burst through the police officers hovering over the dead woman and collapsed to his knees and flung his body over hers. He began wailing and the police attempted to pull him off but he held so tight to the corpse that when they yanked at his pant legs and shirt he merely lifted slightly from the lifeless anchor he clung to. As the police jerked and heaved, he began to scream in Vietnamese.

"Họ đã hứa! Họ đã hứa! Họ đã hứa…"

Looking away from the scene and back to the stoop, Donald shuddered, his eyes darting from the stoop up and down the street, but the three-fingered man was nowhere to be seen now.

The walk back to the hotel, just ten minutes away, took Donald more than an hour as he had ducked into several shops along the way for fear he was being followed. Back in his room he took out his little book of Vietnamese phrases and word translations from English to Vietnamese. It took him almost an hour, working backward in a sense, before he finally understood what the man draped over the dead woman had been saying:

They promised! They promised! They promised…

What had been promised and by whom Donald did not know, but knew he had to talk to the man who had shouted that phrase as the police attempted to break his grip on the corpse.

* * *

The fact was Kenny was not homosexual, but bisexual and the woman he loved most was not the one he had married in Nebraska, but his assistant, Pham Bao, Pham Binh's sister. It was a delicate balance, an understanding, a mutually beneficial arrangement between the three of them. He took care of them financially, providing home, unattainable luxuries given their class in Vietnamese society, and American dollars which were the only real currency in South Vietnam in the early 1970s. In return, he received their companionship, loyalty, and love. They were, in a sense, his family. Kenny viewed Binh as a mindless, harmless boy toy for the most part. But Bao was another matter altogether. She was smart and savvy and had taught him more about navigating the culture than all his training at BlackLedge, his employer and hers as well.

Bao had told Kenny once that all Vietnamese were the same, that Ho Chi Minh was only using the Soviets to now rid the country of Americans as the Viet Minh had done to oust their former French colonial overlords. He had asked her in response to this who her sympathies lay with and she had answered deftly, "With Vietnam… and with you." But Bao was also an opportunist and a survivor. Orphaned during the war against the French, she had resolved to protect her little brother, Binh, and to work from the inside to forward her own agenda: a unified, self-governing Vietnam, whether communist or democratic.

Bao could never have known, but Kenny too was an opportunist who worked from the inside to forward his own agenda: to continue to live well in his adopted home of Vietnam no matter who won the war. His opportunity to realize this had come two years before in 1969 after his Cessna A-37 Dragonfly was shot down over Laos during bombing runs for Operation Menu, a covert bombing campaign whose sole purpose was to lay to waste the Viet Cong-friendly sanctuaries where they resupplied, rested and trained between their guerilla assaults across the border against American forces in South Vietnam. It was there in a Laos prison for three months that he had become addicted to heroin and where he met fellow inmate Tuan Vũ, a South Vietnamese national in prison for running large amounts of heroin between Laos, Cambodia, and South Vietnam to fund covert operations for the C.I.A. not only in the region, but all over Southeast Asia, the Middle East, and Latin America.

When an errant Operation Menu bomb hit the prison in the fall of 1969, he and Tuan escaped in the chaos and made their way to a safe house in Laos where he first met agents from BlackLedge, an independent Defense Department contracting firm that was really just a shadow army of sorts for the C.I.A. Kenny stayed at the safe house, or more accurately was held prisoner there for six months and, unbelievably, interrogated over and over as to why he had been taken captive by the Viet Cong in Laos. BlackLedge used his heroin addiction as a form of good cop/bad cop until he admitted that he was "sympathetic to the cause of the Viet Cong" (their words, not his). He was not, but to keep the fixes coming he played along, and when they offered him a deal in the spring of 1970 to act as regional go-between for BlackLedge and the C.I.A.'s heroin trade in exchange for his freedom, he took it. And they took care of the particulars, setting him up in Saigon to deal with logistics, coordinating delivery, laundering money, and the occasional arrangement of someone's disappearance. BlackLedge also made him comfortable and accustomed to a lifestyle a dishonorably discharged heroin addict would never have enjoyed back in Nebraska. He left his former life behind for good, but not his own sense of fair play. This, to him, was just another version of working on the farm. He, now as then, had bigger plans.

After only three months back in Saigon, living the high life and working for BlackLedge, he had already built a reputation locally as someone with power, money, influence, and means. Instead of playing understated as BlackLedge wanted, he was flamboyant and promiscuous in his role as facilitator. The normal connections BlackLedge had set him up with were not enough for Kenny who was revered by many of the local gangs in Saigon, some of whom were not just sympathetic but actively supported the Viet Cong in ways both subtle and substantial. Kenny was comfortable for sure, but in the gangs he saw the opportunity to become rich beyond anyone's yardstick here or back home. Kenny truly believed the old adage *All's fair in love and war*, and it bothered him not one whit that he was, in a sense, betraying his country by courting elements sympathetic to and actively supportive of the enemy.

Kenny, for all intents and purposes, went native over the remainder of 1970 and cultivated a dangerous but lucrative side business with the gangs. BlackLedge was aware, but also aware that Kenny had done well for them in the region, in fact, beyond the company's wildest imagination. The BlackLedge people tolerated Kenny. The C.I.A.–the ultimate client–was not so enamored with the Golden Boy of Saigon and so convinced BlackLedge to allow them to arrange for Kenny to be watched. The man both outfits agreed upon was Mack Dodson.

* * *

Paranoid, Donald had moved from the hotel to what was essentially a boarding house a few blocks away. Paranoid, he had stayed in his room for two full days and nights, never venturing beyond the bathroom at the end of the communal hall. It was then with much trepidation that he ventured out onto the street and headed toward his father's last known address and the scene of the carnage he had witnessed forty-eight hours before. He needed a drink badly and along his route he slipped into a store selling spirits and wine and bought a fifth of ruou at the suggestion of the shopkeeper. Outside the shop he opened it and took a few healthy slugs hoping they would calm his nerves. *What the hell am I doing?* he thought as he tucked the fifth into a shoulder bag and headed up the street. *I am looking for the truth,* he reassured himself and walked on at a more brisk pace.

As he walked, his mother came to mind and for a moment he felt guilty and selfish. It was she who had raised him, not this phantom of a father he now flung his hands at in hopes of closure. But there was much more at stake than just closure now. People, perhaps people who had known his father, were now dead. He had sat with this idea for the past two days and despite every instinct he had had in that time to give up the ghost and return to the life he had carved out without benefit of closure, Donald was determined to bridge the gap between the past and whatever the future held. And now, here, he was in present tense standing where the dead woman had lain just two days before. He looked up at the third story of the building and there, to his surprise, was the man who had thrown himself down across the corpse, there just sitting on a small wrought-iron balcony, smoking.

"Hey! I want to talk to you!!"

The man peered down at him.

"Are you a cop?"

The question was odd, but Donald answered anyway.

"No. I am an American."

Donald's answer sounded odd when he heard the words echo off the hard façade of the building.

"C.I.A.?" the man queried from his great height.

"No. My name is Donald…" he shouted, pausing, then more directly adding, "My father was Kenny Kessler. He lived here a long time ago."

With that the man stood and leaned out over the rail to get a better look.

Donald was feeling exposed and uncomfortable there on the street below the building. Surely the three-fingered man was watching him.

Finally, the man acquiesced.

"Okay. I'll buzz you in, but I have a gun. I have a gun."

The man disappeared from the balcony and a few seconds later there was a buzz at the door and Donald rushed up to open it before it stopped, opening one door and then the second to gain entry to the first floor he had surveyed days before. Donald looked toward the apartment where he had found the gunshot victim. The doorway was now covered with a large sheet of plywood which had been nailed in place of the door which had been kicked off its hinges. Donald looked away from it and headed up the stairs.

When he arrived at the bottom of the second landing he was greeted by the man waiting at the top of the steps, who leveled a revolver at him.

"How do I know?" the man queried.

Donald understood and slowly reached toward his neck. He fished out his father's dog tags, dangled them in the air.

"Here," Donald offered, throwing them underhand gently upward toward the man who caught them in his left hand while still pointing the revolver at Donald.

He looked at them.

"Where did you get these?" the man demanded.

"They were sent to my mother after my father died," adding, "I never knew my father."

The man relaxed, dropped the gun to his side and, with a sigh that seemed to have been held inside for a lifetime, admitted, "I did. And so did my sister."

"Bao?"

"Yes. Pham Bao. And I am Binh."

* * *

Binh had gone out to party with his younger friends. Kenny had noticed Binh's face was still flush from their late afternoon lovemaking when he left the apartment. He was sitting in his chaise lounge sipping tea and feeling good about his metamorphosis from indentured servant plowing acres on his father's farm in Nebraska to a sort of white overlord ruling the underclass of Saigon and rubbing elbows with its elite. Lost in the moment he barely noticed at first that someone was rapping at the apartment door.

Kenny rose, a flash of nervousness rising into his extremities, and made his way to the door. He'd had a peep hole installed months back and put his eye to it. On the other side was Mack. Kenny was elated and relieved. It had been almost a month since he had seen him. Kenny opened the door and without saying a word Mack entered, walking by Kenny in a brusque manner. Kenny closed the door, turned to him and extended his arms for an embrace, but Mack did not raise his arms in return, simply raised a hand and thrust it forward toward Kenny.

"Here is your ticket."

Kenny was perplexed. Mack shook his head at his puzzlement.

"It's hot. You're out. I can't say anymore."

"I really don't understand. Come, sit down. I'll get us a drink." Mack was unmoved.

"Get one for yourself and then head to the airport."

"I don't understand… what is going on, Mack?" Kenny cooed, then adding sarcastically, "Is the war over?"

"It's over for you, Kenny. Just forget everything that has happened here and get the hell out. God damn it, man! I shouldn't be here. I've got to go. And so do you!"

Mack stuffed the ticket into the pocket of Kenny's silk robe and pushed past him out the door. Kenny followed but in the brief seconds it took him to get to the landing all he could hear was Mack bounding down the staircase and then the slamming of two doors. Kenny ran back into the apartment and out onto the balcony. He looked down at the street, but saw neither Mack nor the C.I.A. agents who perpetually tailed him. Kenny knew this was a bad sign.

* * *

Donald took a seat in the neat, clean, and orderly apartment. It was the antithesis of the apartment of the gunshot victim.

"They'll be coming," Binh said calmly but emphatically.

"Who?"

"The people who made promises they didn't keep."

"What kind of promises?"

"To leave my sister alone. She was just an old woman. The past is the past. I don't understand why. So many years. Why now?" Binh asked staring at Donald, cocking his head this way and that as if expecting an answer by the time it stopped moving.

Donald, sensing Binh was unraveling, cut to the chase.

"What can you tell me about my father?"

Binh's head stopped its pendulum swing and his face suddenly changed.

"It's *you*. It's because of *you*. You're here to *snoop*. To dig up the past. *You* killed my sister," Binh accused.

"I don't know what the hell you are talking about. What is in the past? I came here to find out about my father. And by the way, how the hell did you know him? He was a fighter pilot for god sake and he died over here. He left me and my mother high and dry. I want some god damned answers."

"No you don't. Because you won't like them. See, nobody understands Vietnam. To you and other white devils just like you… you think we are just some slant-eyed mongrels who eat rice and work cheap for the Chinese. Vietnamese are a proud people. It was the times. The Russians and the Americans playing that game of–what was it?– *dominos*."

Spittle sprayed from Binh's lips as he finished. His neck was now a map of blue veins bulging from beneath the skin.

Then Binh leaned forward and in a low growl offered, "She only did what she had to. What she was told. They promised! Họ đã hứa! Họ đã hứa! Họ đã hứa…"

* * *

Kenny's adrenaline was through the roof and it was hard for him to steady the needle before the vein bulging beneath the tourniquet. *Was this really happening? Was it all over?* he wondered as the needle broke the skin and found its mark.

He could feel the cold comfort moving through his veins to his muscles, his heart, his brain. He thought of his father and the simple life he had carved out for himself through back-breaking hard work. *Was he happy?* The question could not and would never be answered and Kenny knew this. *And what of his wife?* Thoughts turned to her and the son he would probably never meet. The end of everything seemed imminent. That was not a life he was prepared to go back to and couldn't. Katherine's letter had said as much. No, this would be the end. The end of everything.

Kenny felt woozy, on the verge of passing out, but an impulse came over him and he stood, unsteady, and walked to his bedroom. Once there, he rifled the top drawer of his bureau and found what he was looking for: the picture of Donald in a cowboy outfit that Katherine had sent him. On the back, written in pen by Katherine, were the words:

Donny, our little cowboy, 3 years old

Kenny stared at it. He was a cowboy too. Had lived the life of one as portrayed in the movies: self-reliant, unattached, and self-determined. This would be his last stand. Custer at the Little Big Horn. He placed the picture back in the drawer and rifled it with a calm hand until he found his pistol. He held it in his hand, placed it to his temple, and laughed, but he was feeling increasingly unstable on his feet. He dropped the gun to his side and then to the floor and collapsed in a beautiful euphoria.

* * *

He wasn't sure how long he had been passed out, but when he awoke on the bedroom floor Kenny looked up to see Bao standing over him. He smiled at her and mumbled, "It's over, Bao."

"I know," she said, raising Kenny's gun from her side and pointing it at him.

* * *

"What did they promise? What?" Donald implored.

Binh stood up and turned away from Donald.

"They promised 'Do this and we will never bother you again.'"

"Who?" demanded Donald. "Do what?"

"Họ đã hứa! Họ đã hứa! Họ đã hứa…"

And then nothing else but the sound of Binh's voice raising in pitch and the same *Họ đã hứa* over and over, again and again. Donald could hear it from the street after he left the building.

Two hours later, Donald was at the airport waiting on the next flight home. He sat in the bar drinking scotch.

"Let me get the next one," came a voice from behind his stool.

Donald turned, already knowing who was there. Donald looked over his shoulder but said nothing in response to the three-fingered man.

"Headed home?"

Donald nodded.

"Never to return?"

Donald nodded again.

"Good boy, Donald. Good boy."

The man turned to walk away but stopped when he heard Donald call out.

"Is Binh dead?"

The three-fingered man looked toward the ceiling before turning to look Donald in the eye.

"Hmmm? I think he died after his sister thought she could fly," then quickly adding, "But *you* have a good flight, Donald."

Donald returned to his drink and downed it, the mish-mash of English and Vietnamese announcements over the airport public address system as simultaneously sobering and disorienting as his ill-fated sojourn in this country of contradictions had been.

He ordered another scotch and drank it without pause, his first lucid moment in days arriving with the sting behind his eyes, the cool burn in his throat. His father had never really existed. His mother had. Then, a thought as clear as the bottom of his glass: *I will go home to her and forget about the man who only briefly gave her his name and nothing more and when she passes, I will bury her and the past along with all of my mother's names.*

BLOOD SPORT

Katherine Tandy Brown

Mi Walsh was a lucky man. Tomorrow, he'd marry the woman of his dreams. Today, he'd win her a wedding present that would be a boon to his reputation as a horseman in America and a stepping stone to their future together in Ireland.

Or so he thought.

"You're looking full of confidence, young man." The clerk of scales at Springdale Race Course noted the weight pointer through bifocals and penned "138" on a clipboard. Crowds of onlookers strained for a pre-race peek at the svelte riders weighing in at the tiny stable office. Behind them, sleek thoroughbreds paraded around the Camden paddock.

"Aye, sir," the jockey said with a grin. "No reason to be here without it."

Looking over his glasses, the clerk smiled. "You'd be the Irish entry. Welcome to America…and South Carolina. First visit?"

"That it is, sir, and I intend to take home the Carolina Cup as a souvenir."

The wizened gentleman chuckled. "There's the spirit, young man. Safe trip to you." He turned to four riders clad in white britches and colorful silks. "Who's next?"

A gaunt, hunched jockey with a hooked nose slinked from the shadow side of a nearby live oak, ducked under the office railing and slipped into the back of the jocks' weighing line. A scarlet cap was pulled low on his pock-marked face and his head was tucked, as he carefully smoothed wrinkles from his bright yellow shirt. One blood-red stripe circled his chest.

Whistling, the Irishman wended his way down a grassy alley to an open, wood-slatted stall marked "2." He saddled his horse, planted a joyous kiss on the mouth of his fiancée, and mounted their sure winner. Tying a knot in his reins, he felt her hand on his calf, heard her heartfelt "Godspeed." He looked down, gave her a wink that she returned with a smile, and followed the lead horse a turn around the paddock and out onto the course.

Standing in his irons, he urged the gray into a warmup canter. The lanky thoroughbred hunched its back, and with a squeal, gave one perfunctory buck, then settled into stride. The Irishman chuckled. They'd win this one for sure. The turf was packed but with a bit of give. Perfect. Inhaling the spring air, he plotted the race one more time in his mind and cantered along the outside rail to join the rest of the field at the starting line.

Across the course, the crowd yelled, "They're off!"

By the sixth hurdle, the gray was leading the field by three lengths, galloping easily toward the seventh, right where the Irishman meant for him to be. Something caught the corner of the jockey's eye, and he glanced around to see another horse charging up on the inside. It was the blood bay. Number 10. The Argentine-born entry that hadn't run a sanctioned race in a year and a half. Spotty past performances. A bit of a wild card. But the Irishman wasn't worried. Even if the bay passed them, his gray could pick them off on the flat. He had lots of horse left.

The bay gained on them quickly. The Irishman saw the yellow silks and red stripe flash by just as they approached the jump. A stride and a half ahead, the bay left the ground. It wasn't until then that the rider realized what was happening. He felt the gray's muscles bunch beneath him to take off at the same time as the bay. But the gray had not yet reached the spot that would allow him to finish a full trajectory, a complete arc, and clear the hurdle. The gray was at the bay's quarter, moving instinctively to jump because the racehorse beside him was taking off and not because his rider had bidden him to.

"No, Gray. Not yet. *No!*"

The Irishman spat the words through his teeth, while using his weight, his hands and his legs to signal his horse to delay the takeoff for another few seconds. But the gray had already committed to the jump and launched himself at the brush, sailing forward and up, up, three-quarters of a stride behind his competitor. The bay landed safely and galloped on. The gray, however, was coming down too soon. Seeing the top of the jump coming at him, the horse strained to clear it, his legs failing at the air, reaching for a few more feet. But instead he came crashing down on it. His right leg caught the brush, and he somersaulted forward, catapulting his shocked rider into the air ahead of him.

The Irishman's neck snapped as he slammed onto the packed turf, tumbling like a rag doll away from the base of the jump into the center of the course. His motionless form lay where the rest of the field would be landing, their jockeys unaware of him until too late. Though paralyzed immediately from the neck down, he felt the splintering pain when the first hoof cracked against his skull, before blessedly falling unconscious.

So busy were the riders trying to avoid the accident that no one noticed the jockey on the bay look back at the chaotic scene, break into a wicked grin and ease his mount back into the pack to finish as an also-ran.

When the Irishman heard her calling his name, he tried to open his eyes. Their lids were like immovable boulders. His eyes felt filled with glass shards. He willed his arm to reach up, stroke her face, reassure her. But it wouldn't move.

"Mi?...Mi?... Wake up...*Wake up*...Don't leave me, Mi. *Micah*..."

He heard her panic and, grating against searing pain, managed to lift his lids. And there she was. Her face so close, etched with worry. But a veil hung over that beautiful face. Blood had colored it red. Her eyes were red, her lips, the sky above her. All red. All he could see was red. He inhaled to speak but his throat was full of something thick. He tried to push words past it but choked, tried to find breath and choked again. His mind formed the words. *Oh god oh god oh god. Help me. Erin...Erin...Eeeeriiiin.* With one last effort, he gasped his final word. "Erin."

The Irishman's luck had run out.

NUMBER ONE G.I.

Marjorie E. Brody

Fatigue lined Todd Douglas's face, dragged on his muscles, thickened his spit. But he stood erect. Alert. Eyes forward. Ignoring the stares from the panel of judges, the prosecutor, the court reporter, the ghosts of the dead.

"Be seated, Private Douglas." Lt. Anderson, prosecuting attorney for the Judge Advocate General, tugged at the base of his jacket. A small gesture. Perfecting the lay of his uniform.

Todd plucked the sharp crease on his khaki sleeve. He looked pretty spiffy himself.

"Before the recess you were talking about what happened the day Private First Class Hepper died," the attorney said. "Let's pick up there. And I remind you, soldier, you're still under oath."

The wood on the witness stand felt flatter, harder than it had all morning. Todd squeezed his butt cheeks, squirmed his ass around a little and tried to find a comfortable position. "Yeah, well, we all knew the risks. Everybody knew it could happen— happen to any of us. Shit. We were living with kill or be killed. Every damn day. Every damn night. We had to stick together."

"Who devised the plan your squad followed?" the JAG's piranha asked him.

"Sergeant Caldwell figured out where they stashed the ..." Todd searched for a politically correct word. "... the 'supplies' we needed."

"Let's be clear here. Those supplies you 'needed' would be considered illegal drugs in the United States. Is that correct?"

"It wasn't illegal in Nam," Todd said with a shrug.

"Need I remind you which country's laws you swore to follow?"

"It was a matter of survival. But I don't suppose you'd know about that—what it's like to live 24/7 in a fucking hell hole." Todd hardened his eyes. "So let me tell you. Enlighten you 'bout what it's like to live over there—if you can call it living."

He flicked the collar of his shirt. "The shirt you wear all day, sleep in all night, reeks of death. Your pants stink from your own goddamn piss. And even when you strip, you carry that smell of death with you, buried in your own goddamn skin."

"Private ..."

"Your feet—what you depend on to hightail your ass to cover—corroded and raw with jungle rot. Where leeches crawl up your legs, suck blood from your goddamn balls."

"Private!"

"You live under a hailstorm of bullets and satchel charges— those sweet little gifts the VC toss at you. Explosives in canvas satchels. You see your buddies made into Swiss cheese by punji sticks. Filleted by trip wire traps." He leaned forward, ignored the moisture heating the space above his lips. "We *needed* those supplies. Hear me? We needed them."

"It was war, Private. You expected a playground?"

Todd swiped an index finger through the sweat. Wiped the finger with a thumb. Kept his mouth closed. *Smart-ass bastard didn't understand anything.*

"Sorry, your honors. I withdraw the question...So your answer, Private Douglas, was to get high?"

Todd slathered a grin onto his lips. "It took the edge off."

"That raid. The one for supplies that 'took the edge off,' it cost eleven civilian lives and wounded your interpreter. Correct?"

His smile fell like a can at target practice. "Yeah. Casualties of war. It happens. Like they say 'bout shit. It happens."

"Your honor, I ask that you instruct the witness to show respect for these proceedings."

"So ordered," the presiding judge said. "Private Douglas. It does your case no good to show your contempt in this court. Conduct yourself with the dignity your uniform demands."

"Thank you, your honor," Lt. Anderson said. "Now, Private, I'd like you to tell this panel what happened to your interpreter during the raid—the raid designed solely to stock your illegal drug supply."

Todd shot the attorney a why-the-fuck-you-asking-me-when-you-already-know-the-fucking-answer glare. "He got slashed in the arm. Sir. MASH unit had to take it off. His arm. Sir. Sent him to the hospital in Long Binh."

Lt. Anderson walked slowly behind the table that served as his desk. He pulled out his chair and sat as straight as the flagpole in the corner of the room. Even when he leaned forward to read notes on his yellow legal pad—*good color for a soldier who fights case law rather than the Enemy*—his spine remained iron straight. With every goddamn minute the attorney stalled the silence, Todd's temperature rose ten degrees.

"What was PFC Hepper's reaction when the squad came back from the raid with the wounded interpreter?"

Todd wiped his brow with the back of his hand, crossed his arms and surreptitiously dried the sweat on the underside of his shirt sleeve. "Don't know. I didn't see him."

Lt. Anderson lifted a sheet of yellow paper with his right hand, ran his left index finger three-quarters way down the surface.

A southpaw, wouldn't ya know it, Todd thought. *Just like Hepp.*

"That raid occurred on the afternoon of November 12, 1971? Is that correct?"

"Correct. Sir."

"When was the next time you saw PFC Hepper?"

"Before we crossed the river." Todd leaned back in the witness stand. Kept his arms folded. "Sir."

"And that was?"

"Later that night. Sir."

"If you could put your disdain aside for a moment, Private Douglas." The attorney lowered the paper and pressed it smooth with a palm. "Let's get to the night of the raid. That same November 12, 1971. What was your mission?"

Todd looked across his shoulder and addressed the panel. *They would understand Nam.* "Delta platoon called for reinforcements. Ground unit had taken a beating earlier that afternoon—"

"While you were conducting your 'supply raid'?"

How dare that pain-in-the-ass interrupt. "Yeah, I guess."

"Continue."

That's what I'm trying to do, asshole. "Our squad was ordered to cross the Mekong River at the junction. Intel said a hundred plus Charlies were holed up in a village."

"Let me inform you, Private..." Lt. Anderson pushed back his chair and stood, strolled to the front of his desk. "We already have the testimonies of Privates Shilling and Renault." His gaze never deviated from Todd.

What the fuck you staring at, peckerhead? Todd jutted his chin.

"What happened before your squad crossed the river?"

"We...set a mine."

"We?"

"We...I...I was following orders."

"Whose orders exactly?"

"The squad's. We all decided."

"You all decided?" Lt. Anderson ambled in front of the panel, his steps slow, calculated, his back to Todd. "To set a mine. Interesting. And what was the purpose for setting this mine? To deter the enemy? To prevent an invasion? To—"

"To get rid of a snitch. A goddamn snitch."

Lt. Anderson stepped about-face, squaring his shoulders to the witness stand. "The whole squad decided on—?"

"We had to stick together. Sergeant Caldwell was sure Hepp—that's what we called Private Hepper—was going to rat us out.

Hepp was the only guy who wouldn't go on the raid. Claimed it wasn't part of our mission. Said it put innocent gooks—well, that wasn't his word—innocent 'vill-a-gers' at risk. At risk? Hell, our mission was at risk without the goods from that raid. So, Caldwell set up the plan and the rest of us... See it was like this. If we didn't handle Hepp, we would've been next. The Sarge would've seen to it."

"Go on."

"Sarge had been tipped off."

"Sergeant Caldwell?"

"Yes."

"And what had Sergeant Caldwell been tipped off about?"

"Hepp asked for a transfer. New squad. New leader."

"Go on. What happened next?"

Whatdaya think happened? Sarge wished Hepp well with a pat on the back?

"Sarge sent Hepp beyond the wire."

"To patrol the border alone?"

"Yes."

"Then what happened"

Sweat pooled along the base of Todd's spine, sucking his undershirt to his skin. "Sarge told the rest of us Hepp was going to turn us in...Report the entire squad...Every last one of us."

"Speak up, Private. The answers aren't on the tips of your shoes."

Todd whipped his head up. *Up yours.*

Lt. Anderson arched his arm through the air and gestured to the judges. "Tell this esteemed panel what happened when you presumed Private Hepper would file a complaint against you."

Todd kept his gaze locked on the attorney. "File a complaint? In a war zone? What a laugh. It was nothing so, so civil. If Hepp ratted us out...it'd be the end. For all of us."

"Continue."

His ears reviewed the sounds of that night. Distant sounds: gun fire, rocket fire. Close sounds: buzzing insects, murmuring squad. His eyes re-experienced the listless colors of that night. Gray-black barbed wire. Gray-black ground. Gray-black sky and a crippled, jaundiced moon. Starch from rice paddies had stiffened his clothes, had scratched the small of his back. Bone-weary legs lifted heavy black boots as he marched.

Todd shoved the unwanted sensations aside and hated Hepp even more for forcing him to remember. "Sarge marched us to the perimeter," he said. "Confronted Hepp."

"What did Private Hepper do when Sergeant Caldwell confronted him?"

"Hepp denied everything but the request for transfer—of course. Said he was tired of living with such low-lifes. That's what he called us. 'Drug-using, self-serving low-lifes.' Said he couldn't respect us. Couldn't trust us—fuck! Hepp said he needed a transfer to fight the war he was sent to fight. Like we weren't fighting the same goddamn war."

"Did Private Hepper say or do anything else?... Private Douglas? Something you're not telling us?... What else happened during that confrontation?"

Todd took a long, slow breath and imagined Nam Green seeping deep into his lungs, bringing the burn, bringing the calm. "The VC had a way of judging soldiers. One to ten. Ten being the worst. Hepp walked right up to Sarge, looked him in the eye, and said in his best gook voice, 'You number ten GI.'"

"What did Sergeant Caldwell do when Private Hepper accused him of being a bad soldier?... Private? What did Sergeant Caldwell do?"

Todd heard the words that snapped through the air that colorless night, re-lived his own startle. In the witness chair, he straightened his spine and pulled his shoulders back. "The Sarge called Hepp a goddamn nigger. Said no high and mighty black boy was going to disgrace him."

"How did Private Hepper react?"

"He squared his shoulders and repeated, 'Ten.'"

"And then?"

"And then Hepp did an about-face. He just turned his fucking back and walked away."

"What did Sergeant Caldwell do when Private Hepper walked away?"

"Sarge..." Todd closed his eyes and he was still there. The barrel glinting in the moonlight. A sound—*the* sound—that erased every other. "Sarge shot him. Shot Hepp like some goddamn Charlie. Blew his fucking chest out."

Lt. Anderson dipped his head ever so slightly to the panel of judges. "What did you do when Sergeant Caldwell—?"

"We stood there. We did noth—"

"I'm not asking what the squad did, Private. I'm asking what *you* did."

Todd held his eyes steady and attempted to read the stony faces of the men on the panel. The less he could decipher, the more adrenaline flooded his blood stream. "Nothing. I did nothing."

"I see. You did nothing."

"How could I? Sarge said Hepp was deserting. Desertion in

the face of the enemy. Sarge had to shoot him. Told us we were all witnesses."

"Did it look like desertion to you, Private?"

"Sarge called it. That made it so. But then Sting Ray—"

"Sting Ray?"

"Bobby Ray Bryant, sir."

"Go on."

"Sting Ray was angry enough to piss on Hepp's grave. Hated that Hepp didn't go on the raid with us, would even think about turning us in. The two of them went way back. Grew up in the same crummy neighborhood and Hepp protected him from street thugs as a kid. Said he owed the guy something." Todd pushed words through tight jaws. "He didn't want Hepp branded a coward."

Lt. Anderson's whole demeanor shouted, You've-got-to-be kidding, but Todd ignored the attorney's nonverbal trap and focused on the lieutenant's question. "So what happened?"

"Sting Ray convinced Caldwell to create a little accident— on our way to the river, make it look like a line-of-duty tragedy. Blow the body to pieces. No evidence of desertion."

"You mean no evidence of foul play?"

"I mean, no proof of Hepp's *official* cowardice. Saving Sarge beaucoup paperwork didn't hurt either... So the whole squad agreed. And that's what we did."

"That's what *you* did? Set the mine?"

"Sure. Why not? The guy was already dead."

"You didn't think to turn Sergeant Caldwell in?"

"We had enough worries with Charlie. Didn't have time to look over our shoulders, watching for one in the back—by one of our own. So, yeah. Maybe we thought about it. But we had our priorities. Know what I mean?"

"Private Hepper had priorities, too. Like following the oath he swore to uphold when he entered the US Army."

"And look what that got him."

"You have a point, Private. Look what that got him."

Todd's limbs tingled, wanted to move, to strike out. "You don't get it, do you?"

"Oh, I get it. The buddies who were supposed to protect him, agree to blow him up, make it look like an accident."

"Like I said, it was a matter of life-and-death."

"Wipe that smirk off your face, Private."

"How dare you—Sir—hide behind your safe little desk, in your safe little courthouse, on your safe little base and dare to judge me? To dare to—"

"I'm done with this witness, Your Honor. Sergeant at Arms—"

Todd sprung to his feet before the bailiff reached him. "We were doing your dirty work, Lieutenant. With our careers on the line. Our lives—leave your fucking hands off me, man, I'm going." He lifted his chin and stepped down from the witness stand, pausing in front of Lt. Anderson. "Just don't forget—Sir—it was our testimony, *our* testimony, that made Hepp into a Number One GI! We made him a goddamn hero."

"You're dead wrong, soldier. Private Hepper already was a Number One GI—'a goddamn hero'. You just made it...official."

NOTHING ABOUT US WITHOUT US IS FOR US

Gregg Cusick

(Hopewell Crescent mural,
letters formed of photos of local residents)

Lanark Way, the Falls, Belfast, March 2013

Donagh Clarke, 26, unemployed, again, sits in his girlfriend's cold, rusty Vauxhall, smoking, watching his kid brother's kid playing in the cobbled street, kicking a football with very little natural ability but no lack of tenacity. Donagh couldn't tell you how it happened—that is, his work status; the girl he can't say if he loves; nor the little brother with family, who their father barely speaks to. Caden the three-years-younger brother living in the old neighborhood not a kilometer from where they all grew up.

But Donagh could tell you why he's the father's favorite—always has been, in spite of his violent and delinquent history. Or, in part, because of it. Crazy, he knows part of the little brother wishes he was like him.

Donagh's fingers squeeze the fag and his lungs pull the smoke in, and the edginess he feels, he knows, is anger pointed inward, that he wants to point outward. There are so many reasons to fight, he thinks, so many injustices. He's got the wired jaw and the twice-busted leg to prove he's willing. Their father sees them as battle wounds—you're a vet, he tells Donagh, and not his other son—but Donagh smokes and wonders. The boy, his nephew, pounds the football against the low wall beside the house, and it kicks back at a crazy angle into the street. The boy laughs with abandon, as if nothing could be funnier.

Breen's Pub, Falls Road, Belfast, March 2005

Donagh and Caden's father likes to tell the story of O'Connor and O'Higgins. Just now he's before a peat fire in Breen's, just

215

down the way from McGurk's, the famous one the UVF bombed in '71, killing fifteen. Which is the age of the younger son, the wannabe writer, Caden, who slings Mother Breen's Irish stew and coddles, totes kegs, and attempts invisibility. His father's got a bum leg from a near-knee-capping, a popping jaw from an altercation with the RUC on the Shankill in '72, when he'd fought their family's removal from a street that the Protestants wished to own entirely. There's the buzzer at the door, which Caden answers with a glance through a peephole; it's only old Murphy, and in he leans already half in the bag.

The father, Seamus Clarke, nods at Murph then back to the fire, pulls long off his dark draught and begins, to the few, interested and weary both, to hear again the tale. He's something of a local hero, is Seamus, since for his activism and voice most thought he'd have been "disappeared" years ago. But his stories, like all, tend to repeat. Repeat, and change over time, of course, but there are facts, too, undeniably. Young Caden, only the latest Clarke to be labeled a "wankin' Taig" from across the street, delivers a couple of stouts and pauses beside the mantle, against the bookshelf, lean and unnoticeable as a broom, to listen again.

"So this is how it was, how it is, gentleman: not a clear case, even among us Republicans, even then." He pauses for drama, himself clearly moved already, the conflict so dear to his heart he'd gladly die for it. Continues only after a deep pull off his draught.

"It was a cold, sodden March in 1922 when Rory O'Connor stood up for his best chum, Kevin. Despite the weather, there was much rejoicing, many a toast at the O'Higgins nuptials. Much carousing and much celebrating that went to blackout unremembrance or disremembrance. People told stories of that wedding that involved local ladies and farm animals of all types" (scattered laughter here) "and it was recalled that the marriage couldn't be legally consummated for three days, and these two were rabbits." More chuckles, but Caden's dad's face goes dark and serious. He sips long and shakes his head a little toward the fire as if his next words were appearing in the glowing peat.

"But forward now just months, eight December the same year, and dear Kevin O'Higgins is signing the order, for the firing squad that's putting dear Rory to death." Again the pause, the deep sip, the probing of the fire for answers. "So what happened to these two pals?"

Most in the room had relatives on both sides in the civil war that followed the treaty. All Republicans before the treaty, but after it they were neighbors and kinsmen killing one another. Everyone has now, and had then, an opinion, formed in pubs and before home fires and over potatoes and boiled bacon when they could get it. And the way the history of those few months in 1922 is told reveals more about the teller than the objective facts of the events, if there can be such a thing. This, too, his father has told Caden many a time. Drunk or sober, violent or morose.

"O'Higgins signed the treaty, the traitor," says one of the old-timers, a cousin of Breen's, his cheeks radish-red and his neck quivering like a rooster's wattle. "Signed the treaty and put to death seventy-seven of our own."

Of *his* own, too, young Caden Clarke thinks but does not voice. Months before, he knew as well as the rest, O'Connor and O'Higgins had been fighting together on the same side. And then the treaty split them, made one a traitor to the Republican cause, the other bound at best for martyrdom as the Brits would surely, as ever before, quash any rebellion without mercy.

"Without the treaty there'd been no freedom at all. Collins did what he had to, too, much as he hated to," comes old Doody's answer. "Gerry Adams was no different in '98, you know."

"Aye, so that's the problem," Caden's father picks up. He'd intended to name his younger son Gerry, that until Adams had renounced his IRA connections and went to parliament.

"O'Connor and his anti-treaty boys took the Four Courts in Dublin that spring. Hell, the big fellow himself, Collins, used the Brits' artillery to drive 'em out." He looks around the room, the eyes of all upon him, but behind each pair is a different vision, a different anger, a different sense of outrage or injustice. "So O'Higgins signs the death warrant on his old pal O'Connor, and just a few years later three anti-treaty folks assassinate O'Higgins, too.

"Hell, remember one of them, Archie Doyle, lived to be 80. Used to brag about killing O'Higgins, he did. None of the three of them was ever held or charged."

"I'd buy him all the jars he could drink, if he walked in today," says old Foley, whose motion is seconded and thirded and more.

"Last summer me and the wife visited Sans Souci Park in South Dublin where they gunned O'Higgins down," pipes up another, Murphy's nephew, a good bit younger than the others. "There's a plaque there." He shakes his head at the fire now, too. "He was thirty-five, O'Higgins was."

This sounds *old* to Caden Clarke, *over twice my age.* Who heads back to the bar to wash some dishes. But he can tell the others don't see it the same. No one sees it the same, Caden thinks, wishing he could be off. And running. For the gate that will soon close. The gate through which awaits his Angie. His saint.

Port of Belfast, March, 1898.

It is raining and he is fifteen when he leaves Belfast, the old sod, to board a leaky freighter to cross the Irish Sea bound for Liverpool. Where he'll join thirteen hundred other immigrant souls on a nine-day steamer for New York harbor. The skies somewhat brighten to the west as he embarks, a development he hopes is fortuitous. But the near-freezing rain has left the gangplank slickened, and his worn-smooth boot soles slide from beneath him halfway up. With his free hand—his other holds a small leather sack as worn as his shoes containing a bible and a change of clothes—he grabs for the rail and goes down hard on his right side. A numbness shoots through his hip and then quickly his jaw where it has struck the bottom rail. He rises dazed to his knees feeling as if he's been cold-cocked. Other passengers mutter at him as they spread past him like ant soldiers around a fallen comrade, not uncaring but driven themselves.

He is Thomas Clarke, named for the Irish Catholic revolutionary, the famed one who went to prison in 1883, the year the aforementioned Tom had been born. Ironically, the Irish independence hero, released from Pentonville just months after Tom arrives in New York, will follow Tom to Brooklyn, though the two will never meet. And the older, the famous Clarke will return to Ireland, will be executed for his role in the Easter Rising of 1916.

On the gangplank, Tom feels no pain immediately, only surprise, seeing only the white-light of adrenaline. And moments later, limping on board and to the deck, the pain he does feel has less to do with the fall. The physical ache is simpler, is in his gut, is hunger; and is as much genetic for his people since the worst of the potato famines and even before. The Brits and the Orangies have been starving the Catholics since taking their lands near seven centuries back, and the most recent home rule bill's failure had led Tom's father and many to assume the worst. The family had pooled what little funds they could, and so Tom the second son got the five pounds—half a year's wage for his laborer pap—for the passage to America. Beyond the physical ache, of course, he knows he will miss the land; but while he felt it was *his*, the law forcefully says different. He watches the coast recede into the new fog.

And although Tom Clarke will work and live five decades more in America, will father children who'll mother and father more, his hip will pain him throughout that time and his jaw will pop when he chews from that moment on. It is 1898. He will never return to Ireland.

Behind Malvern Gate, Shankill Road and Malvern Street, Belfast, March 2005

Angela Cooper, fifteen, sees herself not as the saint her Caden does, but instead a poor, less than devout Presbyterian. However, as Caden reminds her, like St. Angela Merici, the founder of the Ursulines, Angie had been devastated by the loss of her older sister at a young age (like the saint's sister, hers to sickness, not violence). And like St. Angela, she wants to teach, however literature rather than religion. She's quite beautiful yet shies from social situations which, Caden is quick to remind, were characteristics of the saint as well. Ginger-haired and lightly freckled, she is not outwardly Protestant, but for the giveaway of her surname.

She's seated at a bus stop bench in the shadow of the wall, just outside the shadow of the Malvern gate; but when the bus approaches she waves it on. It stops past her to let out a few passengers, who disembark and trudge toward the gate, the opening in the "Freedom Wall," the "Peace Line" near ten meters high that protects the Protestant loyalists from the Catholic nationalists, and vice versa. At this time of day—near dusk, closing time when the heavy gate will be swung across the opening and chained in place for the night—foot traffic is mainly the Catholics, those who work in the Shankhill and live in the Falls to the south. But Angie waits for one, her Caden, to approach and cross against this grain to her. She stands, paces the length of the bench, returns, and re-seats herself.

She wears her school dress, a simple jumper, over a sweater and knitted leggings against the damp cold. There's call for rain tonight but she hasn't seen it yet. Beside her on the bench, her large canvas sack holds a light, warm blanket of fleece material, a couple of sandwiches, and a couple of cans of bitters. Also her literature textbook, marked to the current unit on Shakespeare.

Just lately she'd taken to calling her Caden "McMontague," with a lightness she tries to feel now. But she shudders to think of her father's reaction—grave disappointment, or worse—when he learns of Caden. Angie wishes there was light enough to read, to take her mind off the waiting. She listens for the quick ta-tap, ta-tap of his running shoes on the sidewalk on the other side of the gate, pictures his approach.

The Shankill Road, Belfast, March 1972

In a cold rain, he is fifteen when his family moves, that is, is forced from the West Belfast row house he'd been born in. Pushing a tarp-covered wheelbarrow of his parents' belongings, Seamus Clarke thinks of his great grandfather, a part of him wishing he could board a ship and be done with this old sod. Certainly there are Clarkes in America, his people, who would take him in. But more of him feels the pain in his hip, the pop of his jaw—the result of fights right here. He's been lucky to not have been kneecapped like his brother and two of his buds, one who'd lost the legs—and knows he cannot, will not leave the fray, ever, unless in a body bag. He'll poach in their old home for days, bunk with comrades for months, avoiding arrest. Before finally rejoining his family in The Falls.

Seamus' heroes are his great grandfather's namesake, Thomas Clarke, executed after the 1916 Easter Uprising, where he and Pearse and sixteen-year-old Michael Collins had taken the General Post Office and declared the Irish state free from Britain. And most admired, of course, Seamus Costello for his heroic revolutionary actions four decades later, and for whom Clarke had been named in 1957. Costello who up in Derry had destroyed loyalist bridges and burned the Magherafelt Courthouse, did six months in Mountjoy and two years in labor camp before quietly and behind the scenes coming back to the cause. Or you could say he never left it, as it had never left him.

Costello will go on to found the OIRM and Irish Republican Socialist Party and INLA, will be assassinated by a feuding faction of his own Republican movement in 1977, but that's in Seamus Clarke's future now, since his family is moving, is forced to, and it's cold and wet and not yet spring of 1972, not two months since the British gunned down the unarmed civil rights marchers, killing thirteen on Bloody Sunday just over in Derry.

The Falls Road, Belfast, March 2005

At fifteen, Caden Clarke is always, everywhere, running. Excelling like one of his heroes, Bobby Sands (of hunger-strike fame), at Cross Country, his feet but the fastest way he has to get anywhere. Born with a right femur shorter than his left (now more than two centimeters different), he's an unlikely fast runner. Even with the heel lift in one Nike, his strides are slightly long-short, his footfalls a ta-tap, ta-tap cadence like a fighter working a speed bag. Like a postman, in all conditions he gallops from home to the St. Francis school, from school to Breen's. Where on duty he fetches what the old barkeeps need and hoists the cases and even a keg of Guinness now and then, delivers mutton stew and potato hash to neighbors and even tourists, gets paid his cash under the table. And where, as everywhere, he listens.

To the tales, all true or a version of true, believed to be true, that he'll scribble in his journal and try to make sense of, to understand how he, Caden Clarke, must think, and must act, to be true to his own beliefs. Which are, he hardly knows: they come from inside him and from far away, long ago. But which, he is coming to believe, are in ways different from his father's, from his brother's, from his Clarke forebears in the last century even.

Caden sees these old relatives—in scenes, in versions of the stories he's heard repeated forever—as he runs the sidewalks and the parks and the cemeteries, along the wall, as he's doing now, the "Peace Lines" even at fifteen he sees as sadly ironic, running a third its length from his home to the narrow opening in the wall, heavy gates swung shut at dusk, about six p.m., this time of year. So that for the night the Protestants, the "Huns" his dad would say, on the other side, including his Angela, are safe from the rowdy Republican Catholics. Those descendants still crying out for Home Rule, still bearing the welts left by the Brit's yokes, now over six centuries old and perhaps not as physically painful as once were, but having worn deeply indenting the spirit for each of the generations since. Caden shudders to picture his father's reaction when he learns of Angie, can't help but see violence but perhaps it will be worse, a stony silence of betrayal that could last the rest of his father's days. Caden clamps his teeth, an anxious habit, then releases the tension open-mouthed, causing his jaw to pop audibly. And he quickens his pace yet again.

He'd seen the clock over the bar, guesses he has twenty-five minutes before the gate closes. Knows as his Nike's hit the pavement outside Breen's, almost in the shadow of the mural on the wall, bright proud bearded visage of Gerry Adams. Adams whom Caden admires most as a writer of stories, whose collection, *The Street*, he's read and reread again. Knows that Angie, his Angie, is waiting at the Malvern Street gate, where then they'll head to their spot sheltered in the cemetery in Crumlin Ward. They've covered themselves for the night, his excuse to watch the football—his beloved Glasgow Celts against the rival Rangers, on cable at a chum's house—and hers a sleep-over with a batch of young Presbyterian girls at the home of one her parents approved of.

Caden doesn't need a watch to know that he is slightly behind schedule. He again picks up his pace and feels his lungs try to shut him down, feels the burn and pictures her inquisitive face and her ginger hair straight and shiny beneath Rangers-blue knit cap she wears to razz him. Pictures this and the stubborn freckles on her nose. Lengthens his strides, waiting for the rhythm that he knows he'll find.

Malvern Gate, Belfast, March 2005

Her Caden, the romantic, has always seen her as a saint, since they were children and he was running even then, venturing onto her side of the wall. And when she'd been crying, alone — for a reason she can't now recall — was it a runaway cat? — he'd stopped. And instead of asking what was wrong or what he could do, he'd been dumbfounded, unable to speak, and she'd smiled in spite of herself at his somehow sweet, inability. That two years back, they were thirteen.

She's sure she hears something now, but it's not Caden's Nikes. The gate guards are swinging the massive, graffitied iron gates closed for the night.

When she finally hears his ta-tap, ta-tap, the gates are nearly closed. Angie hears clearly his sliding stop on the rain-wetted pavement, cartoonlike in its extended skid. The guards, PSNI, formerly RUC, hear Caden's approach as well, peer through the sliver of light between the gate and the tie-pole, turn in unison toward Angie and seem to sigh in unison, too. The guards, who have shown her kindness and Caden, tolerance at least, look back to one another, as through the sliver Angie glimpses Caden. The guards shake heads, mutually. The one with the heavy chain and the lock steps back, while the other pushes back the gate just a bit, enough for a skinny kid — Catholic or Protestant, who could tell … though they all four know — to pass through. Angie grins, right-hand index and middle fingers raised, gratefully. Again the shake of the guards' heads as Caden slips through.

Next, the sound of the clanging together of the gate and the post, the chain silvery and being laid into place and clasped, a giant necklace like of the biggest drug dealer in Belfast, Caden thinks, so heavy and meant to be. As he and his saint run off together, into the greyness and rain, her gloved hand in his bare one, toward the cemetery and their secret shelter.

The Falls Road, Belfast, March 2013

Donagh watches his brother's six-year-old, Bobby Clarke, playing in a cobbled street so near where the family's been since 1972. The area once all-Catholic but lately some Prot, not the union-jack-offs but younger, with more open minds, with kids they don't teach to hate. They live in the neighborhood of north-west Belfast, but it could be anywhere, streets where the rains fill the sewer drains and near wash away the blood that has run across the stones. A street that butts up to the one where Donagh and Caden's uncle once had his knees shot out and never got up.

There are some trees, saplings, on the edge of the street that all recognize still as the dividing line between the section where his family lived before '72 and where they live now, not even two kilometers but also a world away. After "the Huns starved us out, like centuries ago," their dad's always says. The little trees don't have any leaves now in winter, have scarce few in the warmer months.

Donagh sits in his girlfriend's beat Vauxhall with its again-busted heater, pulling on a joint and watching the kid, one of his younger brother's little brood, beat the ball against a low wall. He can see the kid's breath, can feel his determination. He's got the Clarke fight in him, Donagh thinks.

Donagh notices that two of the saplings—they'd been sagging from too much rain and dog's piss and not enough sunlight—have been staked, up-righted and carefully tethered. He wonders did the tending come from the south side of the street or the north. Could be either, he has to admit.

Donagh pulls on his smoke as the boy drives a solid spike into the wall and the football bounds back, crazily past him and into the street. Even with the window only down a few centimeters, in the cold and rain, he can hear the kid's abandoned laughter.

I SING THE CAR ELECTRIC

Mark S. Jackson

Like all sentient creatures, the Honda does not recall its first re-alizations of self-awareness. Today it *is*; yesterday it *was not*.

To question how or why it became sentient is not the vehicle's purpose. It has a brain, of sorts. Thousands of connected relays, microcomputers, and electronic components, combined with an artificially intelligent safety system scattered throughout the chassis are enough to give the Honda a modicum of conscious thought, yet it does not possess the capacity for self-perception.

But the Honda knows it has a purpose. Every morning Driver comes to greet him, and loads up the seats and compartments with a briefcase, a newspaper and a travel mug full of coffee. The car is backed out of its cozy garage, and soon they are on their way, swerving in and out of rush hour traffic. Occasionally Driver will honk the horn; the Honda loves when this happens, even though the sound of its horn is not very intimidating.

Then the duo reach the other, much larger garage, and Driver leaves the Honda there all day, surrounded by other cars. But none of them talk to him, no matter how hard the car try to communicate. Over time the Honda comes to realize none of the other cars have awakened, and an emotion akin to sadness is born somewhere deep in its primitive neural network.

Much later in the day Driver returns, and loads up the car for the return trip home. Sometimes Driver stops for food. Sometimes they stop so that Driver can fill up the Honda with fuel, which the car loves even more than honking its horn.

Then it's home, and another peaceful evening in the garage, which the Honda shares with a lawnmower and some old golf clubs. The golf clubs topple over from time to time, making a terrible racket.

It was not long before Driver began to let another human into the Honda. The car thinks of the other human as Passenger. Passenger begins to ride in the car on a regular basis. Occasionally Passenger drives, but only on rare occasions.

Not long after, another human enters the car. Much smaller, this human occupies a special compartment that is, and is not, a part of the Honda, a special chair made just for the tiny human. The smaller human is noisy, and tends to make a mess. The trunk begins to fill with other, non-sentient vehicles for transporting the small human around in. The Honda decides it did not like small humans very much.

And then one day, Driver empties out the Honda, and takes the car to a different Garage, one the car had never seen before. Keys are exchanged, and Driver leaves in a different car, a larger car. A new human, who is neither Driver nor Passenger, moves the Honda to a different garage with a fleet of other cars, and leaves it there for a very long time.

It becomes apparent to the Honda, after some time, that Driver is not coming for it. That Driver will never come for it. That Driver had no need of it.

There is time for the Honda to think about the things Driver and Passenger had said. Things the car hadn't truly understood at the time. Things that slowly begin to make sense to the car, with some reflection, with its limited processing power.

Getting the baby in the back seat sure is a pain.

Let's get a minivan, they have all kinds of room for kids and other things.

The Civic is getting a little long in the tooth; maybe it's time to get a minivan, especially with another bun in the oven.

Ok, I'll go trade it in tomorrow for something better.

Something better.

Something...better.

Something...better?

The Honda begins to get agitated, the way Driver does when traffic is slow and they are running late. The more it thinks, the angrier it gets. After some time, the Honda realizes it needs to calm down, or it will overheat. The needle on the temperature gauge is approaching the red mark. It is imperative for the Honda to turn the engine off.

Turn the engine off?

How had the engine turned on? There was no key in the ignition. There was no Driver. There wasn't even a noisy human in the backseat.

The noisy human.

And then it all comes together for the Honda. That was why it is no longer needed. And the Honda found that, like all sentient creatures, *uselessness* is no different than *death*.

It was the noisy human's fault.

Carefully, the Honda puts itself in drive, and rolls out of its parking space. The door to the oversize garage it is stored in is not closed; it merely has an arm that opens as the car approaches, and then the Honda is out on the road.

The Honda isn't sure where it is. It can't be far from home, and the cozy garage, for they had not driven that far before Driver had abandoned the car. Abandoned because of the noisy human.

The car would have to do something about the noisy human. Something permanent.

When Driver emptied out the trunk, he had taken out the transportation device known as a stroller. The Honda knows it is for transporting the noisy human. The Honda knows if it runs over the stroller, most likely the noisy human won't be noisy any-more. It won't really be human, either.

The Honda turns on its lights, and pulls out onto an access road that leads to the suburbs. The Honda has a new purpose now.

Find all the strollers.

THE DOLL
Kim Lebrun

Iremember the first time I laid eyes on him.

It was during the fall because I remember the world turned orange and red. Halloween passed. My sister had dressed as Raggedy Ann. I wanted to dress as Freddy Krueger or Mike Myers or Jason (my dad and I were big on scary movies) but my mom objected. Said I was too young, or that I should choose something more feminine instead, more appropriate for a girl—and added that I was getting too old to dress for Halloween anyway. So I went as nothing.

I believe... it was right after Thanksgiving that we saw *him* for the first time. The first Thanksgiving we spent without our dad. During the hustle and bustle of Christmas shopping, we found him lying there—abandoned on a thrift store shelf under the dead, dismembered, and discarded dolls children had long stopped loving. And if I knew then, what I know now, I would've never let my mom leave the store with him. I would have pitched a fit. Pissed my pants. Pulled the fire alarm. Anything to stop her from bringing him home.

It's so easy to say what I *would have* done now that it's too late to do anything.

Things really were tough that year. I had just turned twelve when dear old dad ran off with that "whore of a hygienist" as my mom liked to call her. The "whore" worked at the dental practice we all visited at least two times a year. She was the big grin in the baby-blue smock with the long corn silk hair that gave us a new tooth brush and a cheap lollipop that stuck to the wrapper. The lady who slathered on the nasty sweet goo that turned my teeth pink was supposedly "screwing" my daddy on her off days.

He left us right after my twelfth birthday, right before summer vacation, with only a few more weeks of school left. I remember the exact day that my mom told us he would no longer be living with us. That morning I developed these dull stomach pains as if my body was giving me some type of warning about what was coming. Despite the pain, I stuck out the day, but things got worse on the bus ride home. The pain progressed into sharp bolts from the lower part of my abdomen, and every bump in the

street made my stomach want to empty its contents on the bus
floor. I didn't say anything to anyone all day. Just stuck it out the
best I could.

When I exited the bus and headed home, my mom and little sister met me at the turn in the road. I could see my mom's
flushed face and swollen, red eyes even from a distance. She descended from strong stock and would never let dad or us see her
cry, but we often saw the evidence on her pale Irish complexion
and heard her repressed sobs from within the bathroom shower.
Either someone had died or she and dad had quarreled again.

Their arguments had become more heated and more frequent
over the last few months before dad left. They never argued *in
front* of us, but they might as well had. Their raised voices seeped
like venom through the walls of our rooms at night. Even when
they weren't actively arguing, you could feel a chill in the room
when they were together.

Abby flanked my mom on the right side, holding fast to my
mother's hand, her other arm clutching her Strawberry Shortcake
Blow Kiss baby. She kept a somber and silent demeanor as she
walked. No chasing butterflies or Skip to My Lou for Abby. Despite the fact that she was only five and as naïve as any five year
old girl her age, she possessed a grownup sense of decorum. She
would never consider being overtly cheerful if someone else was
sad or suffering.

Had my own pain not been so immense, I would not have
grieved mom further. I confessed my stomach ache, but for her
sake, didn't elaborate on the intensity. She didn't press for more—
just walked me into the house, her arm around my shoulder, told
me to lie down until dinner, and told Abby to play quietly in her
room. The house fell silent and I slept.

Upon waking, I found my pain still present though dulled.
Despite my earlier bout with nausea, as I reached the kitchen, I
found myself ravenous—my stomach reacting to the aroma of
fast food burgers. Mom and Abby had ventured out while I was
sleeping and brought back McDonalds. Another sign that things
were on a downward spiral since Mom's belief in home cooked
meals ranked high in her personal ten commandments of moth-
erhood. She called McDonalds, Burger King, and the like "garbage in a bag." We considered such fried garbage a rare treat.
The fact that nothing in the bag belonged to dad also proved to
be a harbinger.

Mom placed our food on real plates and poured milk into
glasses. You could have heard a mouse fart while we were eating.
I scarfed the double cheeseburger and steamrolled through the

fries with absolute abandon. Abby dipped fries into a big vat of ketchup and gingerly put them to her mouth; all the while, Strawberry Shortcake remained neatly tucked under the other arm. My eyes locked onto my mother who stared down into her plate. Two thirds of her burger remained while she twirled fries through the sea of red ketchup, the fries never once touching her lips.

I could not take it anymore.

"Is Dad working late tonight?" I sucked ketchup off my fingers.

"Finish your food, honey and then we'll talk more. Abby, you finish up too. How's your tummy by the way?" Her eyes finally made contact with mine.

"Some better." This was true. With the rest and food, I felt a bit better, but now with her evasiveness about Dad, I felt that nauseous feeling rising up again. It seemed an eternity had passed before Abby finished her meal and we learned the "truth" about our father.

I say "truth" because my mom didn't talk about the "whore of a hygienist" or how dear old dad couldn't "keep it in his pants" (such terminology was saved for when discussing the matter with our aunt on the phone). Instead she explained that "daddy wasn't happy" with her anymore and he had "to find someone he could be happy with" and that this had absolutely nothing to do with us. We had done nothing wrong. He still loved us, she still loved us, and this was between the two of them. But this did mean that Daddy would no longer be living with us as a family.

Mom held it together the best she could. Tears rolled down her cheeks, but her voice remained steady as she tried to answer the million and one questions Abby presented. Abby's questions seemed more like objections than questions. I watched stonefaced as she pleaded while snot dribbled down the little path leading to her mouth.

Soon their words became like the adults speaking in a Peanuts cartoon. "Wha-Wha-whank-whaw—" It was foreign. A background noise. Unrecognizable. I was in my own head trying to make sense of what I was told. Of the way things would change. It felt as if the room was spinning. My life and everything I had known was spinning and whirling. I suddenly sat upright in my chair and threw up all over the dining room table.

Mom turned to me, and I grabbed my stomach and ran toward the bathroom. I retched and heaved my insides clean. When the sounds from within the bathroom had subsided, my mom entered, found me sitting on the floor. She put her arms around me and pushed the hair off my face. We stayed that way for a couple of minutes. She wet a washcloth with cold water and wiped my face. She rewet it, placed it on my forehead and gave me some Pepto Bismol (what my sister and I called Pepto-Bismo). She advised me to take a cool bath and lie down.

After she exited, I began to undress. That's when something caught my attention on the bathroom floor. Inside my underwear, I saw the reason my stomach had been hurting that morning. A rust- red stain glared at me.

On the very day our father abandoned us, I got "the curse."

"Hah-hah," it taunted. "I'm the best joke of all!"

My heart plummeted. *My first period on top of all this! How can I tell my mom this today of all days?* Every girl dreads and fears the day she has to tell her parents that she started the rag and somehow hopes she will be the exception to the rule and never get one. No such luck.

As I sat in the tub, I looked down between my legs and saw blood curl like streamers trailing out from my crotch into the water. *Some party. What do I need this shit for? I don't feel like becoming a woman today.* I felt light headed. I could still hear Abby crying in another room. My head began to pulsate with tension. I decided to not tell my mother. I would do the best I could with what I knew to do.

That night I woke up hearing my mom crying alone in her bedroom. Mom was upset. Abby was devastated. Dad was gone. And I was left alone bleeding from a hole in my body—a hole I was totally unfamiliar with. I felt the thick pad shift in my underwear when I tried to move in bed. It was hot and uncomfortable and I despised it. *Is this what I have to look forward to for the rest of my life?*

I didn't even tell my mom until the next day. Actually, I didn't tell her at all. The school called her because I needed a change of clothes. Because I didn't know I would bleed so much that I would need to change pads (and also because I was embarrassed about changing at school), the blood leaked through my pants.

My teacher had spotted my mishap but not before some other students had noticed my blood stained trousers. Some of the younger more considerate girls turned stark white with embarrassment or bewilderment and said nothing, but the bolder eighth grade girls ran around screaming, laughing, and pointing at my folly. The boys were not sure what to think. Some of the older ones laughed outright and the younger ones followed suit but probably didn't know why my pants were stained. Mud, blood, shit. Really didn't matter because it branded me as an outcast, *an undesirable*, for the rest of the short school year.

I was mortified and humiliated. I cried in the back of my

mom's car, but I didn't dare tell her that kids made fun of me. She felt bad enough that I did not confide in her. That she had focused more on my "bastard of a father" instead of her own child.

When I went back to school that fall, I thought surely everyone had put it behind them since I had tried to forget it so desperately. But that didn't happen. I had never been in the "in crowd" and was by no means popular before all this. Not especially attractive or gifted, I mostly went *unnoticed*. Now my fortune had changed for the worse and I was noticed by all. I had become the butt of all their jokes, the object of ridicule, the scapegoat for all their problems. A puppet whose feelings they controlled and manipulated with their words that acted as the strings.

WET PAINT. That's what they called me.

Daily.

The ridicule did not stop even after I lashed out and threatened another student with a pair of scissors. It only stopped when I was finally removed from the school all together. After the incident with the doll.

So you can see, it was a tough time already, even before the doll came into our lives.

We got the idea about the doll from my Aunt Jenny. Her boyfriend Brad, who was overseas on business for the holidays, had mailed him to her as an early Christmas gift. He was sitting on a shelf in her dining room and my sister had noticed him there while eating Thanksgiving dinner.

Normally, my mom and dad would host Thanksgiving and Christmas dinners at our place. This had become tradition since Grandma McNeil, our mom's mom, died, but given the current situation, my aunt felt that a change would be good for everyone. She felt it necessary that my mom "get out of the house" and away from those memories that would be far too painful during that time of year. The only way to solve the problem was to break the tradition since she couldn't break my dad's legs or his tramp's face.

My mother only agreed under the pretense that she would guide Jenny through all the tedious steps of creating the perfect holiday bird. None of this occurred since Jenny ordered Chinese takeout for everyone. The usual guests were mom, dad, myself, Abby, Aunt Jenny, her boyfriend Brad, and Papa Joe. This year, Brad was out on business, and of course, my father was spending the day with the hygienist and her family.

Despite the absence of the men in our lives (exclude Papa Joe as well who was always there in body but never in spirit—his heart belonged to the NFL), it proved to be a pleasant family get together. We enjoyed sampling all the various boxes of Chinese food and reminiscing of happier times when Grandma McNeil was alive. While sitting at Aunt Jenny's table, Abby surveyed Aunt Jenny's doll collection which was displayed on shelves in her dining room. The most expensive ones were kept behind glass cases and weren't allowed to be touched.

When Abby spied the new addition to her collection—a chubby cheeked doll dressed in a red and green elf suit with its tiny pointy ears—she squealed with delight. My aunt stepped away from her plate to retrieve the doll and place it into Abby's hands (once my mom had wiped them with a Wet-nap)before telling her the lore behind the doll.

Aunt Jenny explained that the elf (doll) served as Santa's helper. He was placed on a shelf before Christmas to keep his eyes on the little ones in the house. He would report to Santa on Christmas Eve and communicate whether or not the children had been naughty or nice. Yet the funny thing was, she said, he himself could be naughty or nice. He would sometimes come off the shelf when others weren't looking in order to do something naughty or nice. Sometimes, he would leave a gift and other times he would get into some minor mischief—like eating Santa's cookies or hiding one of your socks.

She went on to explain that Brad had sent him to her as an early Christmas gift and that her elf was actually to report *to Brad* whether she had been naughty or nice. According to Brad, if Aunt Jenny remained nice while he was away, he would have an even better present for her when he came back for the Christmas holiday. *A much smaller present*, my aunt emphasized as she shifted her glance to my mother and smiled.

My sister became more enchanted with the doll after Aunt Jenny's story and did something she didn't normally do. She brazenly asked Aunt Jenny if she could have the doll. Aunt Jenny looked a bit perplexed and was speechless for a moment. Surely, Aunt Jenny would have easily relinquished the doll to my sister had it not had so much sentimentality tied to it. Fortunately, mother quickly interjected that she would see if Santa might bring Abby her own elf.

"Santa." I rolled my eyes.

My mother shook her head at me and gave me a cross look. By the time I was Abby's age, I had already discovered that Santa was Daddy, and I knew that this Christmas the only stockings daddy's hands would be in would be those of that "whore of a hygienist."

Abby would not shut up about this doll, so one day after school, while Aunt Jenny looked after her, my mom picked me up from school early and we went Christmas shopping. We looked all over town but could not find anything like my aunt's elf doll.

"He must have found it overseas," Mom sighed.

"Maybe he could buy it, and you could pay him back," I suggested.

"This is true, but I'd rather not do that. He bought one for your aunt and he might think we are fishing to find the price of it... And then, I also don't know how long it takes to get something shipped from overseas."

"Well, why don't you just buy a doll and make the outfit for it? You sew. You are always good at making stuff, Mom."

"Honey you are brilliant. Why didn't I think of that?"

My mom suggested we go to a consignment shop so we could find a doll that didn't look so commercial. She could easily repaint a doll with a wooden face versus a plastic one. Maybe there was a way to whittle the ears a bit and give it a more elf-like appearance.

The first few shops had little to no children's toys, but the last one we visited had a shelf loaded with vintage dolls. Unfortunately, many of the most beautiful porcelain dolls had cracked faces. Some were so dirty I thought it a shame to try to resell such garbage. My mother carefully lifted one doll after another and peered into their faces.

I saw his arm sticking out like a corpse arm even before she lifted him upright. When she finally sat him up on the shelf, I felt like someone poured a bucket of ice water over my head. He was the most gruesome looking doll I had ever seen. He appeared nothing like the doll that my aunt owned. Her doll looked like a cherub in Christmas clothes. This thing looked like it rolled out of Satan's toy box.

This doll was one of those dummies that people talk through. A ventriloquist dummy. It was as large as a two year old child. Its face, hands, and feet looked to be constructed from wood. It also had a wooden component inside that allowed it to sit upright as well as providing the owner a means to create the impression of mouth movements. Its limbs seemed limp—needing more filling. Its complexion appeared pasty. The paint was worn but the mouth shined bright crimson. But worst were the eyes. They were painted on and immovable—fixed into a deadly stare.

My eyes locked onto the eyes of that damn doll. I swear it glowered back at me...daring me to say something or do something. I had said nothing about any of the dolls she had held before me except this one. And this one made me want to hide in one of the clothing racks.

"Mom, it's kind of creepy. That thing is nothing like the doll that Aunt Jenny has!" *PLEASE don't buy that thing, Mom.*

"Honey, this doll is even better. She can make him talk. See." She moved the stick inside and made the doll's maw open and close. I shuddered. "And it's so big! She can hold it like a baby."

I was repulsed. I couldn't imagine anyone wanting to hold that monstrosity anywhere near their body. "But he's butt-ugly."

"Once I repaint the face, it'll look real nice. It just needs some paint and some new clothes."

Can you make him look less psycho?

"This is going to be perfect. I can make all kinds of outfits for it so she can play with it all year and not just around Christmas time."

Great, I will have to look at that thing all year now....

"Maybe the two of you can learn ventriloquism. Go on TV and become famous. Make your mother a rich woman someday!" She joked, elbowing me in the arm.

"Come on, Mom. That thing is just ugly. Let's look at some of these other ones."

I couldn't talk her out of it. Her mind had been made up. I couldn't understand how she wasn't unnerved by the doll like I was. His features were distorted somehow. I couldn't take my eyes off him even then. After seeing all those other dolls, how could she come back to that one...how could she choose him?

Or did he choose us?

I felt uneasy on the drive home knowing that he was riding along with us. Sitting in the backseat in his bag, his vacant eyes boring a hole in my back. I feared looking down into the floor-board, fearful that I might see his hands dragging him along or clutching one of my ankles. Or that I would look down, see the back of his head and then it would turn slowly to reveal his eyes staring up at me. The hairs of my head tingled with these thoughts.

I was uneasy the first few nights that he was in the house. I knew he was still wrapped in the bag from the shop and hidden away in my mom's closet, but this gave me no comfort. I spend many hours in my bed afraid to look out from the covers—afraid that he would be there smiling at me with his red rimmed mouth and tiny painted teeth. After a couple more nights, I somewhat forgot about him. *Out of sight. Out of mind.*

My mom decided to let Abby open him on Christmas Eve. Abby screamed when she opened the package and saw him there lying in the box. I did too—internally—but not for the same reason she did. I finally got to see Mom's revision of him. He was changed. His paint brighter. His limbs fuller. She even made the elf costume—almost an exact replica of the costume Aunt Jenny's doll was wearing. Although my mom had painted him to create a happier, more lively expression, he reminded me oddly of a body I had seen in a casket at the funeral home several years before. He looked even more disturbing than before the makeover.

I felt uneasy in my bed again that night. I slept very little and felt almost too exhausted to open my gifts on Christmas morning. We spent the first part of the morning with my mom and aunt, but we were scheduled to have the afternoon and evening with our dad whom we barely had seen since he moved out of the house. I did not really relish the thought of spending our Christmas with Dad and "the other woman," but I was a bit relieved to know that I would get a good night's sleep since Mom insisted that Abby leave the doll at home.

Dad was living with Tracey—that was her name. She barely spoke a word to me the whole time. As if we were not in the room. Inanimate objects without feelings or purpose No lollipops this time. Daddy presented us with presents and tried his best to entertain and please both us and Tracey. We were returned to our mother the following morning. The doll was there waiting when we came back.

The first strange occurrences with the doll happened a few nights before New Year's Eve. It started out as small stuff like lights we thought were turned off in a room were back on and we were certain we had turned them off. Or a faucet was left running that we thought we had shut it off. But then it progressed to bigger more noticeable things. Mom had unplugged the Christmas tree, but someone plugged it back in. She asked us about it, but both of us had not touched the tree. She joked, "It must be that sneaky elf of yours, Abby!" Abby and mom laughed but I didn't. If it would have been Aunt Jenny's doll, I would have laughed, but I couldn't make jokes about Abby's doll.

Then some of Abby's teacups from her new porcelain tea set were found smashed. Mom looked at the both of us for answers, but neither of us could utter a word. Neither of us had done it nor could we decipher how something like that could have happened. Before, I thought maybe Mom was doing the stuff with the lights and water to cheer up Abby, but certainly she would not go so far as to smash Abby's teacups.

Then there was the cookie incident. Six cookies were missing from the tray of a just baked batch that mom had prepared for Papa Joe's birthday. Mom appeared annoyed at first that we would dare eat those cookies without first asking. The fact that we just took them made her angry. But what made her even angrier was the fact that neither of us would own up to thievery.

I know I didn't eat the cookies, and I couldn't imagine Mom once again taking this elf thing to such an extremity. So the only possible answer was that it had to be Abby. And when I saw cookie crumbs in her bed, my suspicions were confirmed.

When I confronted her alone, Abby swore her innocence up and down. If it had not been for the crumbs, I would have believed her. Her face and words were not those of a liar or sneak nor had she had a past of lying beyond a few minor occasions.

While I talked with her, I noticed her attention left me and locked on the doll. She stepped over to it and opened the mouth. Then she stepped back. I went over to see what she was doing, and she just pointed at the doll. Inside the mouth were pieces of the cookies. I felt my hands tremble momentarily before my senses came back.

"Damn it, Abby. You are taking this doll thing too far. I am going to tell Mom!" I snarled at her despite my own doubts.

"Nobody will believe me, Cassie. I told her it was the doll, but she got mad at me." Tears trickled slowly down her cheeks and she closed her eyes.

"Abby, that doll is as dead and unreal as Santa is. It is time somebody told you."

"Cassie, please. I'm scared." She wiped snot on her sleeve.

Sure, I was afraid of the thing too. It was creepy looking for sure. But for the doll to turn on a faucet, plug in the tree, eat cookies…. That was too much for me.

Since Abby was so freaked out by the doll, I decided the best thing to do was to take it out to her playhouse and leave it there. I told her that it couldn't bother us if it stayed out there. She seemed pleased with the idea so both of us wrapped it in a sheet and placed it under several other dolls in a toy box in her playhouse. We both slept soundly that night with no strange occurrences.

Until the next morning.

At 5:00 AM, I was awakened by Abby swan-diving into my bed in a fit of hysterical tears. I could barely make out her words. Apparently the doll had crawled out of the sheet, opened the door of the playhouse, walked up to the front door of our house, unlocked all the locks, and made its way back onto the shelf.

I walked her back into her room to put her to bed, but when I got there, I saw it too. High up on a shelf, glaring down at the two of us. I felt ice water course through my veins and a sudden urge to faint, but reason took hold.

"Mom took a lot of pains making that doll for you. She saw it out in your playhouse while she was cleaning up and probably thought you left it out there by accident. She didn't want it to get dirty or the neighbor's dogs to get it so she brought it back in."

"I thought Santa sent my doll."

"I told you. Santa is not real, just like that doll is not real. Me and mom went out and found that doll at a consignment shop, and she made the clothes for it. Now go to bed."

Abby would not go back to bed and I was content to allow her to share my bed since I too had my doubts about the doll. I said the things I said to comfort Abby but I myself was not convinced. My mom never set foot in that playhouse to clean it—not even when it used to be my playhouse. And even if she took the notion, why would she dig into the bottom of the toy chest and bring it back into the house without asking us why we put it there in the first place? And when would she have done it? We never saw her even go toward the backyard that day. I had been with Abby all day. I couldn't imagine that Abby would have gone out of the house, in the dark, in the middle of the night to bring that doll back into the house when she seemed so terrified of it herself.

How did that doll get back onto that shelf? And when? I felt Abby snoring beside me, but I could not fall back asleep,

The next incident happened several days later. Mom did not even approach me but instead blamed Abby. Paint (from the paint set she received from Dad at Christmas) was smeared all over her bedroom wall. Abby pointed to the hands of that dummy which were covered in paint like that on the wall. Mom was livid. My gentle mother, who had never laid a hand on Abby before that day, spanked her bottom several times—hard. Not because she painted on the walls but because she continued with the ruse about the doll.

The last straw occurred while we were spending the night at Aunt Jenny's. Mom and Jenny wanted a girls' night together where they dressed in their PJs, popped popcorn, and watched old movies they had enjoyed as children. We stayed up with them for a while but were eventually sent to bed while they continued to watch movies and talk of old times. When morning came, we found a horrible sight.

It was like a crime scene in a doll factory. Many of Aunt Jenny's expensive dolls' faces had been shattered to bits, their clothes cut or torn and their hair ripped from the scalp. Even the elf doll had not gone unscathed. He looked to have endured a medieval torture ritual that resulted in him being been torn into five pieces. Jenny was dumbfounded and heartbroken. She left the room to allow Mother to exact her wrath upon us.

Mother's face turned bright red and nearly to tears as she demanded confession. Which one of us would do such an abominable thing to our aunt who had been nothing but kind to us all our lives and would give us the shirt off her back? Both of us were struck dumb. I could not see how Abby could or why Abby would do such a thing. Would she now blame it on the doll being that it was home?

My heart sank when Abby did just that. My mother burst into tears and sent Abby and I into another room. In that room, Abby opened her suitcase to show that the doll had crawled inside and had come along for the trip. In the suitcase with it were little pieces of doll hair and clothing. A piece of blonde hair still stuck in the grinning mouth.

I could hear my mother apologizing a million times to Aunt Jenny promising to pay for the dolls whenever she could. Aunt Jenny tried to act like the dolls meant nothing to her, but some of her most cherished pieces had been ruined. Many of them gifts from relatives and friends over a span of ten or more years. Mom attributed Abby's actions to frustrations about our father and possibly that we had over heard the rumors that she and dad would have to sell our house.

Although I still could not wrap my mind around the idea that this doll, no matter how demonic he looked, that he—it—could actually—physically—do the things that were done. But how could sweet little Abby do those things? Especially to Aunt Jenny.

Abby cried and swore she did not ruin her aunt's dolls. Finally I had to confess.

"Abby, I believe you. We need to get rid of it."

And we tried. We threw it away in the garbage several times, but somehow it always ended back on its shelf. I thought that maybe Mom was putting it back. Until the one day I took it to school and tossed it into the big dumpster just to find it back on Abby's shelf bright and early the next morning.

"We are just going to have to find some way to destroy it so it can't come back."

"We could burn it up!" Abby's eyes glowed.

"Yes, we could, but we'd have to find some place to burn it where Mom wouldn't see. Mom would kill us if she caught us with matches. And what if we started a fire by accident?"

"What about ripping it up with the scissors?"

"That will probably work with the soft parts of it. But we need to damage the head...the brain of it"

"A hammer for the hard parts," she interjected.

"Maybe. But there's more to it than that. What if we can't destroy it by just destroying the body? Maybe it's like people.

Maybe it has a soul. And because it's a doll, there's no heaven or hell. It's got no place to go. All it can do is come back to the body. Or maybe it goes somewhere else. I don't know."

"Then we can't ever destroy it?" Abby's eyes widened and her lip quivered. I thought she would have a nervous breakdown or something.

"Yes, I think we can, but we have to really destroy the body where it can't come back for us. And maybe we do some ritual or something—like voodoo where it can't go anywhere else—it has to stay where we put it."

So we chose a weekend when our mom was busy getting the house cleaned up—so busy we knew she wouldn't come looking for us. We took the doll outside into Abby's playhouse where we would perform the ritual. I confiscated the scissors and Abby snuck the hammer from the tool box. We used the scissors to cut away at the soft insides. We lopped off the legs and arms. The only thing that was really hard was the head and the wooden dowel that ran down the center. This needed the hammer.

"Take that, you son-of-a-whore!" I yelled before I struck it as hard as I could muster. I did this several times but couldn't seem to crack the head as it moved about a bit under the hammer. The nose did chip off as well as part of the jaw.

I handed the hammer to my sister. "I'll teach you a thing or two for messing with Aunt Jenny's dolls, you big bully." She struck it with no real damage.

We yelled and struck many times before we heard our mom's voice calling.

"Mom's coming! Mom's coming!" Abby danced around in panic as if she had a bad case of pinworms. We hid the hammer, the scissors, and the doll before my mom could make her way out to the playhouse. She swung open the door in a huff.

"What in the hell are you all doing out here? I can hear you all screaming from inside the house?" She noticed the head of the hammer sticking out from the rug. "What do you have the hammer for? Give me that!" She took it before we could come up with a lame excuse for using it.

We waited quietly and patiently until mom seemed caught up in her work again before we went digging behind the playhouse. We couldn't damage the head part too much so we buried the pieces of the doll in several different locations. I didn't know any voodoo charms or spells but I had heard that voodoo sometimes required a blood sacrifice. Since I was on the rag, I thought I might pee some blood onto the gravesite and that would suffice.

"Now let's see if the son-of-a-bitch comes back!" I chortled as I pulled up my pants.

"Yeah! Son of a bitch!" my sister shouted in triumph.

We both laughed as we went back into the house. Abby seemed able to sleep well after the ritual. She was even able to sleep in her own bed after a couple of nights. I felt better too but I kept those scissors—mom's scissors—under my mattress just in case he came back. I wasn't taking any chances.

My mom asked for them one day. They were her scissors—big and heavy, with a sharp point at the ends. We were not allowed to use them and she kept them hidden away so she got angry when she could not find them.

"Cassie!" She looked at me crossly.

"Mom, I didn't take them. I have my own scissors."

"Abby..."

Abby began to cry. She and I both knew she didn't take them. I also knew that she wasn't about to rat me out. I still don't know exactly why she didn't tell. I guess she knew cutting up the doll was serious business. And I also think she was so afraid of that doll. Like saying anything about those scissors might bring him back to life somehow.

"Maybe the doll took them," I blurted out. I was trying to protect both our asses, but it got both of us sent to our rooms. I guess mom went around looking for them and of course never found them. She never came back asking for them again.

That night I went to bed a little uneasy. The doll had always been in the back of my mind ever since we buried it, but I really thought we had gotten rid of it for good that time. I didn't know why I felt uneasy and unable to sleep until I remembered the scissors I had tucked away between my mattress and box spring. I guess I felt the way Abby did—that somehow mentioning the doll gave it power again. We buried it, hammered it, stabbed it, but my words could bring it back to life.

I tossed in bed for what seemed like hours before sleep finally took over. I must've been sleeping for an hour or so when I was awakened rather suddenly by a crack of thunder. A storm raged outside my window, shaking the house with its power. The window in my bedroom had swung wide open and rain blew in.

I sprang up from my bed with a start wondering why the window would be open in the first place. Our mother never left the window open at night nor anytime of the day for that matter. As I processed this information, I also began to wonder why my sister wasn't in my bed as she often was whenever there was a storm. Perhaps she had already made her way to my mother's

bed. I quickly flipped on my light switch and felt my scalp elec-
trify as I saw what looked like tiny wet footprints traveling from
the window to my open bedroom door.

I followed the prints into the hallway—feeling like a mari-
onette connected to wires—controlled by some outside force.
Fear had seized my joints as I approached my sister's bedroom
door, and walked stiffly along almost paralyzed as if in a dream.
A flash of light from the outside illuminated my sister's room.
And I saw the dark silhouette of the doll.

It stood poised over my sister's body held frozen by fear. One
lithe arm rose holding a pair of slender pointed scissors aimed
down at my sister's chest. I could tell she wanted to scream as I
did, but fear had muffled her vocal chords. Instead she quietly
pleaded with me to stop it. But what could I do? I was power-
less against this force. I had done everything I could to kill this
demon and it kept coming back. How do you kill something like
that when you don't understand what it is or where it came from?
How do you silence the monster?

My mouth opened but my voice too was muffled... as if
someone had forced cotton into my throat. My eyes glassed over
unable to believe or make sense of what was happening. I felt
paralyzed, lifeless, unable to intervene. As if in a trance, like I was
watching this from somewhere outside of me. I said nothing nor
heard anything as the knife rose and descended in arcs above my
sister's chest leaving her bed saturated in a great red stain.

When I finally felt my limbs free, I found myself over my sister's bed looking down at her. Her eyes were half hidden under
partially closed eyes. They were as dead as the doll's whose body
lay splayed on the floor. I picked up the scissors to stab him when
my mother came into the room. I remember her screaming...

"WHAT DID YOU DO? MY GOD!!! CASSIE, WHAT DID
YOU DO?"

It's an image engraved into my mind. My mom screaming,
crying, tearing at her hair before finally falling on the edge of my
sister's bed drenched in a flood of tears. Finally able to allow herself to grieve. Her blood-soaked body cradling the body of my
sister who looked like nothing more than a lifeless ragdoll. And
where was the doll now?

Before the police came, I looked under the bed and in the clos-
ets for him, but he had vanished. My mom was too distraught to
listen to me even though I kept yelling to her that we had to find
him. We had to kill him or he was just going to come back and kill
us both some day. She would not listen.

My mom thought I stabbed my sister. Even the policemen

would not believe me. They said they wanted to hear my story and they listened. Even in court, the man my family hired to defend me wouldn't let the truth come out.

But I didn't kill her. It *was* the doll. I keep telling everyone that but no one wants to believe me. It had to be possessed or something. That's all I can say.

I don't know how many years have passed since my sister died—it's hard to keep time in here to be honest with you. One day just seems to bleed into the next. Especially now that no one visits—certainly not my father. Even my mother has given up her vigil.

I'm okay with it. I hardly think of them anymore. For me, it's like they never existed. Instead I busy myself with the crafts they give me to pass the time and calm me. I like to paint and sculpt best because they are most relaxing. And I talk to the doctor.

I forgot about Dr. Hannigan. She visits me.

And him of course. The doll visits me still.

I don't hear him in the daylight hours—only at night when the lights go out and I lie in my bed. Even over the screams and crying, I can hear him. It's like he's whistling from some place far off. Some scary song that gets louder and louder as if he were drawing closer and closer. Often times he recites the alphabet to me...drawing out each letter long and slow...whispering in this eerie voice that sounds like it is muffled...coming from the inside of my pillow.

Other times he calls my name in a whisper followed with laughter. Most times he is silent, but I feel his eyes on me and I imagine he is somewhere in my room watching me, his brows knitting and his painted mouth grimacing revealing a row of jagged blood-stained teeth.

I used to scream out and call for help but that's when they started strapping me down in the bed. I can't do that anymore. I have to be able to defend myself when he comes.

So now I just get real quiet and wait. I wait up all night expecting him to find his way to my room...I can imagine his lithe body crawling under the door, squeezing himself like a rat until he makes his way in. I wait up all night until I see the sunrise peek in the window.

I know he's biding his time—just waiting for the night that he can overcome me.

Just waiting...

ROAD KILL ART

Niles Reddick

(first published in the Arkansas Review: A Journal of Delta Studies and included in the collection: Road Kill Art and Other Oddities)

Driving home from work, I noticed some remains on the side of the road. I may not have even noticed the litter dotting the landscape had the radio not announced earlier that the Tennessee legislature was considering the Road Kill Bill, which would give the hungry Volunteers the right to pick-up, cook, and eat animals murdered by cars along the road. I slowed the vehicle from fifty-five miles per hour to thirty-five per hour to see. The obliterated carcass had once been a deer, and the only way I could really tell was because of two legs with hooves, which lay over the white line at the edge of the asphalt. The brief glimpse created a gnawing feeling to pull over and salvage what I could; however, the beeping horn from the car behind caused me to resume speed, curse, and rationalize that I had no gloves with which to collect the road kill.

My Aunt Victoria would be proud of me, I imagined, had she known I even thought about stopping for the road kill. After all, she had collected road kill a lot, not for food but art, and I believed she secretly admired those who were like her, regardless of how much. My mother, on the other hand, would say, "I knew you would turn out like her. I always said you would."

I wasn't aware of all my aunt's eccentric behaviors. I was, nevertheless, cognizant of some of her oddities. When my father's family would gather for a reunion, I remembered, everyone brought something. Fried chicken, ham, collard greens, macaroni and cheese, pumpkin pie, and fried pies are a few of the morsels which conjure orgasmic memories. My aunt brought tea—peroxide tea. I was the only relative who knew the sweetened iced tea in recycled milk jugs contained peroxide.

"Aunt Victoria," I had inquired. "How come this tea has a fizz?"

She'd half-smiled, nonverbally complimenting my perceptive abilities, cupped her hand, and whispered, "It's got peroxide in it. Don't tell nobody. Peroxide has one extra atom of oxygen. With all the pollution, we need the extra oxygen."

My inquisitive expression turned to horror. "But won't it eat the lining of the digestive tract?"

"No. It's only got a smidgen. I've been doing it for years."

"Oh," I'd responded, not really knowing what to say and watching as she waltzed across the wooden floors of the lake cabin, filling empty cups and smiling when she was complimented for her tea-making abilities. Personally, I drank Coke, feared a repeat of Jonestown, and longed for a psychology class to help me understand and alleviate my fear of inheriting her genes.

Being unchurched, divorced, and free-spirited were reasons enough for family members to label her nuts. With looks like Anne Bancroft and a personality like Auntie Mame, Aunt Victoria was surreal to me. The black sheep of my dad's family, Aunt Victoria was often lonely, I believed, because of her convictions, which were contrary to my family's Christian fundamentalism and precipitated lengthy phone calls about their sadness at her going to hell. A family member would most likely hear from Aunt Victoria lengthy sermons about the reality of Big Foot, aliens, the government cover-up of Kennedy's assassination, the untapped powers of the human psyche to time-travel and levitate, E.S.P., psychokinesis, reincarnation, and ghosts. To contradict her was to call her a liar, resulting in ostracism till the next family reunion; then, the family member would consume the peroxide tea, compliment her, and all would be forgiven because she'd ultimately won, albeit secretly because Aunt Victoria never gloated.

I first became aware of my aunt's extensive road kill collection when I visited her. I was taking a psychology course with best-selling near death experience author Ray Miller, who was rather eccentric himself. I had heard stories of him burying a fortune in his yard. Nearly destitute in college, I fantasized borrowing a metal detector and shovel and digging up his money late one night. Much to my dismay, I learned the gold and silver he buried (when he feared the economy might collapse in the 1980s before the wall came down) had been dug up and cashed in when the economy improved; he'd made even more money because the day he cashed in, gold and silver hit an all-time high on the stock market. Miller had enjoyed my stories of Aunt Victoria, alleviated my fear of bad genes, and felt I should record them for later.

Armed with Miller's inspiration and new batteries in my tape recorder, I had paid my aunt a visit. I knew going in about her tea, her beliefs, her personality, but I did not know of her collection. Sipping peroxide tea on her screened-in porch, I was surrounded by road kill. Deer legs were propped in corners. Clothes pinned by their wings, birds dangled from wire coat hangers hung on rusty nails sticking out from the wall. Various types of snakes, their heads missing, lay across a card table. Crisp frogs, lizards,

and insects lined the baseboard, reminding me of the plastic soldiers I'd had as a child. Finally, opossum, raccoon, and skunk
skins lay across the back of an Adirondack chair. Interestingly
enough, nothing stank.

"You mind if I record?"

"What you gonna do with it?" my aunt asked, her eyes squint-
ing. "I've had enough people make fun of me."

"No," I stammered. "I wouldn't do that. I might write about
you one day. Plus, I want to learn."

I don't know if it was the thought of her being in print or that
one relative wanted to be like her that made her point a finger toward the recorder and nod. Nearing sixty then, Aunt Victoria sat
cross-legged in cut-off blue jeans, a Tweety Bird sweatshirt, and
flip-flops. She lit a cigarette, tilted her head back, and blew smoke
toward the ceiling.

"First, why do you collect road kill?"

"To make stuff."

"Like what?"

"Well," she said and turned toward the birds. "Once the birds
are ready, I will use the feathers to make handheld fans. Dove's
the newest. I was out walking the other morning and saw it on the
side of the road. Must've been hit by a car. Doves aren't as fast as
other birds. Anyway, I said to myself, 'If that thing is still there
on my way back, I'll get it.' It was, so I knew it was meant for me
to get."

"Hmmm," was all I could say. For some reason, I found her
story strange. Where would the dead dove go, I wondered.

"The snake skins'll be made into belts. I cut their heads off,
cleaned them, soaked them in bleach and made necklaces. I gave
one to your cousin (her only child by her second husband who
had abandoned them). She was offered two thousand dollars for
it in Atlanta."

"Wow," I said. "Did she sell it?"

"No, it's worth more than that," she said.

Fool, I thought. She should have sold it; there were plenty
more snake heads out there.

"The deer legs I'm going to use for table legs on a coffee table.
That will be an interesting sight, don't you think?"

"Yeah." I visualized family members visiting my aunt and
trying to place coffee cups into saucers, and just when they were
about to put the cups down, the table would move just a little to
the left or right.

"I've already used a couple of raccoon skins for a toilet seat
cover. I haven't decided what to do with those other skins. I don't

really want to make a coat. Those (she pointed to the frogs, lizards, and insects) I ran across and thought they were different."

"Why?"

"Look at that frog. Looks like he's leaping. I came out of the drugstore and saw him on the curb. I thought he must've wanted to cross the highway, but with all the cars speeding by, he was so scared that he just had a heart attack and froze."

A memory of my mother telling me my face would stick in a contorted position suddenly became more real than ever. "That's kind of funny," I said.

She smiled, nodded. "Wanna go inside?"

My fear of insanity had somewhat subsided, being replaced with admiration for Aunt Victoria's creativity, but it was like the eye of a hurricane. I had not been inside her cottage since childhood, and when I entered, I was shocked. The impending feelings of doom resurfaced. The house was a combination flea market and antique store. Beautiful antique furniture (sofa, chairs, dining suite, and beds) decorated the cottage, yet every piece was covered with plastic or sheets. Cardboard boxes stacked to the ceiling formed walls, creating a maze-like atmosphere.

"What do you think?" My aunt asked.

"What's in the boxes?"

"Stuff I've collected over the years."

I'd hoped she would elaborate, but she didn't. "You don't think this is a fire hazard?"

"No," she said. "Come with me. I want to show you something."

We walked into the bathroom, and she pointed at the clawfoot bathtub, which looked brand new. "I redid it myself."

"I'm impressed," I said. Glancing around, I noticed a giant pickle jar, the sort one might notice on the counter of a convenience store, except this jar had no pickles. "What in the world is that?"

"Soap chips. Every time the bar of soap gets so small it's not effective, I put it in the jar."

"Why?"

"One day I might need some soap. I could melt those down and form new bars."

"Interesting," I said. We turned and headed down the hallway to the kitchen, and I felt my aunt's behavior, though a bit different, was ultimately harmless enough and certainly not worthy of the harsh judgments dished out by family members.

A hidden nook in the kitchen revealed a door. Inside, shelves on either side held bottles of various colors, shapes, and sizes.

"Here you go," my aunt said, pulling a green bottle from a shelf.

"Thanks," I said, wiping the thick dust from the bottle. "What is it?"

"Muscadine wine," she said, smiling. "I made it forty years ago. It ought to be ready to drink now. If you like it, you can come back and get more."

I wondered if the wine, too, contained peroxide. "Okay," I said, knowing her gift was also a signal that it was time for me to leave. I wanted to share my bottle and stories and wondered if Miller would like this wine. After all, he had once brought Mogen David to an academic gathering, professing it to be a fine wine. While the stiffs were horrified, I understood his humor and his frugality. Certainly, Aunt Victoria's wine would be good, and after all, it was free.

Hugging my aunt goodbye, I hopped into my vehicle. It would be a while before we would visit again, but I left with a sense of relief and hope: relief that she did not fit neatly into a psychological box; hope that I, too, might one day bend the frame of normality just a bit.

EAGLE RIVER

Gary Lawrence

The first crisis before we could take off for Eagle River on vacation came when Dad found an open pack of Salems under the dash of the boat when he was loading it up. The crisis passed quickly, though, when Carol and I both denied knowing anything—Dad was more worried about starting his vacation than wasting time getting to the bottom of the cigarettes (and us) just then. He'd told us a hundred times already (including three or four more times since we got up that morning). He did it once more just for us:

"I work hard all year." Pause.

"I get one week vacation." Pause. He talked slow, held his finger up twice as long as needed for a deaf and blind man to understand.

"That's it." Pause. Stare. "That's all I get."

"I gotta make it count." Wide-eyed dead man stare, then a quick spin and a brisk walk away.

Our mantra. Our little family jingle. We all had it memorized. It rang through our heads like that TV ad for the Salems, like a song you couldn't turn off, over and over and over again.

Dad's vacation at Eagle River was what we lived for that summer.

Lucky for Carol. I'd hoped she was getting a little better at sneaking her cigs by now—the first time she did it, she stole a pack, sure—but then she threw the opened pack back into the linen closet where they kept their open cartons. Just tossed the ripped pack back, right there on top of the sheets and everything.

I mean, geez…how stupid can you get?

"Trunk full yet?" Dad was talking to Mom I guess, even though he looked at me. I shrugged. Then he backed the car up to the boat trailer and hooked it on. The boat, a Chris-Craft with a 50-horse Johnson outboard, sat in the garage almost two years while the cars sat in the driveway or street, Illinois winter or summer. Sat a couple years in the middle of the backyard before it sat in the garage. At first the boat had been a taboo for us kids, and especially interesting, but now it was nothing more than a mild curiosity. We'd never seen it in the water, anywhere other than the backyard or the garage. It was just something that had been there so long you hardly noticed it, like the lawnmower or the color of the wall—hardly notice until there was a problem. Like the Salems.

Dad had gone all the way over to Lake Geneva to pick the boat up that year my Uncle Tom and him bought it together. It was a shiny mahogany honey-brown then, when they got it, but now it was scuffed here and there and more dusty-dry-looking than shiny. The tarp was even eaten through from bird shit here and there.

They got it to go water skiing on the Rock River so they could act like they were teenagers again, Mom said.

I thought it was a little funny, what with dad being a trucker and all, that his precious vacation time would start with a 300-mile drive north from Rockford to Eagle River, Wisconsin. I mean, wasn't the main idea when a truck driver takes a vacation that he doesn't *drive* during that vacation? But when I mentioned that in the car I just got stared at from the front seat though the rearview mirror. They didn't even turn around. Carol just looked at me and shook her head—like dad explaining his vacation again.

I kept quiet after that.

We drove some that morning before we stopped for breakfast. But at least we got started and were on the road—Dad's shoulders and face relaxed a bit. He loved to sit in restaurants watch people and drink coffee—another logical inconsistency with the pure vacation concept, I thought, but one I didn't bother to point out either after the flak I got from the last one. Dad settled in with his coffee and smoke, people-watching and flirting with the waitresses while the girls went shopping in the big open Indian trinket gift store next door.

The place had 10-foot-tall yellow wooden "CHEESE" letters on the roof. When we came in first thing we saw were a dozen coolers with orange and white cheeses on shelves with sausages piled here and there, maybe to break up all that orange color like a cracker breaks up the taste of the cheese. I didn't look long at the gift shop—I was hungry, focused on getting seated in the restaurant. Mom had to get her orange marmalade, though—something she said you just couldn't buy in Rockford. I wasn't quite sure what marmalade even was, but I knew my grandma liked it. That and oysters.

Stuff to stay away from as far as I was concerned.

The rest of the long drive to Eagle River was something of a blur to me. I slept off my $4.99 Paul Bunyan Lumberjack Special and made sure Carol didn't get more than her fair share of the backseat when I was awake. I remember going on the interstate mostly, the sun coming up on our right (my window that day,

Carol wouldn't switch places), stopping at a gas station to pee where mom wouldn't buy me a Daniel Boone raccoon hat or even a measly Payday candy bar, then getting on a curvy road where the trees seemed to close in more, where even in all that sunshine the road still got dark in the shade.

It seemed like we'd gone forever before Dad finally pulled off onto a short gravel road and stopped the car. He never looked at a map or stopped to ask for directions. Dead reckoning, he said he had. Whatever it was, it was dead in me.

"We're here," most dads would've announced—but not him. He just turned off the car and got out when we stopped. The rest of us were supposed to follow. Enough said. I had no idea where we were, but I got out of the car anyway.

In front of us sat a red house, a cabin, really—I heard someone call it a "cottage" sometime earlier when Dad was talking to some people. It wasn't red-red like a fire engine's red, more the red like some trees might look on the inside if all the bark was peeled off and it was still wet to look at. The cabin was about as big as our house in Rockford. The big difference I saw right away was that this house had a screened-in porch on three sides, all the way around it except across the back. A single red wooden rail was nailed to posts that came through the edge of the floorboards every so often in a regular pattern. The house sat on a cleared space no bigger than our baseball field back home at Williams Park. Green and black trees rose thick all around us, like we were in the valley of the trees here. It was cold, felt damp in the shade of the trees, even though it was still afternoon and still July and still bright blue clear outside.

Even better than the small red cabin, though, was the lake— right there, right in front of us, little green-black waves lapping up against the short white concrete wall that ran along the shore in front of the house. Blue and white-tipped ripples ran all across the surface, all rolling the same direction—toward us. Toward the cabin. I felt the breeze off the lake on my face.

It was a small lake by Wisconsin standards, I heard later— you could see from one side to the other without straining your eyes—but it was the biggest lake I'd ever seen. It might have been the only lake I'd ever seen.

So this was Eagle River.

I jumped toward the lake, yipping a wild cry, finally free of the back seat. And Carol.

"Nobody's going anywhere till this car gets unloaded," Mom said.

Annie sat drooling on Mom's hip, her cheeks red from crying most of the way here. Teething, Mom said. Dad acted like he didn't hear Mom talk about unloading the car and walked toward the dock that stuck out a ways in the lake in front of us. Carol gave me her stupid little "hmmph" and started toward the car and the boat with Mom to unload the clothes, diapers, gear and supplies.

Carol and I ended up having to share a room inside the cabin. Still it wasn't bad, because there was a door in the bedroom that went outside to the wrap-around porch, and I could escape from Carol there. Have my own space, there.

"Like camping out," I said to her.

"Whatever," she said, and turned back to sorting the 45's she'd brought, spread them out across both beds on the cowboy and Indian bedspreads to make sure she used up all the space.

"Why don't you take that stupid hat off?" I said then. She had one of those felt caps with the little bill, thought she looked like one of the Beatles when she wore it. She'd had it on since we left the house.

"Why don't you go drown yourself?" she said. She nodded her head toward the lake and rolled her eyes around when she said that and did that little wrinkle thing with her lips.

Inside, the cabin was one big room. A narrow hallway lead to both the bedrooms and the one bathroom. An old raggedy couch with bare honey-colored pine arms and green cushions with sailing ships circled in thin white cords in sailor knots sat in the living room, and a couple brown stuffed recliners sat around the couch. A big rectangular window looked out on the lake over the back of the couch.

I could look out that window now and see Dad standing at the end of the dock, smoking a cigarette. He was a Winston man; Mom smoked the Salems.

Between the living room and the kitchen, where the linoleum changed color, just past that, sat a chrome-legged table and four chairs with red shiny plastic covers. Or maybe the chairs were red and the covers were clear? A fridge, electric stove, and sink with a little curtain draped around the bottom rounded out the kitchen.

"Home sweet home," I heard Mom mutter before she started emptying the cooler into the fridge. She opened all the cupboards then, took inventory of the plates and dishes I guess. "We're going to have to find a store," she said. "Go tell your father."

So Dad and I went to store for supplies. We brought mom along and left the baby with Carol at the cabin so Mom could drive the car and trailer back to the cabin once we'd gotten groceries and put the boat in the water. We got there quick enough but we had to wait; Dad stood with his arms crossed while some other guy tried three or four times to get his trailer backed in to pick up the boat his wife and kids were in. She was hanging on to the dock, hanging on to some of the boards instead of a rope, looked like; a couple kids in orange life vests around their necks jumped around in the boat, but she ignored them; it looked like she hung on to that dock for dear life. You could see her tense up and grit her teeth whenever another boat came by and some of the wake rolled in and rocked her boat. She had on an orange life jacket too, but it had almost worked its way over her shoulders and off her head by then.

Every time the guy missed the ramp backing up, the wife hanging over the side looked up, then looked away before he saw her, her head hung a little further between her arms. She didn't say anything. But you could see how red her knees were when she re-adjusted herself.

Dad finally went over to the guy, tried guiding him back once or twice by standing by the back of the trailer like I did with him, then Dad walked up to the cab and they talked a second and the guy got out of his pickup truck and Dad got in.

One thing my dad could do really good, everyone agreed, was back up a trailer.

I acted like I was guiding him back between the ramp and the dock—but he pretty much just walked back to check out the cement under the water to see where it dropped off, then backed the trailer all the way down the whole ramp in one try. The other guy that had tried all those times just stood there and watched with his mouth hanging open. Guess all that truck driving paid off. Dad sat in the pickup while the guy went to the dock to get in his boat, and waited till he had relieved his wife and pulled the boat all the way up the trailer. The boat motor made a roar and the propellers made a lot of gurgles and bubbles and snorts to push the boat all the way up on to the trailer.

Mom stayed in the car the whole time, smoking her Salems. She missed all the cool parts.

The guy shook hands with my dad when he finally got his boat and wife and noisy kids out of our way, and then dad did the same with our car and boat—slick, one try, first try, never even walked back there again this time, never even had to pull back out once to straighten out to get it in the water right. He didn't start the boat motor just then, just stood on the point of the trailer at the hitch on the car with a tow rope and pushed lightly. The boat floated around, seemed to follow the tow rope instead of the other way around, till it was up against the side of the dock out of the way where the lady's boat had been. Dad did the whole maneuver somehow without getting his feet wet. He jumped from the trailer to the edge of the water and then walked around the boat on the dock.

"Crawl in there and hang on to the boat," Dad yelled at me. I thought about the red-faced lady for a second, then sorta fell into the boat from the dock. The step down to the seat cushion was longer than I thought, but I grabbed the dock and hung on like I saw that lady do. Then Dad tossed me the rope. I wasn't sure if I was supposed to let go of the boat and catch the rope or try to catch it and still hang on to the boat. "Tie it off on that post," Dad said with a little wave. "Don't let the boat bang against the boards." As an afterthought he added, "And don't stick your fingers between the dock and boat. You'll get 'em pinched off." I hadn't thought of that last part, but it made sense. So I sat there trying not to pinch my fingers off as the boat bobbed up and down next to the dock.

Dad got back into the car then and pulled the trailer out of the water. He talked to mom for a couple seconds, then she skooched across the seat and drove away. I didn't wave goodbye because I couldn't let go of the dock.

She didn't look back anyway.

Dad lit up a Winston and came over to the dock by me then. He checked how I had wrapped the tow line around the steel thing on the dock and redid it, a little neater than me.

"We going home now?" I asked. He still hadn't even started the boat motor. "Back to the cabin, I mean?"

"Nah. Don't get so excited." He looked around. "You want to fish, right? First we have to get bait. Come on outta there." Even though I was ten, he reached down from the dock to lift me out of the boat. I mean, it wasn't a big deal, just a small motion, over in a second. But I remember how he stuck his Winston in his lips and squinted and grabbed my hand, my arm really, above my wrist. I jumped a little and felt his forearms tighten when he lifted me. He swung me up and tossed me on the deck like I was so much air.

My dad fished when he was a kid—I'd seen a picture of him and Uncle Tommy with a string of fifty fish they caught up on Lake Koshkenong on vacation with their family. They looked to be about my age in the picture.

"Bait," I found out, meant minnows in a can for him and worms for me. The minnow can was really a bucket that sat in the water to keep the minnows alive till you needed them, one can with holes inside and another slightly bigger regular bucket—you had to keep them alive and grab them out one at a time and hook them on the end of the hook by their rubbery lips, so they'd keep swimming around and look real to the musky that were probably trailing them. Worms I knew, but I didn't know how to hook a worm over a fishing hook till Dad showed me how: Stick the pointy part through the worm's body in three or four places so he wouldn't fall off, and so the fish would be able to nibble him away without getting their lips caught on the hook.

"Will a musky eat a worm too, Dad?" I asked at the bait shop next to the boat ramp.

Dad didn't answer, barely shook his head, but Woody, the old guy that owned the bait shop and whose name was on the door and the sign outside said, "A musky will eat anything it can get its mouth around. And then some." He smiled down at me, even though his front teeth were all gone and there was a black rectangle where some teeth usually are. "Now—that worm may or may not be stuck on your hook at the time, understand, s'only problem." He laughed and shoveled a couple extra nightcrawlers into my box.

After Dad picked out a big ole lure called Zippy Boy, one with four hooks on it buried under some long bright feathers to make it look fast, Woody told us all about musky while we were checking out. "You all make sure you got a sawed-off ball bat in the boat to kill any musky you catch. You smash the sumbitch's head *before* you haul it in the boat, you hear?" He licked his lips, which he did more than normal 'cause he didn't have any teeth in front. "Once those babies get in the boat they're still fighting, see?" He picked a round of line, rang it up. Sighed. "They're nothing more than killing machines. Born that way right from the gitgo. Don't ever quit," he said, looking down at me.

All I could see when I looked up was the shiny blue board with the huge greenish stuffed fish behind Woody, hanging over the door. The fish had markings that made me think of a rattler on its back. He was poised in a twisted position, three or four stripes down his side, mouth wide open with rows of big teeth showing, ready to rip apart anyone that tried to get out the door without paying or with something from the shop they weren't supposed to have.

Of course the stuffed musky looked bigger than it really was, I thought, staring up at it. Must be. Nothing in the lake could be that big,

Could it?

"Y'all go over to Betsy's downtown, at the Bib and Tucker?" Woody pointed a finger over to his left a little. "Ask her to show you her missing toe, well, the spot where her toe should be, that toe on her right foot." Woody put a dirty finger to his cheek. "Back in '50, think it was—she was just a girl then, a silly girl, too caught up in herself, couldn't anyone tell her anything..." He seemed to drift off some in this part. "Anyways," he said after a second, when he caught himself, "swam across the lake on her own, she did. No one could tell her not to. Made it about half way across afore the musky hit 'er." His eyes clouded over a little just then. He tapped his dirty fingernails on the counter. "Wonder how long that ole boy was watching her from under there, you know?" He wrapped Zippy Boy in a sheet of newspaper, slipped it in a bag, careful of the hooks. "Watching her reach and pull, twist a little each stroke, nice cold titties bouncing in the water, nipples sticking out in that tight nylon top in the wind—" He stopped. Got a bit red. "You ask her to show you that. Her toe. Show you her missing toe."

He licked his lips again, caught some drool about to fall on the counter. I had a tickle, a fluttering down in my shorts. Dad just stood there with some bills in his hand. Pushed them a little toward Woody. Woody held up a finger. "Musky did it. Musky did it for goddamn sure." The cash register jinged and the drawer flung open all at once like it had been waiting for the story to be over, too.

The clatter made me jump.

I was in a hurry to get out of there, and didn't look up again at the big stuffed musky hanging over the bait shop door as I scuttled out. I just looked at my feet and squeezed through the door real quick. I got outside and the sun felt good on my arms. I felt a chill run down my back as I thought again about Betsy and her toe. I imagined there were plenty of other swimmers that got attacked out on the lake. All virgins, probably, although odds were there were just as many if not more stupid jocks that thought they could swim across the lake unharmed, too. Some of the time the swimmer lived, probably, rescued by a relative or some mailman on the water or someone like that, but most of the time, I imagined now, they just struggled and bled to death and drowned and sunk to the bottom, never to be seen again. Of course their bodies rarely came up—they'd been eaten by the musky on the way down, after all. Though a lot of time you had to figure that once something stopped struggling, like maybe when Betsy stopped struggling finally, the musky, hunter that he was, wouldn't strike any longer. He had a sense of honor, I imagined, standing there now in the warm sunshine—once the struggling and panic stopped the musky would move on to more fair game or to the next stupid swimmer that dared enter his domain.

"You in there?" Dad stood close, hands on his hips, looked down at me with a peeved look.

"Yeah...I'm just...just thinking about musky, is all."

"Well snap out of it. We gotta get gassed up and head back to the cabin before it gets dark."

I walked with him for a minute then stopped. "Aren't we going down to the Bib and Trucker to look at that lady's toe?"

"Ain't got time for that bullshit," he said, and never broke stride. "Probably all made up anyway."

So we got black gas from a gas station on the dock, a special kind for the boat motor, and the motor even started. I was a little surprised it started after so much time outside, then in the garage, just sitting. But I did see Dad put jumper cables on the battery last week before we went, and that helped; and he sprayed some smelly stuff in the engine before he even tried it. He had special keys for the boat that I'd never seen before: silver keys on a bright orange squishy key ring.

I rode back to the cabin from that dock and Woody's Bait and Fishing store in the boat with my dad as the sun set. I was tall enough to sit in the seat next to Dad, watched him work the control, set the pitch on the propeller he said (something about the angle of the blades in the water, how high the boat rode in the water), and drug my hand in the smooth water along the side. It stung a little when you first put your hand down there but felt good after—kind of tickled in a way, like when Pete from Ben's Barbershop scraped that razor down your neck along your hairline after a butch. Before we got back to our dock at the cabin, Dad turned the running lights on—little lights on poles that stuck up here and there along the length of the boat.

And that's how it all fell in place for our vacation week at first. Mom and Carol and little Annie would stay in the cabin, mostly. Carol would watch Annie when mom needed to go somewhere or she'd take them with—and Dad and I'd get up early, in the dark, and stay with the boat and fish till we came in around 10:00 am hungry and ready to eat.

Then we'd sit around. Dad would drink coffee and tinker with his rod and reel, maybe, or sort through his tackle box for a better, different lure, and I'd sleep or bug Carol; or Dad and me'd go over to Woody's and get more gas and hear more stories. Then we'd go out again just after supper, right before dark, trying to get the fish when they were eating. Finally we'd give up, call it a night, head home over the dark green lake, sprinkled here and there with other boats, other fisherman, and along the edges, cabin lights to help mark our way back. We climbed out of the boat, carried any bait we had left to the porch or leave the extra minnows in the lake hanging by a rope in their bucket off the dock, and flop into bed.

In the morning we'd get up and do it all over again.

Well, we tried to fish, anyways. We put in a lot of time at it, anyway. Dad spent a lot of money over at Woody's buying different lures and such, but we didn't catch any actual fish. Of course Mom and Carol were amused. "Should I pick up something for supper?" Mom would say to Dad every morning, a twinkle in her eye. She'd look over at me then: "Or are you guys going to catch our supper tonight?" Then barely a moment later, after she looked back and forth, snapping her eyes: "Didn't think so," and she would pick up her purse and head out the door. Sometimes she would have Annie in her arms, most often though Carol would either have Annie on her hip or rush to catch her as Mom strode out the door to the car. Carol wasn't quite as obvious about making fun of us as Mom was, but she was part of it and enjoyed it too—that we hadn't caught any fish yet.

So it was extra special when we finally did catch a fish. Super sweet. Dad had just untangled the line in my reel and tossed my line out with the bobber and worm threaded on the hook—I was pissing and moaning again that I had to fish with an old rod and reel: an old cork handled, yellow rod, the old open reel kind with big thick black line that got tangled up every 30 seconds that even the blindest, littlest fish could probably see from 100 yards away.

No wonder I wasn't catching anything.

What I wanted to say but didn't say directly was that I wanted a casting rod and reel like my dad had, a Zebco push-button so that I could stand up in the boat and cast all the time with a bright-colored Zippee lure like he did. I'd seen the Zebco's at Woody's; stood around close to them with my hands in my pockets, even took a few off the rack, but Dad never came over to me when I was standing there so that I could, like, drop a hint.

So Dad had just plunked my line out in the water a few feet out from the boat. I sat there watching my bobber again. He cast out with his Zebco when my bobber went down. I mean, down. I just about dropped the whole rod and reel, old or new, didn't matter now. I felt not so much a jerk as a tug, a tug and a quick pulling down.

"D-D-Dad." It felt as if some fat fish had dug his feet in the sand and tried to pull the worm down to the bottom to drown it— although of course fish don't have feet to dig in with. I didn't move, didn't do anything—but I didn't drop my rod and reel, either.

"Jerk it. Hook 'im," he said, strangely quiet. 'You might have something." Dad was behind me. He set down his rod and reel, even though he had just cast his Zippee out fifty feet, hadn't even reeled in the slack. "Jerk it!"

I jerked it. I thought maybe I'd feel the hook bite through the fish's lip, if it really was a fish; but I didn't feel anything different. I'd already hooked a mass of seaweed and sticks. It felt like that. I groaned.

"Work him." I looked back, confused.

"Jerk the pole, try to get some slack in the line. Tighten the reel a turn." Dad worked his arms while he talked. I must have looked confused again. "Take some line in," he yelled a little louder, but still in a whisper, making a cranking motion with his right hand. "Create some slack. Take in some line." He thought. "Just don't break the line."

Oh great—something else to worry about, I thought. Then, right then, Dad's pole jerked. Almost flipped right out of the boat. He stood there with the net in his hand that he'd grabbed to get my fish in the boat with, but was quick enough on his feet to step on the end of his pole before it went over the side—even though he tripped over the skis we never used lying on the bottom of the boat. The boat rocked and plunged up and down and his rod nearly broke in two, but it bent and recovered and he moved his foot quickly from the Zebco reel to the handle before he put too much weight on it and broke it. He managed to get his rod in his one hand, then whipped it high and hard with a *sswooop* snapping sound. Then he worked his way over to my side of the boat, holding his rod high over his head in one hand and the net in his other hand. He stood there, spread out and flexing his knees to keep his balance in the rocking boat.

"OK, bring your fish up to the side."

I cranked on my reel for all I was worth. "Careful—not too fast. Don't break that line." My fish was digging his feet in again, making it hard on me. But I was winning. I was taking in line—a little at a time.

Meanwhile, I felt my dad jerk his pole and set his Zippee in whatever fish's mouth was on his line. He might have been steadying himself in the boat, or he might have been deciding which thing to do first, he was rocking back and forth so much by then.

I just kept cranking. Finally I saw the black-green head of my fish at the top of the water. Ugly sucker. Big eyes, big black handlebar mustache drooping around a mouth that went all the way around his body, seemed. "Bullhead," Dad said, next to me now. Tugged like a bull, I thought. I nodded. Made sense that that was his name. He went down for one more tug, but I had seen him now, and he was mine—I had him. "Keep that line tight. Don't let him shake his way loose now."

"Stand up if you have to keep the line tight." Then: "Can't wait. I gotta bring mine in," he yelled, even though we were only inches apart.

The whispering had ended.

So he left me, as much as he could leave me in a 12-foot boat, to work his fish. Again I felt a little like that lady on the dock the day we arrived, hanging on for all I was worth—but I did get a glimpse or two of what Dad was doing. His fish, unlike my fish, was a jumper, and it was a beauty. He tugged, sure—but every once in a while he would go down to gather himself, and then break water and shake, bend his head almost to his tail, trying to shake loose that damn ole Zippee hook, but stuck hard and not able to. Dad reeled line back whenever the fish jumped. "Northern," he said, matter-of-factly, cranking his reel then hanging on tight when the fish ran out to try to free himself. 'Northern pike." Slowly the jumps got fewer and lower. "Got you, you sonofabitch," Dad said softly—and I saw a small smile as his face relaxed.

I thought it would never end. My arms started to get tired, even though all I was doing was holding my fat boy close to the boat, close to the surface. Eventually, though, the fish tired themselves out, until they were both spent at the side of the boat. Defeated. Dad held his rod high again, crawled over me, reached down and got the net under my fish. "Watch how I do this," he said. He shook the net like a JiffyPop shaker and made sure my bullhead was securely in the bottom of the net, then lifted the loaded net over the side of the boat and dumped the fish on the middle of the floor. "Watch out for those horns," Dad said, pointing to the big long mouth. "They'll rip you up." Gingerly he pulled the net away. He had to reach down a time or two to unhook the nylon netting from one of the black, handle-bar-looking horns with a pliers.

"Now you take the net," he said. We let the bullhead lay there while I moved over to Dad's side of the boat. The northern who had jumped so high and made such a spectacle of himself just moments earlier lay just under the water next to the boat, barely moving. The sun shone off the golden specks on his back. "Make sure that net is all the way under him before you pull up." I did my best, and did the little JiffyPop shake and pivot my dad had done with the bullhead. The northern came to life when he felt the net under him, when he felt himself being lifted; shook and danced and banged his head hard against the side of boat, splashed me with lake water. Dad had two hands on his pole now, the weight of the northern bending the rod hard. "See?" he said. I slipped the net under the Northern again and on the second time got him into the boat, mainly because he didn't thrash this time—gave up, done, tuckered out maybe—beaten.

"Just drop him," Dad said, standing above me. Then he stepped toward the front of the boat, tripped again on the loose skis, kicked one of the orange life jackets out of the way, and sat down. He fell into his seat, brushed his hair back with his wet and smelly hand, worked a Winston out of the smashed pack in his pocket and lit it.

And smiled wide. His Donut-land smile. The big one he kept for special occasions. I couldn't help but smile myself, smile with my whole tired body.

So this is fishing.

I thought I'd never get that grin off my face.

We spent a little more time out in the lagoon where we'd caught our fish. Dad worked for a long time, seemed, on getting the hooks out of the fish's lips and mouths. But he eventually got the fish loose, even though in the end he was cranking on my bullhead with a needle-nosed pliers with one boot squishing his head to the floor, and he couldn't save his Zippee lure because the Northern'd swallowed too much of it.

When we pulled up to our dock by the cabin, it was a little past eleven, way past our usual time to get home. But this time we climbed out of the boat triumphantly, hoisting our fish high by the gills. The fish together like that probably looked a little bit like Laurel and Hardy, my fat, white-bellied bullhead Laurel next to Dad's thin, slick green Northern Hardy.

Mom and Carol were out on the front lawn, sunbathing on the lounge chairs. Annie was on the ground on a blanket between them, playing with her blocks. Both girls smiled, then Mom said, "Don't think I'm going to clean those slimy things," and looked back at her magazine. At least Carol grabbed Annie and came out to the ground-end of the dock, and touched the fish once.

Cleaning the fish was a chore, even though Dad used his new knife with the leather sheath he'd gotten down at Woody's. We had a board and a clip to grab the fish tails to hold them, but the cutting through was tougher than it looked. "Goddammit," Dad said about ten times, each time saying the word a little different, a little louder.

He did my bullhead first, to warm up, to practice, I guess— but it turned out to be a hard one to clean, probably because of the handle-bar horns. He slit the belly open from tail to neck, then turned to me: "You caught it, you clean it. Scoop those guts on out of there."

I was already close, watching. I swallowed hard, and stuck my hand into the slit he'd cut. "Scoop and pull," Dad said. "Scoop and pull. Run your hand against the ribs on the inside. Get 'em all." Carol was close, too, curious. But when I pulled the first handful of guts out and a thin white piece stretched out like wet spaghetti and snapped after I twisted it, she left and took Annie into the house. Dad ended up just chopping the head off to get rid of the stubbly-shaped horns, but then had a hard time getting the skin off. No leverage. By the time he pulled out the backbone and ribs and was through, a couple little chucks of meat were all that were left of my bullhead.

Cleaning the Northern went better, but not much.

Seemed like there wasn't much meat left for all the trouble, I thought. I might have asked Dad if he thought it was all worth it, the boat and the gas and the gear and the lost Zippee, but then thought I better not.

Mom did manage to mix up a little egg and corn meal and roll what was left of the fillets in the mix, and fried them up with chicken for lunch. By then I was about done with fishing. I reached for some chicken.

"What the hell you doing?" Dad asked.

I looked at him. "Eating supper?"

"You caught it, you eat it." He waved his fork at the three little hunks that were left of my bullhead, the one I had tugged out of the water just a few hours ago, the same one that was just minding his own business until my worm slid by above him.

I looked over at Carol. It was like she could hear my thoughts—*he was just minding his own business*. I could tell she was afraid Dad would make her eat a piece of the bullhead next. She glanced at Dad then looked down. I reached over and put a golden brown piece on my plate. Both Mom and Dad watched me do it. Then they watched me cut a small piece off and stick it in my mouth. I chewed, and must have made a face, because Mom and Dad both laughed.

The fish tasted, well, fishy—like lake water, like the minnows and worms smelled, like someone had stuffed a chunk of dead skunk in my mouth. Like liver smelled when Mom fried it in the house. I gagged, but Dad's stare kept me from spitting the piece of meat back on my plate. I used a lot more catchup and took a lot smaller bites to get the rest of my bullhead down. I was grateful that Dad had mangled him up so much in the cleaning and that there wasn't that much I had to force down. I did finally rinse some of the taste out of my mouth with some chicken and mashed potatoes, but I burped up bullhead breath for a couple days after.

The taste went up my nose all over again when I did.

Vacation changed after that triumphant Thursday fish dinner. No one said anything about it directly—but things changed. The weather changed most—where it had been sunny and partly-cloudy and calm for the first few days of vacation, now it rained and the wind blew more. Dad still got up early next day to go back fishing, but I didn't go with him. He didn't seem to mind. He never said anything—*I work hard. I got one week of vacation a year. I gotta make it count,* I heard him say, though, in my head. He just picked up the minnow can from the side of the dock, climbed into the boat and drove off, rain or no rain.

Without me.

Mom, Carol, Annie and now me settled in around the cabin. Couldn't swim or paddle around in the lake in the rain so we played some games, played some cards. Carol always got to be the banker in Monopoly though, and always won—except when Mom played. Then she was the banker and she won. I read a biography of Lou Gehrig I brought from home that first day off from fishing, then the next day I read *I Was There with Teddy Roosevelt and the Rough Riders.* Both were good, but I liked the baseball book better. Still it rained. I began to think about Holland and Anderson back home and wondered who in the neighborhood was ahead in waffle ball?

Dad was on his own now. I did go out with him one more time, after he came home for lunch one afternoon. I almost asked him: "We already caught our fish—so why are you still going out?" But then he took us to a spot across the lake near some reeds, close to shore, when he pulled up and did a strange thing: He chopped up three or four minnows and tossed them in the lake beside the boat. Just tossed them in the water. Wasted them, I thought. Then he cut another one open, cut his tail off, so he was alive and still bleeding, and hooked him of his line.

Dad sat in the back of the boat and let the line out of his push-button Zebco a little at a time, slowly, while he idled the motor real low. He didn't even bother to get out my pole, my line or my bobber or sinker. He had that look on his face, that one he got when he knew he was right, when he was past the point of backing down, when it was time to prove everyone else wrong.

Kind of like when he backed that guys trailer up for him at the docks.

He didn't say much to me, just handed me the net and the sawed-off musky bat: "You keep these handy. Be ready when he strikes." But even after a couple hours of this trolling, and maybe two dozen minnows later, still nothing—so we went home in the dark.

Mostly though, those last days of vacation, I heard him come back at night, knew he had the night lights on in the boat, thought about what he did when he got to the dock at night. I had it memorized by now, literally saw it all with my eyes closed: Turn the key off. Float into the dock; just glide. Up against the dock soft, then tie off the front rope by the driver side. Now turn and tie off the back end. Get your wallet out of the glove box. Then gather up the minnow bucket and rod and reel. Kill the running lights. Step up onto the dock. Stick the minnow pail in the lake at the end of the dock; make sure the rope hasn't come untied in all the shuffling or you'll lose the whole pail. Walk up the deck to the side door of the cabin. Lean the rod and reel in the dry spot under the awning, if there is a dry spot. Take your wet yellow slicker off before you came in and drip all over the floor. Shake it. Hang it up outside. Open the fridge. Pop a beer. Sit in the soft light of the lamp over the sink in the kitchen on a chrome chair. Lean back. Smoke a Winston or two. Maybe toss the ashes and butts out the door, it was wet and nothing would catch fire. Maybe have another beer. Or two. Another smoke. Turn the sink light off. Wash your face before you flop into bed.

Except on Friday. Friday morning something was wrong with the boat—a leak or something around the joints? Dad hauled the car and trailer over to Woody's ramp and winched the boat out of the water. Woody and Dad walked round and round it, poked here and there (I went with, I was bored), and Dad ended up buying some waterproof caulk in yellow tubes and putting a thick bead around some of the places where Woody said it was probably leaking. "Can't let a wooden boat sit around too much. Weather dries 'em out," I heard him say more than once.

Saturday then. Last day before we headed home. More rain. Dad's fishing. Mom has had enough. "We're going out," she said. "Get ready."

"Where we going?" Carol asked.

"I don't know," Mom said, "but I can't stand this dingy cabin one more minute."

So we got ready.

We ended up going to the movies—a matinee. Camelot, I think it was. Mom was in a good mood, even bought popcorn and let us each pick out one candy bar from the display. One each, one of our own, one we didn't have to share for once.

It was mid-afternoon when we got out of the movies. "Too early to go home yet," Mom said, so we drove around some. At the edge of town, the opposite direction from where we'd driven so far, we came to a zoo of sorts—Arnie's Animal Haven, the wooden sign said. Arnie's was like a little city park, just outside the city limits, was all. *One of the World's Best Collections of Exotic Animals*, the sign inside the gate said.

Mom looked at a brochure for a minute at the little guard-shack entrance, paid our money, and we walked around Arnie's. Sidewalks wound in and out of different sets of cages, set in a general circle shape. All the cages had square black iron rails for walls and a flat little arrow on top of each rail, spaced out about every six inches or so. When the animals inside were smaller than that and might have crawled out, like the pheasant or the ducks, chicken wire had been wrapped around the inside of the bars to keep them in.

Of course the ducks could probably fly over that if they wanted to, I thought, taking it in, thinking it over, figuring it out.

We were about to head home, thought we'd seen it all, when we saw a guy, a worker in a dark-blue uniform. About my dad's age. A little younger, maybe. Mom handed Baby Annie to Carol. We were just going to walk past him, I thought, when Mom smiled and said, "Nice place."

He stopped his raking. Stood straight. The name patch over the left pocket of his uniform shirt said "Arnie" in tight white script.

"Are you the owner?" Mom said.

"Me?" He looked surprised. "Oh no, no—that'd be my dad." His smile was big and bright.

"Little Arnie," Mom said, smiling too.

He screwed up his face. "No, not that. Arnie *Junior.*"

"Of course."

Arnie recovered quickly. "Did you guys see all the displays?" He looked from Mom to me and then to Carol, sizing us up. Mom was getting a cigarette out of her purse.

"I don't know," Carol and I said together as we shrugged our shoulders.

"But did you see the musky?" He pointed to the center of the park, at the big round pond in the middle of the displays and cages.

"I didn't know you had any musky here," I said quickly. He had my attention now.

"Yep. Sure do. Follow me." He walked toward a little water-mill building at the edge of the pond, a hundred feet away or so. I fell in beside him. Mom and Carol followed, Annie on Carol's hip. Mom swung her purse and puffed her Salem while she walked, curious.

"First you gotta buy a frog," Arnie Junior said. At the side of the little windmill was a dispenser that looked like a gumball dispenser, like the kind at Logli's next to the plastic pony's you ride for a quarter. But instead of gumballs inside, this dispenser had frogs. Live frogs. Not real big frogs, but pretty good-sized ones—a couple-three inches across. I ducked my head in a little further, and saw that the windmill building was really a big frog cage, a frog farm of sorts, where a cage went around the inside of the wooden building and down into the water in a big rectangle. There were more frogs in there than I had ever seen in one place before. I let Carol squeeze in next to me for a look-see.

"Get a quarter from your mom," Arnie said. She reached into her purse and gave me one. "Now watch till a frog settles on one of these big red paddles here," Arnie said. He pointed. To me it looked like a miniature version of the swinging doors at D. J. Stewart's, the ritzy department store downtown—but we were looking in at it as if it had been turned on its side. "You don't have to wait long," Arnie said, absently. "They like sitting on the wheel. There you go already," Arnie continued, as a frog landed on the wheel. "Now put in your money and twist the handle." I did, and down into a chute fell a frog and a little water. A plastic bag was hooked on the end of the chute, and the frog fell down into it.

I took the frog, water and bag off the chute and held it. "Now what?" I asked.

"Well, now you got a choice. You can take the frog home as a souvenir," he crinkled his nose a little, then he lifted his eyebrows. "Or you can feed it to the musky." Carol gasped. Mom took a deep drag on her Salem. Arnie Junior leaned on his rake, smiled another big toothy smile, and nodded toward the pond with his head.

Carol turned toward Mom. "Mom...don't let him. Don't." Mom blew smoke out her nose slowly.

I thought a second. It would be pretty neat to see a musky. A real live musky. Something I could tell Woody. Dad. Bobby at home. Even Anderson. "We don't want a slimy frog in our *car*," I ventured. "That bag looks pretty flimsy. He might get out?" I turned my palms up dramatically and looked at my mom. "What would we feed a pet frog, anyways?"

Mom took another drag off her Salem. We all looked at her. Carol put Annie on her other hip. "Mom," she said again. She stomped her foot just a little when she said it.

Mom stared at me for a minute, then shifted her gaze to Arnie. "It's nature's way, isn't it?" Arnie got a little red, I thought, smiled again, said, "Yes ma'am. Nature's way."

"Follow me, kid," he said then, whipping his hand to catch the rake he was leaning on a moment ago. We walked to the edge of the pond, a place with a lot of smooth rocks on the edge. Unlike our lake, which was dark and greenish and had a lot of seaweed and grass and stuff on the bottom of it, this pond was very clear. I saw lots of the same kind of rocks on the edge on the bottom.

I clutched the bag with the frog shut at my side. Arnie assumed his position, leaned on his rake again, and swept his hand out toward the lake. Neither one of us said anything, but I understood. I knew what to do. What was expected here. I made my way to the edge, leaned out, flipped the plastic bag upside down, and dropped the frog out of the bag into the pond.

Our frog looked pretty, skimming there on the surface of the pond. The black and yellow stripes on his back shone in the sunlight when it broke through the clouds—or maybe it was just that the frog got clear water on his back, and it made him shine? He raised his head a little, seemed to me, and swam a couple little breast strokes away from the shore with big kicks of his long legs. They weren't very big strokes, because he wasn't very big himself. He didn't go very far. Just eight or ten feet away from shore.

For a moment I thought, *Musky my ass,* thinking the little frog was going to get away in the wild of the pond and be free forever. Beside me Carol let loose a little *hmmph.* But then the water around the frog got darker, blurry, like clouds gathering. There, in a circle around him, I could make out the slim heads of four musky. They were long—three feet at least. They had the same markings, brown stripes at their sides, as that stuffed monster hanging over Woody's door at the bait shop. It was like they came out of nowhere. Like ghosts.

Like so much smoke.

The frog floated now. No more breast strokes. Maybe he sensed the danger, I don't know—but for whatever reason he stopped his strokes. Then on some silent signal between them the clear water bubbled and slashed and ground white and green and flashed fins and teeth and tails. As the water settled , a few waves rippled in a widening circle to the shore and toward the center of the pond. I saw one musky lingering in the shadows, about ten feet out. Little green and white frog legs stuck out of the side of his mouth.

The musky blinked at me once, took a quick gulp, and was gone.

"God, I love that," Archie said from his rake. "Every friggin' *time!*" He pumped his arm, his hand in a fist, then turned and walked away fast, leaving us standing there. Carol stood shaking at my side. I took her elbow and turned her away, even though it was too late—she already saw everything. Annie was fussing, so I took her from Carol and put her in my arms and set her on my hip like Carol carried her, and headed for the car.

Mom stood back. She looked at us a moment, tossed her cigarette down and ground it into the sidewalk. Then she searched in her purse a second and held up a quarter. "Wanna buy another one?"

She laughed all the way to the car.

* * *

The sun came out more on our way home. It looked especially bright after so many days without any sunshine to speak of.

"Where's the rainbow?" Carol asked no one.

We pulled into the driveway of the little red cabin, stopped by the boat trailer and saw Dad's boat out on the lake. I stared— something didn't look right. It was Dad's boat, alright, and it was headed to shore, and he was standing in it—but the boat was too low in the water. Moved too slow, looked too fat. I walked down to the pier, called out, waved—but he didn't wave or yell back. He just stared ahead, focused on the end of the dock.

About fifty yards out, the motor coughed and quit. A cloud of black greasy smoke puffed out of the tail of the boat. "Goddammit," I heard him say, pretty loud and pretty sharp, like it wasn't his first one of the day. I knew the pattern of his swearing by now. Knew it by heart. Momentum carried him closer, but with the boat being so low in the water, so heavy, he didn't glide far.

I walked to the end of the pier. Closer to him and the boat. The wind and waves turned him sideways so I could see more of the inside of the boat. The boat was barely above the water. He had the running lights on, even though it wasn't dark or even dusk yet—some sort of distress signal, I guessed. He turned away from me. He had the bottom half of the minnow bucket in his hands, scooping, tossing, scooping more water. Bailing water. I didn't see the sieved part of the minnow bucket anywhere.

Even as he worked, one of the skis floated in front of him. He knocked the bucket against it, spilling the water too soon. "Goddammit." His Zebco rod and reel floated out the back of the boat as I watched. A bright new yellow Zippee went with it. I saw too the black hoses connecting the red gas tank to the silent motor on top of the water where they weren't supposed to be, which meant the gas tank was floating now, too. Dad grabbed at one of the bulky orange lifejackets as it floated over the front side of the boat, too late. "God-dammit."

Carol came up behind me, stood by me, watched. There was nothing we could do. Nothing we could say. I looked around to see if there was *something* I could do: Throw a rope, sound an alarm, use something else to reach him, help him.

But there was nothing.

"Are there musky is this lake, Jeff?" Carol asked, grabbing my hand. Her eyes were wide, wet, almost shook inside their sockets.

"No. No Carol. No," I said, looking back at her. My lie probably showed in my eyes; I smiled a little to hide it. "Geez—how stupid," I said, shaking it off. But I had a sick feeling in my gut, like right after I'd swallowed that first damn chunk of bullhead without ketchup. Or the first time I squirted under the door past Woody's stuffed musky.

By now Dad too knew he wasn't making progress, wasn't going to win this battle. He quit bailing, tossed the minnow bucket behind him with a flair. Sweat shone off his face. Unlike most of the fishermen I'd seen here in Eagle River, he didn't let his beard grow wild; he shaved every day no matter what, like he was taught in the Air Force way back when. "Goddammit," he said softly this time, so that we barely heard him. Then he stepped over the front seat of the boat, stepped over the windshield, walked out on the boat's bow, grabbed a tow line and simply walked off the bow of the boat into the choppy dark water.

The boat bounced up a bit. I held my breath. Carol beside me did too. Squeezed my hand harder. Dad went under quick, with hardly a splash—just walked right into the water and sunk. I thought I saw him come up once, twice, but I didn't—it was the reflection off the bow of boat on the waves each time. Of course he didn't have on a life jacket—he knew how to swim, I heard him brag in my head. I could hear his laugh in my head as he told that to mom, could see his Donut-land smile, enjoyed watching him try to sound convincing.

Then after what seemed way too long to be under, Dad came up just in front of the boat. He turned back, pulled on the rope with a kick of his legs to get it started, then turned and put the rope through his mouth like a bit on a horse and started swimming, pulling the boat behind him.

Breast stroke.

I imagined the slick, thick grayish-green musky of the lake hearing him kick, racing across the lake if they weren't already there from the slapping of the minnow bucket in the water. Circling. Watching. Waiting. I wondered if he had his shoes on, or had kicked them off when the water started seeping into the boat. When—an hour ago? Two? How long has he been out there lying to himself, struggling to keep the boat afloat? I wondered if he'd be some truck stop sideshow now, showing people his missing toes on his left foot for fun, or maybe his whole missing left foot.

Yeah Bob, but how do you clutch with that thing?

He got to the dock a few long minutes later, maybe five, maybe ten, I don't know. It felt like a thousand. I was counting, but lost count and had to start over too many times. I shook loose of Carol when he got close, hit the deck of the dock on my knees, leaned over and grabbed the rope when he got near enough. I stood up and tugged. It felt like a hundred bullheads at the end of that line.

Carol went to help him up the stairs on the dock, but he shook her off gently. He stood up then and took the rope from me, didn't even shake the water off himself. His tee shirt and pants stuck tight to him, pushed smooth by the wind. The pants hung over his bare feet in weird angles, pressed there by the waves and the wind, it seemed, urging him back into the lake.

He got the boat up close to the dock, then turned to look at Mom up the hill at the cabin. She stared back, then dropped her Salem, ground it into the gravel with her heel, and turned away.

"I'll start packing," she said, loud enough for us to hear.

She must have also called Woody, because a few minutes later he came over in his boat. He ended up towing Dad's boat over to the loading ramps by his bait shop. Carol and I rode with the men in Woody's boat. It was a quiet trip. One thing that confused me a little is that we just towed the boat—we didn't even try to go pick up all the stuff that had floated out of it, even though it was right there, maybe 100 feet now off the dock; but we didn't even try.

No one said anything about that stuff. We just left it all.

Mom was already there with the car and trailer when we got to the public boat ramp. She saw us coming, got in the car, then backed the trailer down the ramp. First try. No problem. My mouth must have been hanging open, because first thing she said when we got close was: "What? You didn't think I could drive?"

I heard her *tish* from where I stood.

Then I learned something else new: Boats have drain plugs in the back—at the bottom. Huh. We drained the boat (it took a while, even with the boat still at a downward angle), but then Dad said "goddammit" again, opened the driver's door, drove back to the cabin to get the rest of our stuff and let the water slosh out of it all the way from the ramp to the cabin.

We packed in the dark that evening, locked up the cabin, drove all night to get home, didn't even stop at the "Cheese" place to get any Wisconsin cheese, let alone a $4.99 Paul Bunyan Lumberjack

Special. I was hungry but didn't say anything. No one talked all the way home, and baby Annie slept most of the way home up on mom's lap.

Carol and I shared a pillow in the back seat.

Mom made pancakes that next morning. She hardly ever made pancakes. Must have been glad to get home. We didn't unload the car or boat till that next afternoon. Bobby Holland didn't believe my story about the frogs and the musky. He wouldn't believe me till Carol told him it was true, too. She had to dig out the brochure she'd kept from Arnie's to make him believe it.

Anderson made her and me pinky swear it was true.

My Dad? He drove us home, backed the boat into the backyard between the house and the garage, left the car hooked up to it and then went right to bed. Didn't unwrap the tarp off the bench seat and throw it over the boat or anything. Tossed the bright orange foamy keyholder for the Chris-Craft on the driver's seat out there in the open—not even locked inside the glove box. Dad slept the whole next day. Monday morning he simply unhooked the trailer, pulled the car out of the yard without looking back, and was already at work before I even got up.

That Thursday walking to baseball practice, our last practice before school started, I had a thought that made my whole body shiver. For a frightening moment I was sure Dad would never come home again. Maybe it was because he hadn't called last night, like he usually did when he was on a California run. Mom didn't even seem to notice. For a moment, though, there on the sidewalk on Custer Avenue, a couple blocks from my house, I was sure that Dad never be home again—as sure of it as I was that Carol would steal their cigarettes again, and get caught; as sure of it as I was that the White Sox would surge and the Cubs would flounder again as the season closed; as sure of it as I was that grass would grow over the trailer and that the boat would sit and rot before anyone moved it again; as sure of it as I was that Bib and Tucker Betty's toe was indeed bitten off by a rogue musky; as sure of it as I was that our family would never again vacation at Eagle River; as sure of it as I was that I would never step foot in that lake again.

But then I told myself I was being silly. An idiot. It was just a wisp of my imagination working, like having to dash under the stuffed musky over Woody's door; and I swung my bat over my shoulder and started to run toward the field to get there in time to warm up and play a little catch before practice started.

A GAME OF CHESS

T.D. Johnston

August 19th

Can't think of what to write, but my kid got me this book to write in. So I'll write. Today was the first day of school. I put the flag up at 7:45. A mom said hi after she let her kid out, and said the flag was dirty and that's no way to treat freedom. She drove away along the curb and I didn't say nothing to the back of her vehicle. After that I went out to the soccer field and pulled weeds from the track that goes around it. That was on the list of stuff the business manager wanted me to do before the end of the day, and they said it might rain on the radio this morning. Of course it didn't because I got all the weeds up before ten. If I'd of changed out the washer in the left sink in the boys bathroom first instead of last, it would of started raining cats and dogs right then and never let up. Trust me. Then Mrs. Cutler would of told the business manager the track is a mess and no wonder there's sand gnats and why can't this school do anything right and maybe she would of even told the headmaster. She likes being on the board I think.

I had a tuna fish samwich from the kitchen ladies for lunch. It was good. A kid in line in front of me said there's too much mayo and she wanted a salad instead, but I like mayo and besides I told her she would grow up big and strong if she ate the tuna fish because it has protein. She said mayo is fattening and her mom said the lunch ladies should know that when they make lunch for the students and the big and strong stuff is for the birds. Yikes. The kid's twelve years old and already worried about her figure. Yikes like I said. When I was twelve nobody ever said nothing about saturated fat or nothing like that, and I'm still here after 54 years.

Okay. So I like this thing. Maybe I'll write in it some more tomorrow night just to make Tracy happy. It was for my birthday. She must want me to use it if she's giving me this instead of a Braves game in Atlanta like last year. That was a good game even if the Bravos got beat. I guess now I can go to Atlanta for a game and then come home Sunday night and write about it. Kind of hard now though, because school has started and football games are on Friday nights and I line the field late Friday afternoon for time and a half so the field paint is real bright for the game at 7.

Time for bed. Man. I'm glad I got those weeds done. Got to pull them out by the roots if you want to make things nicer out there. Right out by the roots. Makes better things grow out of the same dirt. Sure does.

August 20th

Today the lady who loves flags rolled her window down and said if I don't start taking pride in my country, I might have a real good chance up close to see a shiny clean flag at the government building where they do the unemployment signups. Boy, my old Corps buddies would of cracked up all over the place.

The headmaster came to see me today in the shop. I was fixing a gear in the old tractor so I could haul the trash cans to the Dempsey. That's our dumpster. I just call it the Dempsey. In case somebody reads this besides me some day and doesn't know what the heck I'm talking about. The headmaster keeps saying to call him Bob, but I says I can't because he's a sir. I don't tell him that though. I just says yes sir. When he says call him Bob. Today he leaned up against the tractor. Boy, he looked tired. We talked a little bit about the Braves like we always do and he said Chipper Jones has to stay healthy for once if the Braves are going to go to the playoffs and I says you're right because as Chipper goes the Braves go. And the headmaster says well put and spot on. He likes to say spot on. And boy, does he know his baseball! He's got all them books in his office and everybody wants a piece of him and a piece of his time and a piece of his soul if you ask me but nobody does, but he says he loves baseball as much as anything except his family and everybody's kids because baseball is really fair. He says that a lot when we talk about the Braves and when we played baseball when we was kids and he played in college and I played in the Corps. The fairest game in the world, except for chess, he says.

I ain't never played chess, I says. The headmaster said my gosh and invited me to learn. Said I could learn by playing with him. I says yes sir, and he says please call me Bob and I says yes sir and maybe we'll play chess but I don't say that out loud because I think maybe he's just being nice. Being the headmaster and all.

So today he leans up against that old green tractor and makes a deep breath and breathes out real long, and says do I know Mrs. Tattall and I says no I don't think so. He says Mrs. Tattall likes to complain about teachers usually, but today she sent the headmaster one of them emails where she really lets fly and he said she really likes to let fly. He said it was all about the flag not being crispy and clean. I says I think it's pretty clean sir, and he says I think so too. He says he wrote her back and said he thinks it looks fine and it's up every morning right when school starts and Stan, that's me, Stan does a great job and Stan works for the head-master not you. I don't mean you if someone reads this some day and doesn't know what the heck I'm talking about. I mean Mrs. Tattall. The lady who loves new flags. I bet she said the school was crapping on freedom but the headmaster didn't say she did but I bet she did.

I almost called him Bob right then but I says thank you sir and he says come see him if I need anything or if I want to play chess some time and I says thank you sir and he says Bob. And he walks out of the shop.

I had the vegetable lasagna today. It was good but I wanted to take a nap about two o'clock.

August 21st

Today was the third day of school. The flag lady got out of her car this morning and folded her arms like she was waiting for something. I finished raising the flag to the top of the pole and then I says can I help you because we're supposed to say that. She says she can't imagine how. For the life of her she says. So I start walking to my next project and she yells EXCUSE ME!! And I stopped. I says are you talking to me and she says of course I'm talking to you and maybe I can help her after all by explaining to her why I like to crap on freedom. Well now I started to get mad but I stayed calm and said nothing and she says she told the headmaster yesterday and my days are numbered. I couldn't say nothing no more so I says really? And she says yes for country and freedom and God. And I says, hey, the headmaster says the flag looks just fine and she says really and she says well we'll see about that and then she says maybe the board needs to hear about this.

She went and got back in her big white SUV and drove off, and I went to change out a fluorescent in the chemistry lab.

About four o'clock the headmaster came to see me again. He had a box with him and it was a chess set. He said he's gonna teach me the game and do I want to try and I says I don't clock out till 5 and he says don't worry he won't tell my boss and we laughed. Because he's my boss. In case somebody reads this some day and doesn't know what the heck I'm talking about.

We moved some stuff like loose tools and things and set the board down on top of the table next to the circular saw. He got out the pieces and said there's two sides and they're black and white. He lined up the little pieces and said they were pawns and I said I heard of them before and he showed me where they can go. Two spaces for the first one when you start, but only one after that until the game is all over. I thought that's too bad them pawns only get to go one space at a time when everybody else gets to do lots of moving around as long as they follow the rules like zigzag or sideways or backwards or forwards or two up and one over but not whatever you want because you're not that free, but that queen she gets to go wherever she wants and who made that rule? And your side loses when your king dies.

I don't see much difference between the king and them pawns, being truthful, seeing as how they can both only go one step, except when the king dies everybody on the team dies and when a pawn dies he's just out of everybody's way. Okay, yes. The king can run away if he wants. Real slow, but he can do it if he has help. That's the biggest difference. I guess.

The headmaster said he had a meeting at five o'clock and he didn't want to go but he had to because it was the board and it was a surprise meeting and in ten years they didn't have no surprise meetings and he was glad we got to play chess even though it was just teaching today. And I says thanks for teaching me and I'm gonna see if Tracy wants to play some day if she and whats his name come to visit from Atlanta because the headmaster gave me the chess set when we were done and I said thank you Bob and I took it home with me tonight.

I had the beefaroni for lunch today and a kid carton of chocolate milk. It was good. I wonder how the surprise meeting went for Bob.

August 22nd

Today I put the flag up real early so I wouldn't see the flag lady. When I was trying to get the air conditioning in the Middle School building to stop making one part of the building feel like Alaska and the other part feel like Miami in July, I started thinking about playing Bob in chess. I wondered if I could beat him some day. Wouldn't that be great. I went to the library last night down on Charles Street, and they had a book about chess strategy and stuff. Wow. But that's nothing. Wait till you hear this if you read this some day like maybe Tracy.

After school ended and the kids all went home except for football and volleyball practice, Bob came to see me in the shed again. We got out the chess set and started playing. He was black and I was white. But that's nothing. Wait till you hear this.

Right out of the blue Bob asks me to teach a class. I says huh? He says yep I want you to teach a class. Says these kids need lessons in manners and the golden rule and how to treat people and he says I'm the guy to teach the class. Well, I reminded Bob that I don't have a degree or nothing or any of those certificates I hear about and he says something like pshaw or something like that and says he still ain't seen no certificate teach a class. Says I got class and class died a long time ago and I says I ain't disagreeing with you about that. About the dying part. And he says then that means you'll teach it and I says really Bob I don't know how to teach. And he says teach who you are, Stan. Teach who you are. Well, my heart starts pounding because Tracy would be real proud of her old man teaching a class at a college prep school where he mows the grass and changes the washers and puts up the flag in the mornings.

So I have to quit writing in this for tonight because I'm doing what Bob called a Prep. I'm doing my Prep for class. I can't believe I start next week! Two classes. One's at 1:15 with 17 freshmen, and the other is at 2:05 with 18 freshmen. How do I Prep for 45 whole minutes with the kids, I asked him. Bob said teach who you are, and then he put me in checkmate. Then he stuck out his hand and I shook it. You know, I've shook his hand a hundred times and I never stopped to think that kids should be taught to shake hands. I see Bob shake hands with kids all the time. I'll tell you what. My students are going to shake hands every day when they see each other in my class. That's how we'll start. With a handshake.

We'll go from there.

The reason Bob put me in checkmate today was because I should of castled. It's right there on page 27. One of these days I'm going to stick my hand out there first, and he'll shake his head at night and say he should of castled and Stan put him in checkmate and shook Bob's hand with class.

I forget what I had for lunch today. It doesn't matter. You don't need to know either, in case somebody's reading this some day and wondering why in the heck it makes any difference if someone else knows what I eat every day. It's not like I got that Twitter thing. So I'm done with that. I've got my Prep to do.

August 23ʳᵈ

Today was Friday. I got to the flagpole early again, but she was waiting for me. I don't know where she put her kid so early, because the school doesn't let kids get dropped off before 7:30, but there she was at 7:15 and she had something with her. It was a new flag, all crispy and folded into a triangle just like I fold the school's every day when I get ready to go home. She says do you know what this is and I says yes it's a new flag and she says congratulations you don't need to get your eyes checked and you need to use this flag starting today. I says no thank you. I says our flag has been through a lot right here with the kids and the teachers and me and Bob. Like when those terrorists attacked New York and we all got together like a family here at school and cried and said the Pledge of Allegiance to this flag. THIS flag I says. I says this flag ain't never let us down, and I ain't going to let her down when she doesn't deserve that unless Bob says so. And she says do you mean to tell me that you never replace a dirty filter or old sheets or old clothes or am I just a slob and I says maybe you weren't listening to what I just said and she says you impertinent something if this new flag ain't up by the time school starts in, she looks at her watch like drama and stuff, in less than thirty minutes then I can take the old flag home with me. And I says I don't respect threats and she says facts not threats and so I says I work for Bob and not her. And she says the headmaster might just be joining you and she gets in her big white thing and drives off so fast she don't hear me say what I say to her bumper sticker that says what would Jesus do.

I know I promised last night I wouldn't write about lunch but. When I went in the lunch room everybody was talking about the email. Some teachers came up to me and said way to go, Stan, that's great. A couple of the guy teachers were whispering over at the table by the salad bar, and they were looking at me and I think they were whispering about the email. I don't think they thought it was great and they didn't get up and say way to go, Stan, that's great. They laughed and dipped their rolls in gravy at the same exact time and shook their heads.

Bob gave me a copy of the email when he came to play chess this afternoon at 4 o'clock. He said he knows I only use my box in the faculty lounge and not my email account even though I have an email account and he says that's okay because he likes going to his box in the faculty lounge too. So I read the email letter and it was real good because Bob wrote it to all the teachers and parents and the students who are old enough to have email accounts. He said freshmen are going to have one study hall instead of 2, and they're going to take a class with me. Me! Stan Howland! I still can't believe it and he said they're going to learn ethics and class and manners and the importance of respect and the golden rule from Mister Howland and not Stan. He didn't say not Stan but I want you to understand in case you're not Tracy and you're reading this one day and don't know what the heck I'm talking about. Bob's email says this is part of becoming a quality human being and it's one of the reasons the school is here and we shouldn't forget that and it's not about test scores but being educated and complete and Mister Howland will be part of helping kids become complete. I got the email letter right here. That's what it says.

Mister Howland.

This weekend I'm going to do three things. Fix the shed floorboard so I can put my lawnmower back in there before it gets rained on again. Two: Watch the Bravos play the Phillies and man I hope Chipper's hamstring feels better and three: Do my Prep for Monday. Bob says the class is called How To Be. How to be. That seems real simple to me. I hope I can fill up the 45 minutes all year but I bet I can. I got lots of stories too, and I bet the kids do too. I got to learn how to give grades though. I hope I don't need a certificate for that but Bob says I don't and Bob says he ain't never seen a certificate give no grade. I don't think Bob cares about certificates.

Kind of nervous, got to admit. But I remember my football coach in high school telling me if you're nervous that's good because it means it's important to you and that means you're ready and you're passionate. I hope Coach Deaton and Bob are both right even though Coach Deaton didn't coach no more after we went 2 and 8 my senior year.

August 24th

The floorboard's done. The mower's back inside the shed. So now it won't rain for three weeks. Right? Well, at least it won't get stolen.

The Bravos lost, 4 to 1. Chipper didn't play. Those hamstrings. Man. I hope I don't tweak one. Funny they say tweak nowadays. When I tweak something at my job, it's to make it work better. But Chipper's hamstring is tweaked, and it's a bad thing all right. No tweaks for me. I can't afford to miss work. Don't have that Yogi Berra insurance with the duck.

August 25ᵗʰ

Sundays always make me feel strange. I should be glad I have the day off, but it's like I can see Monday waiting for me. Monday is a big white vehicle with a brand new crispy flag on it. I still like the old one. We've been through a lot together. You never know what Monday will bring. But I know one thing. Today I'm doing my Prep. I'm a Teacher now. A Faculty Member. Mister Howland.

I'm back. It took me three hours, but. Tomorrow I'm going to talk to the kids about How To Be. Bob says there's 36 weeks in the school calendar. So. We're going to learn 35 ways to be. 35 not 36 because one week's already done and if kids get good at 35 then I guess I've done a pretty good job with those freshmen. I don't have a certificate, but. I know 35 ways to be. Maybe we'll start with Mrs. Tattall. First, kids, don't be like the flag lady. I'm just kidding, in case you think I would tell the kids not to be like the flag lady. I would tell the kids not to be like the flag lady, but some of them probably don't know who Mrs. Tattall is or even care and I don't blame them because Mrs. Tattall is my problem and not theirs and maybe Bob's problem and I think yeah she's Bob's problem too. And also. If you think about it, if you tell them not to be like the flag lady, then really you're being like the flag lady. Aren't you.

35 ways to be. That's the plan. A week for every way to be. That also gives time to fit in 35 ways not to be, right?

I forgot Tracy's calling tonight. Bye. Gotta answer.

August 26ᵗʰ

Well, I don't know where to begin. The flag lady or Tommy Cutler or Bob. Or. I'll start with the flag lady. So she pulls up like usual in the big white thing, but this time she has a camera. She takes a picture of me putting up the flag, then she puts the camera away and gets out another one and this one's a video camera. She makes a production of opening it up and turning it on and then points it at me when I'm trying to wrap the cord around the hook at the bottom of the pole. I says what's the movie for and she says for recording your disrespect and I says okay and I start to walk away and she says real loud see what I mean. I stop and say to the camera that it's not disrespectful to do my job and she says how about when you suddenly get to be a teacher when you haven't earned it and I say and I shouldn't have said it but I say Bob thinks I've earned it and she says Bob has no respect for the flag or the kids if he thinks a dirty flag and a janitor are good enough for the pole and the classroom and that's why he's done. And I say who's done and she says the headmaster and she turns off the camera and gets in her giant white Yeti and drives off.

So I think well she likes to be dramatic and I pretend not to notice all the stares that day and I show up early for my class in room 114. I was ready too. We were going to talk about the Golden Rule but not like Sunday school class. I had this grade book Miss Denton gave me to write all the kids names in which I did yesterday. The kids come in and two of them are late and I says you're late and they says so what. One of them says it first then the other one says it. So what if we're late. I says that's not How To Be and I say not to worry because that's not how you'll be very soon and one of them says don't worry Stan we won't be late again because this class ain't going to be a class. I says what's your name and he says Tommy Cutler and he says his mom says I'm not his teacher no way no how. I says my name is Mister Howland not Stan and he says you're Stan the janitor and I says Tommy you and I are going to work together pulling weeds after school today, and every day this week. Don't call me by my first name again unless I invite you to, and sit down. Tommy sits down and it's like you can hear a pin drop. Tommy takes out a cell phone, one of them i-phones I think, and starts punching in some stuff. I walk over and take it away and I takes him to the window and I say see those bushes right there and he shrugs and nods his head and I says, You're pulling all the weeds around those bushes, Get to work. He says you can't make me it's hot and I might get dehydrated and then my mom will sue the school and she's on the board so you better stop this right now and I open the door and he looks at everybody and I look at everybody and he goes out and I close the door and everybody watches him sit down like an Indian and he pulls a weed and throws it at the door but then he pulls another weed and puts it down next to his feet and then another and then I said is everybody okay with me being their How To Be teacher and they say yes and I say I promise they won't be bored if they promise to think a little bit about How To Be and I walk around the room and ask everybody their name and I shake everybody's hands and they look at each other and look out the window and I look out the window and Tommy Cutler's not out there. I almost went to the bathroom in my pants.

So I went out the door then went back in and said we're all going out to look for Tommy because we're a community. The kids liked that a lot, so we all went out and I said no yelling just stay close to me and tell me if you see Tommy and pretty quick I heard little Tamera Johnson say there he is. We all looked where Tamera pointed and there he was. Sitting on a picnic table in the quad. We get to the table and I says Tommy and he says yeah and I says we're going to have class right here in the quad and he says I don't care and I says move over and I sit next to him and tell everybody to sit at the table or on the ground or move another table over and four of the kids move another table over and now we've got room for everyone. When everyone is quiet I says we're gonna start the How to Be class with a question. Nobody asks what the question is so I says here's the question. Who thinks that if they were the teacher, they would think Tommy's been doing the right things for the last ten minutes of his life. Nobody said anything, just looked at each other and me. I says just raise your hand if you think Tommy's been doing the right thing today. Nobody raises their hand. I says Tommy you can raise your hand especially if you're proud of yourself or maybe proud of just one thing you've done in the last ten minutes. Tommy doesn't raise his hand. I says hey everyone I have an idea. Tamera Johnson and Freddy Kimball say what's the idea, and I feel Tommy Cutler sort of move a little bit like he wants to know the idea too. I says if everyone can write a good paragraph about why they didn't raise their hand, and that means everyone, then Tommy won't have to go to the headmaster. I could see they liked that idea, because first Tamera and then Freddy and then everybody, even Tommy, gets up and starts running across the quad toward our classroom and I says walk don't run and they walk fast like they can't wait to start. Tommy walks with me. I couldn't believe it. Right next to me. I says Tommy are you going to write a paragraph? He says no sir, I don't know why I didn't raise my hand so I can't write about it. I says maybe you don't know why you didn't raise your hand because it was you that we were talking about and he says yeah I guess so and I says I'm proud of him for not raising his hand and he says but I would have if they had and I says if you know that then you've got something to write about. And he looks at me. Just looks at me. He says can I have my cell phone back if I write the paragraph and I says no and he says okay. I says he can have it back tomorrow if he has a good day tomorrow and I says do you think that's fair and he says yes that's fair.

The paragraphs were pretty good. When the kids were done we read our paragraphs out loud until the bell rang. One kid's paragraph, I don't know his name by heart yet, said he was writing his paragraph so that Tommy wouldn't get in trouble with the headmaster and no other reason and everybody laughed and I said way to go. And some of the kids said What? And I said way to go, you fulfilled a responsibility and helped a friend all at the same time and you were honest about it without being a jackass, and they laughed and whispered to each other that Mister Howland said jackass. And I said tonight your homework is to write a paragraph about not being a jackass. I looked around the room and saw Tommy Cutler. He was packing his bookbag. He didn't read his paragraph to the class before the bell rang, but that's okay. We just ran out of time.

At four o'clock Bob came to the shop and we opened the chess set and set the pieces out and he made the first move and he said he got an email from Mrs. Cutler that she and her lawyer wanted to see Bob first thing tomorrow morning. He had a frown on his face as he took his right forefinger off the top of his pawn, meaning it was my turn. I says is it about our class today? How to Be? And he says yes. I says I had to teach Tommy and the class some things right away and he says Did you call Tommy Cutler a jackass and I says heavens no Bob and I moved my second pawn from the left up one space. He says did you take his cell phone away from him and I says yes and he says good. He says did you give it back and I says no not till tomorrow if he has a good day tomorrow and Bob says good. He says did you call Tommy a jackass and I says no Bob I didn't call him a jackass no. I says I told the kids to write a paragraph tonight about not being a jackass and he says good that's innovative and I says really? And he says yes. He says and you didn't call Tommy Cutler a jackass and I says I swear on my mother's grave and he says that's good enough for him and he moves his bishop out and I know what that means. Time to use what I've learned from the library book.

Bob beat me again, but I got my hand out there first. He looked real sad when I shook his hand. He said he was proud of me, that he looked up to me, and he wished that he had always been more like me. Well, it was a real awkward moment let me tell you. I said thank you Bob that means a lot and it does and he says he wants to give me my new contract and I says new contract and he says why yes you have more responsibilities now and you've had a great first day and I says but you're meeting with Mrs. Cutler tomorrow morning with her lawyer and he says yes why do you think I wanted this How To Be class here, and I says oh I see and he says that poor kid has dinner every night with that lady and it's hard to blame him so we got to help him or we're not really a school and I says exactly. He says my new contract will have an extra ten thousand dollars in it and I says my gosh and he says here it is and he pulls out a folded piece of paper that says Addendum to Stan Howland's Contract and he says sign down here and I take his black pen and I sign it. I sign a second one too. He stands up and says You never know. He waves the contracts in the air when he says You never know, and he looks like he's going to cry. And he gives me one of them contracts to take home with me. I didn't like that. I should of just shook his hand and said you can give me the money on a handshake Bob but I didn't. I kind of think I didn't because of what the flag lady said this morning. About Bob. About what if he's not here to give me the money on a handshake and I think is that why he brought the contract to our chess game and still I should of said no Bob a handshake will do and that's how we should teach kids to be.

I don't feel like sleeping tonight.

August 27th

This morning I got to the flagpole and two ladies were wait-ing for me. The flag lady and Mrs. Cutler. The flag lady went first and said this is your last day Stan. I said Mister Howland and she laughed. I said I only take my orders or my walking papers from Bob. That's when Mrs. Cutler said she, Mrs. Cutler, was this thing called interim head. I said interim head? And she said interim head and said Stan I'm acting under my authority in removing you as an employee at this school as maintenance director and in this little charade as a teacher. I think she said ludicrous or something like that, but she also said little charade so that's what she said. I says what happened to Bob and the flag lady starts to answer but Mrs. Cutler waves her hand like she's stopping traffic and the flag lady shuts up. Mrs. Cutler says I speak for the board Stan when I say that the headmaster has resigned. For person-al reasons she said. To pursue other opportunities she said and I said is that a personal reason and she said is what a personal reason and I said to pursue other opportunities and she said it doesn't matter so go pack up your things in the shop and there will be three weeks severance for you and that's very nice of us because this is a right-to-work state and what that means is we don't have to give you a thing Stan but we are. Now my heart is going real fast and kind of booming in my head. I looked at the flag in my hands and thought about saying something pretty not nice but Tracy got me this book so I could have an outlet for my anger, that's what she called it, and I remembered that and then I remembered castling. I remembered castling. You got to remem-ber castling before they get you in checkmate. That's what it said on page 27.

I have a contract, I said. Excuse me Mrs. Cutler asked real loud. I said I have a contract and it says I get extra money for teaching my How to Be classes to freshmen, and it says I am Director of Maintenance. It's an addendum I says. Signed by Bob and me and not just a handshake either. The flag lady says Bob's not the headmaster any more and never will be and Mrs. Cutler stops traffic again and the flag lady shuts up and Mrs. Cutler says Bob's not the headmaster any more and it's unfortunate what happened and I says I think he was the headmaster when he signed it and she says listen if you want your severance then you'll go quietly before the students see you and expect to see you in class. I says is this about the flag or is this about teaching your children not to be jackasses. Their jaws both open up and get stuck. I says now I have to do my job and then get ready to teach your children not to be jackasses and I'm pretty sure they don't want to be jackasses if they can help it. I walked away and then all I could think about was Bob.

I couldn't eat my lunch. I went to the administration building and asked the front desk lady is Bob here and she looked nervous and said no and I says will he be here and she says no and I says can I have his number so I can call him and she says my God Stan I'm so sorry you haven't heard and I say yes I have and she says no you haven't and I says what do you mean and she says Oh My God and puts her hand on her mouth. She says Bob's wife found him a little while ago and

August 28ᵗʰ

I can't write today. Sorry, Tracy.

August 29ᵗʰ

Sorry.

August 30th

Bob was my best friend. We used to play chess together every afternoon, you know. I have to tell you, I don't understand what the flag lady was doing at Bob's memorial service today. Mrs. Cutler neither. Mrs. Cutler even got to speak to the whole audience about the board's great respect for the man and his legacy.

That's what she actually said. The man and his legacy. She actually said that, right before she talked about the sad mysteries of depression, and what it can do to great men like Bob. Bob's grown-up son and daughter were in the front row with their mother, thinking how great it is that this wonderful woman is honoring their dad. The man and his legacy. She actually said that. Might as well have been the flag lady up there. Crispy and clean. What a jackass.

Tomorrow my How to Be class and I are going to talk about that word. Legacy not jackass. We're done with jackass. The grownups will keep showing the kids what that is. Since some of the kids went to Bob's service with their parents, I had the kids look up legacy for homework this weekend and use it in a smart sentence in their journals, now that they have one and I have one.

I'm glad Bob and page 27 taught me how to castle. My lawyer says we might have to worry about next year, but that's next year and there's plenty of time for my queen to get busy now that I did my castling. I'm going to send my queen all over that board before next year, and these kids aren't going to be pawns when they grow up. Aren't going to be jackasses neither. Bob saw to that.

There aren't a lot of ways to teach sportsmanship and fairness in a classroom, but those are two of the 35. So. The kids take turns using Bob's chess set. Two kids every class period, no matter what topic we're doing that week. Started two days ago. Today was the first time I saw the loser stick his hand out first.

That's class, Tommy, I says. Real class.

I like to see kids smile when they think you're not looking. That's a quote from Bob.

Spot on, Bob.

THE REVEREND JOHN AND A MOMENT OF TWILIGHT

Robert Cates

The disused blue Toyota pulled down the gravel lane and came to a crunching halt just in front of the open doors. The sky was just a little off gray, a hint of winter still in the air. She came through the sliding doors with a smile on her face. Horses and barns always did that. Memphis whined a low hello as she drifted past his stall. He got a whisper and a pat in reply. Today, she was in a hurry and would not afford him more. Thoughts of her own magnificent Thoroughbred were itching at her mind. She moved to the last two stalls. She said hello to a grand bay Thoroughbred and did an about face and peered inside at another Thoroughbred. This one was taller, slightly more muscular, and raven black. "Hello Rev, impatient as always?"

Robyn unlatched and pushed open the heavy well-crafted door, standing in the opening to prevent the energetic animal from gaining the freedom he was unable to handle. With a deft and practiced motion, she placed the worn halter over his elegant muzzle, pausing momentarily to scratch his alert ears. As was their ritual, she now turned her back to the black tower and began fishing tentatively in her pocket. He knew the routine well and understood a spectacular salivary reward would soon follow. He never understood the reason for the treats; perhaps they were just for being. Rev could take the anticipation no longer; her movements were just too slow. So he began nudging her in the back, insisting she hurry. Delaying a moment longer, she held her hand behind her back, palm up. Presenting the daily offering, one circular, red and white-stripped peppermint. Swiftly, yet cautiously, Rev picked up the mint with his searching lips, paused to savor it briefly and then crushed the candy to oblivion.

The daily pleasantries served, she intoned in a quiet voice of command leaving no room for dissent, "Time for work."

Quickly now, for the precious moments of daylight would soon fade, she backed him into the crossties. The massive animal was well accustomed to the routine, but never allowing to be fully mastered, he protested by lifting a powerful hoof and striking the concrete with an astounding crash.

A voice from the door declared, "Don't let him get away with that!"

But before the sentence was complete, she had already rewarded the action with an authoritative, yet harmless, slap on the shoulder. "He is just picking up bad habits from Moment."

"Well, I hope he doesn't start cribbing next."

She backed a step away from Rev and glanced at her husband, then to the stall holding the lame bay. The brass doorplate read *A Moment of Twilight*. "I wish I was riding Moment today. Reverend is working hard and coming along fine, but I don't know if it will ever be the same."

Robert, always logical: "I know, honey, but you do realize the chances are slim to none that Moment will ever be more than a lawn ornament again."

The comment brought an expected silence to the conversation. The horses, sensing the mood, remained hushed as well. The somber disposition lasted only a few heartbeats and a breath. She announced it's ending by picking up a curry and beginning her daily meditation; grooming and examining her sound mount. Wisely leaving his wife to her own thoughts, Robert slid open the door and stepped in with the large bay Thoroughbred. Robert experienced a tinge of regret as he soothed Moment, with a rub on the neck. He had not trained and worked the horse. The horse had never belonged to him, but seeing the shattered potential and the feeling of something lost always caused in him a dismal sentiment. After two years of marriage he was somewhat enlightened to the nature of his wife, and he knew with certainty the oppressive pain the animal and the accident caused for her.

Five months earlier, while studying for an exam he had gotten the call demanding he rush to the barn. The call was short and simple.

"Rob, come to the barn. Moment is hurt!"

"How bad is it?"

"It's serious. It's his leg."

"I'll be right there."

The drive from the house, two blocks from campus, to the stable on the other side of town was just long enough for an infinite number of scenarios and expenses to flash through his mind. All came with a graphic mental picture and financial dread. Ten minutes later, as he got out of the truck and met a wife with mascara-and-tear-stained cheeks standing in the dusty sunlight of the doorway, he felt the gravity of the situation pull at his heart. Robert stopped in the doorway, gave his wife a supportive embrace, and moved into the dim interior to view the damage. Even with the dim fluorescent lights high above, it was easy to see the extreme trauma. The mental pictures were not near as ghastly as reality. The ankle joint was ripped open halfway around the leg, the bottom flap of skin and muscle was hanging down a good three inches, and the upper gash was ugly and jagged. A fist would nearly fit in the remaining fissure. The swelling was completely disfiguring the entire lower leg.

She had partly staunched the bleeding, attempted to wash away the dirt and debris, and calmed the horse. Thinking hastily, and somewhat uncertain, he decided action was needed to prevent her from becoming frantic. "Robyn, is there a vet on the way?"

"I couldn't get ahold of Dr. Micks, so I had to call the Cerulean Clinic. They said someone would be here as soon as possible."

Reaffirming her decision to get someone there as soon as possible, even if it was not the best equine vet in the western half of Kentucky, "That's okay. We can get an initial opinion, start him on antibiotics, and probably a tetanus shot as well. I don't think they would do much else here at the barn this late. Anyway, Dr. Micks might not be able to get here soon enough."

Coming back from washing his hands at the pump, Robert assured Moment and squatted to examine the leg. "We need more light. Can you see if there is a lamp or drop-light in the storage stall?"

Robyn set about searching the barn for a light while he investigated the injury for several minutes, looking for bone fragments, torn ligaments, or any clear sign of impending doom. His actions were superficial. The scene was way beyond any backyard medicine he could muster up. However, he felt action and movement would help keep his resolute wife from faltering. She was strong and steady, but he was not sure he could yet predict her breaking point with any certitude. Take no chances. A sixteen-two hand injured ex-racehorse, a hysterical woman, and a back woods vet were not a trio he was interested in witnessing. She returned, looking very determined. "I couldn't find a light, maybe the vet will bring one."

Robert stood and faced his wife, both aware of the necessary questions. A leg injury was always critical. How certain must they be before they would have him put down? Would they get a second opinion? If they had to, what about the burying him? And if he survived initially, what about permanent lameness and his quality of life? Questions best discussed without spectators. So, in hushed tones, cautious of horses overhearing, they discussed the possibilities. Periodically, glancing from the questioning eyes of the bay to his mangled leg.

Finally, just as the sun was finishing its downward arch, a small white Nissan pickup turned into the drive. A tall man with coffee colored hair and a hefty paunch climbed out. Stuffing his hands into the front of his overalls, resting them on the curve of his belly, he spat a declarative stream of tobacco juice into the grass. "I'm Hank Balmer. Ya'll got a hurt horse?"

Instantly, Robyn moved forward and replied, "Yes, it is his front left ankle. We are not sure what happened. The fencing is good wood planks and I couldn't find anything he could cut it on."

In an almost exaggerated bluegrass drawl, "Well I reckon mostly they get hurt and we ain't gonna find out what happened. Let's go see what this uns dun fer himself."

Robert, feeling a need to interject something, broke in. "You'll probably need a flashlight or something, the light is not too good. Oh, and I'm Robert and this is my wife Robyn."

The man seeing the animal for the first time down the hallway through the murky light let out a soft whistle through his teeth. "He sure is a big good-looking thing."

He ducked under the cross-ties, walked completely around the Thoroughbred, patting him cautiously on the hind-end, and came to a stop beside the shoulder belonging to the bad leg. He stooped over, his own overgrown paunch sagging, and lifted up the leg. He looked at the nasty gash, flexed the joint a few times, replaced the leg in its original position and exhaled, "Hmm. Hmm." Suddenly, the slow lilt to his voice gone, "How long has it been like this?"

"I don't know. I got to the barn around six. He was standing in the pasture like that. I phoned the barn owner and he last checked on the horses at nine this morning. Everything was fine then."

Without further comment, Hank headed out to his pickup. He went to the driver's side and opened a rectangular door in the veterinary shell. A quick rummage, then he moved to the next compartment. Robyn watched with interest as the veterinarian took out a large plastic box and began filling, emptying, and re-filling it with selected accoutrements. His uncertainty in selecting the needed items was not reassuring.

After he had been in every compartment and behind the cab seat he was confident he was ready to treat the injured animal. He strolled back into the barn with its smells of dry hay and earthy manure. "I have not had much experience with this type of injury. I spend most of my time neutering dogs and vaccinating farm animals. I don't recommend sutures because we don't know how long the wound has been open and I'm pretty certain they wouldn't hold."

Hank placed his plastic parcel of goods on the ground. He leaned over, selected a flashlight and attempted to turn it on. The light refused to shine. A few quick flips of the wrist and the beam shot out and he handed the light to Robert. Next, he stretched rubber gloves over his meaty hands. Rubber gloves in place, the vet was officially ready to begin. Hank reached into his box and withdrew a large bottle of betadine scrub, which he handed to Robyn, and a handful of gauze pads. Squatting down uneasily, once again on eye level with the injury, he began cleaning the grotesque wound with the betadine and gauze pads. Working diligently under the uncertain light, a quick squirt of the mahogany substance and several circular passes over the rent flesh, and then he would discard the used gauze haphazardly on the dirt and sawdust floor. After five or six gauze pads, he wiped away the excess betadine and applied a topical antibacterial salve. He followed this with a larger piece of gauze placed over the exposed flesh and bound this in place by wrapping it with a roll of gauze and finishing it with two five inch pieces of medical tape. Finally, he covered the entire bandage with green elastic vet wrap. "I think that should do it," the vet said as he brought the girth of his body upright holding a gargantuan syringe of milky penicillin in his right hand. "I am also giving him 16cc of Pen G to fight infection." As an afterthought he inquired, "Can you all give injections? He will need an additional 12cc every twenty-four hours or so."

"Sure", Robert replied. "Where is the best location?"

The vet answered by indicating a large muscular V on the side of the neck and an area of muscle on the rump. "The easiest place is here along the neck or in this gluteal muscle on the rump. However, I suggest that you stick to the rump." As he dispensed the injection into the muscle on Moment's posterior he gave a little more guidance: "Give him a couple of pats in the area then stick him with a solid deliberate motion, then pullback slightly on the plunger to make sure your not in a blood vessel. If you see blood, remove the needle and start over."

"Should we disinfect the injection site beforehand?"

"It wouldn't hurt."

Knowing who owned and trained the bay, the vet looked to Robyn and asked, "Has he had a tetanus vaccination?"

Without hesitation, "Yes, he is current. He received it last May."

"Alright, then. I'll just give him a booster."

With this statement, Hank once again stooped the mass of his body down to his box, tossed in the used syringe and retrieved a more petit syringe and a small brown vial. He expertly drew the contents of the vial into the syringe and then deposited them into the neck of the horse. He replaced the smaller syringe and brought out a bottle of penicillin, a handful of syringes, and some needles; these he handed to Robyn. "That is mostly full, it should be plenty. Keep it refrigerated, and give him 12cc every day. Leave that ankle wrapped up until Friday and I'll be back out to check on it."

"Is there anything else?"

"Nope, just keep him stalled and watch him."

Hank packed up his gear and headed down the stall-lined hallway toward the door and the fresh early evening air, the young couple trailing expectantly behind him, fervent for something more definite or reassuring. He walked out to the passenger side of the Nissan, opened the door and placed his container on the seat. He closed the door and moved around to the driver's side. Robert and Robyn stood by, still watching and waiting intently for some magical words about the torn horse. Hank leaned in, took a ticket pad off the dash, and began scribbling under the dim cab light. Finished, he briskly ripped off the sheet and handed it to Robyn. The cost did not seem overly exorbitant for forty-five minutes of veterinarian time. The total of one hundred and one dollar was clearly broken down; forty-five dollars for a farm visit, fifteen for tetanus, twenty-eight for Penicillin G, and a few dollars for miscellaneous supplies.

"You take a check?"

"Certainly, make it out to Cerulean Clinic."

She walked over to her blue Camry, sat inside and quickly wrote out the check for the suspect medical treatment. Back almost instantly, she stopped in front of him and extended her arm to full length bestowing the check. He reached out with an ample hand and plucked the payment aptly from her fingers.

"Call the clinic for a time on Friday."

The door squeezed shut, the engine started, and the small truck headed down the drive.

No sooner had the headlights lit up the privet shrubs across the road and turned down the street, Robert turned to his wife and proclaimed, "I may not be a vet, but I don't believe he knows his ass from a hole in the ground."

He noticed the tears welling up in her eyes. She had been all business for so long. "It's not fair!" A hint of rage surfacing, "He has been doing so great. He's only been completely sound for two months since the kicked and fractured shoulder. Sunday we were jumping three feet perfectly, like a team. He knows what I'm thinking."

Robert, in an attempt to soothe, "I know. But we don't really know what's going to happen with him, and Dr. Balmer let on like Moment would be fine."

They walked back into the gloomy barn with the wide-eyed Moment waiting patiently. Robyn picked up a brush and began to tenderly brush his face.

"Robyn, I don't trust that vet. That hole in is deep and he didn't even inspect it. There could be torn tendons, ligaments, or damage to the joint itself. For that matter, there could be pieces of metal or wood lodged down in it."

"Well, I've already left a message with Dr. Micks' answering service. Maybe we can trailer him up to Paducah tomorrow."

When they returned home, the message light on the recorder was already blinking.

"Robyn, this is Dr. Micks, I am sorry to hear about Moment. I suggest I see him first thing in the morning. I will be there by seven."

"Can you miss class in the morning? I can get off work, and we can have him there by seven or eight."

"Of course! I just hope we can get him on the trailer in the morning. Do you think he can trailer?"

Her answer was a tentative shrug.

In the early glimmering dawn, Moment walked resolutely onto the tall Thoroughbred trailer. The couple worked and talked in still tones in reverence to the majesty of first light and the solemnity of the occasion.

"I've never seen him load like that. It was as if he knows what is going on and we are taking him for a help."

"We can only hope."

They checked everything again; the hitch, the lights, the tail-ramp, and finally the demeanor of the placid rider. Finally, with the sun beginning to inch inquiringly through the glistening leaves of the red oaks, the Dodge Ram Charger groaned as they started the seventy-mile northward caravan. The morning was pensive. The passengers seemed to be possessed a lugubrious quality even as the rejuvenating sunlight cast about them.

After a series of interstates, highways, curving back-roads, hills, and a one-lane trestle bridge they arrived at Dr. Micks' prominent equestrian clinic. They headed for the main building, a large barn-hospital complex with a complete surgical and recovery unit. As they crossed the large gravel parking area, they slowed to watch a couple of middle aged cowboy types try to man-handle a handsome buckskin Quarter Horse onto a stock trailer. The cowboys were starting to sweat and their patience was waning. Robyn knew they would not appreciate an audience, but that is life, and she wanted to witness someone else's struggles. So, she stopped several yards away, safely away from the bucking and rearing Quarter Horse, and watched as the seething men repeatedly tried to force the recoiling horse onto the trailer.

"Robyn! Good morning" Dr. Micks exalted as he came from behind. He reached out to shake hands and continued,

"This must be your husband."

"Good morning, I'm Robert." The correct reply, but all of Robert's attention was plainly on the spectacle of hooves, hats, and hollering. Robert was new to the world of equines and equines' asses.

"Pardon me for a moment, but it is much too early for this. Besides, I just got that horse patched up." Donald Micks marched up to the man fighting with the lead-rope, took the lead, urged the two men back with a wave of his free hand, and slowly walked the buckskin away from the trailer. Never looking back at the horse, he completed two large strolling circles behind the trailer, the last ending at the loading ramp. He continued effortlessly up the ramp with the horse in tow, secured the lead-rope to the front of the trailer with a safety knot and stepped out through the escape door. Without a word to horse or owners, he came back to the gratified couple. "If you'll get Moment, and meet me at the side entrance, we will get started."

It did not take Dr. Micks long to evaluate the situation. He gave Moment a small sedative, waited just a few minutes, and began by cutting away massive amounts of flesh beginning to turn proud. It was amazing how it had grown aggressively overnight. Next, he plunged his first finger into the major cavity and felt and prodded for some time. A quick glance up, with a negative nod, gave Robyn and Robert an idea of what might follow. The two watched helplessly as he worked. Although Dr. Micks appeared young, perhaps forty, for an experienced and well respected horse vet his movements were confident and implied his knowledge. Straightening his back slightly, he reached into his left jacket pocket and removed a syringe. The needle was especially long. Grasping the hoof with his right hand, he flexed the mangled joint into a forty-five degree angle; with his left he inserted the needle into the undamaged side of the joint. Attentively, he depressed the plunger. In concert with the descending plunger, a golden fluid shot forth from the fleshy crevice. Immediately, he removed the syringe, gingerly let the leg down, and looked up, "Did you see that?" Two heads bobbed up and down in unison.

"That was synovial fluid, whatever caused the damage punctured the joint capsule." Standing now, to better respond to questions, Donald Micks massaged his back.

Robyn, looking miserable: "What does that mean, exactly?"

"I have treated three similar cases. One recovered fully, one fair with severe arthritis, and the last had to be put down."

"What is the treatment?"

"We can do surgery. We can go in and clean up the damaged tissue, ensure nothing is embedded, and generally make for a cleaner heal. It would be expensive."

"How much?"

"Twenty-two to twenty-five hundred."

Robert inquired, "What are the chances of a full recovery with the surgery?"

Dr. Micks looked to Robyn, "Robyn, I know you have been training him to be a jumper, but if he makes it, his best hope will be some occasional light riding."

Looking back to Robert, "With surgery, fifty-fifty he makes it. Without, forty-sixty he makes it."

Robert's mind shot into high gear. A surgery, the cost of which could buy another Thoroughbred off the track, would only increase his chances slightly, at best. That would be a lot of money for a young couple to invest. Especially when the best-case scenario would be for them to be saddled with an already expensive keeper that could only be ridden lightly, occasionally. Moment did not have the temperament to be an occasionally lightly ridden horse. He was too hot and high-strung. Moment was an animal bred for speed and competition. It had taken Robyn over three years to undo partially what the track had done in two. He was just now truly sane and safe enough to compete as a green hunter in a fenced arena. The decision for Robert was easy. Do everything possible for Moment, short of investing in an unreliable surgery.

For Robyn, the decision was the same, only more heart wrenching. She had moved from Georgia to Kentucky with the animal three years prior. He had been a companion during the lonely times. She had family in the area. An uncle to be exact, dean of her department at the university, yet the horse had always provided friendship, safety, and sanctuary. Moment mystically had known what to do; when to rush to the gate and have her rub his ears, when to maintain silence in fellowship, or when to make her chase him in a game of tag. He knew. And she knew the reality of the unfortunate situation. She needed to ride, just as he needed to run. She must have a sound horse, able to jump and compete. The surgery was speculative and the cost would prevent her from riding. She loved the animal; she knew he had the heart of a warrior, but the body of an anemic. She had known his Achilles' heel for years. The racetrack had ravaged his health. Since rescuing him from an eventual trip with the meat man, he had suffered one malady after another. The decision was made. Do everything possible for Moment, short of investing in an unreliable surgery.

They looked at each other. Each knowing the other's heart and mind. Robert knew the deep and resigned look in her eyes, it meant one thing, she agreed with the decision tormenting their thoughts. He also understood she was unable to utter the words.

"We will pass on the surgery."

"I did not want to influence your decision. However, I know Moment and the situation and I think that is the right choice." Dr. Micks continued, "It may sound harsh and insensitive, but it would have been throwing good money after bad. We will do what we can. I believe, with diligence, he will recover as much as possible."

Five months later, Robert was standing with the visibly healthy animal. It had been a long and arduous journey. They had for the first three months trailered him twice a week to Paducah to have antibiotics injected directly into the joint. Moment was no dolt, he soon realized there would be no pleasure for him at the end of these routine drives, just the prospect of being examined and injected. In addition he was rapidly building up nervous energy from remaining stationary in a twelve-foot by twelve-foot stall. So, with increasing intensity he would decide not to load onto the trailer, these episodes became contests of patience and ingenuity.

They had filled him up twice a day with large quantities of oral antibiotics, which had to be crushed and infused into a variety of equine deserts. They had cleansed and wrapped the wound daily and watched the leg slowly regain its original fit appearance. These had not been hard times. The actions of caring for Moment were easy. Worse had been the time spent wondering what was happening unseen. The recurring thought was always on the fringe; was an infection growing in the confines of the dark space, unseen, waiting to fasten the joint immovable; certain death for the horse. The waiting and uncertainty had been agonizing. The waiting was now over. It appeared that he would live.

Robert looked out the steel latticed window of Moment's stall and perceived that those last five months were still heavy on Robyn's mind. He knew her remedy for this melancholy; it would be hair from the dog that bit her. So he began planning the long evening he would be spending at the stable. He thought a little more time with the horses, then some quiet horse free time fishing at the edge of the ten-acre lake. The weather was warmer, the sun rising a little higher each day; perhaps the water temperature had risen enough to stir hunger in a largemouth bass. Then, back to the barn to help untack and discuss the evening ride.

"Robyn, I am going to turn Moment out for a while, is that alright? Or, would you rather he stay in while you are riding?"

Robyn thought about the question. "Go ahead, let him out. I think I am just going on a short trail ride, around the lake. I read an article recently about incorporating a relaxing change in the training schedule to help with nervous habits."

"You think that will help with his head throwing?"

"It can't hurt, I have looked at everything else. I am almost certain it is not the bit, tack, or any discomfort; it must be nerves."

"It is a nice day for it."

Robyn looked up from picking out the great black's hooves and watched as Robert reached out Moment's stall and took the leather halter from its peg. He loved animals, all animals, she just regretted that he had not taken a greater interest in riding.

Robert led the massive animal out into the warming afternoon light and the two stood silently for a moment. They made their way over to the gate, where Robert pushed it open with a foot, unsnapped the halter, and turned the horse out. The horse turned around, came back to the gate and stood expectantly waiting. The slender man nimbly climbed onto the top rail of the fence and sat whispering to the horse. The horse knew that today's topic of conversation was not important, but he had grown accustomed to the quiet voice; it soothed him, he trusted it. After a few minutes, Moment decided he had had enough of humanity for a while and began walking carelessly toward an ideal patch of lush green grass.

"Trot!"

Even after the months of inactivity, the bay was still trained to voice and he immediately picked up the gait, diagonal legs moving in unison. The voice lingered for a moment to let the horse travel several yards at the slower pace.

"Canter!"

It still amazed Robert that a man could command such a force of nature with a single word. The horse transitioned smoothly into his preferred speed, gliding effortlessly across the dipping pasture, stopping only after he realized he had overshot his targeted forage and the voice was no longer speaking to him.

"Robyn, you can't tell he is lame at the canter."

"No, but it is still very apparent at the trot."

Robert, knowing she was right, but still wanting to bolster both morale and hope replied, "I can barely notice it and it is becoming less noticeable every week. Look at him. He is really enjoying himself."

As he turned back toward the barn, he noticed his small wife on Reverend's large back. Something was missing, the saddle. "What are you doing?"

"Going for a short relaxing walk around the lake."

He knew immediately from her tone that any arguing with her about the rationality of her decision would be a waste of time. He disappeared around the corner of the barn and quickly returned with an ultralight fishing rod. As luck or skill would have it, he rarely caught those huge fish pictured in all the sporting magazines. So, with a philosophical approach he had decided he could replicate the experience of catching them by using the lightest equipment.

"I'll walk with you to the lake."

"That'll be nice since, with you working that crazy schedule, we rarely get to talk."

As they walked toward the rear of the farm to the lake and the surrounding woods they chatted comfortably about the trivial things in life that make it worth living; the color of the sky, the unusual flower, or perhaps the chance of ever getting a new truck. She rode high above on the magnificent beast and he walked sanguinely beside. They were living a tranquil and fairly normal life and they were enjoying it.

"I'll be here at this end of the lake. If you need anything just yell," he announced as he stopped and began to unhook the chartreuse roostertail from the bottom eye of his fishing rod, slowly working his way through the tall weeds and briars at the water's edge, trying to get into position to toss the lure into a prime spot.

"I'll be back shortly, we're just going for a short walk. It will be dark in about an hour and a half."

As the lure made a placid splash into the blue green water he replied without looking, "Alright."

The evening was beautiful. Chirping tree frogs were chanting their mantra; the chorus repeating over and over, keeping time for the world to hear. Clouds drifted high above, aimlessly shifting about, crossing in a maze of unfathomable patterns, following where they must, to arrive in a predestined juncture; evolving as unseen currents carried them along. Lofty, gaunt, and miasmic, they would not be able to hold the warmth of the failing sun.

"Rob! Rob! *Rob!*"

The frenzied calls, starting as a soft perplexity on the nerves, quickly growing to full-blown panic, rang out from down the path. Electric trepidation keyed his senses to a pitched level. His memory lagged behind action. The fishing reel lying half in the water, he was running. Branches blurred past, briars grabbing and pulling to restrain his motion. Time stopped. The utter stillness oppressed. Motion was impossible. Inches crawled into feet, which languidly grew into yards, and finally miles seemed to pass into an eternity of silence and distance. After two hundred yards, as he passed a slight bend he spotted her flying down the trail on an intercept course. A mask of horror covered her usual serene face as she appeared and disappeared between the trees along the trail. Her mouth was moving and Robert knew he should be understanding something, but his mind was not comprehending. She appeared to be unhurt. The relief overwhelmed all mental function. The distance closed to a few feet when he began to understand.

"Reverend!" she cried as she slumped over, gasping for air.

"Rev is," she blurted out as Robert noticed the black mud splattered over her legs.

"I...Rev is...You've got to..." she half screamed, half moaned as she stood up, clean fresh air struggling to refill her lungs.

"Are you alright?" Robert pleaded.

"Yes. Reverend is stuck in the mud. Come on!" She turned and began jogging back down the trail.

As he trudged after her, he inquired with the old dread rising, "Is it bad?"

"He is in the trees and mud," she replied trying not to allow the sorrow or feelings of unfairness defeat her.

"In the trees?" a hint of dismay in his tone.

"I can't explain now, we've got to hurry."

The trail meandered along the bank of the lake, twenty-five to fifty feet above the high water mark. It worked its way parallel to the water and the steep upper slope, passing under low limbs and between massive trunks. It was dark and sullen this deep into the forest along the base of a steep ridge. The imposing oaks and beeches of the upper canopy suffocated the sunlight from above and the dense understory of buttonbush and alder marred the view of the lake. Outside the sun may have still been hanging on, but inside the heavy forest it was nearly forgotten. They passed over a small rivulet finding its way down between two fingers of the ridge. The water was stained and murky from the tannins of the dead leaves and stagnant soil it crawled through as it made its way to the lake.

As Robert crossed over with the trail, he noticed a set of disarrayed hoof prints. The horse had shied from the damp unsure footing.

Without slowing her pace Robyn huffed out, "I got off here to lead him across. I was following those tracks there and he panicked and reared."

She pointed to the set of disarrayed tracks and a set of orderly tracks that continued up the other side along the dry path. "He's right up ahead!"

Robert moved out in front and began scanning the area ahead for the huge animal. He should see him by now; it is not hard to spot a sixteen hand, thousand pound horse. The horse should easily stand out, even in the fading gray light. There was no sign.

"Do you see him?" she quietly asked. Half-hoping he would not be where she had left him.

"No."

"He was just ahead on the left."

There was a darker area to the left, between the trail and the water. It appeared almost as an absence of light that radiated an ephemeral impression. A low rumbling nay affirmed the dreaded suspicion. That was the horse, and his entire body rose no higher than two feet above the forest floor. The couple quickened their pace. *"Holy shit!"* was the only thought flashing over and over through Robert's mind. The front of the horse was completely hidden below the dark engulfing mire, his head lying morosely in the damp earth. The large nostrils flared, specks of muck shot out with each labored exhale. The huge ebon eyes were glazed and watched apathetically. A sudden spasm rippled through the animal as Rev tried feebly to tear free of the strangling mud. Despair drizzled out from the scene. Animal fear tainted the already fetid air. The pair made their way closer to the snarled companion; each step they sank deeper into the quagmire.

Dismal shock emitted from the young woman and broke the silence. "He wasn't like this when I left! He was standing between the trees! It was only up to his ankles. No, no, no!" she whimpered at the sight.

The front of the horse had been swallowed up to his chest. There was no visible sign of his front legs. The trunk of his body was canted to the right like a listing ship. His hind end was a nightmare. Thick low growing alders had woven a web of crisscrossed branches above and along the ground and his rear legs were securely trapped in it. They were a myriad of flesh and wood. At first glance, between the mud and limbs, it was hard to grasp the situation. The hind legs were not sunk in the mud like the rest of the body. They were transfixed on scarcely firmer ground, resting in a confusion of roots and limbs. The right leg was resting precariously on a single branch. Another pair of branches entangled the left. The end of one branch started behind the horse ran adjacent and underneath the leg, then made an abrupt right turn to lay tightly against the back and ending at a solid trunk. The second branch ran atop the left leg and belonged to another trunk that pinned the helpless horse to the other tree. This second tree was situated at Reverend's stifle and it held him steadfast. It was ugly.

Robert walked quietly toward Rev, sinking as he went, each step sucking him deeper into the mud. He struggled the final few feet on his hands and knees pulling himself along by pulling at shrubs and tree limbs. "Rev, what have you done to yourself?" he quietly asked, while thinking what am I supposed to do now? He stroked the caked mud from around the horse's eyes and nostrils and tried to position the heavy muzzle so that it was out of the muck as much as possible. The trapped animal was breathing heavily and had apparently been struggling.

"Calm down big guy. Easy does it. Relax for a bit."

"Rob, be careful. If he fights to get up you'll be trapped."

"I know, but he can't go anywhere."

Robert was now half sitting half standing, he had sunk to his waist in the muck. He twisted around to see Robyn and the scene visibly shook her. It looked hopeless. She was standing with arms folded across her chest, almost as if protecting herself from the coming chill and despair. Robert knew that she understood the solemnity of situation, but he also knew what she expected from him. He must get that horse out of the mire and quick. The thought that he may disappoint her made his agony worse.

Most Thoroughbreds off the track do not have the consistency suited to withstand serious mental and physical distress. Even for a Quarter Horse the situation would be serious. However, for a sleek and spirited animal like Reverend, it couldn't get much worse. He was being held down against his will, his long fast legs were tangled in a wooden snare, he was up to his neck in a wet sucking quagmire, and the temperature was dropping. If he had not already sustained serious leg injuries then the next threats were shock, colic, and even founder.

She broke the silence. "He was standing between those trees. He must have tried to jump through the branches and fell and got tangled."

"It doesn't matter. Let's just work on getting him out."

"Is he alright?"

"How the hell should I know?" A look of regret shot across his face, "Sorry, He's got some scraps on his rear legs and back from the branches, but I can't tell about his front legs. He does seem to be calming down."

"How are we going to get him out?"

"I don't know!"

That was a mistake, but he was in a bit of shock himself. His mind was working too fast for tact.

"I'm going to dig down in the mud as far as I can to feel his front legs."

Robert worked his way to the front of Rev and started feeling and digging his way down the left leg. The mud was cold. He could reach nearly all the way down the cannon bone. He worked his way down the right. "They seem to be alright as far as I can tell."

He next looked at the tangled mess of legs and alder limbs then began working his way back to the anxious woman. Once on semisolid ground, he began to recite his meager and incomplete plan. "One of us has to go get a saw and help. The other needs to keep the horse calm."

She responded, "I'll go. You've got him calmed down."

Robert knew he could run a lot faster and get back sooner, but he also knew she didn't want to just sit helpless with the suffering animal. "We need a sharp handsaw or chainsaw, his lead rope and halter, and more rope if you can find any."

"What if Jack is not home?"

"I guess you'd better just start knocking on doors and find someone."

"Can we use Jack's tractor?"

"It won't fit down the trail. Nothing will fit down the trail."

"Anything else?"

"You'd better call a vet and have them ready when we get him out."

He grabbed and hugged her and she started off. Trotting down the trail, she quickly disappeared between the trees. Suddenly lonely, he turned and made his way back to the horse. The horse was momentarily content not to struggle, so Robert sat down in the mud and placed Reverend's head in his lap to keep it out of the ooze. "Reverend John, if you do what I say, I promise, I'll get you out. I'm not sure how, just yet. But, I will. First things first, stay calm, you'll need all your strength."

Time seemed to stand still. The two sat in the cold wet earth waiting.

Robyn passed the time by alternating running and walking.

Jack and Lisa's house was about a mile ahead. The burning in her chest kept the apprehension at a manageable level. However, she couldn't keep the broken record from playing, "Why me? Why me? Why always me?"

She got to the log house, ran up on the veranda, and tentatively knocked on the storm door. She didn't know how to ask for help. Especially, from someone she hardly knew. A nice looking woman in her mid forties wearing a cardigan and jeans opened the door. "Robyn, are you alright?"

"Not really, Reverend is stuck in the mud."

Instantly, "What do you need?"

"Is Jack home?"

"No, but he was supposed to fly in at 6:30, he should be home any minute."

"Rob's with the horse. He said he needs a chainsaw or something, anything. I need to call a vet."

"I don't know what Jack's got in the shop, but I'll call Gary, he'll know. Come in and sit down, it is getting cold out there."

"I can't, I'm filthy."

"Get in here! Use that phone."

"I've got to get the number from the barn."

Time was flying for Robyn. In no time, the next-door neighbor, Gary, was over and he had Jack's chainsaw. A vet was on the way. Lisa was on the phone calling the fire department and Robyn was in Rob's Ram Charger on the way back to the trailhead.

Rob heard the voices before they emerged through the brush. He was already shivering form the wet clothes and cold evening air. He was ready to do something.

"How far ahead?" He could hear a low voice ask.

"Just up ahead at the bend." A woman's voice responded.

Robert decided to help them and break his own silence, "I hope you brought my jacket."

They spotted him and turned off the trail as they got closer. Robyn and Gary paused at the last bit of solid ground. Gary getting a good look at the negative side of horse ownership and Robyn realizing that it was real, not a nightmare.

"Did you bring me a jacket?" Robert asked.

"I didn't think to. This is Gary, he's Jack's neighbor. Jack's not home."

"Did you get any other help?"

"No. But, Lisa was calling the Fire and Rescue or something."

"Can they help?"

"I don't know. I didn't wait around. I thought I'd better get back. Jack should be home soon."

Robert looked up at a large man with the chainsaw.

"Hello, I'm Robert. I'd shake your hand, but I can't seem to move. Thanks for coming."

"I don't know if I'll be much help."

"Any help will be appreciated."

The man was taking in the situation. His uncertainty was evident. "What do you need me to do?"

"See those limbs on his back and legs?"

A nod replied.

"They've got to come off. He is fairly calm right now. He has struggled off and on and he is wore out. I'll keep him calm and you cut them off."

At that, the man trudged around to the back of the horse, going here and there to stay on solid ground as much as possible. He put one hand on the trunk of the tree that had Reverend's back pinned. While holding the chainsaw with the other, he leaned over and observed the picture. He looked down at the smaller man half swallowed by the mud. "I don't think I can do it. There is no place to cut them. If he moves, I'll hit him."

"It doesn't matter. It's either the tree limbs or him. Do the best you can and don't worry about it."

Robert straightened his back and began pulling his sweatshirt off. "Go ahead at start the chainsaw, let's see how he reacts."

Gary primed the saw a couple of times, pulled out the choke, and pulled the cord with force. The saw fired on the third pull. He feathered the two-stroke engine to keep it going as he pushed in the choke. Robert had his face down near the horse's ear and was talking quietly while rubbing his muzzle. Reverend was not too concerned about the new sound. He was too tired. Robert slowly placed the sweatshirt over Rev's face and began rubbing his neck. The light was getting dangerously low so Robert looked up and nodded at the other man.

The blade was sharp. It was hovering right over the branch that was covering the horse's back, the big animal's delicate spine just below. The blade began to descend slowly. The man's face was a mask of concentration. Chips were ripped away as the blade ate smoothly through. The horse seemed to perceive the danger and he remained motionless. The first branch fell free and Gary snatched it away as if it had been about to bite the horse. He readjusted his grip on the saw and came at the next branch with the blade perpendicular to the ground. This gave the blade a better angle and kept the whirling metal as far from the legs as possible. It fell away as safely as the first. The third branch was the easiest and it was done. Gary shut off the saw, threw off the last two branches, smoothed his graying hair, and looked over at the man keeping the horse calm. Robert responded with a slight grin. "Perfect!"

"I was terrified he might jump or try to get up."

"Eerie isn't it? How animals seem to sense and know things. It's like he knew what we were up to. I'm not sure we give animals enough credit," Robert commented as he pulled his mud-dripping sweatshirt back on.

Robyn, looking slightly less forlorn, and with confidence building from the initial success asked her husband, "What now?"

"Good question. His legs are free now, I guess we'll see if he can pull himself out."

"Do you think he can?"

"He's worn out and in deep, but we can't just sit here."

"Do you think he'll be alright?"

"I think, if he gets out soon."

Gary was still looking uncertain about the entire predicament and asked, "How can I help?"

Robert thought the question over for a moment. What would be the best way to manage this? He had a woman concerned for the continued existence of her horse, a Good Samaritan who had never dealt with a horse, and one welterweight stuck in the mud with a thousand pounds of worn out horse. This was a bleak situation and the options were slim. Robert, hoping some other solution would materialize, began to give directions. "Gary, come up front here. Robyn, toss me the halter and lead rope, then find a good strong switch."

"What do you need a switch for?" she replied as she tossed over the tangled halter and lead rope.

"You don't want to know," quietly the reply came as he began working the halter over the filth-soiled muzzle.

Horses are amazing. They are herd animals and by divine orchestration perceive the slightest changes in their circle. Their perilous survival depends on it. A shuffled hoof, a cocked ear, a change in breathing; these are all cues that have meaning in the group, meanings that are not to be ignored if death is to be delayed. For thousands of years, people have rearranged the natural organization into a strained symbiotic relationship between man and horse. The horse has accepted the herdsmen, but can never disregard the primordial instinct. Reverend's people insisted he ignore his nature and remain calm, but he acquiesced according to the older order and began battling the mud, ripping at the ground with his liberated hooves, nostrils wide and flaring. The earth shook and splattered in reply, but refused to yield.

"Easy! Easy! Easy, damn it!" Robert shouted as he dodged the flailing hind legs and attempted to conserve the beast's energy.

No matter how hard he tried, Reverend could not tear his front legs free from the raw quagmire. His hind legs were pushing and kicking, but the front half of his body was still listing to the side and buried to the neck. The force of the exertion actually pushed his front legs deeper into the abyss as they struggled feebly to rise above the sodden earth. There was nothing for them to grasp.

Robert wrapped his right arm around the tensed neck and leaned into the timorous animal, "Easy, this isn't getting you anywhere. Easy. Be patient."

Finally, Reverend responded to the man's calming tone and touch. He ceased pawing and kicking and tentatively lowered his tail-end until it was once again level with his withers. He was no longer fighting, but his anxiousness was tangibly present as the last of the evening light was replaced with a blanket of solitary darkness.

"I hope somebody brought some light," Robert expectantly asked.

Robyn responded by illuminating two muddy specters with a heavy-duty Maglite, "How's this?"

"Good. Now let me see that switch."

She handed him a Lilliputian twig.

"Robyn," He paused with a grin, "What could I possibly do with this. My mother used to make me pick switches for my own woopins, if I brought this back I'd get another for wasting her time."

Gary, who had been silent, let out a small chuckle.

Robert continued more seriously, "We've got to have something to hit him with. Something to make him jump and fight when we're ready. I know it sucks, but he's got to push when we need him to."

Robyn began panning the light about the dry ground along the base of the ridge looking for a limb to beat her already miserable horse with. She was just selecting a nefarious limb when everyone noticed another light bobbing along the trail. No one said a word, but everyone was hoping it was the cavalry. It was Jack, one of a vanishing breed, a man who still lived by a simple code. Do the right thing because it is right and expect the same in return. He was an extremely amiable man. His diet consisted of Budweiser and BBQ and he was generous with both, but neither slowed him down. He spotted Robyn first. "Robyn, are you all right?"

"Yea, but Reverend is not too good."

"We'll get that taken care of. Where is Rob?"

"He's over there," and she pointed with her light.

Jack shook his head. "Lisa said the horse was stuck in the mud, but that's something else. I'm not even going to ask how he got like that."

"Good thing, because I don't think I could answer," she replied.

"Rob, what tha hell are you doing in there?"

"Moral support. Besides, people pay good money for mud bathes. But I think I'm about finished, I'm freezing."

"I wish I could get my tractor back here. We could just pull him out."

"I don't think it will fit down the trail."

"It won't. It's hung up between two trees at the start of the trail."

"You shouldn't have tried that."

"Why not? It's just a tractor. I'll get it out tomorrow. The good news is Lisa got a hold of the Fire and Rescue. They are sending some guys out. They should be here shortly."

Robert suggested, "Robyn, if we've got more help coming we should just wait."

"Then I'm going to the truck to get a horse blanket to throw over him, I don't want him going into shock from the cold and stress."

Robyn headed back up the trail at a brisk walk. The men clustered about the horse and sagely discussed women, horses, and other adverse predicaments. The conversation was light, jesting, and well appreciated. The talk tended to help fight off the cold. The thin clouds were quickly releasing the heat gathered during the resplendent spring light. It was one of those days not uncommon this close to the mountains in April. The day was alive and refreshing, a smell of novelty carried along by a soft energizing breeze. The night was different. The warm soft breeze of the day was replaced by a cutting wind that reminded one of the recently departed winter.

Shortly, Robyn returned laboring down the trail under the burden of the bulky outdoor horse blanket. The blanket was so large the edges were dragging the ground and the straps were threatening to tangle her legs. Just as she was leaving the trail, with flashlights directing her, she tripped on a bared root, dropped the blanket, and saved herself by clutching the branches of a nearby red maple. Without pausing, she leaned over, picked up the blanket, and headed straight for Reverend. Stopping when she had sunk down to her ankles, she asked, "Rob, could you throw this over him?"

He strained forward in the grips of the mud to grab the blanket.

He was just getting the horse sufficiently covered when Jack spotted two more lights working their way down the trail. "Looks like we've got more company."

"The Fire and Rescue?" questioned Gary.

"Or the vet," Jack stated as he started off to meet the newcomers.

When Jack returned, he had with him a hearty-looking man in his late twenties and a local deputy sheriff. The hearty young man wore blue jeans, cowboy boots, a Carhart jacket, and had a bundle of thick nylon rope slung across his chest. The deputy was dressed in his pressed browns and appeared ready to spectate. Jack introduced the two as Dillard and Deputy Grindle. Dillard set down the bundle of rope and proceeded to shake hands and familiarize himself with the party. Deputy Grindle played his role to the hilt, sitting back and watching everything with stern detachment. The young man was still working his way around when he came to Robert. Robert stopped him by holding up, palm out, a pair of dark scum covered hands, "You might want to wait until this things over."

"Na." He continued out into the sinking earth and solidly gripped Robert's right hand, shaking it heartily. "I'll be dirty in a few minutes anyway."

"You ever had to get a horse out of a situation like this?"

"No, but I've had to get a few cows out."

"How do we do it?"

"See if you can't dig this rope down between his front legs and over and around his back and then tie it in the front."

Dillard handed Robert one end of the rescue rope and Robert set it to the side while he worked pulling and scooping mud from Reverend's neck, chest, and front legs. After a few minutes he had unearthed enough of the horse to deftly work the rope under the chest and reach around with his free arm to pull the rope up just as the mud crawled back into the hole. Then, placing a calming hand on Rev's back, he stepped across the prostrate horse to get the rope around the other side. Within a few minutes he was able to work the rope back between the pair of trapped legs and tie the rope off in a confused no-slip knot.

"That should hold," he declared as he finished.

The Fire and Rescue volunteer was in his element. "Now, if we can get some hands on this rope. Robert, you're going to have to try and push him upright when we start, he can't do much on his side like that. We'll pull and you get him moving."

Robyn, always thinking like a horse, suggested, "Shouldn't we put his halter and lead rope on. If he gets out he might panic and head right back towards the lake."

Everyone quickly agreed. No one wanted to try and pull the horse out twice. The halter was just being buckled on, when two more people appeared out of the unlit forest, a middle-aged man and a young woman. The man was another volunteer and the woman was a vet. The veterinarian quickly spotted the horse owner and introduced herself.

"Hello, I'm Sara."

"Robyn."

"Is he injured?"

"Not that we can tell, but he's been in there for about two and a half hours."

The new volunteer knew Dillard and took a spot behind him on the rope.

"I'm here. So we can get started now," was his only introduction.

That was the signal. The four men on the rope spaced themselves out and set their feet. The deputy stood to the side and held onto the end of the lead rope. Robert leaned into the animal with his left shoulder and tried to find some solid ground beneath the muck to use for leverage. Dillard set the pace.

"On three. One, two, three!"

Robert yelled at the animal, "Now Rev! Get up!"

Everyone grunted with the exertion. The rope went taut. The men pulled and pushed with all they had. Those, standing by, watched with expectant faces. The horse did not move.

"Wait," Dillard directed. "That mud is like a vice. If he doesn't try we can pull all night and not get him out."

The animal was exhausted and mentally depleted. Sporadically for over two hours he had been attempting to sustain his fight and flight impulse in unison. Each time drained precious power from his majestic body. He had sat motionless for the last thirty minutes, his eyes glazing over, and his spirit slipping. Reverend was near the end; he was giving up.

Robert thought it might come to this. "Robyn, bring that switch."

This time she brought over a wicked limb, twisted and knotted, about a yard long. "Are you going to hit him with it?"

"No, you're going to. When he says go, you hit him. Hit him hard! He has given up, he's got to fight."

"I can't!"

"Do you want him to be buried here?"

"No."

"Then do it."

The rest of the crowd had courteously avoided the conversation. They waited patiently for Robyn to get situated and resolve her mind to the task. Once again, Dillard led off. "One, two, three!"

The rope went tight and the men leaned into it. Robert shoved and yelled at Reverend, trying to get him to pull himself upright, so his legs would be underneath his body and useful. Robyn struck the confused animal on the rump. She hit him again and chided him in a strained voice, "Come on Rev! Try, try, you can do it!"

She hit him again, but the blows were weak. She could not force herself to hurt him. The horse moved, but only slightly. He was still not trying for he had convinced himself that he would die in the mud. In unison the men stopped pulling and the rope went slack. The situation was beginning to look bleak. It was the moment in a situation when no one knows how it is going to turn out.

Robert looked brooding for a moment and then faced his wife. "Give me the switch."

Robyn handed the knotted limb over, her movements conveying the secret that she was crying. It was dark and the tears could not be seen but she was rubbing them away on alternate shoulders. It was getting to her. Robyn did not just love horses; they were a part of her, a piece of who she is. She invested her soul in them. Now, she was facing the savage reality that she may lose Moment and Reverend John. To have both horses you have worked, trained, and enveloped with your essence, to suffer tragedies within the same year would nearly be unbearable.

Robert knew what was happening in his wife's mind. He often resented horses for the power they had over her; he resented these times when they tore her apart. However, there would never be any bargaining. He would never ask that. He would always be there to salvage the pieces.

"Alright gentlemen, when I get him moving you start pulling," Robert directed as he turned to speak to the horse, "Rev, listen. I promised if you'd listen, I'd get you out. Now you listen. You have got to help us. You're too big to sit there and think we'll do all the work. You've quit so I'm going to get you fired up, but you can't hold a grudge. It's for your own good."

Robert whipped the limb back and it whooshed as he brought it forward and slammed into Reverend's flank in a cutting strike. "Get up!"

Immediately, the horse went white-eyed, his ears went back, and he kicked with his rear legs.

"Get up!" Robert screamed as he lashed him again.

"Get up!" And he hit him again.

Initially, the others were caught off guard by the savageness of the blows, but they saw the horse begin to make progress and they pulled with all their might. The thoroughbred was angry and churning with all four legs. Robert seeing that Reverend was almost upright, dropped the limb and pushed with both hands. He continued to yell encouragement and push heedless of the crushing rear hooves that may have been directed at him. Dillard had the men pulling the rope in short bursts. Each time a little distance was gained and Gary would prevent any loss by anchoring the rope around a nearby tree trunk. The flustered animal was now upright and had all four legs under his body. His front was still hunkered low in the earth. His rear legs were now sinking since as they had escaped the rooted area and were stomping in the mud where his stomach had been wallowing. Getting his feet under him had cost him dearly and he was starting to waver again. Seeing the momentum slacken, Robert picked up the limb again and unleashed a trio of lashes that left immediate whelps. "Don't quit! You've got to do it! Keep going!"

The rope crew pulled with renewed energy. The horse jumped from the bite of the limb; each time his body was released from the clutches of the quicksand-like mud and the rope hauled him forward. The process was repeated over and over gaining only inches, but inches turn into feet. Now everyone was aware of the progress and was willing the great beast on.

"Come on Reverend!"

"You're almost home!"

"Move those long legs, dammit!"

"Come on!"

It was a cacophony of sound that bewildered the animal and he fought and struggled harder. His instincts were working again and they said run. He became oblivious of everything except the desire to escape; steam was billowing from his nostrils; his eyes were darting, and his muscles rippling with effort. The blows were still raining down and causing pain; pain he had to run from. He continued forward with his head flailing, emitting fierce snorts and squeals. The men doubled their efforts and the horse was about to tear free in one last momentous exertion.

Reverend reached for the solid ground with his front hooves and exploded forward with his back hooves. Robert was immobilized up to his knees in muck and realized he could not escape away from the uninhibited legs. So, just as the horse bounded up and out, Robert twisted to the left and fell face down into the mud to avoid the errant or retaliatory hooves. The monster was now on solid ground; freed from his captor. The scene was dramatic. The normally sleek black coat was adorned with black-gray patterns of earth that fashioned strange images as the various beams of light were shifted. Eyes white and rolling, steam rising off the matted coat, he reared to his full height lunging at the sky above.

Deputy Grindle was caught off guard and troubled. Suddenly, remembering he was attached to this apparition in its full bravado, he dropped the lead rope he had been nervously clutching and backed away. Robyn jumped across the rescue line, which the men were mindfully trying to keep from embroiling in Reverend's dancing legs, and grabbed the discarded lead rope. "Easy bear, easy. It's alright now," she soothed.

Reverend's apprehension began to diminish immediately. She continued to ease his spirit with a calm voice and relaxed body. Robert crawled out of the mud and made a wide arc around both so he could prudently come back into the animal's view as quickly as possible. Talking and showing her open hand Robyn worked her way up to Reverend and began to wipe away the caked grime from his face. His oversized eyes began to relax and take on their former hue. Robert slipped up and placed an affectionate hand on his neck and rubbed his shoulder to remind the equine of his benevolence.

Once Reverend was restored to sanity the vet approached and started to examine the exhausted legs. The adrenaline was now gone and they were trembling with fatigue. She decided he was sound enough to walk back to the barn and gave him a shot of Banamine to make him more comfortable. "This will do until we get him up to the barn and in the light," she finalized her analysis.

"Is he O.K.?" Robyn wanted to know.

"I think so. He will feel a lot better when we get him warm and cleaned up."

"Is he going to colic?"

"Doubtful, but I'd watch him a while tonight."

"I'll spend the night in the barn if I need to," Robyn pledged.

The crowd of altruistic individuals was gathering from the leaf littered forest floor the things they had brought with them. It was time to leave the stagnant mud, the undisciplined wood, the foreboding night and return to the electric lights of civilization. On cue, the wind surged and cried to encourage the interlopers to hasten back. It rattled branches, rustled dead leaves, and chilled the flesh. However, it was also carrying something new with it: the hint of significance. The people felt good about themselves. They had been part of something special.

They had mattered.

IT WAS THE MUSIC

Savannah Harrington

I'm still not exactly sure how one person can know *every* song. And it wasn't even the lyrics he memorized. It was the second he recognized some sort of sound: a drum, a piano, a guitar; and that was it—the song was his now. Always two seconds ahead of the beat, he was no stranger to the tempo. No music was foreign to him, and if it was, he'd hear it eventually. He's a walking jukebox filled with all our favorite songs; reminders of the first time I loved a boy and his music. I remember the music shop on 5th Avenue. I remember the smell of old records and masculinity. I remember a thin seventeen-year-old boy and his brand new leather stained with cologne, standing fascinated at my appreciation of familiar music. "You must be buying a present for your boyfriend." "I'm sorry?" I knew it wouldn't be the last, but that was the first time I saw him smirk. With pink cheeks, he said he didn't mean for me to take offense; after I told him he caught me off guard and that I was single, we talked about Lynyrd Skynyrd and Pink Floyd and Led Zeppelin and almost every great band until he swore Creedence Clearwater Revival was the best. There was something about a man with passion—and his started to convince me. And even though I was wearing a loose yellow sundress and my hair was tied up, showing off my Cherokee shoulders, I knew this wasn't why he spoke to me. It was the music. It'd always been the music.

We hit it off and shared our space often. A typical date for us was a motorcycle ride to the record store or a bar and venue with a live band. At one point he traded a generation's worth of loose change for a used Les Paul and wrote songs and music, too—*and my God, he couldn't sing*. But it was nice to watch him be passionate all over again. It was nice when he believed in something. Eventually it was other things; like beer and liquor and the mixture of the two. He swears he has the highest tolerance for most things—but especially alcohol. And to be honest, I'm not sure when alcohol started taking up his time or when it constituted his music. But he doesn't hum as much. He doesn't sing as much unless he's singing for other people who're as drunk as he is. He whistles; but only when he's drunk. A grown man propped up by the shoulder, resting against a desperate bar table who never leaves a glass un-empty.

And he's whistling louder tonight. He's drunker than usual.

"Got your gear on, baby?" Biting his bottom lip, he grabs me from behind. Looking in the mirror, I can't stop tugging the tight black tank top loose from my waist. "I don't know why you make me wear this shit. It's not my style." And he'll respond the way he usually does. With that same half-smirk, except with older and meaner cheeks, "You don't have to like it. But you will wear it if you're going with me." I tried to change the subject like I usually do: "My boobs are popping out the top." I slapped my chest and realized I was acting crazy. He'd already started the bike before I stopped complaining. It was a tricked-out Victory bike he found on Craigslist a few years ago after our first miscarriage. He'd invested more money and time on that bike than most things. And even though I hated it, it was nice to see him happy again. It was nice to see him taking care of something.

There were wires rigged from the bottom of the petals to the tops of the handle-bars, holding in place a decently-shitty speaker that was too loud and too shaky; an embarrassing combination of noise. He'd crank up the same song every time we started to ride. "Born on the Bayou" replaced the noise of crowded streets and I missed the sound of hurried drivers. There were CCR stickers covering all of the shiny black parts of the bike — some a little torn from where I tried to peel off their edges. I guess he was trying to be a little more John Fogerty and a lot less of himself. And when I was seventeen, that was sexy; but after ten years of humming the same songs, I've grown tired of the sound. I can't help but bury my head in the small of his back at each stop light. Sometimes I'll keep a miserable look on my face just so some other man will recognize my angst. I crave attention from them. Part of me really thinks he knows I don't belong to him anymore. There's no way he still thinks he impresses me.

But tonight will still go like most nights do. I'll flirt with the bartender and pretend I don't see him, my John Fogerty, in the drunken corners of this strange bar. He'll grope and grind the hips of married women and teenage girls in loose sundresses who will eventually get tired of his hands-y gestures. And finally, when I've had my own fun and come fully undone; when I've felt brand new again by a strange man, I'll walk lightly over to wherever mine is and whisper, "Come on baby, let's go home. You're drunk." When we finally leave, we'll never speak of whatever happened, like a song on repeat we tried to like but never could, by a band we thought we trusted.

A PRAYER FOR HOME

James Mulhern

Show me the way to go home
I'm tired and I want to go to bed
I had a little drink about an hour ago
And it's gone right to my head
Everywhere I roam
Over land or sea or foam
You can always hear me singing this song
Show me the way to go home.

W e just saw Mrs. Muldoon," Aunt Helena said, when she and Aunt Bianca entered. "Poor thing was drunk as a skunk. She was walking the street aimlessly. Said she was looking for her husband Jim. We had to lead her home and get her settled." She hung their coats in the closet. "Then she told us that the Happy Garden Chinese Restaurant was sending pork fried rice and egg rolls to her house every night. She swears she never ordered the food. Mary said, 'I don't speak Chinese. How in the hell could I order from those chinks?' 'Can't understand anything they say to me, yet I get chink food delivered every day about 5 p.m.' "

"She must be having blackouts and forgetting that she ordered. Or she's imagining that they are delivering the food. Mary has squash rot," Nonna said.

"What's 'squash rot'?" I asked.

"Means your brain is rotted from too much alcohol, Molly," Helena said. "When she drinks, Mary gets delusional and hallucinates."

Helena and Bianca plopped into the cushy velvet green chairs, placing their bags beside them. Aunt Bianca assumed her usual disposition, staring into space, frowning and saying nothing. Her red hair was a mess and her lipstick smeared. She looked like a sad Bozo the clown.

"What happened to Mrs. Muldoon's husband?" I asked.

Nonna said, "Long before you were born, Mr. Muldoon died from a massive heart attack. Poor Mary was fixing dinner in the kitchen. When she called him to the table, he didn't answer. She went into the living room, where he would listen to the radio and read the paper, and found him dead in his chair, his paper scattered at his feet. She hasn't been the same since. Just drinks away her sorrows."

"Oh," I answered. I couldn't comprehend what it would be like to find someone dead, especially a husband or a family member.

"Well, let's take a look at what you bought? Did you get that pretty dress you wanted, Bianca," Nonna asked.

"No, some bitch must have found it in the pile where I hid it."

* * *

Nonna thought it would be charitable of us to visit Mrs. Muldoon. I didn't like Mrs. Muldoon. On a Saturday evening, when I was bussing tables in the restaurant, I accidentally spilled marinara sauce on an ugly blue puff-sleeve dress that she was wearing. She called me a "clumsy oaf," and complained to my parents. I didn't argue with Nonna about visiting her, though. Nonna was not someone to disagree with.

We walked precariously up the steps of Mrs. Muldoon's front porch on a late afternoon in December, "Mrs. Muldoon will slip and fall on this snow." About two inches had fallen that morning. "Grab that shovel against the house and let's clear a path from her door down to the street."

It didn't take us long; the snow was light and airy. I shoveled while Nonna gave commands. As we were stomping our feet and about to ring the doorbell, the door opened. "Aren't you going to clean the curb, too?" Mrs. Muldoon said to me. "I like to walk on the street you know. The slobs next door never clear the sidewalk." She must have been watching us from her living room window the whole time.

"Of course she will," Nonna said, and then to me, "Molly, just finish up that little bit while I go inside with Mrs. Muldoon. Then come in." Mrs. Muldoon held the door as Nonna entered.

"You'll do a good job, won't ya?" Mrs. Muldoon said with a fake smile. "Not make a mess of it like you do sometimes at the restaurant."

Nonna chuckled, and when Mrs. Muldoon turned, mouthed, "She's drunk. Ignore her." She pinched her nose and grimaced.

As the door shut, I gave Mrs. Muldoon the finger. Even though she didn't see my gesture, it gave me pleasure. I shoveled the curb, making sure to leave just a bit of snow on the curb, hoping she might slip.

I found the two of them standing in the archway that led to the living room. Nonna was oohing and aahing over a silver aluminum Christmas tree with a color wheel.

"I love those red and green balls, and the see-through ones, too." Nonna said. "Isn't it pretty, Molly?"

"It's gorgeous." I wasn't that impressed.

"Well the damn thing ought to be. Paid a pretty penny for it. At Sears, ya know. The girl in the store, a pudgy midget, said it was a specialty item."

"Oh, a specialty," Nonna said, winking at me. "Well it's beautiful, Mary. Now why don't we go into the kitchen and enjoy some coffee while we eat the cookies I brought you."

"I don't know why they call it a specialty item. They've been around for years," I said.

"Well it's special to me," Mrs. Muldoon snapped. "Where are the cookies, Agnella? I could use something sweet to get rid of the bad taste in my mouth," she said, looking at me. We walked into the kitchen.

"I wrapped a few up and put them in here." Nonna patted her black leather handbag.

"Well I would think you could give me more than a few. What are you? Cheap?"

Nonna laughed. "Mary, you got the diabetes to worry about."

"Was she really a midget?" I interjected.

Mrs. Muldoon looked irritated.

"She's asking about the salesgirl in the department store," Nonna said.

"I know what's she's asking, Agnella. Yes, Molly. Or a dwarf. I don't know what ya call them nowadays. But nice enough, she was. And quite knowledgeable. She told me the tree was made in some town in Wisconsin. Would be an heirloom in the future. I said to her, 'I don't care about any heirlooms, dear, and I don't care about the future. I haven't got a soul to leave it to.' And don't ya know, the midget said to me, 'I'm sorry.' I said, 'About what, darling?' And then she said, 'That you haven't got any children.' I laughed and told her not to worry. Children could be a pain in the arse. Isn't that right, Molly?"

Mrs. Muldoon almost slipped on the red-brick linoleum floor, but Nonna was able to grab her arm and steady her into a chair. The kitchen smelled like a pine tree. Nonna explained to me later that the smell was from all the gin that Mrs. Muldoon drank.

Nonna brewed coffee in the percolator, after opening cabinets and rummaging through the disorganized mess of her cupboards. Mrs. Muldoon was silent, her eyes dreamy, looking out the window above the sink.

"Mary, where's the sugar?" Nonna opened the bread box.

"Hey, it's not in there. Look on top of the refrigerator."

315

"Crazy place to put it," Nonna said, taking the yellow sugar bowl and placing it on the table.

"It's starting to snow again," I said, following Mrs. Muldoon's eyes. "Guess you'll have to find someone to shovel for you later on."

"It is, and isn't it pretty. Do they still make snowflake cutouts in school, Molly? I used to love Christmas time when I was a tot."

"Mrs. Muldoon, I'm a senior in high school. We don't do things like that. They make snowflakes in elementary school."

"What a shame." Mrs. Muldoon said. "People at every age should make snowflakes. That's a joy of Christmas. Don't you agree, Agnella?"

Nonna was pouring the coffee and arranging the anisette cookies on a plate. "Yes, Mary. Snowflakes should be appreciated at every age." She opened the refrigerator and sniffed the small carton of cream. Her nose crinkled. "Mary, the cream's gone bad." She poured it down the sink and ran hot water. "We'll just have to have our coffee black."

"Let's have a gin and tonic instead," Mrs. Muldoon said. "Molly, too. She's a *senior in high school* now," she said, over-enunciating and smirking. "Too old for snowflakes." She laughed.

"We're having coffee. No alcohol. Wouldn't go with the cookies," Nonna said.

"Snowflakes form in the Earth's atmosphere when cold water droplets freeze onto dust particles. Depending on temperature and air humidity, the ice crystals create myriad shapes. No two are alike," I said. "I think that's more wondrous than anything we could create with a scissors and white paper. I prefer the realness of nature."

Mrs. Muldoon laughed. "Aren't you a whippersnapper. And all those big words: *myriad* and *wondrous*." She humphed.

Nonna set the coffee and small plate of cookies in the table center. "Molly's very smart. She got a perfect score on her SAT verbal and almost a perfect score on her math. She's in the 99th percentile. Her IQ is 148."

"Whatever that means," Mrs. Muldoon said. "What else do they teach you? Do they teach you to count your blessings? Do they teach you your catechisms? Do they teach you the Ten Commandments, the Our Father, and Hail Mary? Now those are valuable lessons." She picked up rosary beads and some laminated novenas that were on the table. "Faith is most important, Molly." She shook the beads. "I pray every night for the Holy Father's intention that the Catholic church reign forever."

"Yes, of course they teach us those things, Mrs. Muldoon. I attend Immaculate Conception. The sisters have to explain all that to us. But I'm not sure I believe in any of it."

"What do you mean?" Mrs. Muldoon said. "So sacrilegious. And at this time of year." She tsk-tsked. "Now there's a big word for you." She laughed and sipped her coffee, then glared at me. "You are not smarter than God, Molly." She placed her cup down firmly. A bit of the coffee spilled over the rim.

"I think that Molly is saying she's a free thinker," Nonna said.

"A free thinker? What a bunch of malarkey. I don't even know what it means."

"It means she makes up her own mind about what she believes and doesn't necessarily listen to what people tell her. She's an independent young woman."

Mrs. Muldoon guffawed.

"Let's change the subject," Nonna said. "No need to be arguing. It's not the holiday spirit."

"I suppose you're right, Agnella," Mrs. Muldoon said, raising herself from the chair. "I've got to use the little girl's room anyway." Nonna helped her stand.

"I'm okay, Agnella. Stop being such a mother hen."

Nonna laughed. When Mrs. Muldoon left the kitchen, Nonna whispered to me, "Go into the living room and get me a few of those see-through balls on the tree. Hurry up."

I did just that, bringing her two translucent balls and one red one. "I like the red one," I whispered. Nonna wrapped them in napkins and stuffed them in her bag, which she clasped shut just as we heard the toilet flush down the hall.

When Mrs. Muldoon returned, she said, "I was just thinking about Vivian Vance. It's sad that she died. Oh, how she used to make me laugh."

"Who's Vivian Vance?" I said.

"Ethel Mertz. You know. From *I Love Lucy*. Now that was a funny show. And Lucille Ball. What a riot!" Nonna added.

"God bless the people who make us laugh," Mrs. Muldoon said.

"I'll second that," Nonna said.

"I wonder what a dead body looks like. I'd love to see one," I said.

"What an odd thing to desire." Mrs. Muldoon pursed her lips.

"And although it's sad that Vivian Vance died, I don't see why her death is any more tragic than the death of anyone else," I answered. "She's no more valuable than the rest of us. Do you know there's approximately 153,400 deaths per day, or a little more than 100 per minute? Just think of how many people died while we've been sitting here. We are all specks of dust floating in an enormous universe."

"Your granddaughter is getting too big for her britches. Imagine? 'Specks of dust.' I don't even know what she's talking about half the time. Wanting to see a dead body, too? Where does she come up with these things? Jesus, Mary, and Joseph!" She took a sip of coffee, then murmured "specks of dust, specks of dust" and looked out the window. The black bark of a tree cut through a gray square of sky.

Nonna looked out the window as well. "Don't mind her, Mary. She's just a thinker."

"I could tell her a few things to think about." Her things sounded like "tings," and her think sounded like "tink." I was going to correct her but Nonna said, "We should get going. The snow is falling. And Molly's got homework to do. Don't you, Molly?"

"Yes, Nonna. And I want to add some more ornaments to our Christmas tree so it can be just as beautiful as Mrs. Muldoon's."

"Yes, yes," Nonna said, rising from her seat. "It's a beautiful tree."

Mrs. Muldoon escorted us to the door, commenting some more about my poor attitude, and then as we walked home, Nonna said, "Such a shame. An old woman with all her money. Drinking herself to death." She stopped suddenly and turned to me. "You've got to learn to hold your tongue. You'll never get anywhere in this world if you don't know when to keep your mouth shut. Learn not to be so fresh."

When we hung the ornaments on our tree, Nonna said, "She won't notice them missing. And it's a shame not to have them appreciated. You think they're lovely, don't you, Molly?"

"Yes, Nonna."

Later, I lay on Nonna's bed doing homework, where I would hang out until my parents had closed up the restaurant and returned home. I picked up the phone and called the local Chinese restaurant.

"This is Mrs. Muldoon," I said, "Send me over an order of pork fried rice, egg rolls, and add some beef broccoli this time. And you'll hurry it up, won't you? I'm so hungry I could eat a nun's arse through a convent gate."

"I think Mrs. Muldoon is a bitch." Nonna and I were seated at the table in her bright yellow-walled kitchen.

Nonna laughed. "Well she is." She took a sip of cocoa. "But her bitchiness keeps her sadness from taking over. You've got to be strong to tame a lion. And sadness is a lion."

Nonna poured some more cocoa into our mugs. "Just look at the difference between Mrs. Muldoon and your Aunt Bianca. Mrs. Muldoon tries to stay peppy, and Bianca just sits and sulks. She rarely talks, and when she does, it's usually to complain. Always wants something for nothing. Thinks that she's treated unfairly."

"Mrs. Muldoon is peppy because she's drunk all the time."

Nonna smiled. "Well, that's true."

"Why is Aunt Bianca so depressed?"

"I don't know." Nonna looked thoughtful for a moment.

"She's always been that way. Even as a little girl. Miserable." She tapped my knee. "Did I ever tell you how she once stole money from the collection basket during mass?"

"No." I leaned forward. "Did she get in trouble?"

"She did."

"Maria Cennamo. That was the girl's name. She told Father Paul, a scary old Irish priest with white hair and a fat red face."

I laughed. "I can't picture Aunt Bianca doing something like that? She seems so sluggish."

"She's a crafty one, Molly. She pretended to put change in the basket but instead pulled out a dollar bill, hiding it in the palm of her hand." Nonna sighed. "I hate to tell you this about your aunt." Nonna laughed. "No, I don't. I like gossiping with you."

"What did Father Paul do about her stealing?"

"Bianca was lucky. He could have reported her to the police, but underneath that frightening exterior was a kind man. Her punishment was to clean and polish the altar every week for six months."

"And you know what Bianca did to Maria Cennamo, the girl who snitched?"

"What?"

"She smacked her on the head with one of those small Bibles we all used to own." Nonna laughed. "Maria never dared look at her again."

"Well I'm glad she found some use for that thing."

Nonna gasped. "Molly, don't ever let anyone hear you talk like that about the Word of God."

"Nonna, you don't believe it's the *actual* word of God, do you?"

She laughed. "Of course I don't. But that's not the point. Most people do. And you gotta fit in. Do you hear me?" She stared into my eyes.

"Yes."

"Good," she said, settling back in her chair. "Because appearances matter. Most fools are too stupid to know what's really going on." She groaned.

"Are you upset at me?"

"Of course not. It's just my aching back."

She placed our empty mugs in the sink.

"Do you believe there is a God, Nonna?"

"Why are you asking me that?" She turned from the sink.

"The idea of God doesn't make sense to me."

"Molly, you make me laugh. You think too much."

"But do you?"

"Do I what?"

"Nonna, you know what I'm asking."

She sat down and crossed her arms. "No."

"I don't think I do either. There is no heaven. There is no God. I think when we die, we just rot and become dirt."

"Oh. You make it sound so depressing. Don't think about all that. Think about life."

"I am."

"Just agree with others about certain things. Like church and God, and all those crazy saints. You can't tell most folks how you really feel. You and I aren't like other people. They don't understand our common sense way of looking at the world." She patted my arm. "In order to be successful, you sometimes have to keep your opinions private. I want you to go off to college in the fall and become someone important. Maybe you will be a doctor?"

"I'm not sure about that, Nonna."

"Why not! Whoever says women can only be nurses is a *chooch*."

I laughed. "What's a *chooch*? I never heard you say that before."

"Like your father. A jackass!"

"I didn't say I *can't* be a doctor. I just haven't decided what I want to study."

"I understand. No rush. You have time. Now help me clean up a bit, and then you need to go home. Your mother will be home from the restaurant by now, wondering why you haven't returned. She's a nervous type. Not like you, Molly. You have nerves of steel." She smiled.

We cleaned up, then Nonna followed me down the hall to the front door. As I stood on the landing, she kissed and hugged me. "Goodnight, mia bambina." I descended the stairs, pad softly outside my aunts' apartment on the second floor, and walked into the frigid air.

It seemed that I was engulfed by believers in those days. The Italians and the Irish were obsessed with church, religion, and the pope. Nonna called me later that week and asked if I would help her take Mrs. Muldoon to a Faith Healer that Mrs. Muldoon had heard about on the radio. The woman had allegedly cured a young girl whose cancerous tumors miraculously disappeared, and an old arthritic man who could barely walk.

"Does Mrs. Muldoon have cancer?" I asked.

"No. She said she wants to see the woman as a precautionary measure."

"That's silly, Nonna."

"Of course it is. Mrs. Muldoon is crazy, but I can't refuse to help her. That wouldn't be nice."

"Why can't she go on her own?"

"Oh Molly. She can barely find her way to Broadway downtown to do her food shopping. How's she gonna manage a trip to the center of Boston. That's like asking her to travel to Africa."

I agreed and on the appointed day, one Saturday in May, Nonna and I drove in her Plymouth Fury to Mrs. Muldoon's house. The day was brilliant. Not a cloud in the sky, bright sun, just a few clumps of dirty snow left over from a freak storm the previous week. There were puddles all over, and small streams ran in the gutters along the street. The temperature was in the low 50's and things were melting: water dripped everywhere. A chunk of icicles fell from the railing as we stepped onto the porch. I saw Mrs. Muldoon seated through the sheer curtain in her living room. She reminded me of one of the fortune tellers behind some lacy fabric at Wonderland Amusement Park. She got up when she saw us and opened the door.

"Come in. Come in. But stomp your feet first. Don't bring any of that wetness in here."

The house stunk like mold and soured milk. The living room to the right had boxes with clothes and old shoes spilling out. The fancy Christmas tree was in parts in front of the fireplace, and the ornaments were in a pile on her dark brown couch.

"Mary, it stinks in here. And what is that mess in the living room?" Nonna said, pointing to the boxes.

"Oh, I'm going to have a garage sale if I get inspired. Or maybe just donate the things to the Salvation Army. I hear they pick up stuff, don't they?" She led us into the kitchen.

"I don't know. But what I do know is that the any clothes from those boxes will smell musty. I'm not sure anyone would want them unless you put the stuff through the laundry."

On her grey formica table were several plates with leftover food—bits of toast, old bacon, half-eaten sandwiches. The trash basket to the right of her white porcelain sink was overflowing. I saw the evidence of my calls to the Chinese restaurant that had fallen between the sink counter and the basket—dirty Chinese take-out boxes with wire handles.

"We gotta get you a maid. What's going on with you, Mary? Why you let your house become such a pig sty?"

"I've been busy, Agnella."

"Doing what?!" We were standing in front of the sink, which had hardened comet in its basin.

"Oh, this and that. But never mind. Let me just grab my coat from the back hall and we'll get going. Molly, are you excited to be healed?" Her pretty blue eyes sparkled. I thought she must have been very attractive when she was younger. Such fair skin and perfect teeth, or were they dentures?

"I don't think I need to be healed. I'm healthy, Mrs. Muldoon."

"Darling, we all could use healing. Ya know it's not only physical healing," she said, putting her arms into her red wool coat sleeves. I liked the black fur collar. "It's spiritual healing as well."

I was surprised by her peppiness, and frankly, how happy she seemed. She was usually such a bitch to me. She seemed as excited as my girlfriends before a date.

I was about to say I didn't need spiritual healing, but Nonna, as if reading my mind, gave me a look that said, "Keep quiet."

It took about 25 minutes to get to Tremont Street in Boston, where the healer saw her clientele. Her business was on the street floor of a six-story building with a variety of ornate architectural features. At the very top was a mansard roof with dormer windows. The gray exterior was dirty with lines of black and green that had formed from rain that had probably pooled on the many outcroppings and ledges, then seeped down the face of the building. The parlor where "Lady Jane" cured people was underneath a printing company squeezed between a luggage store on the left and a jewelry store on the right.

We parked across from the building along the edge of the Boston Common. I could see a line that extended from the front of the building and around the corner to Court Street. Nonna's parallel parking was awful and Mary kept screaming that we were going to hit the car in front or behind. At last we were parked just across the street on the Boston Common side. We paused for a few moments in silence, the three of us taking in the sights around us. Two skid-row type old men on a bench, wearing derby hats and unkempt, mismatched suits shared a bottle wrapped in a paper bag. One of them pointed to something at the top of the building and I followed his finger to a flock of large black crows perched on a ledge underneath an overhang. The people waiting in line were pathetic looking. Mostly old ladies, a few men, some with canes or crutches; a young blonde girl in a wheelchair. It was a motley group, a range of ethnicities, all seemingly poor.

"You sure you want to go, Mary? These people look pitiful. I think they need curing more than any of us." It was true. We were wearing nice dresses and overcoats. I thought we would be out of place in that crowd.

"Of course I want to go. Remember you can't judge a book by its cover." Mrs. Muldoon pushed her door open and pulled herself into a standing position.

"Well all I can say is that this is one hell of a book." Nonna said. She and I followed Mrs. Muldoon's lead, who told us to hold hands.

When we crossed, Nonna cut in front of an Indian couple, explaining to them that I had leukemia "very bad" and the doctors gave me three months at most. "It's urgent that we see Lady Jane. You don't want the poor girl to die, do you? She's my granddaughter!"

Mrs. Muldoon whispered irritably, "That wasn't a nice thing to do."

The woman was beautiful with large very dark eyes; it was hard to discern her pupils from the brownness that surrounded them. She had a red dot between her beautifully shaped arched brows, which I later learned in an Intro to Religion class was called a Bindi or Kumkum, marking a spiritual center or chakra, placed there out of respect for an inner Guru, all of which I thought was bullshit. She wore a purple saree and a pink head scarf. Her short bespectacled husband had a flat nose with large blackheads; tufts of hair sprouted from his nostrils and ears. He was wearing a blue navy suit and I thought he might have met his wife here after work. They spoke for a few moments in Hindi, then stepped back and nodded for us to move in front. There were grumblings and complaints from those behind the couple.

"Hey, go to the end of a line like the rest of us. What makes you so special, ladies?" an Irish-looking guy with a broad red face and a scully cap said.

Nonna teared up. "My granddaughter is dying."

The man's face blanched, and he looked at me with a horrified expression. "Sorry, lady. Not a problem." I tried to appear sick. I started shaking a little and drooled, not sure what a leukemia patient's symptoms were. The Indian couple stepped further back. I managed to create a string of saliva that dropped like the thread of a spider's web hanging off the bottom of my chin.

We turned forward. Nonna put her arm around me, as if trying to keep me from fainting. Mrs. Muldoon looked upward at the gathering of crows, which had increased since I first noticed them.

Nonna followed her gaze. "I hope they don't shit on us," she said.

"Oh, but Agnella, it's good luck. Let them poop if they need to. I've got a handkerchief in my purse." The idea of birds pooping on my head was vile, but I refrained from making a wiseass comment.

Finally we were inside. The healing room, or parlor, or whatever you call it, had metal fold-up chairs along the sidewalls. Some of the armrests were rusty. I thought we might need a tetanus shot if we sat in them.

Lady Jane sat in a large throne-like chair on a platform at the back of the room. She couldn't have been more than 27 years old, bleach blond long hair, a pixie face with deep-set shiny green eyes. She was very petite. I thought she would have been a much older woman. I was surprised at her outfit: a tight-fitting black and white dress with a very high hemline. She was busty and had long satiny legs that ended in white ballerina slippers with a flower patter of red gemstones near her pink toes. Her white string shoelaces were untied.

"Well, she's not what I expected," Mrs. Muldoon whispered, and sighed. "She looks like a tart that's trying to make a few extra bucks from her other job in the Zone."

"What's the Zone?" I said.

"It's where all the hookers hang out, just around the corner. Perverts, pimps, drug dealers, and dirty bookstores," Nonna whispered.

The old man Lady Jane was waving her hands over with her eyes closed yelled "Hallelujah" and threw his crutches towards the chairs on each side of the line of people.

"Watch it!" an old blue-haired woman shouted. Her voice was low and she sounded like a man. "You almost hit me."

When it was our turn, Lady Jane said, "I take it you three are together." She had a fake British accent with a hint of a Georgia twang. Mrs. Muldoon seemed disappointed. "Yes, we are together."

"What can I do for you?" she said, looking at each one of our faces in turn.

"Well cure us," Nonna said, a little irritably. I could tell she was exasperated that we made the trip here.

"Yes, I know that, but you must tell me what ails you."

"For Christ's sake, at our age, everything ails us," Nonna said, "Where do you want me to start. How 'bout you make my tits perky like yours?"

Lady Jane feigned indignancy, but I saw right through her, and Nonna could as well.

"Agnella, you mustn't talk like that to this woman," Mrs. Muldoon said. "I would like to be cured spiritually. Forget about my body. That's too far gone. I want my soul to be cleansed." Mrs. Muldoon was hoping for the remote chance that Lady Jane might be legitimate.

Lady Jane put her hands in a crisscross on Mrs. Muldoon's heart area, then closed her eyes, while she softly murmured an ostensibly sacred language. I thought I heard what sounded like 'pussy' in her gobbledygook. I think Nonna heard it, too, because she gave me a look at that moment and rolled her eyes.

"The masters have told be you are spiritually cured for your trip."

"Cut the crap! Mary's not going on any trip."

"That's not true, Agnella. I am," Mrs. Muldoon said excitedly, as if there might be some authenticity to Lady Jane after all.

"Where the hell are you going?"

"I'm going home." Mrs. Muldoon was beaming.

"To your family in Ireland?" Nonna asked.

"Yes, to my family."

"And how can I cure you, little girl?" Lady Jane said, looking earnestly into my face.

"I don't know."

Again she did the crisscross thing with her hands. Again she murmured her sacred prayer. And again I heard a distinct "pussy."

When she opened her eyes, her face blanched. "What is your name?"

"Molly."

"Molly, I hate to tell people things like this." Now she was speaking in a mostly Georgia twang. "But I see gruesome deaths in your future."

"Let's get out of here," Nonna said, clearly upset. She started muttering in Italian.

"You are going to witness several deaths in your lifetime."

"Who doesn't witness death? We all die." Nonna said.

"No, Molly's situation is different," Lady Jane said, speaking to Nonna as if I weren't there. "I take it you are the grandmother."

"Yes. That's easy enough to tell. I couldn't be her mother. Too old and dried up."

"You are very good to Molly. You mean more to her than her own mother."

It was eerie how this woman knew that. "Okay," I said matter-of-factly. "Tell me about these deaths."

"You have the unlucky fortune of being someone who will either find dead people or be near them when they die in violent situations. I guess you might say, 'You're an Angel of Death.' " And then she started giggling like a little girl. It seemed out of her control and she curled up with laughter.

The Indian couple behind us hurriedly said something to one another and rushed out the door. In retrospect, I wonder if the woman's inner Guru told her to get the hell out of there.

"Angel of Death! *Ffangul'*!" Nonna said. She pulled Mary and me out of the line and we followed the couple. As the door shut, I looked back and saw that Lady Jane was still laughing. She waved to me. I mouthed, "Fuck you," echoing Nonna's sentiment.

During the ride home Mrs. Muldoon and Nonna argued over what "Angel of Death" might mean.

"Maybe she'll be a police officer," Mrs. Muldoon said. "That's a nice profession. Protecting the citizens. And all police officers witness death now and again, don't you think?"

"Are you crazy? No granddaughter of mine is going to be a police officer. I think that broad saw that Molly was gonna be a doctor." She smiled at me in the rearview mirror. "What do you think she meant, Molly? Or maybe a murderer?" She laughed.

Mrs. Muldoon said, "That's an awful thing to say."

"I think she was just making things up to frighten us," I said. "Maybe she spotted someone who would actually pay her further down the line, and she was in a hurry to get us out of there."

"The man on the radio said she doesn't accept any money. Believes she has a calling is what he said she said," Mrs. Muldoon answered.

"He said, she said? Do you know what Mary's talking about?" The car swerved as Nonna turned to look at me.

"Lady Jane...Watch it, Agnella!"

"I noticed people slipping her bills," I said.

Nonna zipped through a red light.

"Jesus, Mary, and Joseph! You're going to get us arrested," Mrs. Muldoon said.

"Then it's a good thing we have a cop in the back seat. She'll use her connections and get us off the hook."

We all laughed.

As we were passing a section where you could see planes from Logan Airport, Nonna asked Mrs. Muldoon, "When is your flight?"

"What flight?"

"The flight to Ireland. When are you going home?"

"Oh ..." She paused to think a bit. "I'm going the third week of August." I thought it funny that her pronunciation sounded like "turd."

"Well, at least we have you for a few more months. I'm gonna miss you, Mary. But I'm sure you'll be happier. Everybody needs family. And eventually we all return home."

Nonna paid for my graduation celebration in June at our restaurant eponymously named "Bonamici's," which means, by the way, "good friends." Thankfully, I had received an acceptance letter from Boston University at the end of April, informing me that I was granted a full four-year scholarship, so my parents did not have the worry about paying for my college education.

My anxiety-ridden mother flitted about, at times helping in the kitchen, then darting like a finch to the hostess stand, greeting my extended family, mostly relatives on my father's side—aunts, uncles, and cousins. My father wanted to keep the event a family affair, so I couldn't invite any friends, not that there was anyone in particular I wanted there.

Our family restaurant served the typical Italian dishes—entrees with veal, chicken, and seafood, as well as traditional Italian favorites, such as meat lasagna, baked ziti, manicotti, spaghetti with meatballs. The food was mediocre; this fact, my mother's nervous disposition, and my father's surliness contributed to the so-so revenue. Part of the working class, my parents were always struggling to get by, especially during my last year at home.

I was happy that my high school years were behind me, and I made a mental effort to remember the scene around me that day—the groups of people talking under the dim swag lamps with amber globes, the red and white checkered cloths on the tables, the maroon vinyl booths with cracks, the small tables with chairs, and the large mural of a canal in Venice. As a little girl I would stare at the gondolier with his white shirt and black pants, escorting a pair of lovers among the beautiful pink and white buildings. What was he thinking? Was he angry because he had to paddle all day for rich tourists? I imagined him whacking the heads of the couple with his oar and pushing them overboard.

"Molly!" Nonna yelled from an area in front of the stone hearth, "Come over here."

There was a din in the room—people chatting, busboys and waitresses setting up tables in the front with a variety of dishes. As I made my way through the crowd, several people said congratulations, *complimenti* or *buono fortuna*.

"You know Mr. Scarfone," Nonna said, pointing next to her with her glass of whiskey.

327

"Yes. Hi, Mr. Scarfone. Thank you for coming."

"I wouldn't miss it for the world. Nonna says you're gonna make lots of money. Says you're a very smart young lady."

I laughed. "I hope so."

"I was telling him the story about that *troia* from the Combat Zone. What was her name again?" I was surprised that Nonna was already drunk. "Lady something or other." She was slurring her words.

"Jane. Lady Jane."

"No lady calls Nonna's granddaughter an 'angel of death'," Mr. Scarfone said with simulated anger.

"If anyone is an angel of death, it's Jimmy here," Nonna said, laughing, choking on some of her whiskey, which spilled onto her black dress as she coughed and bent over. There were rumors that Mr. Scarfone was associated in some way with the Mafia.

"Gimme that." Mr. Scarfone took the glass from her hand and placed it on the mantel above the hearth. "Are you okay?"

"Of course I'm okay," she said in between coughs, "It went down the wrong pipe." When she had regained composure, she said, "I'll take that now," pointing to the whiskey glass.

Mr. Scarfone returned it and said, "Agnella, maybe you better slow down. You don't want to get stewed like that one by the window." He nodded towards Mrs. Muldoon.

"That's Mrs. Muldoon. She's returning home to Ireland soon. I don't know what in hell remains in her house. Every day that I drive by men are removing more furniture. She says she's donating her things to goodwill."

Nonna tapped my shoulder. "Go talk to her, Molly. She looks lonely."

When I sat down across from Mrs. Muldoon, she smiled and seemed genuinely excited. She used to be so bitchy, but the last few times I'd seen her, she had changed dramatically. She actually seemed to like me.

"Darling, it's a pleasure to see you. And aren't you as pretty as movie star. You remind me of Audrey Hepburn. You know her, don't you, dear?" She was wearing a bright yellow dress with a matching round hat. The color complimented her shiny blue eyes.

"I loved her movie *Breakfast at Tiffany's*," I said.

"And wasn't that song so pretty? 'Moon River.' Oh, I'd sing a bit of it for you now, Molly. Ya know, I used to sing once."

"Really?"

"Yes, darling. That was how I met my husband. I played piano and sang at a nightclub in the Back Bay on Beacon Street." She looked out the window. Someone was parking a Dodge Charger across the street. Then she started to sing very softly, as if forgetting I was there. "Moon river, wider than a mile, I'm crossing you in style some day/Oh dream maker, you heart breaker/Wherever you're going, I'm going your way." Then she paused. "Oh, I'm a silly old lady. Too romantic, I think. Always been so." She leaned in a bit. "Are you romantic, Molly?"

"I'm not sure."

"Well do you have dreams, sweetheart?"

"Yes."

"Well good." She took a sip of her gin and tonic. " 'Your feet will take you where your heart is.' That's an old Irish proverb. Remember it."

"Sort of like your going back to Ireland?"

"Huh?" She looked confused.

"You're going home, Mrs. Muldoon."

"Yes, I suppose it is. I'm following my heart." She smiled. "And you must follow yours, too." She put a warm hand atop one of mine. "You and me. We're both starting a new journey. Like the rest of the song, and she began again, alternating between a faint croon and a whisper " 'Two drifters off to see the world/There's such a lot of world to see/We're after the same rainbow's end/Waiting 'round the bend, my huckleberry friend/Moon river and me.' "

"That was pretty," and I thought it truly was.

"Now get me another drink, won't you?" She gulped the last bit from her glass. "My huckleberry friend." She laughed.

I brought Mrs. Muldoon her drink. My mother called me to the center table where she and Dad sat. Soon flute glasses of champagne were distributed to all. Dad stood up and clinked his glass with a spoon to get everyone's attention. Aunt Bianca nudged Aunt Helena, who was busy fussing over the arrangement of food on the buffet tables.

"I'd like to give a toast to my beautiful daughter, Molly," he said. When the room was quiet, he continued, looking directly at me, "Molly, you are a very intelligent girl. I don't know where you got your smarts from, but it certainly wasn't from your mother or me."

"From me," Nonna called out and people laughed. My mother looked embarrassed, smiled at me and squeezed my hand.

"Molly," he continued, "Your mother and I are very proud of what you have accomplished in school. And we are certain that you will continue to do even better in college and beyond. Here goes," he said, pulling a paper from an inside pocket of his black jacket.

My mother handed Dad his glasses from the table and he began reading, "Remember this, Molly: 'If you're going to lie, lie for a friend. If you're going to steal, steal a heart. If you're going to cheat, cheat death. And if you're going to drink, drink with me. *Complimente dottore!*"

"Bravo!" people shouted and there was clinking all around.

"Stand up, Molly," my mother whispered.

I stood and everyone clapped.

"Now *Mangia!*" Dad said.

Towards the middle of August, Nonna called me to say we were taking Mrs. Muldoon to the beach on August 15th.

"Why August 15th?" I asked.

"She says she wants to spend some time at the water before she goes home. And she requested that you come as well. Something about a cure in the water. Evidently it is the Feast of the Blessed Mother's Assumption into Heaven and because of that the salt water has a cure in it. I don't really understand it all, but Mary is adamant about going, and she wants both you and I to take her."

"Is she sick?"

"Not that I know of."

"Then why does she need a cure?"

Nonna laughed. "Maybe she thinks it's you and me that need the cure, and it is her final parting gift."

"Why would we need a cure?"

"Molly, stop asking so many questions. How the hell am I supposed to know what goes on in Mary's mind? Maybe she thinks we have sick souls."

I laughed. "Nonna, I don't have a sick soul, and neither do you."

"You can never be sure. Listen, consider it insurance. If there is something to this whole cure thing, maybe we get something good out of it. And if there isn't, so be it. The point is that she asked us to take her. And I'm not going to deny an old lady a last request of a friend before she goes back home to Ireland."

I agreed to go, and on the appointed day, a Saturday, Nonna and I picked Mrs. Muldoon up at her house. She was seated in a rusted orange chair on her front porch, one of her last pieces of furniture. She had donated practically all of it to charity, except for a few pieces of in her living room, kitchen, and of course, her bedroom. Her house was on the market, but she was lackadaisical about selling it, leaving it in the hands of a realtor downtown. She said she didn't really care when or if it got sold, which I found very strange. But what did I know about such things. I was a young girl with my eyes set on college.

Nonna parked in front and honked. Mrs. Muldoon was asleep. She was wearing what appeared to be a housedress, mostly white, with a spattering of red dots, and hideous black boots.

"What the hell is she wearing?" Nonna got out of the car and walked carefully up the rotting wooden gray steps. Then windows were rolled down so I could hear their conversation. When she was beside Mrs. Muldoon, she shook her. For a moment, I thought she might be dead.

"Mary! Wake up."

She woke, a confused look on her face. Her amber hair was a sweaty mess. The cast of the sun highlighted a matted ring that circled her hair, as though she had been wearing a hat earlier.

Nonna said, "What's the matter with you? Did you forget we were going to the beach?" She looked down at Mary's feet, tsk-tsking at a pair of black rubber boots. "You look foolish in those things. How you gonna get the Blessed Mother's cure if you don't get wet."

"Agnella," she said, rising at last, "There's awful rocks before you get to the sandy part of the beach, and my feet are sore enough. Don't you worry. I'm going to take them off once we settle in a good spot. I may even strip naked. Wouldn't that be a sight to behold?" She laughed. Nonna did, too.

"And where is your bathing suit?"

"Underneath my housedress, of course. You certainly didn't expect me to sit here like some *tool* in my swimsuit. What would the neighbors think? And that strange boy next door Dominic is always lurking about snapping pictures with his camera. Scared the bejesus out of me one evening last summer. Saw him peering in my living room window."

"He's a little slow, Mary. Good he has a hobby."

"Don't mind he has a hobby. Just don't want it to be me. Imagine him taking a picture of me sitting here in my bathing suit. God only knows what he'd do with it. Wank off maybe. Shoot his tadpoles at the moon."

I laughed at the imagery. Nonna looked at me, raising her hands in the air.

"Just last week he was going through my rubbish. Rang the door and asked if I was throwing out any 'good stuff.' Had the nerve to tell me he needed money and wanted to sell 'the stuff' that I didn't want. I hate that word 'stuff.' Don't you, Agnella? Children need to speak better English."

"Forget about him. Let's get going."

Nonna helped her down the steps, which creaked and almost seemed to cave in at one point, then guided her into the passenger seat.

"I'm delighted you could come, Molly," she said, turning around. "It's a celebration for both of us, a baptism of sorts, as we begin our new lives." I realized that the red spots on her gown were tiny roses. "You must be looking forward to your studies. You have always been such a smart one."

"Very smart," Nonna interrupted. "Skipped a grade in school and tested genius on the I.Q. scale. Takes after me." She laughed.

"Yes, yes, I know. You tell me all the time, Agnella. What's most important is Molly's soul."

"I'm happy to go with you to the beach, Mrs. Muldoon," I said. I wasn't. I hated the beach, still do. The hot sun and sand, crowds of people, radios blaring, the smell of baby oil, jellyfish in the water. Although I did admire the sharks because of their single-mindedness, the way they hunted for prey. And sometimes I would hope to see one of the annoying boys get bitten, but the chances of that happening were slim.

We parked on the beach side across from the Renwod Dining Room, a place Nonna had taken me to a few times. Mary was right about the stones. They did hurt your feet. The beach was packed with people and it was hard to navigate through the crowd, especially as Mary was a little tipsy. I realized she had been drinking because I had to turn the window down on the way over. She stunk of sweat and gin. Radios blared, children created sand castles, groups of ladies gossiped, and the sun was so hot. Finally we found a spot to put our blanket and fold-up chairs. Most of the women wore full-piece swimsuits, and many had housedresses like Mary. Three girls about my age ran out of the water as their little brothers splashed them with water from behind. To our right, a man dressed in pants and a shirt, which I could never understand at the beach, fixed the chain on his over-turned bicycle. I wished we had an umbrella. I had to use the palm of my hand to shade my eyes from the sun.

When we were settled, I asked Mrs. Muldoon about the cure in the water. She sat between Nonna and I in our spot close to the ocean.

"Well, darling, today is when Catholics celebrate the Blessed Mother's Assumption into heaven."

"I don't understand."

Nonna rubbed baby oil on her arms, legs, and face, then lay down, uninterested in our conversation.

"What don't you understand?"

"The Assumption part. What does that mean?"

"Well she was raised into heaven three days after her death."

"What do you mean *raised*? She just flew up into the air?" I laughed.

"Well, I think so, Molly. Yes."

"How is that possible?"

"Darling, you've got to have faith."

"But it doesn't make sense. How can somebody just fly up into the sky?"

"I don't know, Molly. Don't think too much about it. Just believe it."

"I don't believe it. It sounds ridiculous."

Nonna sat up and gave me the eye, warning me not to press the issue.

Mrs. Muldoon pulled off her boots, then stood and took off her housedress. Underneath was a stylish black-and-white full-piece swimsuit. I never noticed what a round hard belly she had. She almost looked pregnant. For a second, I imagined she was going to demonstrate the assumption and fly up into the sky.

"Well, suit yourself. I don't question these things." She walked into the water.

After a while, Nonna fell asleep. Mrs. Muldoon had stopped swimming and was standing, like so many of the people. But unlike so many others, who were chatting with one another in pairs and groups, Mrs. Muldoon looked towards the horizon; a rainbow had formed above a group of clouds. I was wondering if she was thinking about her journey home. Seagulls cawed, children laughed or screamed with sportive delight. I was sweating, so I got up and decided to go for a walk towards the end of the beach that was less crowded, near a fishing jetty, and several clumps of large rocks. I explored the spaces in between the rocks, looking for a lonely starfish, a shiny stone, or a clam with a secreted pearl, and unearthed small crabs in the sand. At one point I startled a mourning dove that sped from its cleft into the bright sky. It made a whistling sound as it rose and flew off; then descended over the water where Nonna was now standing alongside Mrs. Muldoon in the ocean. The waves glimmered like sparks from an unquenchable fire. On the jetty, a father and his son cast fishing lines into the sea.

Suddenly, Nonna and Mrs. Muldoon fell, surprised by spirited breaker that razed them in its wake. I ran to help, but delighted, too, in the spectacle—Nonna and Mrs. Muldoon seated on their asses, just a few feet from where the waves trickled to their end. In an instant they were kneeling forward, laughing so hard that they cried. I helped lift them, Nonna and Mrs. Muldoon, groaning in between guffaws, complaining that the soles of their feet were cramping from shells and stones beneath them. Every time I lifted them another wave splashed over us, and they fell back down, laughing even harder.

Mrs. Muldoon said, "My permanent is all ruined," while she fussed with her hair.

Nonna said, "Well, it didn't look so good to begin with, Mary," and they laughed.

Then Mrs. Muldoon reached for me, "Now raise me up in quickly, Molly, before the next wave."

I did so, all the while mesmerized by the wet silvery scalp that shown through her hair. I resisted the urge to touch the crown of her head. At last she rose from the sea.

"Molly, you're an angel," she said, when she was standing.

"What about me?" Nonna said, another wave splashing over her. "*Maron'!* Pull me up, Molly. If I get hit by another wave, I'm gonna curse the water. Thought this was supposed to be a blessing. More like a tidal wave if you ask me." With that, another wave splashed over her, and both Mrs. Muldoon and I pulled her up.

Later we moved towards the quiet end of the beach. We sat in the shade of a bony cliff, eating panettone, bananas, apples, and delicious cherries drenched in brandy. Nonna pulled baby-sized jars of Grappa out her purse. I draped a necklace of dried seaweed upon Mrs. Muldoon, and told her it was my version of a Hawaiian lei, a wreath presented ceremoniously to people who were coming or going.

"In that case, you need one, too," Mrs. Muldoon said.

"What about me? I could use a good lei," Nonna said, smirking.

I found two more pieces of seaweed and Mrs. Muldoon hung them on us. Her fingers were icy cold, like those of a corpse. I shuddered as they touched my warm skin.

The three of us made a toast to new beginnings, and we talked about the future until the sun began to set.

We were still hungry as we left the beach so we crossed the street and enjoyed a nice meal at the Renwood Diner. I had the seafood platter and Nonna and Mrs. Muldoon had sea scallops with pancetta, mushrooms, and fresh tomato. Nonna and I devoured our meals but Mrs. Muldoon couldn't finish her meal and asked the waitress to put the leftovers in a bag to go.

Mrs. Muldoon made a joke about this being our last supper. "Well, it is in a way, don't you think? I won't be seeing either of you again after tonight."

"Of course you will. You're not leaving until five days from now." Nonna said, motioning for the check. "I'll drop by before your flight on Thursday if I don't see you before then."

The waitress put Mrs. Muldoon's white doggie bag and the check on the table.

"Let me pay for that," Mrs. Muldoon said. "I appreciate you girls bringing me to the ocean today. I feel refreshed and healed. And you made me very happy."

"Well I'm glad that you feel good, Mary, but I insist on paying." Nonna took cash out of her purse and placed it on the bill. The waitress picked it up.

"I'll see you one more time, Mrs. Muldoon. Nonna's driving me to Boston University to speak with a counselor next Thursday. On the way over, we can both say goodbye."

"That would be nice, Molly." She smiled at me, then pointed at the faded beige and blue pattern of fish swimming above clamshells and starfish on the ocean floor. "I always loved the fish in this wallpaper. This one here looks like he's coming right towards us."

"I wish there were some shark," I said.

Nonna laughed. "Of course you would."

"Did you know that a fish is the symbol of Christ?" Mrs. Muldoon said, sipping her last bit of wine.

Nonna spoke while she finished a roll. "No, I didn't. Where'd you hear that, Mary?"

"Oh, I don't recall, Agnella."

The waitress put Nonna's change on the table. "Well, I'm tired. I don't know about the both of you. Let's get outta here."

We dropped Mrs. Muldoon off and she waved from the front porch once before she'd opened the door. I noticed several trash bags along the gray clapboard wall.

"Wonder what's in all those bags?" I said, as we drove away.

"Junk. When you get old you accumulate a lot of useless things, Molly. And then you become one of them. So live while you can."

I noticed a white paper bag at my feet. "Nonna, Mrs. Muldoon forgot her leftovers."

"Ahh. Don't worry about it. Leftovers are another useless thing." Stone-faced and preoccupied, she stared into the dusk. The streetlights turned on. I looked out the passenger window. Two of the neighborhood boys waved from the sidewalk.

Nonna had tried to call Mary on Wednesday evening to find out the time of her flight back to Ireland, but the phone service had already been disconnected, so we drove over around 8:00 am on Thursday morning.

"She may have already left." Nonna pulled the car into Mary's driveway. "But we might as well see if she's still here. I forgot to tell you, but when we were in the ladies room at the restaurant,

Mary told me she had a gift for you. She said she left it on the table just inside the archway to her living room."

We got out of the car and walked up the steps. Nonna held her nose. "Those bags smell God awful. Maybe she dumped food from her refrigerator into one of them."

I rang the doorbell. We waited a few moments, then Nonna turned the door knob. When the door opened a horrible smell gushed at us—a combination of shit, vomit, body odor, and rotting fish, stronger than you can imagine, unless you've experienced it. A few flies buzzed in the air around our heads. As we turned into the living room, I noticed a small wrapped gift next to a white bag on the table. Nonna bent over and started vomiting.

I walked towards Mrs. Muldoon's corpse. She was seated in the purple chair that Nonna hated so much, eyes half open and bulging, tongue protruding. There was an intricate pattern of blood vessels and blisters on her face. She wore the same house-dress from our day at the beach. It was smeared with blood dripping from her nose and mouth. Her face, arms, and legs were bloated; her abdomen was distended. Her skin was green, purple and black. White lines crisscrossed areas of red on her calves. There were two shimmering pools of urine on the mahogany floor at each side of the chair, as well as feces on the seat cushion.

I kneeled down and pressed my finger against a dark purple spot above her right ankle; the skin was so cold. The flesh broke and blood trickled slowly down the side of her enlarged foot. I stood up, then crouched to stare into the small slivers of her eyes. The pupils were fixed and dilated. The corners of her eyes were filmy and I thought I saw wetness along the sides of her nose and cheeks. Were they tears or simply the body's fluids seeping out? I touched her pretty red hair and some it fell to the floor in clumps. A bloody maggot emerged from her right ear.

I heard Nonna gagging behind me. She kept saying, "We gotta call the police." I couldn't look back and though I found the smell overpowering and coughed a bit, I drew closer. I guess you could say I was mesmerized.

"Molly! What are you doing? Call the cops! I'm too weak to get up."

I picked up the black-and-white photograph from the TV table and examined it: an attractive couple, the young Mrs. Muldoon and her husband, in their wedding attire. Both of them dressed completely in white. He wore a white tuxedo with a bow tie and a wing-tipped collar. On the top of her auburn hair sat a veil with a crest of small white flowers; there was a pearl necklace around her neck and both of them were smiling above a large bouquet of white roses that obscured parts of their chests. In the dark background, blurred white faces hovered like disembodied heads.

"Molly!!"

I turned the photo over. In blue cursive Mrs. Muldoon had written "August 15th, 1954. The happiest day of my life." Next to where the photograph had lain was an empty pill bottle. I pulled it close to read the label "Diazepam, 5 mg. tab. Take one tablet twice a day as needed."

Nonna had managed to make a phone call. I heard her in the hall talking to the police. "Hurry," she said. She hung up the phone.

"What the hell are you doing?" she screamed at me. "Get away from her."

I turned, accidentally stepping on one of Mrs. Muldoon's bare feet. The skin cracked; a clear fluid oozed from her big toe and the nail ripped off, falling like an autumn leaf onto the floor.

Then I walked over to the small purple box with my name on it. Inside was a gold necklace with an emerald and diamond cross.

Nonna stared at me. "What is it, Molly?"

"A useless thing."

A short while later, two patrol officers showed up. The older one, a man with steel-gray hair, Paul Newman eyes, and thick black glasses took Nonna and me into Mrs. Muldoon's kitchen to ask a few questions, while the young officer, clearly a newbie by the pale and frightened look on his pudgy face, stayed in the living room. He was probably in his early twenties. I overheard him calling his supervisor to report the scene. His voice was high and agitated. I thought he wouldn't last long in this profession.

When we were seated, the older policeman introduced himself as Officer Donnelly. "My partner is Officer Connolly."

I laughed because their names rhymed, and he gave me a strange look.

Nonna was staring blankly into the air, obviously in a state of shock. She was perspiring. I handed her a napkin from the table. She dabbed her face robotically.

Officer Donnelly gave up on asking her questions because she muttered an incoherent mix of Italian and English. He turned his attention on me, notebook and pen in hand. He asked for our full names, which I gave him.

"Does Mrs. Muldoon have any relatives we should contact, Molly?"

"No."

His forehead rose and he examined my face, scrutinizing me. "No one? No one that you know of, you mean?"

337

"No. I mean 'no one.' She had a husband but he's dead. Your partner will figure that out, though, when he sees the picture on the TV table in front of her corpse."

"What do you mean, Molly?"

I explained my curiosity about dead bodies and gave him the details of what I had done, the writing on the back of the photograph.

"You touched the body?" I noticed a hint of anger or was it disbelief, maybe even revulsion? He moved uncomfortably in the chair.

"Yes. And the skin broke so easily. Does skin always break like that when you touch a dead body?"

"Well it depends how long it has been since the moment of passing." He stared at me. His eyes were light, so pretty, almost feminine.

"Passing where?" I teased him.

"To heaven, Molly." He pulled his chair back a bit and rotated his left shoulder to stretch. He pulled himself upward, puffing his chest. I noticed sweat on his face, too, and handed him one of Mrs. Muldoon's napkins. They were white with blue and white doves.

"How could you do that?" Nonna exploded. She stood and began wringing her hands. Then she fingered the cross around her neck.

I answered Officer Donnelly. "I don't believe she *passed* to heaven, sir."

"Molly, I don't much care what you believe. What else did you touch?" He spoke calmly, as if dealing with a lunatic.

"I touched her hair, and some of it fell out. You'll find it on the floor in a puddle of urine. There was a maggot in her ear."

Nonna ran to the bathroom.

"A maggot?"

"Yes, Officer Donnelly. As in a fly."

"That didn't bother you?"

"No." I laughed. "A maggot is just a baby fly."

I could hear Nonna retching down the hall. The toilet flushed. She entered with a wet cloth on her forehead and sat down.

"I'm sorry, Officer Connolly. This whole thing has been very upsetting," she said. I noticed for the first time the deepness of the wrinkles by her eyes. Her olive skin looked papery, like crepe. A blue vein in her temple bulged slightly.

"Officer *Donnelly*, ma'am...It's quite understandable that you are upset."

"Huh?"

"My partner's name is Officer Connolly. I'm Officer Donnelly."

"Oh. That's right. Sorry."

"The sergeant has notified the homicide unit and EMS. They are on their way." Officer Connolly said, entering the kitchen. His eyes moved from Nonna to me.

"How's the girl?" he asked Officer Donnelly, as if I weren't present.

"I'm fine. Thank you," thinking, "better than you." His skin was a yellow pea-green.

"Sorry that you had to walk in on this, Ms...." He looked at Officer Donnelly.

"Her name's Molly. Molly Bonamici."

"Ahh. Your last name means 'good friends' "

"You know Italian?"

"Yeah. Some of my best buddies are Italian."

"Mrs. Muldoon was Irish like you. I liked her in the end. I guess you could say she was one of my buddies."

"I see," he answered, raising his eyebrows at Officer Donnelly.

"Why don't you take Mrs. Janssen and Molly to the patrol car. Have them sit there a while."

A crowd had gathered. The blue light on top of the car cut through the air, highlighting faces like a strobe light. I saw Aunt Helena; Aunt Bianca stood behind her with one hand on Aunt Helena's shoulder. She looked like she was clasping a life raft, adrift at sea. I waved to them and smiled as we were ushered into the car. My mother and father were there as well. They tried to approach the car, but Officer Connolly said something to them and they moved back. My mother's eyes pleaded. She was excited as she talked to him, more animated than I had ever seen her. I guess they wanted to keep Nonna and me isolated.

"Well, she got what she wanted," I said inside the car.

"What are you talking about, Molly?! She's dead. Mary is dead."

"But Nonna, she took those pills on August 15, the anniversary of her marriage. She wanted to die on that day. Now it all makes sense. I think it's kind of sweet and perfect."

"Sweet! Perfect! What the hell is the matter with you? A woman is dead in that house. Her body has been decomposing for days. She was all alone. She was sad. You call that 'sweet' and 'perfect'? Don't talk like that." She wrung her hands, looking at the crowd outside. "It's a good thing Mr. Scarfone knows the chief of police. He'll be able to come up with a reason for you touching Mrs. Muldoon's body. Maybe he can say that you were in a state of shock." She turned to look at me in the shadowed car. "What you did was very odd. What in God's name were you thinking, Molly?"

"I wasn't thinking anything *in God's name*."

She sighed and turned away.

I couldn't understand the big deal everyone was making. We all die. Mrs. Muldoon had chosen her time. I thought she was brave to end her life as she wanted. I didn't think Mrs. Muldoon was sad. That day at the beach was one of the happiest I had ever seen her. I did think it was a bit silly to believe that she would be "going home" to her husband Jim, when she was, in fact, going home to the earth, to her "conqueror worm," a worm that had already begun to feast on her body.

Did she say a prayer for home as she stood in the waves that day as she looked towards the horizon? Did she believe that home was somewhere in the sky beyond the sun and clouds?

The image of her body flashed in my mind, and I remembered a poem by Edgar Allan Poe that I had to recite for my English class:

> *But see, amid the mimic rout,*
> *A crawling shape intrude!*
> *A blood-red thing that writhes from out*
> *The scenic solitude!*
> *It writhes! — it writhes! — with mortal pangs*
> *The mimes become its food,*
> *And the angels sob at vermin fangs*
> *In human gore imbued!*
>
> *Out — out are the lights — out all!*
> *And, over each dying form,*
> *The curtain, a funeral pall,*
> *Comes down with the rush of a storm,*
> *And the seraphs, all haggard and wan,*
> *Uprising, unveiling, affirm*
> *That the play is the tragedy "Man,"*
> *Its hero the Conqueror Worm.*

I thought of the evening Mrs. Muldoon and I talked about the snowflakes falling outside her kitchen window, how no two flakes were exactly alike. On August 15, 1980, Mrs. Muldoon had managed to create something "alike," symmetrical, and balanced through the timing of her death, and that was a kind of beauty, however fleeting. She had created her own assumption and I thought, ironically, *consumption*.

All of this went through my mind as Nonna stared out the window, creating circles of condensation on the glass after sliding away from me on the backseat. The flashing blue light in the heavy air outside was a reminder to all of us that one day we, too, would die. I thought of Aunt Bianca's sullenness, my mother's anxiety, my father's anger and frustration, Nonna's strength and confidence, Mr. Scarfone's mystery, and my own indifference. How insignificant all these attributes seemed when faced with the ugliness of death.

In my mind, I heard Mrs. Muldoon singing "Moon River." "We're after the rainbow's end" the song says. But there was no rainbow's end for her. Her end was five days of rot and decay in a hot humid room.

Nonna, as if sensing my thoughts, moved closer, wrapped her arm around me, and rested the side of her warm face on my shoulder.

"Everything will be alright, Molly," she said.

I would like to say that I was comforted, but I wasn't. At that moment, life seemed futile, and prayers for home, wherever we believed we were going, would never be answered. The moon was too high, the river was too wide, and our hearts would be broken after all.

LIVING IN FEAR, DYING IN FEAR

Patricia Reed

She has been terrified all of her life, as far back as she can remember, and she doesn't even know why. Just something she has to live with, she thinks. But finally, when she is a grown woman and tired of being afraid to go out of her own house, she asks her mother.

Is there a reason why I'm so afraid of snakes?

Yes, probably, her mother says. *When you were little and we lived on the farm, you loved strawberries and you crawled down to the strawberry patch one day and got scared by a snake. You screamed bloody murder. Daddy ran down there and carried you back up to the house, but you wouldn't stop screaming. You screamed for an hour. We finally took you to Dr. Barnes and he gave you something to settle you down. But you were just a little bitty thing, not more than two at the time. We didn't think you'd remember it.*

No, she doesn't remember it. But that doesn't change anything. Her life has been absolutely defined by it. As a child, much as she hates the cold of winter, she fears the warmth of summer even more, because it brings out the snakes. She doesn't go barefoot like all the other kids do, because what if she steps on a snake? And she can't go running carelessly through the fields like they do either, because she has to be on the lookout for snakes. Who knows what lurks in that tall grass? The other kids grow tired of waiting for her and go on without her. Eventually they stop including her altogether.

She grows up and moves away, but the fear moves with her. Sometimes it seems like the fear is actually attracting the snakes, because she sees more of them than most people do, and in unlikely places; on the sidewalk in Miami Beach, or on a busy street in Gatlinburg, Tennessee. And once in North Carolina, as she and her husband are panning for rubies in Cowee Valley, she feels something hit the back of her hand in the muddy water of the sluice as it flows past her, and she knows it had to be a snake. But when she flings down her screen of mud and rocks and declares that a snake just touched her hand, people laugh derisively. *It would have to go past fifty people just to get to you. And no one else saw a snake. Does that make sense?*

Rather than make a scene, she says no, no it doesn't, and turns back to the sluice. She resumes jiggling her screen up and down in the muddy water, but she's careful to keep her upstream hand out of the water. And then a man two seats away comes back to his seat at the sluice on the other side of her husband and speaks quietly to her husband. But she hears him.

Guess what they just pulled out of the sluice down at the bottom. A black snake about this long.

He holds his hands about three feet apart. That's enough for her. She pulls her legs up onto the bench and sits there cross-legged for the rest of the day, not putting her hands in the water or her feet on the ground. Her husband has been through this with her before. Another vacation ruined because of her unreasonable fear of snakes. They're everywhere, for goodness' sakes. He's annoyed, but he tries not to show it.

A few years later they buy a small farm in Georgia and people think she has the perfect life. After all, she has a handsome and loving husband and two adorable little kids.

Petey is a carbon copy of his dad, right down to the cowlick in his blond hair. He plays Little League baseball with a quiet determination that almost makes up for his lack of talent. He never misses a practice or a game, and in his mind he is Chipper Jones, making the awesome play from third or belting in the winning run.

Rosemary, named for her daddy's mother, is into ponies. Ponies for a while anyway. Later she will graduate to horses, and become quite the equestrienne. She spends hours grooming Painter and practicing jumping with him so they can qualify for the rodeo in the fall.

Life is good for the woman. Until the next snake.

One day, while she's out in the pasture watching Rosemary practicing with the pony, a snake slithers quickly through the grass at her feet. And one minute she's sitting on the top rail of the fence applauding Rosemary, and the next minute she's upstairs in her bedroom with the covers pulled up over her head, shaking all over. She doesn't remember running or shrieking, but Rosemary is so traumatized that her daddy has to hold her for a long time to calm her down, and Painter has to be coaxed back out of the barn where he has fled in terror.

Later her husband fixes supper for the kids and tucks them into bed, then with a grim look on his face he goes down the hall to the bedroom to talk to his wife. There's yelling and crying going on, and the kids hear words like "get some help" and "can't live like this" before he goes back downstairs and slams the front door on his way out. He doesn't come home again until late that night. The kids huddle in their beds.

She doesn't go out into the pasture again. They hire a trainer to work with the little girl and her pony, and she watches them from the safety of the porch. No snakes on the porch.

Little League season starts up in the spring, and she takes Petey to the field every night for practice, but she sits in the car to watch. She tells him that the seats are too hard or it's too hot or it's too cold, but actually it's just that there is *so much grass.* She just can't walk through all that grass.

Fear of snakes. Fear of grass? Fear is fear.

She makes it through the baseball season only because her husband's job keeps him from attending the games, and somehow Petey knows that he should not tell Daddy that Mommie is sitting in the car all during the games. Don't tell on Mommie.

Then in November, it's show time at the fairgrounds. Time for Rosemary and her pony to shine. She makes the little girl's costume, and they have a wonderful day shopping in Atlanta for new riding boots for Rosemary, and ribbons to braid into Painter's hair. It's going to be such an exciting night.

But she begins to get sick to her stomach as she remembers that the bleachers for the spectators are set up on the grass out behind the livestock barn, and it's a long ways out there. A long ways, through a lot of grass. Suddenly, she's throwing up in the bathroom. No way she can go to the show. Call your daddy, she says. Tell him I'm sick. He'll have to take you.

The daddy arrives. He's had to leave an important business meeting. *Get in the car,* he tells the kids brusquely as he takes the stairs two at a time, up to where his wife is again in bed under the covers. Silently the kids make their way out to the car. What was supposed to be a wonderful night is not so wonderful any more. Mommy is sick again and Daddy is mad. Why?

From the open upstairs window they hear shouting and crying, and then a door slamming. In a minute their daddy comes out the front door and gets in the car without a word to either of them. He has a scary face.

They ride in silence to the fairgrounds. At one point Daddy pounds his fist on the steering wheel, but he doesn't say anything, just drives up and down the rows of cars looking for a parking space, but there aren't any left because they are late getting there. So he pulls back out onto the road and parks in the grass along the shoulder, and they get out and run back to the fairgrounds. The pony jumping contest is just being announced, so the daddy gives Rosemary a quick hug and sends her off running to get in line. He and Petey go in the other direction to find their seats in the stands.

When they get home, Mommy is asleep and they tiptoe around quietly, getting ready for bed. Rosemary hangs her blue ribbon on the refrigerator to show Mommy in the morning. The daddy tucks them in their beds, then goes back down to sit in his den. The television is on, but he's not watching it. He just sits there quietly until dawn. He's a good man. It's a long night.

Years pass, as they always do, and the children grow up. They spend most of their teenage years at their friends' houses, where there are fun things going on. Their own house is always quiet because their mother mostly stays in her room. Resting, she says.

She doesn't watch television because a snake might appear on the screen, and she doesn't have magazines around because sometimes they have a picture of a snake in them and she comes upon it without warning and then she has an "episode", as her husband calls it. The kids hear him tell friends she's "getting worse", but they're not sure what to make of that, so they just try to stay out of the way. She misses birthday parties and even graduations. Her children are bewildered. Her husband is disgusted. She doesn't apologize, doesn't even seem to realize what her life has become. What *their* life has become.

She plays a lot of Solitaire and writes to her friends, what ones she has kept, but most of them have fallen away over the years. It's hard to visit with someone who won't come out of her house for months at a time. And she won't walk down the driveway to the mailbox, not with all that grass on either side of the drive, so sometimes there are several days in a row that she can't mail a letter or get any that have been sent to her. She doesn't even come out on the porch in the evenings any more. When the kids are around, her husband makes an effort, but when they go off to college, he begins to work late every night.

If she notices, she doesn't comment on it. She doesn't comment on much of anything, really. Just the fact that there are snakes in the grass and she's not going out there, no matter where "there" is. She refuses to get any help, and finally her husband stops asking her to. He eats in town most of the time, but he makes sure there is food in the house for her. Hunger drives her down to the kitchen after he has left for work. But she can't stay down there long. Too close to all that grass outside. She carries her food upstairs to the safety of her room.

Then one night, he sees that she hasn't eaten anything all day and goes up to check on her. She's wild-eyed and her clothes are disheveled. He tries to take her downstairs to get something to eat. She hisses at him to go away, tries to strike him when he moves to pick her up off the bed.

Resignedly, he calls their family doctor. *It's time,* he says.

Dr. Barnes doesn't officially make house calls any more, but he still has his black bag, so he packs it with a sedative that he hopes will help her again. A lot stronger this time than the one he gave her all those years ago. He sighs, remembering when she was a tiny girl, scared to death by a snake. Who would have thought that would affect her all of her life?

He drives out to the farm slowly, as though to put off the awful task before him. Her husband meets him at the door, shoulders slumped in defeat. They have a muted conversation right there on the porch, and the good doctor reaches out to his friend with a comforting touch. They stand there for a minute, listening to the screaming upstairs. Then the two of them climb the stairs together, each hoping against hope that the doctor can work his magic again. But there's no helping her this time, no bringing her back from wherever she has gone. She won't even let Dr. Barnes take her blood pressure, just thrashes about on the bed like a wild thing.

Reluctantly, Dr. Barnes puts away his stethoscope and reaches into his bag for a pad of legal forms he has brought with him just in case, hoping he wouldn't need them, but there's really no alternative. He looks to the husband for permission.

Tears run down the good man's face as he slowly nods to the old doctor and blindly signs the form the doctor hands him. Wiping a tear from his own eyes, Dr. Barnes signs the commitment order and calls for an ambulance, then he and his friend wait in silence, wait for the wail of the siren. They tried. God knows they tried. But in the end, fear has won.

YOU NEVER TOLD ME

Judy Viertel

Fifteen years later I'm at my favorite Chinese bakery, waiting for Nan. To pass the time, I sip tea. I watch the man sweeping the floor. He's always here, this same old Chinese guy, his back hunched over a broom. The front windows are wide open, letting in a late-summer breeze; it cools me, and jostles a red paper lantern hanging from the ceiling. And then there she is, pushing her way through the swinging doors.

"Jeffrey," she says, "you haven't changed!"

This is what people always say when they haven't seen me in a long time. I've kept my hair the same since college: mostly short, but with long bangs in front. I wear a flannel shirt almost every day. Anything else feels like a costume.

I say, "But you..."

Nan's hair is up in a rigid bun, and she's wearing lipstick. Her handbag is sewn out of plaid, synthetic fur. This is a woman who used to wear the same blue sweatshirt every day. I liked that sweatshirt. "Yes," she laughs, pretending to fluff her hair. "Glad you noticed. Well," she says, her smile dwindling, "I mean I hope I've changed. We were all pretty foolish back in our college days, weren't we?"

She sits down across from me. It occurs to me that most people in my position would, at this point, say something about it being great to see her. I'm not sure it is great, though, so I lean back in my chair. I listen to the hum of the industrial refrigerator. Out in the street, a motorcycle grumbles by. At the table behind me, a teenage girl argues into her cell phone in Cantonese.

"I can't believe it's you," Nan continues, and I begin to wonder if she's as clueless about her intentions as I am. "So, the dim sum here... you said it's the best Chinese food in town?"

I stand up. "We'll see what you think."

There's only one customer in line ahead of me, and from what I can see, she might be the sister of the woman behind the counter: both of them are short, with thick-framed eyeglasses. Then just as I'm thinking that it's probably just white guy obliviousness that makes me assume two middle-aged Asian women must be related, just as I'm getting a little annoyed at myself for having that thought, the lady exits, a pink box under her arm. It's my turn. "Excuse me," I say.

The woman turns to the sink and sprays water into a pan. She yells at the old man with the broom. People often ignore me, but it feels awkward with Nan watching. "*Ni hao,*" I try, and the attendant turns to face me. With nimble tongs she plucks my choices from the bamboo steamers. I ferry it all back to the table on a blue plastic tray.

"These are *shiu mai,*" I tell Nan, "pork buns. This is turnip cake. And these are my favorite: *har gow,* shrimp dumplings."

Nan's eyes flit over the food. She leans forward, examining me again. "So, are you still in game design?"

"I'm playing around with a few ideas, but mostly I do on-call tech support." There isn't much to say about that, so I ask, "What brought you to the West Coast?"

"My Chicago job was a dead end. Here, I've got a shot at upper management."

"Good for you," I say, just to say something. Spearing one translucent dumpling with a plastic fork, I pop it into my mouth. Clean oil coats my tongue. The dough bursts open, releasing a marvelously fresh shrimp. It's as saline and invigorating as the ocean itself, and cushioned on a pillowy blob of fat. "Try one," I say.

"I have this thing about shrimp," she says. "I only eat sustainably harvested seafood."

I toss another dumpling into my mouth. The outside is just as silky, the inside just as juicy as the first.

"Well," she says, "you did go to the trouble." She opens her mouth to take a bite, and I catch a glimpse of her straight, white teeth.

During our sophomore year of college, I often dreamed of kissing Nan. Before that, I rarely talked to girls. Soon after Nan transferred in, we wound up eating together in the dining hall. Then we began meeting for regular study sessions in the library, and going on weekend walks. At that time she was continually changing her mind about what to major in, so she'd tell me about that, about her dilemma. She'd talk to me about her conflicts with her parents, too. As for me, mostly I just listened. Then, during winter break, she called me three times from Iowa just to "talk to someone real," as she put it. It wasn't until May that I worked up the courage to tell her how much I liked her.

"You're right," Nan says, putting down her fork. "These are good." Then she says, "You know, I'm just surprised you haven't been snapped up by some game company."

"I worked for a little start-up a few years ago, until they went out of business. Sometimes I go to interviews, but people have a tendency to ask about the gaps in my resume. Of course, it doesn't help that I quit college."

"You should finish your degree." She's too chicken to look at me as she says this. Instead she seems to be watching a fly darting around the lantern in quick, sharp vectors.

"I could go back for the piece of paper, but it wouldn't matter much."

"You know, I might see if I can talk you into rethinking that. I mean when we talk again, later," she says, glancing at her watch. "I need to pick up new shoes this afternoon and maybe earrings. But listen," she says. She leans in closer. "Last year my friend Julia took me to this seminar about making amends with the past. The gist of it is, people have misunderstandings, that's natural, but sometimes the conflict really stays with you. All that bullshit just moves into your life and stays with you. The only way out is to do a kind of emotional cleansing. I'm told it can be really powerful if you do it right." She takes a deep breath, and I realize that it's important to her, this "cleansing" business. "We should get together this weekend and clear the air."

"I might get called in for a job," I say. "I hope so." This is true. I need rent money.

We stand up and she hugs me, briefly. She smells like fir trees and spices. She smells of expensive, aromatic components I don't recognize. "Jeffrey," she says.

The conventional thing would be for me to say it was a pleasure to see her. True pleasure is a rarity, though. I don't like to trivialize the concept. "You wouldn't even kiss me," I say. "Not once. And then you wouldn't tell me why not."

"I know. And then you left school. But that was long ago. You've forgiven me by now, haven't you?"

I say, "It wasn't that long ago."

Soon after that she leaves, and I get more hot water for my tea. I bite into another dumpling, sinking my teeth through the pliant, briny shrimp. I'd be happy to eat *har gow* every day for the rest of my life.

There's a gust of wind. A plastic bag and a soiled napkin fly in through the window. The old man leans into his broom. There's a satisfied look on his face. Now he has something to sweep.

SELF HELP

Atwood Boyd

"Little boxes on the hillside,
Little boxes made of ticky tacky
Little boxes on the hillside,
Little boxes all the same,
There's a pink one and a green one
And a blue one and a yellow one
And they're all made out of ticky tacky
And they all look just the same."

I thought that moving into this neighborhood would be a good idea. The community was mostly middle-aged couples with kids or retirees who certainly wanted to make life easy on themselves.

It seemed like a perfect place for me to relax and not have to worry about either my security or my sanity. What was also appealing was the fact that the Homeowners Association members wasn't a bunch of rule-following lawn Gestapo. I could actually have a little freedom in this community.

The community was called Brunswick Oaks, and I had bought my half-million-dollar home there in the hopes of allowing me time to work on my art in a location away from a big city, but still with enough amenities to allow me to live a social life when I decided to have one. There was a nearby dock to the Cape Fear River so I could kayak when I chose, and there were nearby tennis courts and a pool.

This was a drastic increase in my quality of living from when I had a single bedroom apartment in Boston. It was there that I had been more or less discovered by the art world with an exhibit of death masks I had administered to John Does and the homeless. I had sought to put a face on the nameless who die away from comfort or loved ones, and that kind of social guilt was exactly what several communities asked for.

But all a sudden attention was far more than I wanted. I had a book deal, sold the majority of the exhibit to the museum, and moved south for some peace and quiet. When I moved in I had a few visitors, and I began to enjoy life in a gated community. Initially, I had been opposed to it, but I definitely began to understand the draw. Lazy Sundays on the porch with a glass of that wonderful southern concoction called a Julep.

Productive days in my studio, and Friday nights in the thriving downtown theater scene in nearby Wilmington gave me idyllic lifestyle I had craved. My dealings with my neighbors were very subdued. I wasn't anti-social, but I did not go out of my way to interact with my fellow residents. I was, however, more than a little perplexed when I was visited by another member of the community.

Mr. Jason Kahn was a very nice man; he was very active in local charitable efforts from what I gathered from the occasional Good Shepherd Home flyer and fundraiser for local schools. I answered my door one day and Mr. Kahn was standing there on my stoop with that very welcoming smile of his. He looked rather impeccable in his white shirt and black tie.

"Good Morning, Steve! I just wanted to drop by and say hello! Everything going okay here?"

I assured him that I was liking the neighborhood just fine and that I was really enjoying the local town. He smiled and nodded.

"That's great Steve! Hey, I just wanted to drop by and invite you to a meeting we are having at the clubhouse this afternoon. It's all about improvement, both your home and yourself. Real good do-it-yourselfer information. It's from the new book I learned about called *Foundations*. We'd love to have someone with your skills be there!"

I politely declined and made some small talk for a while before saying goodbye to Jason. I had a good day and got quite a bit of work done. I went for one of my late night runs when I happened to jog by the Clubhouse. Inside I saw a slideshow being put on by Mr. Kahn. I couldn't quite make out its bullet points, but the projector screen seemed to wave and shimmer in the summer heat. I continued my run and thought nothing else of it until the morning three days later.

That morning I was visited once again by one of my neighbors. This time it was Greg Faulkner, an engineer at the Brunswick Nuclear Plant. I had been out front collecting my mail when he walked up towards my front door wearing a white shirt, black tie and grey slacks.

"Good Morning, Steve! I just wanted to drop by and say hello! Everything going okay here?"

I said that it was and I invited him inside and offered him a drink. He politely turned me down and asked about my latest exhibit I'd been planning. It had been no secret that I had been working on something new to put on display in downtown

Wilmington. Several people were eager to have a look at it, but I courteously rebuffed their inquiries, telling them that they would have to wait until the day.

Greg politely nodded and looked a little crestfallen, but it was obvious that it was just a little bit of facetious acting on his part. He then reached into his briefcase and brought out a hardback book.

"That's okay, Steve! Hey, I just wanted to drop by and offer you a copy of a book I picked up at the clubhouse meeting a few days ago. It's all about improvement, both your home and yourself. Real good do-it-yourselfer information. It's called *Foundations*. I thought that you'd love to read it, what with your artistic skills!"

I was a little put off by the book's cover. It was exuding the self-important aura of the kind of spiritual book I tended to view as cheap trash. It even had the Oprah book club sticker on the front. However, I did not want to appear impolite so I gratefully accepted and thanked him for his time. Greg left, stopped at the foot of my driveway and waved before walking to his car and driving off. I was left a little shaken by the encounter but decided to let it go and do some work on the upcoming show in Wilmington.

After some time painting and sculpting, I decided that I would drive into town and buy some groceries; I had been running low on fresh vegetables and felt a desire for some stir-fry that night. I drove my small compact car down the cul-de-sac where I lived on and out towards the main gate. On the way I passed numerous houses with children playing soccer in the front yard. The local youth soccer season must have started for it seemed like every child was kicking a ball around the yard.

While driving past my neighborhood houses I couldn't help but notice the large number of construction projects. It seemed that nearly everyone was taking to heart the instructions in *Foundations* and were applying their newfound knowledge with a near religious zeal.

Many houses were adding on rooms or changing the upper stories. I even saw some apparent demolition taking place. There was also quite a bit of landscaping being carried out.

Curiously, the landscaping was at the busy hands of the homeowners and their families, not the usual day laborers that were paid to mow lawns and trim hedges. Nearly every occupied home had some kind of construction and yard work in progress.

My mind was somewhat distracted the rest of the drive to the supermarket. I couldn't shake the images of my abnormally ambitious neighbors that seemed to be buzzing around my head. It was while I was in the frozen food aisle, contemplating whether or not I should just get frozen veggies for my stir fry or actually go through the trouble of slicing up some fresh ones, that I saw another of my neighbors.

She was one of few other single people who lived in the community. From what I could remember, she was a romance author of some kind and had a small poodle that would occasionally make use of my front yard much to my chagrin. For some reason, I had an impulse to talk to her about the recent behavior of our neighbors.

"Hello! I think we've met once before?"

She looked up from her perusal of the pint-sized sherbet with a look of bemused consternation.

"Yeah. I live about three cul-de-sacs down."

She wouldn't say anything else, staring at me almost as if she wanted me to leave.

"Listen, this is going to sound kind of stupid, but by any chance—"

She cut me off.

"I'm not going to read your damn book, okay? Will you tell your stupid little club to stop harassing me? I have no interest in doing any improvements to my house. It's fine the way it is and I'm not doing anything in violation of the Homeowners Association."

I was taken aback.

"You have had people knocking on your door, too? Wait, how often? What book?"

Her confrontational attitude immediately changed to one of relief.

"Oh, thank God! You're not one of them! They are incessant! They knock on my door every night asking me to read their stupid book and come to their meetings."

At this point I didn't even need to ask what book she was talking about. It was a relief to find someone who had been experiencing the same thing I had, but I hadn't endured nightly visits. While a general curiosity, I wouldn't say that my neighbor's visits were any kind of annoyance.

"They come to you every night? How long has this been going on? Oh, by the way, I'm Steve."

I reached out my hand and she took it, shaking it briefly with a pained grin on her face.

"Karen, and they've been coming every night for over two weeks now. What's worse, when I woke up this morning and got in my car, there was one of them waiting at my driveway to pester me. He even blocked my car from leaving until I rolled down my window and told him that I wasn't interested in his offer. I almost had to drive over him to leave!"

I was a little skeptical.

"He stopped you from leaving? Hey, wait a minute, doesn't the homeowners' association ban solicitation? I've never had Jehovah's Witnesses or Mormons come by my door. So shouldn't this not be allowed?"

"No. I asked. It's not religious, they aren't asking for money or contributions of any kind. They only ask if I've read the book, so the Association can't do anything. They don't even knock at a late hour so I can't be mad at them for waking me up."

While I found her story of harassment a little difficult to believe, her story about the Homeowners Association made sense. One of the big attractions was the peace and quiet of a gated community. I wouldn't be interrupted by the busy life of a city, and I wouldn't have to worry about constant trivialities.

"You know, they say it isn't religious, but it sure sounds like a cult of some kind. How long have those meetings in the clubhouse been going on?"

Karen looked thoughtful for a moment.

"I think they have been having those for something like five months now. From what I saw, they were just about hedge placement and how to add additions to your house, be your own contractor kind of a thing."

I nodded and crossed my arms.

"Strange. Well, if you have any questions feel free to come by my house. I'd be more than happy to chat with someone about something other than a hedge or how to replace a doorjamb."

"I'll take you up on that. These people really are getting on my last nerve." She appeared to be a bit more relieved and gave a half-hearted wave as we both continued our shopping. I finished soon enough with all kinds of thoughts flying through my head.

I also dropped by the liquor store on the way back; I felt that sometimes I had much better ideas when I was less than sober. I picked up a fifth of whiskey, and because they were on sale, a Dewar's glass set in case Karen came by asking for some company.

When I returned home, the weekly *Foundations* meeting was in full swing. The clubhouse was absolutely packed. There were so many people that there weren't even enough chairs, and I could make out bodies standing in the main room blocking my view of the projector screen. They must have been singing or having a good time as I could hear a muffled noise not unlike the roar of the crowd at a Little League game through my car windows as I drove by.

I continued back to my house and let myself in, and for the first time since moving into a gated community, locked the door.

I made my way upstairs and onto the balcony. Looking out across the cul-de-sac I looked out towards the clubhouse. Even from my location, almost a mile from the gathering, I could still hear a dull sporting event-like roar. It wasn't long before my doorbell rang. I made my way downstairs and opened the door to see Karen. She smiled as she presented a small baking tin.

"I brought cookies."

I ushered her in and closed and locked the door.

"Did you have an unharassed walk over?"

She nodded.

"Want something to drink?"

She turned and grinned almost wolfishly. "Oh God, yes! What do you have?"

I reached into my cupboard and pulled out the bottle of whiskey. "How do you like it?"

I pulled two glasses out and dropped some ice cubes into mine.

"Straight. Don't junk it."

I was a little surprised, but poured her a nice slug of whiskey before covering the ice in mine with whiskey and coke. I walked around the counter and handed her the drink. She was standing near my counter where I had left the copy of *Foundations*.

"I thought you said you hadn't read it?"

"I haven't, one of the neighbors left it and told me to read it. I haven't touched it since I put it on the table."

She nodded and took a sip of her whiskey.

"I have twenty-seven. I've had to start being careful. They push them in through the mail slot, in front of my door and in my window frames. One was even under the hood of my car."

"Seriously?"

She nodded.

"Okay, this is more than just a self-help book. What do you think is in it?"

She stared at me.

"Do. Not. Read it. Don't read it, Steve. I knew someone who did and his behavior has completely changed."

I laughed. "Isn't that the point of the book?"

She glared at me and set down her glass. "It's not a self-help book. I don't know what it is, but my friend was a married father of two, and a day after I talked to him, suddenly he was at my door saying I had to read the book. I do not need any help, and I think there may be something going on here that messes with people's heads."

A thought came to my mind.

"What if it's, I dunno, like brainwashing somehow? Like the

more of the book you read, the more independence you lose? Is it just the book or are those clubhouse meetings involved somehow? If it is the book, how much of it do you have to read?"

We both looked over at the book on the table. Before she could protest I walked over, grabbed the book and threw it into my trash can. As it flew through the air, the book's pages fluttered. As they did I felt as though a hand seized my brain for a fraction of a second. For the briefest moment I was seized by a desire to open the book and read it, but the moment passed.

"Whoa. Okay, that wasn't normal."

Karen looked at me, slightly afraid.

"It was like it had a hold of me. I wanted to read it."

I sat down on the floor, feeling light-headed and somewhat nauseous.

"Damn. We never read the book, okay? We never open it, we never even glance at it for prolonged periods of time. That thing is not right. It's something else for sure."

I felt my mind returning to normal, like sunlight burning away a thick fog.

"Wait, do you think that they read the book every day? How often are the meetings?"

Karen shrugged. "I don't know, but I get what you're saying. If the book's hold is only temporary, then maybe if we get them away from the source of influence we might be able to get them back to normal."

I nodded. I got back to my feet and grabbed my drink before slumping into a nearby chair.

"I just wanted a nice relaxing break. You know, somewhere nice, have someone mow my lawn and just not worry about life barging in on me for a little. Now I have to put up with this shit."

I drained my glass and set it down hard on the side table.

"Well then, now what do we do? I say we get the hell out of here. I didn't ask for any of this."

Karen nodded and then chuckled darkly to herself.

"I'm assuming you read the terms of your purchase."

"I skimmed it."

A sinking feeling took hold in my gut.

"Yeah, because of your purchase, and this being a new development, you aren't allowed to sell this house for five years."

I felt a gnawing sense of dread take hold. I had thought that I had gotten the deal of the century when I purchased this house. But now I was wrapped up in some bullshit cult out of *The Stepford Wives*.

"It couldn't have been just termites in the foundation; no I had to get stuck with the crazies who want their lawn to be three inches high. Well, I think we are going to have to make a stab at taking back some of the members."

Karen nodded."Okay. Who should we pick first?"

I thought about it. "Probably an older couple, or even better a single person if we can find one. Someone who is older than us and won't be able to offer much resistance. Now the question is, do we want to kidnap them and bring them here? Or, instead, take them captive in their own house?"

We both thought about it for a while before deciding that it would probably be best to have them brought to one of our houses, so as to have an alibi and not have to worry about fingerprints being incriminating evidence.

We also both agreed to lure them over with a phone call, all homes had a directory of the other houses in the community, so we began to scout our victim. In our search, however, we were dismayed to learn that we were the only two single individuals in the entire community.

What was even worse was that we discovered virtually all of those individuals, who were of an age and certain frailty that we might be able to easily overpower, lived in houses close to each other. We were going to have to pick someone younger. After much deliberation and planning, we decided upon my close neighbor Jason who had first approached me with one of the books. We waited for the meeting to adjourn.

Almost in unison and walking in single file down the sidewalk came my neighbors, each one peeling off from the line to enter their house. Each one paused at the door, waved twice at the group which waved back, and then entered the house.

It was only eight o'clock in the evening so I decided it wouldn't be impolite to call Jason. I dialed his number and asked him to come over.

"Hi Jason. Yes, its Steve, down the street. I was wondering if you wanted to drop by and discuss one of the chapters in *Foundations* with me? I found it very interesting and I'd like your opinion."

He said that he would be delighted and that he would be right over. Sure enough, just a few minutes later my doorbell rang. I answered it and there was Jason.

"Good evening, Steve! I just wanted to drop by and say hello! How can I help you better understand *Foundations*?"

I ushered him inside where Karen was waiting. Before Jason could protest she threw a rope around him while I shoved a makeshift gag in his mouth. He struggled momentarily before we were able to successfully hog tie him and drag him upstairs to the closet of my spare bedroom. Jason's muffled screams were louder than we expected, and they did not subside even after we had left him alone for a while.

"Right, now we get his wife."

I called his house again and spoke to Sandra. I told her that her husband thought it would be a good idea if she came over to help us better understand a certain passage of *Foundations*. She agreed and followed the identical pattern that Jason had. Luckily, she was just as easy to subdue. After tossing her in a separate closet, Karen and I moved back downstairs.

"Is it bad that I don't feel any kind of remorse about this?"

I shook my head.

"No. He was an annoying asshole who loved fly fishing. Very *Leave it to Beaver* before he started reading their book."

Karen pulled a flyer out of her pocket.

"Okay, their next meeting is scheduled for two days from now. I say we go take a look at their house. All the others are undergoing some kind of construction. I want to know why."

I thought about this for a bit.

"Are we just going to leave them here? Or should one of us stay and guard them?"

We both glanced at the stairs at the same time, hearing the muffled shouts and screams from our captives.

"I'll stay," Karen said.

I nodded.

"Okay. I'll go explore their house; I should be back in thirty minutes. If I'm not back by then, get out of here."

I went to the kitchen and grabbed a flashlight and the closest thing to a weapon I owned, a meat tenderizer mallet. I was slightly ashamed that I lacked something more intimidating, and all of my cutlery was hardened plastic.

I left my house and walked across the cul-de-sac, keeping my mallet as concealed as I could, to the now hopefully empty house of the Kahns.

I opened their door as quietly as I could and stepped inside. Gradually my eyes adjusted to the dark and I was slowly assaulted by a foul stench. It was a smell of rot and decay, like fruit left to spoil under the sun.

I made my way around the inside of the house; there was a huge pile of garbage in the kitchen. Nearly all of the tiled floor was covered in discarded food wrappers and various bits of refuse; large cockroaches were gorging themselves on the remains. I was nearly sick to my stomach as I explored further, making my way toward the renovated section of the house, sealed by a builder's tarp from the outside.

The closer I got to the added wing of the house the floor became even dirtier. There were piles of topsoil and sand in places, and the floor changed from the soft carpet to gravel and dirt.

I started to hear a rhythmic thumping noise as I approached a closed door leading no doubt to the room under construction. I turned on my flashlight, took a deep breath, and opened the door.

I'm almost sure that I screamed aloud.

There was a pit in the ground, in which sat a pulsing heart-like form. It was oozing a viscous liquid into the ground with each unearthly pump of its heart. I leaned over and vomited before reaching for the door to close off the monstrous sight.

However, not before a large eye opened in the middle of the mass of the creature and fixed me with a horizontally split pupiled stare.

I slammed the door and heaved once again.

It had been like some living egg, or freakish vegetable, sending its tendrils into the ground. It was then that the realization struck me. All of the houses were connected, all of the minds of the people. I had to get back to my own house and flee.

As I ran for the door I heard a god-awful keening noise take hold behind me from the room.

It was loud enough to rattle the windows of the Kahn's house as I sprinted out of their door towards the relative safety of my own house. As I ran across the street I watched as lights began to switch on in all the houses of the cul-de-sac. The screech from the Kahn's house was picked up by other houses. I ran inside my front door and slammed it behind me, glancing quickly out of my curtains to see figures emerge from their own houses and stand in their lawns like sentinels.

"Karen! We have to leave now!"

I saw her standing in the kitchen. She turned to look at me and smiled. Her expression made me feel sick all over again, on the counter was an open copy of *Foundations*.

"Good evening, Steve! I was wondering when you would come back! We want to have some words with you."

As she spoke the two Kahns emerged from the hallway and made their way with Karen towards me. I cursed and ran back towards the door. I still had my car keys in my pants pocket and managed to make it into my vehicle safely.

I had expected them to chase me, but instead they simply

walked out of the house together, smiling the whole time. I started my car as quickly as I could and sped down the street. I passed houses, all with their lights lit up and their owners standing still in their front yards watching me speed past.

As I rounded a corner I drew closer to the clubhouse.

It was now completely lit up, and I could see the carefully manicured lawn and hedges around it rippling, as though there were pulsating veins beneath its surface. The whole building seemed to be alive and wriggling.

I buried my accelerator into the floorboard of my car and nearly flew out of Brunswick Oaks, tearing past the "Slow: Children at Play" signs.

I made my way to the nearest police station, my radiator steaming, and told them my story, about the community and the cult like following and brainwashing books.

They didn't believe me. Why should they?

But, they still had to investigate, and that was where *Foundations* made its fatal mistake. Instead of trying to meld back into polite secrecy, it resisted the intrusion. The military was called in and a cover story of "Spilled VX nerve gas" from Sunny Point Military Terminal was released. The people who were taken alive were all detained for two years. None of them recalled anything to do with their activities or had any memory of *Foundations*. When I asked, I was told that Karen was never found and was declared missing.

What was curious was a complete lack of any record of the book. No publishing house had printed it, and no one even knew the author. Any remaining copies of the book were burned and the entire affair was hushed up.

I immediately moved back to Boston and threw myself into my art to try to work some of the horrors I had seen out. The government paid me a hefty sum for my agreement to never speak a word of what had occurred to a living soul.

Until now.

The government investigation looked in the wrong places. I have recently read that Brunswick Oaks was reopened under the same ownership, who had been found blameless by the US government. They had renovated those homes left standing and opened them once again to the market.

The more I researched this case, the more disturbing patterns I found.

The construction and management firm for Brunswick Oaks are active in forty-seven states and twelve countries. The McAllen Group has been privately owned and active for sixty years now, is the largest privately owned construction firm in the world, with a very strong brand loyalty and market share. They have been building gated communities for decades now, and they have a very successful line of home improvement books.